T0110216

"RICHLY ATMOSPHERIC . . .
He does a splendid job of making you feel the sadness of thwarted dreams and the isolated beauty of the mid-California coastal town where the Mexican past blends with the cappuccino present. *The Perfect Witness* is tense, well written, with deeply engaging characters and a striking sense of place."

—*Detroit Free Press*

"Often the best courtroom thrillers take us beyond the usual murder case to grapple with larger and more complex matters. . . . Siegel perfectly captures the kind of webbed connections between politics and law enforcement that can paralyze the workings of constitutional protections. . . . It's a story in which triumph may come from failure, and losers get a second chance."

—*San Francisco Chronicle*

"Every page is alive with the feel of reality—from the lies and betrayals of the court system to the beauties of the California central coast and its entrancing past and present. . . . Siegel's story [has] the feel of Steinbeck's Monterey. . . . I hope this is the first in a long series."

—DARCY O'BRIEN
Winner of the 1997 Edgar Allan Poe Award

"An abundance of plot twists."

—*Chicago Tribune*

Please turn the page for more reviews. . . .

"GRIPPING, EMOTIONALLY CHARGED . . .

Siegel conveys a strong sense of place, and he convincingly captures the conflict between flagging idealism and hard reality in his protagonist. . . . The plot twists are genuinely surprising. . . . [A] compelling debut."

—*Publishers Weekly*

"A dogged defense attorney's running battle with an unimpeachable prosecution witness raises disturbing questions about the nature of the judicial process in this first novel. . . . Not a whodunit, but a sharp, unsparing exploration of the conflicts between justice and advocacy in the adversarial system."

—*Kirkus Reviews* (starred review)

"Intriguing and shocking . . . An electrifying debut novel in the legal thriller tradition of Scott Turow and Philip Friedman . . . A beautifully crafted sense of place surrounds prizewinning journalist and nonfiction writer Barry Siegel's debut thriller in a cocoon of credibility, adding weight to a strong story. . . . As sharp and surprising as the book's resolution is, it's the image of the fading, changing town of La Graciosa that will stay in your memory."

—*www.amazon.com*

"MOVE OVER SCOTT TUROW AND JOHN GRISHAM!

The Perfect Witness may be the perfect courtroom thriller—taut, suspenseful, relentlessly paced, and written with the special authority of a veteran investigator who knows the territory backwards and forwards."

—JACK OLSEN
Author of *Hastened to the Grave: The Gypsy Murder Investigation*

"*The Perfect Witness* is at its heart a classic courtroom tale, but it's also something more. . . . Mr. Siegel has a good eye for detail and a nice touch with legal matters."

—*The Washington Times*

"An outstanding debut. . . . The very involved plot turns on the testimony of a pathological liar who is the prosecution's primary witness."

—*Mystery Lovers Bookshop*

"An engrossing legal thriller with all the twists and surprises of the genre."

—*The Register Herald* (Beckley, WV)

By Barry Siegel
Published by Ballantine Books:

THE PERFECT WITNESS

THE PERFECT WITNESS

Barry Siegel

BALLANTINE BOOKS • NEW YORK

This book contains an excerpt from *Actual Innocence* by Barry Siegel. This excerpt has been set for this edition only and may not reflect the final content of the forthcoming edition.

A Ballantine Book
Published by The Ballantine Publishing Group

www.randomhouse.com/BB/

Library of Congress Catalog Card Number: 98–93885

ISBN: 978-0-345-48514-4

Manufactured in the United States of America

For my mother and father,
Rae and Earl, with much love

PART ONE

ONE

At half past six on a misty spring evening, a siren sounding along an isolated reach of the central California coast jostled Greg Monarch from his customary late afternoon reverie. He looked out his office window. It was dusk. Time to lock up, time to leave his cramped, airless law office. At the door, in his hurry to flee, Greg fumbled with his keys, then stepped outside.

A thick bank of fog, the region's seasonal signature, hung low over La Graciosa's central plaza. A steady rain, less common, relentlessly fed the rising, agitated Graciosa Creek, which normally snaked lazily through the middle of town but now slapped at its earthen barriers. Greg, listening, imagined the torrent's hurried journey through Chumash County's rolling chaparral-dotted ranchlands, past the modest hills called *cerros*, past the ancient volcano called King's Peak, past the fragrant oak-thick woods of Apple Canyon, reaching finally its destination at the mouth of Port Graciosa. The sea was a good ten miles away, but by the time he'd claimed his regular stool at JB's Red Rooster Tavern, Greg could smell kelp, the scent carried inland on the mist. He turned, leaned back against the bar, and looked around.

JB's was what you'd expect from a hundred-year-old tavern in this part of California. The long mahogany and maple bar, a Brunswick-Balke-Collender original, featured carved nudes on the posts supporting the rear mirrors. Across the room, two billiard tables stood under boxy light fixtures made of white cedar. In a corner sat a potbellied stove, topped by a hanging kerosene lamp. The rough plank walls were covered with branding irons, trapper's tools, mining equipment, snakeskins, and the obligatory steer horns. The neon Rockola jukebox represented J.B. Baylor's one grudging bow to modern times, but he balanced it with a true treasure, a Fischer upright piano, made of maple, ivory, iron, and pine.

Dave Murphy was just setting up shop at the piano. He'd brought his wife, Shirley, this evening. As usual, she sat alone at a small table, twisting her loose blond hair, looking through the picture window that gave onto the creek, waiting until Dave called her to the microphone to sing what she liked to call her "dirty blues." Watching them, JB's customers leaned over narrow communal tables, their hands wrapped around open bottles of the local Graciosa Brew. They were a cross section of Chumash County—ranchers, cowhands, and fishermen mingled easily with merchants, realtors, even the teachers and students who strayed over from the nearby state college. Most lived only blocks from where they were born. Only occasionally did strangers appear at JB's; those who did rarely stayed long. To its patrons on this damp, foggy night in late April, JB's felt like a refuge.

Greg cradled the glass before him but did not pick it up. Almost nightly he came to JB's, yet he drank sparingly, and rarely talked. Usually he found pleasure enough sitting on his stool, listening to those around him, nursing a single glass of whiskey until last call. Only when the piano player started his country-blues ballads did Greg stir. He'd look around then, and tap his fingers to the music. This evening, as he did so, some patrons offered him familiar nods. Others studied him with vague curiosity.

Then, shortly after ten P.M., Jimmy O'Brien pushed open JB's door. "I'm fat and dumb, and I'm about to be drunk," he announced to the room as soon as he'd thrown off his dripping slicker. Noticing Greg, he headed his way, at the same time signaling the bartender with a flurry of waves and pointed fingers. By the time Jimmy had settled next to Greg, a double shot of Black Bush sat before him. He studied Greg's still-full glass with pained wonder. "So, Monarch," he finally inquired. "How far ahead of me are you?"

Jimmy had a big gut, a broad face, and a bushy mustache. By not caring what impression he was making, he managed to move in many different circles. This often proved handy, since he was a reporter for the La Graciosa *News-Times*. Greg suspected that Jimmy knew more sordid details about Chumash County than even the gentleman-rancher land barons who controlled most of its acreage.

"I'm smashed," Greg answered. "You'll never catch up."

"Let's see," Jimmy suggested, rattling the cubes in his already empty rocks glass. "J.B., J.B.," he cried, "how about you just run an IV line from the bottle to my arm?"

At the piano, Dave was playing "Heartbreak Hotel," accompanying old Doc Lewis, who believed he could do an estimable Elvis impression by bending his knees and lurching about. Doc usually made it to JB's eight A.M. Happy Hour for a toddy of milk, egg, and whiskey, after which he practiced fine medicine but found it difficult to string together a whole sentence without a cussword. Jimmy watched the burly, gnarled old coot until the performance grated so much he felt it necessary to intervene. "No, no, that's not Elvis," he declared, grabbing the microphone.

Well, since my baby left me, I found a new place to dwell, it's down at the end of Lonely Street called Heartbreak Hotel . . . Jimmy at least knew how to bend and lean into that microphone, Greg had to admit. His voice didn't sound all that much better than Doc Lewis's, but you could tell whom he was imitating.

Greg's mind drifted. Then another siren shattered his reverie. He winced. They were always testing something or triggering false alarms out there at the Devil's Peak Nuclear Power Plant. At this time of night, the noise jangled.

"Hell's going on," muttered J.B. Baylor, standing behind the bar. He didn't like the power plant's siren, because it possibly signaled an accident, which might oblige him to close the Red Rooster early. He flipped on the portable radio he kept behind the bar. First they heard nothing. Then came the standard announcement. *This is a test* . . . J.B. shrugged, turned off the radio. Such was life in the shadow of Devil's Peak.

By the time Greg started thinking about dinner, Shirley was at the microphone singing "I'm in the Mood for Love." Jimmy was standing by the potbellied stove, spraying spittle and spouting Yeats to a handful of puzzled cowhands. *Why should not old men be mad? . . . Some have known a likely lad . . . That had a sound fly-fisher's wrist . . . Turn to a drunken journalist. . . .* Jimmy couldn't help it; his great-grandfolks hailed from Sligo, where they used to visit the poet's grave every Sunday, and monthly climb his tower.

It was well past 11:00 now. Forget dinner, Greg decided. He wasn't hungry.

Soon after—later, Greg would wish he knew just precisely when—J.B. called Jimmy to the phone at the far end of the bar, near the jukebox. Greg watched Jimmy totter over, playfully poking at those he passed, then pick up the receiver. Within a minute, Jimmy had stopped winking and waving at his friends. He was leaning over the bar now, taking notes, his eyes narrowed. When he hung up, he stood for a moment absorbed in his thoughts, the blood drained from his wide face. Then he slowly walked over to Greg.

"Jesus, Greg," he whispered. "Postmaster over in Crocker? Old man Wilson? He's dead. Murdered. They just found his body on the floor of his house, out back of the post office. Pretty well beat up. Bullet in his brain."

Before Greg could respond, Jimmy moved on, quietly sharing his news with others in the tavern. Soon, JB's had settled into a mix of strained murmurs and stunned silence. There'd been only three murders in Chumash

County in a dozen years, after all, and not one in the past four. Poor old Jenny Branson driving herself off the cliff at Clam Beach had been about the worst thing to happen around La Graciosa recently. That just about everyone knew old Bob Wilson made this even harder to take.

The U.S. Post Office in Crocker, up the county road ten miles, had been open since the turn of the century. Bob Wilson had been its postmaster for nearly forty years, half his life. The job hadn't exactly worn him out, since the Crocker post office, smallest in the county, never had delivery routes. Ranchers and cowhands just wandered into town when they could to pick up their mail from boxes built into the post office wall. With only about fifty letters to sort each day, Wilson spent a lot of time on his sunporch visiting with passersby. Some brought a bottle to share; more than a few, particularly in the years after Wilson's wife died, brought casseroles or stews. "The avocado man," the kids called him, because of the grove out back of his house. He'd leave the pick of his crop in a basket on the post office counter. Take what you like, he'd tell visitors. Can't eat them all myself.

Who would want to kill poor Bob Wilson? That's what most of JB's patrons were asking now as they gathered around Jimmy. Hands raked through crew cuts; feet shuffled. *Who found him? Was it a robbery?* Only Greg stayed on his stool, clutching his whiskey glass. The questions swirling about the tavern appeared to trouble him. He turned toward the piano.

"Shirley," Greg called. Dave's wife once again was sitting by herself, her eyes turned toward the surging creek. "Come on, Shirley, let's play pool." She obliged, as he knew she would, rising plump and dreamy, saying nothing. Together, they circled the billiard table, cues in hand. Greg moved easily; middle age had not yet consumed him. Apart from a few strands of gray, he recalled still the earnest, lanky youth he'd once been. Only the strained set to his jaw gave him away. *I'm in the mood for love,* Shirley hummed softly as she took a shot. Greg hummed back with a familiar, crooked grin, but his eyes roamed the room. Swaying toward him, Shirley sang it out this time, *I'm in the mood for love*. Her fingers rose to Greg's brow. "What's bothering you so?" she whispered in his ear. Then, louder, she sang, *Back to you babe . . . Come on, come on*. Greg did not answer. He was listening over his shoulder to the murmured news about the postmaster's murder.

A crowd still stood gathered around Jimmy, speculating and asking questions, when Greg left JB's at half past one. The rain had eased but the fog lingered, clinging to the plaza. He negotiated the brick pathway lining the edge of the creek, watching as the storm-tossed residue from upstream upheavals—mattresses, boxes, highway signs—swept past him on the ten-mile march to the sea. Reaching the footbridge that crossed the creek near his home, Greg stepped gingerly, for the rising waters were almost at his feet. On the other side he climbed the sloping lawn to his wood-frame cottage, stopped on its splintery porch, and settled into a redwood chair overlooking the creek. There he sat for half an hour, staring into the dark, listening to the torrent. Then he turned to the bedroom and fell onto his mattress without undressing.

There was no telling how long the phone had been ringing before Greg heard it. When he finally did, he glanced first at his clock. It was almost half past four. He reached out, punched the speaker button.

"Where you been, Greg?" a gruff voice asked. "Nasty night like this, you could catch your death of cold."

Greg wished he had the glass of Black Bush he'd left half-full at JB's. Just enough to wet his parched throat. "What's this about, Buzz?" he asked.

Buzz Johnson, the huge, dour, thick-browed investigator for the Chumash County sheriff's department, was the sort of man who would enjoy waking a fellow up in the middle of the night simply to badger him. So perhaps it was about nothing. But the gloat in Johnson's voice aroused foreboding in Greg.

"We've got your law partner down here at the station," Buzz said.

"He's not my partner anymore, Buzz, you know that. What did Ira do this time? Wrap his jalopy around a lamppost?"

"Not quite." Buzz sounded gleeful. "You hear about our murder? Wilson, postmaster over in Crocker? Picked up Ira an hour ago. Looks like his latest drug deal blew up on him."

Greg squeezed his eyes shut, as if that could ward off Buzz's message. He said nothing at first. When he did speak, he kept his voice even. "Not my area of the law, Buzz. You know that. Don't do criminal work anymore. Contracts and wills, that's all these days." Greg opened his eyes and studied the phone. "Besides, as I mentioned, he's not my partner."

"You're his one call, Greg. He picked you. He wants you."

"Then why isn't he on the phone?"

Buzz chuckled. "Let's just say he's . . . indisposed at the moment."

Greg could imagine Buzz's expression. The thin, cruel circle of a mouth, the pale, lifeless pig eyes, the broad, primitive forehead—those familiar features had been unavoidable in Chumash County for more than a decade.

Ira Sullivan indisposed? Yes, no doubt.

Wearily, Greg pushed himself off his bed. "Okay, Buzz, okay," he muttered. "I'll be right over."

TWO

That La Graciosa's jailhouse occupied a former house of God never failed to amuse the town's more secular elements. The 200-year-old *asistencia* had in fact hosted myriad enterprises—barn, schoolhouse, hospital, bottle shop, charnel house—since the days when it served as assistant chapel and backup headquarters for Mission San Luis Obispo de Tolosa to the north. Now it sheltered not just the jail but also the sheriff's station, the district attorney's office, and La Graciosa's solitary courtroom.

For a town forged in the Spanish mission era, this wasn't entirely surprising. There weren't many other large old structures to choose from, and La Graciosa didn't have the tax base or inclination to build the sort of modern granite box that made other communities so proud. What wasn't made of adobe and tile in La Graciosa was made of split timber, reflecting the mission era's eclectic mix with frontier ranching days.

Cupped between the Santa Lucia Range to the northeast and a lesser row of volcanic peaks on its seaward side, the town sat in an insulated canyon, bypassed by the Southern Pacific Railroad at the turn of the century, and by the interstate highway decades later. Cut off in this manner, wrapped in a perennial haze, it had never grown beyond a small ranching, farming, and fishing outpost. A small brick central plaza, a handful of cafés and bars with patios backing onto the meandering creek, a few merchants with storefronts on tree-lined streets thick with camphor, jacaranda, and redwood—that was it.

That, and the Devil's Peak power plant perched on a shoreline cliff fifteen miles to the northwest of town. Although the mountains hid it from view, Devil's Peak was hard to ignore, what with the recurring sirens and the ubiquitous warning signs posted in various public places. *If you hear a steady siren every three to five minutes, turn your AM radio to 940 or 1420 for information*. Most in La Graciosa did ignore Devil's Peak, though. There was little alternative, if you wanted to live without distraction. Devil's Peak wasn't going away; Devil's Peak was a critical pillar in the region's economy.

The fog still hung low when Greg reached the sheriff's station shortly after 5:00 A.M. The *asistencia* stood just off the town plaza, a fortlike quadrangle with adobe walls and clay tile roof. The jail and sheriff shared the west wing, a low, long run of rooms fronted by a colonnade of eleven pillars. Once a convent and quarters for padres, these rooms' windows conveniently came with mission-era grilles, meant to protect the priests from black bears, and young Indian girl novices from local ranch hands.

The notion of Buzz Johnson sitting where the novices and Franciscan Grey Friars once sat made Greg snort with amusement.

"What's so damn funny, Greg?"

Sheriff Dan Wizen stepped out from the gloom. He'd been leaning against one of the pillars. He was working a toothpick in his mouth and tugging at the tan cowboy hat he favored for all occasions, but the effect was not as menacing as he intended. Greg had never managed to work up much fear of Wizen. A family man with four children, the sheriff spent most of his time worrying about his future. Well he should, Greg reasoned. Local voters couldn't be expected to keep electing his sort forever.

"Hard to say, Sheriff," Greg replied. "Humor is so subjective."

"Didn't know you had a sense of humor, Monarch."

"I've been trying to work on one."

Sheriff Wizen frowned. "But this is not a time for jokes."

"No," Greg agreed. "The postmaster has been found dead, I'm told. Death is always hard."

"Not just dead, Monarch. Murdered."

"Even worse."

Wizen glared, then nodded Greg toward the main entry. Together they walked through a warren of small rooms. Each had whitewashed plaster walls bordered at top and bottom by ocher bands. The floors were pink-hued, hand-laid cement; the painted ceiling beams were cracked and peeling. As he wound further with each step into the bowels of the *asistencia*, Greg fought a rising irrational urge to turn and bolt for the street. Too late for that, though. They'd reached the sheriff's office. Once the padres' study, it was larger than the others, with a big window overlooking the quadrangle's inner courtyard. Chumash County's district attorney, Dennis Taylor, stood by the window. Detective Buzz Johnson sat at a table.

"Gentlemen." Greg nodded.

Buzz curled his lip, shifted his bulk, didn't bother to answer. Dennis Taylor played it differently, striding quickly across the room, offering a serviceable smile and a firm handshake. The forced ebullience only partly obscured Taylor's cold, flat eyes. He had a salt-and-pepper beard, a perpetually hurried manner, and an incongruous reputation for chasing skirts. What bothered defense lawyers most, though, was Taylor's habit of gaming them. Making deals, then backing out once they were before a judge—that went way beyond the pale, even among vicious, double-dealing adversaries. Taylor was a man on the move, at thirty-five unencumbered by doubt or remorse. Greg almost preferred Buzz.

"What's this about?" Greg asked the D.A.

"Not much I can tell you right now, Monarch." Taylor smiled faintly. "And not much I have to tell you."

"That's true," Greg allowed. "Except as to why you're holding Ira."

"We found Wilson dead on his living room floor," Taylor offered. "We think Ira killed him."

"Why do you think that?"

Taylor's eyes danced. "Intuition."

Greg nodded. "Your premonitions have always served you well."

"The evidence also helps sometimes, Greg."

"So quick an arrest. You must have caught Ira standing over the postmaster's body."

Taylor hesitated. "No."

"Where, then? Where did you arrest him? I'm entitled to know."

"At his home."

"When?"

A shadow crossed Taylor's face. "Middle of the night, Monarch. My detectives don't punch a time clock."

"How long after you found the postmaster's body?"

Taylor glanced impatiently at his watch, then at Buzz, as if they had a meeting to attend. "Sorry, Monarch, we're sort of busy right now."

"You've been busy all night. My compliments for such an effective investigation. So swift, so decisive."

"You are irritating me, Monarch."

"My regrets. A man of your stature should never be irritated."

Taylor suddenly grinned, showing two rows of perfectly white teeth. "What an interesting surprise, Greg. I thought you gave up the practice of criminal law. I thought you handled wills and contracts now."

"That's not a secret in La Graciosa."

"Yet you are here, yapping at my ankles."

"Ira asked for me, Buzz woke me up. So yes, I am here."

"Do you plan to represent Sullivan?"

"The county public defender is a young man full of energy and ambition. He will do an excellent job."

"Better than you would, if the past tells us anything."

"No doubt."

"I ask again, why are you here, Monarch?"

"The *asistencia* is such a pleasing place at dawn."

Taylor turned toward the door. Greg stepped in front of him. "I'm also curious," he said. "Do you plan to file your own charges, or take this to a grand jury?"

Taylor held up his hands. "All I can say is, this looks like murder one, special circumstances. A cold-blooded shooting during a robbery."

Despite his many triumphs, Taylor had never won an aggravated first degree murder case. What Taylor's expanding résumé sorely lacked was a death penalty conviction.

"That would be a first," Greg observed. "Wouldn't it?"

Taylor blinked and flushed, but said nothing. Greg stopped trying. "Can I see Ira now?" he asked.

Sheriff Wizen led Greg across the inner courtyard and through two doors to the jail. A dozen cells in all, really just rooms with barred windows, sat six on each side of a hallway. Wizen unlocked the door to one of them. How many nubile Indian girls have dwelt in this room, Greg wondered as he stepped inside. He wished one were there right now.

Instead, Ira Sullivan lay stretched on a cot in the far corner.

"Hey," Greg began.

Ira lifted his head. Buzz had been right; Ira was indisposed. A big raw abrasion decorated his left cheekbone, the unmistakable result of a collision with a boot, if not a pair of brass knuckles. His lips were split, his nose caked with blood, his eyes groggy.

"You look like a fuckin' mess, Ira."

Ira winced, then pushed himself up and swung his legs to the ground. "You would too," he muttered, "if you'd spent the evening with Buzz."

It wasn't just Buzz, though. They both knew Ira's decline had started well before last night's encounter. Ira looked worn down, as if he'd been traveling for ages. He glanced around the room, refusing to fix his eyes on Greg.

"Ira," Greg sighed. "Jesus."

They'd grown up together, they'd gone to school together, they'd hung out a law shingle together, Ira always leading the way. With his angular face and gentle smile and dark forelock hanging over sunny blue eyes, he charmed almost everyone he met. Even back at La Graciosa High, he knew how to act, how to talk. Amid a campus full of teenagers wrestling with adolescent demons, his easy grace set him apart.

There is no telling why people falter. Looking back, some in La Graciosa swore they early on could see a dark side to Ira's many successes. At parties sometimes, he'd just disappear; you'd find him hiding in the john or behind the garage, flipping through a magazine. On camping trips upcounty, or weekend visits to San Francisco, he'd occasionally just pack up and leave, say he had to get home. In their dorm at Chumash State, Greg would find Ira alone behind his bathroom door, soaking in his tub for five or six hours at a time.

Others, who knew Ira only passingly, thought Vietnam explained everything. Between high school and college, he'd enlisted and made the Green Berets. During eighteen months overseas, he'd done lots of high-altitude parachuting behind enemy lines. Ballsy stuff, everyone agreed. To evade enemy radar, he'd free-fall from 30,000 feet, waiting until he was 2,000 feet from the ground before opening his chute. Maybe he'd gotten addicted to the adrenaline rush? Maybe he'd just gotten sick of seeing his buddies' heads blown off?

Greg knew better. Ira had managed well enough after the war. Despite his quirks and odd drives, he'd settled, added maturity to his gloss. College, law school, a modest but honorable practice, even a nice family. No, it wasn't Vietnam.

Greg couldn't repair what truly haunted Ira. He couldn't

even talk to him about it. He could only think about it, imagine it, replay it in his own mind over and over.

Ira and his six-year-old son, Jeff, his cherished pride, his constant companion, fishing at Los Osos Lake, at the southern mouth of the valley, halfway between La Graciosa and the sea. Springtime, surrounded by a rolling field abundant with brilliant orange poppies and broad swaths of purple lupine. Dappled woodland sunlight filtering through the oaks. In the hills just above them, a railroad trestle spanning a ravine, the tracks emerging from behind an outcropping. Ira, lazily dreaming.

Did he just lose track of Jeff? Or did he somehow misjudge the danger of letting him scramble up to the trestle? Greg didn't know, never would. He knew only that a train sounded its whistle suddenly, hurtling around the bend. Jeff was midway across the trestle. Ira lurched up. *Run, Jeff, run,* he cried. Jeff was only six, though. The boy stumbled, picked himself up. The train, screeching, trying to stop, bore down on him. *Jeff,* Ira wailed. Greg couldn't help wondering whether father and son's eyes met in the moment before the train slammed into Jeff.

That was four years ago. Ira had never recovered. At first he'd just disappear without explanation, take those six-hour baths, drink too much. Occasionally, though—and then more frequently—the sadness and guilt deepened into something darker. His wife, Susan, finally packed and left. Greg hung in longer, but when Ira started regularly missing court dates and failing clients, their partnership collapsed. For a while Greg tried to help, but he found himself unable to rescue his friend. Eventually Ira more or less drifted away. On occasion Greg would spot him drinking at the Foghorn Pub, a ragged biker bar over in Pirate's Beach, where Graciosa Creek reached the ocean. What Ira had been up to in recent months, Greg didn't really know. He'd heard the stories circulating at JB's, though. Handful of busts here and there, they said. Twice for possession with intent to sell, once for a drunken fight in a bar.

Greg repeated himself. "Jesus, Ira."

Ira looked at him now. His eyes were moist. "What's this Jesus stuff?" he said. "Jesus doesn't have much to do with this. Unless Dennis Taylor is the Son of God."

"Who knows," Greg pointed out. "Anything is possible."

Ira bent his head ruefully at that, empty of whatever brittle anger had been driving him these past months. He ran a hand through hair still thick and dark. Greg recognized the gesture. Long ago, it had been Ira's absent-minded preparation for battle, just before entering a courtroom. Greg used to derive comfort from it, knowing a reliable ally stood by him.

"We've certainly proved there are endless possibilities, haven't we?" Ira said. "My God, how has it come to this?"

Greg thought of the day he finally told Ira their partnership was over. Ira hadn't argued. Instead, he'd studied Greg gently for a moment, as if it were Greg who'd just received bad news. He understood, he'd finally reassured his new ex-partner. It had to be.

"Are you all right?" Greg asked.

Ira glanced toward his cell's small, barred window. "It must be dawn by now. The sky. What it must look like."

"What do you want from me, Ira?"

Ira turned away. "Nothing. Nothing at all."

"You're in trouble. Taylor needs a last notch on his belt. Murder one, he's saying. Special circumstances."

Ira didn't move. There was a grace in how he held himself, Greg thought. Still a grace.

"Taylor does have his needs," Ira said. "Our D.A. is a man of destiny."

Greg moved to Ira's side. "You have a will needs revising, terrific. But not this, Ira. I'll get you someone. I'll get you the best."

Ira, a profile in the shadows, whispered his reply. "You once thought you were going to be the best."

"Events proved me wrong."

Ira forced a laugh. "Ah yes, events. They've disappointed both of us, haven't they?"

Greg thought of late nights in their law office. The next day's legal strategy mapped out, they'd talk then not of their work, but of their fears and doubts and dreams. One night they shot pool until dawn, plotting new lives as wilderness guides. Another night they talked for hours about Ira's parents: his father's rages, his mother's chilly disappointment. On a spring evening four days before he was to wed a woman he'd met the previous Christmas, Ira suddenly confessed that he'd rather stay single. I can't be your best man anyway, Greg replied. I don't own a blue suit. The next morning, Ira called it off.

In later years, after Ira had married Susan, they mostly talked about children. Their absence in Greg's home; their arrival in Ira's. Jeffrey's arrival, that is. He hadn't known he'd like being a father so much, Ira confessed. Now his only worries were about his boy. He didn't know what he'd do if anything happened to Jeffrey.

"Blast events," Greg said. "Blast events."

"Too ambitious a goal."

"What, then?"

"This one event."

"There are many fine criminal defense attorneys in California."

"Can't afford them."

"Chumash County's public defender is quite equal to the task."

"Anyone else would just be a hired gun." Ira hesitated. He looked scared, and full of longing. He hadn't really understood Greg's retreat, hadn't ever accepted its need. "Only you care enough, Greg. We could be partners again."

Greg turned away. "There are far better than me at this. That's why I stopped. I'm a small-town civil attorney, nothing more."

Ira looked about his cell, as if searching for the proper response. "Funny stuff going on," he said finally. "They didn't even want to hear my alibi. Didn't care where I'd been."

Despite himself, Greg responded. "That so? Why would Taylor do that?"

Ira held his palms up, said nothing.

Greg began another question, then stopped. "I'm not taking on a capital case, Ira."

"Just listen to me. That's all."

"There's no point."

"Yes, there is."

Greg glanced at the cell door as if contemplating an escape. Then he slowly sat down. The least he could do was debrief Ira for the public defender. "Okay, Ira, what can you tell me about this?"

He'd instinctively slipped into the calculated mode of a criminal defense attorney. *Control the client's dialogue.* That was the defense attorney's motto. You're not a priest, you don't want to hear confessions, you're not there to give absolution. Don't ask your client for the full story, don't ask if he's guilty, don't let him tell you. If you know the whole truth, you can't play the game. You ask narrow questions, you avoid issues, you interrupt. Then you explain the law to your client, and wait for him to supply a story that fits. By using such techniques, Greg estimated that maybe 90 percent of defense lawyers ended up trafficking in perjured testimony. Their hands were clean, though.

Ira touched the raw wound on his cheek. "I don't really know what's going on," he said. "I spent the evening at the Foghorn. Got wasted, walked into the dunes with a couple of guys and a jug of Early Times. We sat under the stars, listened to the surf."

"And then?"

Ira studied his feet. "That's the problem. Can't say. I'm afraid I blacked out. Next thing I know, I'm on the sofa in my living room. And Buzz is pounding on the front door. It's the middle of the night. They have the place surrounded with rifles. A minute later I'm on my stomach, handcuffed, with Buzz's boot in my ear."

Into the Chumash Dunes. Not a bad place to spend a

night, Greg thought. More than once, he'd lost himself in those great white voluptuous mounds that reached south along the coast from Pirate's Beach. Bordered on the inland side by an eighteen-mile run of marshes, lakes, and headlands, the dunes provided blessed refuge when the world was too much to bear.

"Did you know the postmaster?" Greg asked.

Ira rolled his shoulders and rocked his head side to side, as if trying to shake off his meeting with Buzz's boot. "I'm not sure," he said. "Fact is, I'm not sure when I ever was in Crocker. Drove through, but can't remember ever getting out of the car. I told them that. They weren't interested. Made Buzz kind of angry. You see the result."

"Tell me more."

Ira shook his head. "There's nothing more to tell."

Greg couldn't judge whether this was true. Yet another reason to back off. It would be a nightmare defending someone who constantly ducked and dodged. He started to rise.

"Oh yeah, there is one thing." Ira spoke quickly, trying to make it sound casual. "In between slapping me around, they talked about an eyewitness. A woman named Sandy Polson. Said she'd fingered me, so I might as well confess. You know, Dennis's usual game."

"Do you know a Sandy Polson?"

Ira looked away. Both of them sensed they were getting too close to the truth now. "Yes, I know Sandy Polson," Ira said. "Met her months ago. She was there last night."

"In the dunes?"

"No, no. At the Foghorn. We talked, we danced."

"Why would she be fingering you?"

"Don't know. But I can tell you this. If she's their eyewitness, I'm in trouble. She's a master."

"Master of what?"

Ira's eyes flashed. Tangled memories from countless Foghorn evenings filled his mind. The drug rush, the liquor buzz, the feel of her body on the dance floor. She tilting her head, taunting him through lowered eyelids, him and everyone else. He'd sensed something wrong, though, something strange about her. He'd held back, turned away eventually. It had never happened. She'd been just a passing acquaintance in the end.

"Master of lying with a straight face," Ira answered. "She's something. No nerves. Never blinks, never apologizes." This time Ira didn't force his laugh; it rang with a caustic amusement directed at both of them. "Don't you see, Greg? In the old days, in our office. She's what we always wanted. She's the perfect witness."

Greg pushed himself to his feet. A perfect witness for the prosecution, a drunk and drugged Ira for the defense. Maybe even a guilty Ira for the defense. How could he have almost taken the bait? He was losing his mind.

"I'm sorry, Ira," he said. "You're asking the wrong guy. I'll find you the right one."

Greg was halfway back home, walking the brick pathway along the creek, before he fully realized that he'd almost, once again, become the defense attorney in a murder case. The notion made him shudder. He'd withdrawn from that world years before, and had no intention of returning. He walked faster.

"Damn you, Ira," Greg muttered. "Damn you."

THREE

On the second Monday after Ira's arrest, Greg Monarch drove northwest along the country road that followed Graciosa Creek to the sea. Despite his efforts to ignore it all, the public dance had started to get on his nerves. With each day now came more insistent demands from citizens agitated by the postmaster's murder. Whether for retribution, protection, or simply answers, Chumash County wanted its district attorney to act.

When would he? Greg couldn't say. The county public defender currently represented Ira; watching from afar, Greg had heard little. He imagined Dennis Taylor was calling witnesses before a grand jury. Taylor liked to know the citizens of Chumash County were behind him. He'd want an indictment.

Coming around a curve, in a pass between two hills, Greg caught his first glimpse of Pirate's Beach, the ramshackle village on Graciosa Bay where the road and the creek ended. He could feel the muscles in his neck relax. Pirate's Beach always beckoned. It was even more lost than La Graciosa. Sheltered between rolling hills inland, the virgin white sand dunes to the south, and a spit of land that reached seaward to the north, its only connection to the world was the country road Greg had traveled. Thousands of years ago, the Chumash Indians fished from the town's natural promontory; more recently, the Spanish padres and *rancheros* used the same landing as a port for shipping supplies. According to folklore, so did pirates and rumrunners, who found the cape a useful place to land on foggy nights.

Swinging onto the single main street, Greg studied the now-dormant hamlet with appreciation. A scattering of simple wood-frame homes dotted the weed-clogged hill-side and descended to a row of ragged seventy-year-old storefronts that faced the sea. Everything looked as it always did—the seedy snack stands and beachcomber shops, the grocery store that first opened its doors in 1922, the solitary two-story Seaside Motel, the lonely fishing pier. What Greg liked most was the rich mix of wildlife that regularly visited Pirate's Beach.

Climbing from his car, he hiked across a rocky ledge to watch. Brown pelicans, great blue herons, sea lions, harbor seals, sea otters, even thirty-ton gray whales on their grand migration between Alaska and Baja California—all could be seen at one time or another from where Greg sat. What caught his eye just now was a peregrine falcon.

The sighting startled him. He knew it was uncommon for a casual observer to spot this rare and endangered bird. He knew why, too: the pesticides used by inland growers. Over the past thirty years, helped by nest robbers and hunters, they'd devastated a once magnificent, abun-dant species. Was this, Greg wondered, what Darwin had in mind?

He watched with fascination as the solitary peregrine cruised offshore, in search of prey. The size of a crow, with a wingspan of three to four feet, peregrines were master hunters. With their extraordinary vision, far better than that of a person using powerful binoculars, they could spot their victim a quarter of a mile away. They had long, pointed wings powered by strong pectoral muscles. They had potent talons. They had bills made for tearing flesh.

Greg couldn't help but feel envious. The peregrines were much better suited for their world than he was for the one he'd chosen. He'd learned as much the hard way. Hard for him, harder for the one he was supposed to defend.

* * *

It had been fifteen years ago. Greg was thirty then, living in Florida on a whim, a hungry young attorney looking for cases. Cases, and causes as well. In those days, he still thought it possible to protect the abject and vulnerable from the vise of institutional power. For a time, coming out of law school, he'd tried doing just that in La Graciosa, he together with Ira Sullivan. Here and there, they'd even succeeded. They'd convinced judges to punish exploitative slumlords; they'd protected street musicians from overzealous patrolmen. With each victory, however, had come a dozen defeats. Often, they were simply outgunned; two pea-green lawyers, defending Chumash County's most weak and impoverished, had neither the resources nor experience to match a wily and well-funded D.A.'s office. Yet even if they'd been better armed, Greg had to admit another problem: Not infrequently, their clients were guilty. This one did deal drugs to schoolchildren; this one did savagely beat his girlfriend. Which cases were victories, Greg began wondering, which losses?

Not justice, but at least the chance for justice—that's what had drawn him to the law. And, in his thirtieth year, temporarily to Florida: It offered a larger, more electric playing field than Chumash County; it also offered, he imagined, more clarity. In the rich, humid stew of political refugees and CIA operatives, Greg thought he might just find something truly worth fighting for. There, one morning, in pursuit of that goal, he'd wandered into a judge's chambers at the Naples courthouse. The clerk asked if he could take over a case from the local public defender, who had a conflict. Greg didn't hesitate. He had only three criminal jury trials under his belt, but this was just an armed robbery at a Best Western, and both guys had already confessed. Not a cause exactly, not a grand, noble battle, but he needed the money. What's more, it looked like a walk.

Not until he reached the jail did he learn that his man's bail was big enough to choke a horse. The cops smirked when he inquired. Don't you know? they said. That Joe Hilliard's got a murder charge on the way. Greg thought of backing out, until he met Hilliard. He was twenty-three, black, scared, and trying so hard to act dignified. "Mr. Monarch," Hilliard said. "I didn't do this. I'm innocent."

Hilliard had no criminal record only because he'd never been caught. He, with his buddy Frankie Frazier, indeed had pulled the Best Western job. He'd started to assault the lady, too, but had backed off when she begged him to stop. Thought of his mom, Hilliard explained. She'd been hurt once like that. Full of remorse, he'd turned himself in the next day. Waved down a patrol car, handed over his gun.

All in all, most defense lawyers would say, not too bad a story. Except there'd also been a rape and murder at a jewelry store that same day, not far from the Best Western. The timing and sexual assault encouraged the cops to link the two crimes. Then a charming, aw-shucks detective nicknamed Bobo started driving Hilliard's buddy Frankie around town, making appropriate noises about getting off easy. Frankie listened only briefly before fingering Joe for the murder.

The trial lasted all of four days. Greg faced Bob Lasorda, a veteran prosecutor with more than forty jury trials behind him. Lasorda had nothing besides Frankie; no prints, no blood, no hair, no fibers. He did have Hilliard's gun, a .38-caliber Smith & Wesson, and the bullet recovered from the murder victim was also a .38. That one was a .38 "special" slug, though, which couldn't fit into the chamber of Hilliard's regular Smith & Wesson. The prosecutor knew this; he had an FBI ballistics report flatly telling him Hilliard's gun couldn't be the murder weapon. All the same, Lasorda in his opening statement told the jury "we have a weapon which the state contends is the murder weapon."

Greg wasn't that green. Knowing about the ballistics report, he planned a dramatic physical demonstration during his cross-examination of the FBI agent who'd written it. He'd ask the agent to put a .38 special cartridge in Hilliard's Smith & Wesson. It wouldn't fit. That would make for a terrific jury show.

It never happened, though. Because the prosecutor had already listed the FBI expert as a witness, Greg didn't subpoena him himself. He just waited for Lasorda to call him to the stand. Lasorda never did. Instead, on the trial's last day, he released the expert back to the vacation from which he'd been summoned. It had never occurred to Greg that the prosecutor would do something like that.

Frantic, Greg tried locating the FBI agent by marine radio where he was fishing out on the Gulf Stream. He begged the judge for a continuance. He introduced the ballistics report himself, as a defense exhibit. Nothing worked. Without an expert on the witness stand to display the gun and explain the technical report, he was hamstrung. Greg moved for a mistrial based on his own incompetence. No, the judge ruled.

The jury took just two hours to convict Hilliard and sentence him to death. That night, Greg went home and drank a fifth of Black Bush. Five days later, when they finally gave out sentences for the Best Western robbery, Frankie drew probation.

Greg never let go. Even after he'd returned to La Graciosa and rejoined his practice with Ira, he regularly flew cross-country to visit Hilliard in state prison. He wrote letters, he beseeched the governor's office, he haunted newspaper city rooms. All to no avail. Over the years, Greg lost at three post-trial hearings; three times the Florida supreme court rejected his appeals.

Joe Hilliard by then had become quite accomplished at appearing dignified. He stood erect, he looked people in the eye, he never whined. Nor did he ever stop insisting he was innocent. Only when they came to him that final night did his eyes flash with anger. He would not order a last meal. Instead, he sat in his bare cell, talking to a minister about an afterlife. Shortly after six the next morning, he squeezed Greg's hand and turned to the guards. *Joe,* Greg whispered as they led Hilliard out the door. *Joe . . . Joe.*

Only Greg blamed the legal system, only Greg blamed the prosecutor, the judge, the detective. Everyone else blamed him. *I know a dozen lawyers in town who could have rammed this case right down the state's throat*—that's what more than a few Florida attorneys said. The prosecutor was just doing his job, they pointed out. A damn good aggressive job at that. The defense attorney must respond in kind. Greg Monarch wasn't up to it; Greg Monarch didn't do his job.

To settle things, just to understand, Greg visited Bob Lasorda long after Hilliard's execution. *How could you do this, how could we let this happen,* he wanted to know. The former prosecutor was by then a widely admired Florida state judge. He received Greg graciously, spoke to him kindly, as a teacher would a student. "Greg, that's the adversary system," he explained. "I do my job, the defense attorney does his job. Don't you see? That's what the adversary system is all about."

Ira Sullivan saw well enough. He consoled Greg, he unequivocally absolved him, yet he dutifully hewed to his own role as unbounded advocate. Defending the innocent and furtive alike, challenging both scrupulous and overreaching prosecutors—however imperfect, he could fathom no other course. Greg played it differently; Greg finally tried swapping roles, hoping it would give him a new perspective. He again left his practice to Ira, this time to work for the Chumash County prosecutor's office. To work, specifically, for the young, just reelected district attorney Dennis Taylor.

He didn't fit in any better there. Halfway through his first year, they gave him second-chair on a manslaughter case. A neighborhood scuffle where the dying victim mumbled something about a trailer-park transient called Bowser. Detective Buzz Johnson quickly arrested the befuddled old fellow, but Greg never could convince himself they had the right man. Nor could a second Chumash County detective, Roger Kandle. While Kandle sniffed around, Greg dragged things out, asked for continuances, lost files. Soon they found someone willing to say he'd seen Bowser way the other side of the county on the murder night. Then they found two more. Dennis Taylor had no choice but to drop the charges.

After that, Greg worked alone in the D.A.'s office, drawing only minor cases. Fifty-dollar convenience store holdups, minors buying booze, they were his province. Passing him in the hallways, other prosecutors turned their heads or studied the floor. Within six months, he was gone, by mutual agreement. "You just don't get it," Taylor told him on his last day. "You're supposed to pick a side."

Greg had been back at his private practice just four weeks when Ira lost his son. In the days following Jeffrey's funeral, the two partners hiked for hours through wooded stream canyons, stared blankly over sheer coastal bluffs, drank whiskey until dawn. Nothing worked. As Ira slowly sank, Greg tried to stay with him, but found he could not. Ira's collapse scared him, in the way certain situations affect people who have always tried to avoid them. By the end, Ira had stopped coming to their office entirely, and Greg had stopped looking for him. Alone, Greg kept the law firm open, but now took only the type of civil matters that involved little contention. Taylor and Lasorda were right, he told himself. Yes, he was obliged to be a relentless adversary. Yet he couldn't work up much enthusiasm for such a role. He refused to pretend they were all engaged in something the least bit righteous.

It could, Greg knew, be called a retreat cloaked in philosophy. He acknowledged no regrets, though. He hadn't folded his hand, after all. He still did his best to help clients, as long as he could do so honorably. He'd found his small corner of the universe. At least some in town appeared to respect his course; he had a fair-sized practice. With his days full of wills and contracts, his evenings listening to JB's piano player, his weekends hiking the hills and beaches of Chumash County, Greg had constructed a way of life he could accept.

Then Ira had gone and gotten himself arrested for murder.

A rustling in the sky over the ocean snapped Greg out of his reverie. The peregrine, from high above, had spotted his prey. The heedless gull never had a chance. Greg watched amazed as the peregrine, its wings folded back, pivoted into a power dive, struck the gull in midair, clutched it in sharp talons, broke its neck with a hooked bill. It was over in an instant. They said peregrines dove at 170 miles per hour.

"Good for you, falcon," Greg muttered. "Good for you."

It was late afternoon; the first tendrils of fog were drifting onshore, carried by a brisk wind. Greg pulled up his collar and headed back to the Pirate's Beach main drag. The smell of grease wafted from the snack stands, the sound of country-rock music from the bars and cafés. Greg walked past Gordo's and Mr. Rick's and Tasha's, turning in at Ira's old hangout, the Foghorn Beach Pub. The Foghorn was a far cry from JB's. Instead of a piano player, it featured a black Lethal Weapon pinball machine. Faded green carpet half covered a chipped parquet floor. The plain, scratched bar faced a long, grimy picture window, so that customers stared out on a blurred view of the beach. A long, handwritten list of rules, meant to ward off fights, adorned the wall by three billiard tables. ALL FOULS AND SCRATCHES RESULT IN BALL-IN-HAND. A JUMP SHOT IS A FOUL. YOU ONLY HAVE TO CALL THE POCKET, YOU DON'T HAVE TO CALL KISSES OR RAILS. Still, at one table two high-mileage gals with raspy whiskey voices were arguing about a break.

In the gloom, it took Greg a minute to realize that Jimmy O'Brien was sitting at the bar. Jimmy O'Brien, who never retreated, who betrayed and beguiled without remorse to get his stories. "Hey, Jimmy," he said softly, putting his hand on the newspaperman's shoulder. "Working hard?"

Then Greg saw the reporter's notebook sitting open on the bar, saw that Jimmy was taking notes, interviewing the bartender.

"Actually, I am working," Jimmy said, tapping his notebook sharply. "Ira hangs here. I'm on his trail. Will be for a while, I guess."

"Why's that?" Greg asked, not understanding.

Jimmy regarded him with wonder. "You haven't heard? Ira's been indicted. First degree murder. The grand jury handed it up late this morning."

Seeing Greg's dismayed expression, Jimmy hesitated, then made his best stab at a Sligo brogue.

"No time for you to be hanging out in bars, Gregory. Dennis Taylor is asking for the death penalty."

Greg stared at the desolate gray beach. *Whatever it takes . . . What else is there to do?* That's how Jimmy had once explained himself. He'd made it sound like fun.

"Taylor usually gets what he wants," Greg said.

Jimmy studied him. He and Greg and Ira had spent many fine hours together. He'd once thought Monarch & Sullivan the most admirable law firm in La Graciosa. "You know Taylor better than anyone," he said. "You know how he works, you know what it takes."

"Which is precisely why I think Ira needs someone else."

"I understand your reluctance. But this is a chance to . . ." Jimmy hesitated.

"Redeem myself?" Greg flushed. "Is that what you were going to say?"

"You won't help Ira? You won't try to save him from this mess?"

"That's beyond me, beyond the possible."

Jimmy put his hand on Greg's arm. "I don't think so."

FOUR

Peering through the sheriff's big picture window, Detective Roger Kandle tried to imagine the ancient Spanish oak that rose somewhere in the thick fog, dominating the center of the *asistencia* courtyard. Behind him, the Chumash County district attorney sat at a desk, murmuring into a telephone. Kandle could hear only passing fragments of Dennis Taylor's conversation, but he knew well its substance. He'd been listening to Taylor all morning. The D.A. was busy fielding dozens of calls about Ira Sullivan's indictment, many from journalists, a few from sources Kandle couldn't identify. To the reporters the D.A. talked vaguely, to the others, with precision. What evidence he had, how the grand jurors responded, future tactics, the timetable for coming hearings—the information cascaded from Taylor in ceaseless waves.

Kandle had seen such displays before, for Taylor was an intense man with unbounded enthusiasm about his job. The D.A. regarded his as a noble mission. The streets were full of wrongdoers, he often reminded his staff, wrongdoers who caused law-abiding citizens much pain and loss. Most did not pay for their sins. Most freely repeated their mean deeds over and over, aided by shameless defense attorneys willing to do anything for their clients.

"Well, Roger, looks like we've really got hold of a sexy one here." As Taylor spoke, he leaned back, swung his feet up on the desk, and lit a thick Macanudo. He indulged himself like this only when far from the public eye. Turning from the window to face him, Kandle realized the D.A., at least for the moment, had run out of phone calls.

"Yessir," the detective agreed. "Sure getting lots of attention. From all sorts of people, it seems."

Taylor ignored the implied question. "Even the networks are calling. The *L.A. Times*, the *Washington Post*. Respectable lawyer kills old-time postmaster—I guess that presses some kind of button in those newsrooms."

"All we have to do now is prove our case," Kandle said.

Taylor jerked his head toward Roger. He studied his detective with a sharp curiosity. "Yes, that's right," he said. "All we have to do is prove our case."

Kandle said nothing more. He felt confused about Dennis. The D.A. was an engaging man, it seemed to him, at least when he summoned a little warmth into those cold, flat eyes. He was also a skilled and dedicated prosecutor. If only he didn't get carried away so often.

Kandle couldn't help wondering whether Ira Sullivan's indictment represented one of those occasions. It wasn't for him to judge; his job was simply to gather the evidence. Yet it was precisely the evidence that puzzled him. Or rather, the lack. They had no prints, no blood, no fibers, no signs of forced entry. They had only some bullet holes in the postmaster's ceiling, which suggested a struggle, and one .22-caliber bullet in the postmaster's head, which suggested a murder. They also, of course, had the statements of two eyewitnesses—for what they were worth. Paul Platt and Sandy Polson. An odder pair Kandle had never seen.

They might never have seen them at all if not for Buzz Johnson's decision to take the back roads to the *asistencia* when they left the postmaster's that moonless night. Winding their way through the dark, narrow roads of Apple Canyon, Roger and Buzz at first weren't even certain what they were looking at. For a moment, they thought the dull white panel poking up from a roadside ditch was part of a discarded refrigerator, or maybe an ancient washing machine tub. Then the two detectives climbed out of their cruiser and crept carefully past tangles of chaparral and clumps of rabbit bones left by feasting coyotes. Not until they reached the rim of the steep, shadowy ditch did they realize they were staring at the rear end of a white Volkswagen Bug.

The car rested on a diagonal, its nose pitched down. Inside, in the driver's seat, a woman sat rubbing her forehead. She looked dazed, but otherwise unhurt. Kandle saw no blood, no sign of injury. For that matter, the VW itself displayed no damage. It looked as if the car had slid softly off the road, its landing cushioned by thick branches.

Noticing them, the woman offered a welcoming smile. "I've had a little accident," she explained. "I swerved to avoid an animal of some sort. Look where it got me."

Kandle had trouble managing a response. Less than an hour before, he'd been standing over the bloody body of the postmaster. A neighbor, hearing first yelling and shouts, then cars driving off, had called the sheriff around midnight. Twenty minutes later, he and Buzz had found old Bob Wilson's still-warm body on his living room floor. There not being much opportunity in Chumash County to see someone with half a forehead blown away, the sight had unsettled Roger. He and Buzz had left the scene quickly, giving way to the more experienced forensics team. Roger felt shaken and distracted now, peering down at this woman. He didn't want to deal with her accident; he wished they had not come upon her on this road.

Buzz Johnson did not share his reticence. Buzz was studying the woman with undisguised delight. It took Kandle a moment to understand why. Not until his eyes adjusted to the gloom did he realize her allure. She wasn't strikingly beautiful, but she had a fresh, frank look about her that was hard to ignore. She had cornflower-blue eyes and tousled tawny hair that spilled to her shoulders. Her hips were twisted in the driver's seat, leaving her thin white skirt hitched up to midthigh. Kandle wondered whether she'd noticed this result of the accident, and sensed that she had. Yet she was making no effort to cover herself. She appeared to be studying them with some amusement, her head tilted, her eyes half-closed. Buzz's delight was building; beads of sweat glistened on his wide, thick face.

"Good evening, ma'am," Buzz began. "Looks like you need some help."

It occurred to Kandle that he should intervene. He was a by-the-book officer, always had been, even if it did cause some eye-rolling in the department. "May I see some identification, please? Your driver's license and car registration? We'll need to make a report."

Buzz groaned. "Shit, Roger, I don't think we need to bother with all that. Let's just pull her out of the ditch and all of us can get on our way. We've got more pressing business."

Agreeing with Buzz, the woman nodded warmly at Kandle. She'd adjusted her skirt now, although not by much. "My name's Sandy Polson," she said. "I live near here. I don't want to be a bother."

Buzz started walking back to the cruiser for a tow chain, but Kandle remained beside the VW. "If you'll just hand over your license and registration, ma'am?"

Sandy Polson sighed and reached slowly for her purse. In the dim light, she had trouble searching its contents. She picked at several items gingerly. First she pulled out an eyeglass case, then a makeup kit. The third time, she found her wallet, but as she lifted it out of the purse, a cloth bundle emerged also, spilling onto Sandy's lap. Its appearance appeared to disturb her. "Oh," she exclaimed, reaching to gather the cloth together again. She wasn't quick enough. Aiming his flashlight, Kandle could see several bundles of cash, hundred-dollar bills, piled inside what looked to be a dish towel.

Just then, Buzz returned to Kandle's side, tow chain in hand. Kandle jerked his flashlight at Sandy's lap. "Look at this," he said. "What do we have here?"

Sandy laughed as she pulled the dish towel around the

cash. "Waitress tips for the past year," she said. "Good thing you boys aren't the IRS."

Buzz shrugged, appeared uninterested. Sandy started stuffing the bundle back into her purse. Kandle reached through the car window and stopped her. It wasn't the cash that bothered him so much. It was the dish towel. Tan, with wiggly, geometric green stripes. He felt sure he'd seen a towel like that before. Not so long ago.

As he stood there, his hand on Sandy's wrist, the evening's third siren began surging through the canyons. He lifted his head and looked in the direction of the Devil's Peak power plant. Sandy and Buzz followed his gaze. It was, Kandle noted, 1:15 A.M. now.

"I'm sorry, ma'am," he said. "We'll have to bring you into the station to answer a few questions."

Kandle watched as Dennis Taylor swung his feet off Sheriff Wizen's desk and reached for the phone. The D.A. punched the button that gave him a direct line to the jail. "Let's get Sandy Polson to the conference room," he barked. Then he paused, looked over at Kandle, smiled faintly. "And let's get Paul Platt in there, too."

Kandle turned back to the window. He could almost see the Spanish oak now in the thinning fog. He'd never been the sharpest in a crowd, he knew that much. Truth was, if he hadn't become a cop, Roger didn't know where he might have ended up. Maybe in the same factory where his dad built window frames for thirty years. He liked being a policeman, but didn't trust his ability to deduce. So he watched his colleagues and tried to move in their direction. One day, he feared, they'd realize his limits. One day they'd tell him to go build window frames.

"Going to question Platt and Polson together again?" he asked.

Taylor walked to Roger's side, studied his profile. Kandle kept his eyes fixed on the courtyard.

"Yeah, Roger, I am. Seems to be working out fairly well."

Kandle had handled some of the initial questioning, in the hours after they'd brought Sandy down to the station. He hadn't been invited to the more recent sessions, though. Something had happened. First came a flurry of phone calls, which the D.A. took behind closed doors. Then Taylor seized the interrogation for himself.

"Their stories holding together now?" Kandle asked.

In the early going, there'd been no story at all. Sandy Polson at first denied any connection to the postmaster's murder. In fact, she expressed utter dismay when Kandle told her Wilson was dead. Stared Roger right in the eye, her expression full of concern and anguish. Made him feel as if they somehow were bound together in this event. She, too, desired to find the perpetrator of this horrible murder. She was on his side, she admired his efforts, she saw what a difficult task he faced.

Who knows how long all that might have continued if not for the kitchen towel. It had taken Kandle only minutes to realize where he'd seen one like it before. By the time they were leading Sandy into the station, he'd figured it out. The cloth wrapped around her $33,000 in waitress tips exactly matched two others that were hanging in the postmaster's kitchen.

After Kandle pointed this out, Taylor grew animated. He leaned close to Sandy. *You can help yourself,* the D.A. advised her. *The only way you can help yourself in this deal is to tell us what happened.*

Taylor didn't stop there, of course. When Sandy still hesitated, he talked about fingerprints, even though they didn't have any. He mentioned hairs and fibers found at the scene, although there were none. *We know you were there,* Taylor warned Sandy. *We know.*

Maybe that's the way it had to be done. Until then, Sandy certainly hadn't been overly revealing. Kandle had to admit—Taylor's way worked, Taylor's way got you where you needed to be. After just a couple brief rounds with the D.A., Sandy began wavering. By 2:30 A.M. she was crying and offering names. Ira Sullivan's and Paul Platt's.

In her first version, she only heard about the postmaster's murder from Ira, who gave her the $33,000 to hold. In her second version, she was up in Crocker with Ira but hadn't seen anything, hadn't gone inside the postmaster's home. Not until her third version did Sandy offer what Taylor wanted—an eyewitness.

Also, not until her third version did they tape Sandy's statement. Since then, Kandle had listened to it at least a dozen times.

She bumped into Ira at the Foghorn earlier that evening. Ira and his young sidekick, Paul Platt. They were both pretty sloshed. Kept talking about something big going on up in Crocker. Just what, she didn't know, but they convinced her to come along. Ira made it sound like a party. They drove together in his green Dodge van. Pulled up at a house behind the Crocker post office. Just a quick stop here first, Ira explained. They knocked at the front door, an old man opened it, Ira pushed his way in. Then everything got crazy. The old man yelling and shoving, Ira pulling a gun, the old man lunging, shots ringing out, she screaming and turning away, Ira and Paul searching for something. She didn't know then what they found, what they took. She didn't even know the old man was dead. All she knew, Ira and Paul were running to the green Dodge van, pulling her with them.

What about the money? Buzz asked her that question; Buzz was the one who took her statement.

Sandy had a ready explanation. When they dropped her off at her house, Ira stuffed the cash in her purse, wrapped in that kitchen towel. Begged her to keep it for him. Big trouble with some drug suppliers, he explained. That was all he said, nothing more. She didn't want to take it, but his look scared her. After they left, she thought it over, then got in her own car, started back to the Foghorn. Meant to find Ira and give him back the cash. But she was trembling so bad, she couldn't drive straight. Went off the road. That's when Buzz and Roger found her.

After hearing this story, Taylor hadn't even waited until dawn. By 3:45 A.M., Buzz and Roger had Ira Sullivan spread-eagled on his living room floor. By 4:00 A.M., they had Paul Platt in handcuffs. Back at the station both denied everything, but Taylor wasn't persuaded. By then, Kandle sensed, the D.A. couldn't be persuaded. By then, the D.A. was spending half his time behind a closed door, murmuring into a phone.

They locked up Sullivan as soon as he started demanding his lawyer; he obviously wasn't going to talk, he obviously wasn't the weak link. Paul Platt was. Skinny, pale, nervous, somewhere in his late thirties, Platt did not appear to be overly bright, or even coherent. He had the jumpy, ravaged look of a chronic drinker.

First Kandle briefly, then Buzz at length, took their turns with him. After two hours or so, near 6:30 A.M., Buzz suddenly emerged from the interrogation room with a big, wet grin creasing his face. A big grin, and Paul Platt's taped confession in hand.

Kandle had listened to that one a dozen times, also.

Platt basically offered the same story as did Sandy. Except his account included two new details. He told them how many shots had been fired—three into the ceiling during the struggle, one into Wilson. He also told them that Ira took a bracelet he found hidden in a kitchen cabinet. Sandy hadn't been able to give them the number of shots, and didn't mention a bracelet. Which made Platt's account all the better: He wasn't just corroborating Sandy, he was adding things no one else knew.

Taylor couldn't have been happier with his detectives' work. They'd provided him evidence of a violent murder during the course of an armed robbery, attended by two eyewitnesses. With that, Taylor announced, he'd get a special-circumstances homicide one on Sullivan. Platt and Polson, he'd decide about them later. Maybe murder two, maybe accessory, who knows. He wanted to keep his options open, hold back some cards. That way he'd have no trouble convincing them to testify at Sullivan's trial.

"Terrific work, guys," Taylor told Buzz and Roger. He beamed and threw his arms around their shoulders. "Absolutely terrific work."

Buzz smiled broadly, Kandle a little less so. Maybe there was something he didn't know, Roger thought. Something he didn't understand.

A glum, rheumy-eyed sheriff's deputy led Greg Monarch down the *asistencia's* winding corridors to a small cubicle. There the officer silently placed before Greg a thin manila file, then turned and left the room.

He wasn't taking the case, Greg had advised the D.A.'s office. He did not represent Ira Sullivan. This was a courtesy visit only, requested by the public defender and urged by Jimmy O'Brien. He would read what the D.A. had on the postmaster's murder, then share his thoughts with Sullivan's lawyer. That was all he'd do.

Sitting in his assigned cubicle, listening to the deputy's retreating footsteps, Greg lifted the folder and held it in his hand. Only now, after the grand jury indictment, was Taylor obliged to share this with anyone. Greg wondered how much Taylor had held back; he knew a few pages would be missing. The file felt slight, even for this early stage. Just a few police reports, no doubt, plus the coroner's findings and something from the forensics technician.

Greg opened the folder and started to turn the pages. It was as he imagined. Greg quickly scanned Buzz's account, the autopsy report, the lab work. Not until he flipped those pages over did he see the statements from Sandy Polson and Paul Platt. He froze as he began to read Platt's. *The old man started yelling and shoving, Ira pulled a gun, the old man lunged, four shots were fired . . . Then Ira found a bracelet . . .*

An unwelcome feeling tightened Greg's chest. The postmaster's daughters, he could see from the reports, didn't tell investigators about a missing bracelet until hours later. A family heirloom, they called it; a vintage scrolled diamond and emerald bracelet their father bought their mother in the 1920s. The forensics technician took even longer to share his findings. Not until late the next afternoon did he decide four shots had ricocheted about the postmaster's living room. So Paul Platt had gotten it exactly right—before anyone else knew.

Greg could imagine Dennis Taylor before the jury. *How could Paul Platt, awakened in the middle of the night, match Sandy Polson's story so closely, without ever talking to her? How could Paul Platt know what even the police didn't know? Above all, why, ladies and gentlemen of the jury, why would Paul Platt say he was at the murder scene if he was not?*

Greg rose, walked over to the expandable brown carton from which the deputy had pulled Ira's case file. In his few unhappy months working in the D.A.'s office, he'd learned a few of Taylor's tricks. You couldn't legally hide relevant documents from the defense attorney, but you didn't have to go out of your way to make sure they were noticed. Instead of handing documents directly to his opponent, Taylor generally favored an "open file" policy. By that he meant defense attorneys were always free to come look at what he had—if they knew where to look.

Greg found the two single pieces of paper stuck behind a divider deep inside the expandable carton. Each contained a brief handwritten statement, dated four days after the arrests. One was from a Simon Hutch, the other from a Rob Linter, both identified as Sandy Polson's "friends" and fellow patrons at the Foghorn Pub. Their statements appeared at considerable odds with what Sandy and Paul had told the police.

Sandy didn't drive to Crocker with Ira and Paul in a green Dodge van, Linter and Hutch each stated. Rather, she drove to Crocker with them, in Hutch's white Plymouth Fury. She'd approached them at the Foghorn, asked for a ride. They'd obliged. Up at the Pozo Tavern in

Crocker, she'd borrowed Hutch's Plymouth, saying she had to "take care of some business." When she came back shortly after midnight, she looked dazed. They sat at the bar for a while drinking beer, then smoked a joint as they drove back down the coast. When they dropped Sandy at her home in the hills above the Foghorn, she grabbed a paper sack from the backseat and disappeared inside.

Linter and Hutch had seen Ira Sullivan and Paul Platt at the Foghorn earlier that night, but not in Crocker. Nor had they heard Sandy mention their names. Nor did they know anything about a green Dodge van.

Flipping the page, Greg found one more document attached to the end of Hutch's and Linter's accounts. It was dated later the same day. Buzz Johnson, it seemed, had acquired a search warrant and visited Sandy's home deep in the woods of Apple Canyon. There, in a paper sack stuffed in a corner of the living room, he'd found a .22 pistol.

Greg slapped the file shut. The postmaster had a .22 bullet in his head; Sandy Polson had a .22 pistol. This wasn't a complicated case; this wasn't even a mystery. This was, rather, the same old stinking song. Lasorda in Florida, Taylor now. What exactly was Dennis up to, though? Why make Ira the killer?

Glancing out the window that gave onto the *asistencia*'s inner courtyard, Greg saw Roger Kandle walk by. "Roger," he called, jumping out of his chair and tapping on the window. The detective stopped, turned, waited for Greg to negotiate the corridor. In a moment, they were facing each other under the great Spanish oak.

"It looks like Ira Sullivan might as well confess," Greg began. "The evidence against him is overwhelming."

Kandle frowned at Greg as if he were trespassing.

The two had never been friends, despite their time working together in the D.A.'s office. Still, they appreciated each other, in a way. For a while, they'd even trusted each other. When the Bowser case came along, only Roger had entertained Greg's concerns; they'd shared a tenuous bond. Then, as others in the D.A.'s office started pulling back from Greg, so had Roger. The two had eventually lost almost all contact. Roger had learned to make his way in the Chumash County district attorney's world.

Greg understood. Despite their differences he couldn't work up much enmity toward Roger, not with his half-bald head, his soft, full face, his way of smiling easily at people. From time to time, Greg spotted him at the beach or park with his family, three young daughters and a wife who all seemed unable to stop hugging him, climbing on him, tugging at him. He always looked good-natured about the assault, not exactly laughing or smiling, but content. Greg envied him in those moments.

"Two eyewitnesses," Kandle muttered. "Open-and-shut, Dennis says."

"It's a wonder Ira's not already sitting on Death Row," Greg replied. "You and Buzz have done some nifty detective work."

Kandle started to back away. Caution clouded his eyes. He'd spent enough time around Greg to understand his tone. "What I think doesn't matter," he insisted. "Only what the jury thinks matters. You know that."

Turning his head, Greg spotted the prosecutor and sheriff looking at them from a window of the *asistencia*'s jail wing. He thought he also saw another head, maybe two. One appeared to be a woman's, with light brown tousled hair. Recalling the floor plan, Greg figured this window gave onto the prisoner's interview room. He walked over, tapped on the window. By now, a couple of deputies were blocking his view; he caught just a glimpse of bodies being hurried out of the room. Then Dennis Taylor and Dan Wizen appeared in the courtyard. Roger joined them, the three half circling Greg.

"A little social mingling with the prisoners, gentlemen?" Greg asked. "A new program for improving jail morale?"

Dennis Taylor laughed heartily, as if he thought Greg a wonderful card. Dan Wizen, as usual, tried to ape the prosecutor, though the sheriff's laugh came out more like a snigger. Roger didn't move a muscle. "Yes, that's exactly right," Taylor said. "We're improving jail morale."

"Didn't there used to be a law or something about this?" Greg asked. "About you being in there alone, questioning Sandy Polson and Paul Platt without their lawyers?"

The smile remained fixed on Taylor's face, although now his upper lip involuntarily curled. The cold, flat eyes were showing. To Greg, everything on his face looked glued on.

"Your integrity is so charming," Taylor said. "Such an idealist. A utopian, even. That's what you are, an absolute utopian."

No longer, Greg thought. That was long ago. That was before he'd retreated, before he'd stopped hoping. It surprised him now to realize how much he missed those days. It surprised him also to realize how excited he felt.

"Since I'm apparently here during visiting hours," Greg said, "I'd like to see my client."

Taylor stared at him. "Your client?"

"Yes, my client."

"I thought this was a courtesy call."

"No longer."

"I thought you didn't do criminal defense work anymore."

"Someone's got to stop this."

Taylor shared an amused glance with Kandle and Wizen. "Are you really sure you want to be the one, Monarch?"

Greg again stifled an impulse to turn and run.

"Dennis," he said, "you don't always get to win."

They brought Ira to him in handcuffs. Greg glanced at the cuffs, then at the deputy, who shrugged and took them off. Ira moved slowly to the chair across the table from Greg. He wouldn't look at his ex-partner.

Ira had been thinking of Jeffrey's funeral when they came to get him. On and on everyone had talked that day about his little boy. His big brown cow eyes, his goofy smiles, the way he cocked his head at grown-ups. Ira himself, standing beside his son's grave, could think only of Jeff acting cranky and demanding; in those moments, Ira would swing him over his head, bring him down, peer into his eyes, sometimes even earn a grudging smile. When the funeral ended, Ira had insisted on staying behind to help the grave diggers shovel dirt. Alone with them, he'd stretched out atop the casket, hugging Jeff's wooden cradle.

"Why are you here, Greg?" Ira asked quietly. "You're not my lawyer."

Greg reached across, touched Ira's arm. "Events," he said. "Let's blast them."

Ira peered at him with curiosity. "I thought you'd gone on strike. I thought you were a conscientious objector."

"Who's Paul Platt?" Greg asked.

"Didn't you take your ball and go home?"

"I'm back."

"How come?"

"Trust me, Ira."

"Not sure I can."

"Who's Paul Platt?"

Ira studied Greg. Slowly, his wariness turned to a grin. He couldn't help it, the sight of Greg once again so animated made him want to chortle. "Don't you want to get out a pad of paper, Counselor? Maybe a pen?"

Greg patted his empty pockets. "I'll remember what you say."

"No, you won't. If I hadn't taken notes, we would never have won a single case."

"This time I'll remember."

Ira's expression turned serious. "Paul Platt's just a guy. Hung out with me sometimes, earned a few bucks. Not very bright. Sort of retarded, really. He needed work, I needed someone real simple."

Greg, settling back in his chair, didn't ask what for. He drew a breath. "Okay, Ira, again. You know any special reason why Taylor would be after you?"

"No, I don't. He and I never had a run-in. Hell, by the time he became D.A., I was hardly even practicing law."

"Anyone else after you?"

Ira tapped the table with his fingers. "I owe money to a few folks. Nothing important. But something funny is going on here at the jail. They've been moving people around in the cells. I've never seen Sandy or Paul, but I think sometimes I can hear them."

"Who are they talking to?"

"I'd swear they're talking to each other."

"How efficient," Greg said. "No middlemen." He leaned toward Ira. "Tell me more about Sandy Polson."

Ira blinked. Again he felt a rush at the thought of that woman. He barely knew her, but something about Sandy made him recall his days free-falling for miles through the thin, cold sky. He wasn't sure Greg would understand. Not that Ira understood so well himself. The combination of danger and allure he saw easily enough. Sandy didn't exactly scare him, though. What she did was make him feel wary.

Once, late on a chilly, wind-whipped night, they'd stepped outside the Foghorn together to find a grizzled beach bum prostrate on the boardwalk, vomit splattered down his flannel shirt, an empty whiskey bottle in his bony hand. When Ira bent to help, Sandy urgently yanked him away, her mouth twisted in disgust. "What a bore," she muttered. "I despise people like that." Then, as if compelled, she turned back and for a moment stood over the poor wretch, her eyes glistening, her cheeks flushed. Finally, she led Ira to the surf's edge, where she sat huddled in a blanket, spent and disarmed. At his mention of the boardwalk derelict she peered blankly, and talked instead about her childhood desire to play the tenor saxophone. "To play that instrument as if it were a glorious human voice" was how she put it. "To share your most private feelings without uttering a word."

Another time, after he'd started buying meth from her, she'd gently cautioned him about a bad batch of Super

Buick circulating on the street up north. Ira wasn't nearly that far gone into junk, so first she had to explain what it was—a brutal blend of cocaine, heroin, and the antinausea drug scopolamine. Then she had to describe what the bad batch did. How users were being rushed into emergency rooms with faint heartbeats and no breathing, how doctors were giving them Narcan to kick-start respiration, how Narcan combined with scopolamine produced screaming, foot-stomping lunatics. How at the push of a syringe, half-dead patients were suddenly turning violent and delirious.

"Stay away from that stuff," Sandy urged, her voice full of concern. "Oh, Ira, that stuff is dangerous."

A moment later, suddenly transformed, she cocked her head and started giggling. She couldn't help it, she explained. Think about all those hospital workers, the laundry crew and motor-pool guys side by side with nurses and surgeons, everyone grabbing straps, ropes, and torn sheets, four of them at a time needed to lash down each thrashing wild-eyed junkie. "Like a scene out of 'MASH,' Ira. Yelling, bodies pouring in by the minute, cars roaring up, drivers pushing junkies out the door, cars zooming away. Like 'MASH,' just like 'MASH.' "

"Where'd the bad stuff come from?" Ira asked.

Sandy gave him a funny look then, like a schoolgirl caught cutting a class. "A supplier I know," she said. "He put it on the street to ruin a competing dealer."

They'd finally drifted apart over a small-time drug deal. Ira passed $5,000 to her from friends who wanted some meth. The night she was to deliver, the pay phone rang at the Foghorn. Sandy listened, murmured a few words, hung up, then walked back to where Ira stood near a pool table. She picked up a cue stick, studied the lay of the balls. "I'm afraid something has gone wrong," she reported breezily. "My guy's been ripped off. Your money's been stolen."

Ira blurted his response instinctively, with little thought. "No way," he said. "No way."

Sandy showed only a flicker of annoyance beneath her

nonchalance. "I understand your feelings," she offered, smiling sweetly at him as she drove the six ball into the corner pocket. "But, Ira, these things happen."

Already uninterested, Ira shrugged and nodded. In those days, little could rouse him to argue. He just didn't care. Maybe she was telling the truth, he reasoned. The moment passed; they turned to their billiards game. But after that, Ira instinctively avoided Sandy. He'd nod at her in the Foghorn, even buy her a drink, but he kept his distance. He sensed it best not to get further ensnared in Sandy Polson's world.

"Tell you about Sandy?" Ira answered Greg. "What can I say? Met her at the Foghorn, but that's not really her scene. She likes slumming, is all. Especially when she's bored and restless, which is often. When she's tapped out, she's a waitress around town. Other times, she dances, she plays pool, she laughs at your jokes. She goes places with you."

"Drugs?" Greg asked.

"Buys and sells a little. Nothing big-time, just among friends, or to pay the month's bills."

"The postmaster's murder?"

Ira shrugged. "That I can't explain. Doesn't fit with the woman I know."

"Carrying around thirty-three thousand dollars cash in Wilson's dish towel looks downright foolish," Greg pointed out.

"Also doesn't fit."

"Fingering you?"

Ira chewed on that one. "That might fit. She always did feel like danger to me."

Greg rose, turned to leave. Then he stopped, put his hand on his ex-partner's. Inexplicably, he found himself thinking of a day long ago. A bully named Biff was pushing Greg around, on their junior high playground. Suddenly, Ira was at his side. He didn't shove or hit Biff, didn't say anything to him at all. Ira just tugged at Greg's elbow, said, "Hey, come look what I got." They walked off together, Ira showing him something, just what, Greg didn't even remember. That wasn't the point. Ira had obliterated the assault by denying it, by sweeping Greg into his own charmed orbit. It wasn't a beating Ira had saved him from, it was humiliation.

From then on, for years, Greg watched Ira do the same for others, casually and without any ado. Awkward athletes, guys without dates, classmates overwhelmed by teachers. It was more than niceness; it wasn't exactly niceness at all. It was an instinct—or maybe a need—for averting another's shame. Others enjoyed watching such degrading moments, but Ira felt compelled to ward them off. As odd as it was for someone so popular, his seemed the manner of one overly familiar with humiliation.

Greg squeezed Ira's hand, as if that could remedy an act of desertion. "We all fail," he said. "No one's perfect."

The usual late afternoon fog was rolling in by the time Greg exited the *asistencia*, but he had one more visit to make before he could repair to JB's for the evening. From La Graciosa's town square, he drove west toward Pirate's Beach, then south toward the county line. To his right, between him and the ocean, rose the startling white Chumash Dunes.

Greg never stopped marveling over these wondrous four-hundred-foot-high mounds of sand. What he loved most was their history. The Chumash lived in the dunes thousands of years ago, then Spanish explorers camped there on their way from San Diego to Monterey. Best of all, during the 1930s and 1940s, the dunes were home to refugees—refugees from the world's madness.

The Dunites were a loose community of some thirty writers, artists, mystics, freethinkers, and hoboes. One was a poet who never intended to see his work published, one lived off hog grain, one had been a gunrunner during the Irish Revolution, one a *Vogue* cover girl. Greg thought of them mainly as expatriates. They built ramshackle lean-to huts amidst the dunes, living each alone, but they gathered at night at a community house for talk, brandy, parties. For a while they put out a journal. For food, they grew vegetables and harvested the clams that abounded on their shores. On foggy nights, when enough women were present, they'd wind up a Victrola and dance by an open fire. It was, to some of them at least, a grand experiment. They were trying to create a utopia.

It didn't last, of course. When World War II came, bringing with it Coast Guard installations full of armament, the Dunites scattered, vanished. Maybe Dennis Taylor was right, Greg mused. Maybe he was a goddamn utopian. If so, he was doomed for sure.

Reaching the Chumash Dunes Trailer Park, Greg walked down a dusty, pitted path, looking for Number 38. This, according to the police report, was Simon Hutch's home. The rolling fog hung thick here. Scrawny dogs barked in the gloom, scratching at screen doors. A woman emerging from one trailer with a laundry basket glanced blankly at Greg before turning to pin faded blouses to a clothesline. Another woman, from another trailer, stared longer at him as she heaved gray, sudsy dishwater into her yard.

Number 38 was at the end of a row, a faded blue trailer with an empty flowerpot on the porch railing and a torn front screen. Simon Hutch, clutching an open can of Graciosa Brew, dressed in shorts and a sleeveless undershirt, opened the door at Greg's first knock. He had dark, bushy hair, a thick, matted beard, a beer drinker's paunch. He did not look all that happy to see Greg.

"Yeah?" Hutch began.

"Simon, my name is Greg Monarch. I was wondering if I could talk to you for a minute."

"I already told the cops what I know."

"I'm not a cop," Greg explained, struggling to keep his voice casual. "I'm a lawyer. I represent Ira Sullivan, who, as you may know, is charged along with Sandy."

Hutch relaxed a little. Lawyers apparently weren't as bad as cops. "Yeah, I know. Weird about that guy."

"What do you mean?"

"What I mean is, we told the cops Sandy didn't go up to Crocker with Sullivan. Rob and I, we told the cops we drove her up to Crocker. Not Sullivan."

Greg nodded. "I know you told the cops that," he said. "But what did you tell the grand jury? That's what I'm wondering. Did you tell the grand jury the same story, Simon?"

Hutch tugged at his beard, genuinely puzzled. "What grand jury?" he finally said. "Rob and I didn't tell a grand jury anything."

Greg labored to understand. "You mean you refused to testify?"

"No, no, you don't get it," Hutch said. "We were never asked to testify. The D.A. never called us before any grand jury."

FIVE

At dusk, on his way to JB's, Jimmy O'Brien stopped to watch La Graciosa's plaza come to life. It was a scene he never tired of witnessing. Each evening at this time, shoppers, store clerks, and families gathered in the town's core to visit as the setting sun washed the sky pale gold. On nearby street corners, local farmers offered home-grown apples and avocados from the backs of pickup trucks. At the outdoor cafés, scruffy college students and well-groomed office workers nursed beers or herbal teas. At the now placid creek, children tossed bread crumbs to ducks as their parents sat measuring the fog curling over the peaks.

If he closed his eyes, Jimmy almost could imagine himself back in the La Graciosa of old. Gone now was the cigar factory, the big wholesale meat market, the dairy, the Greyhound bus station. The Thurston family had sold their department store to a national chain years ago. Henry's Hardware, where you could buy everything from kerosene lamps to washboards, was now an empty lot. The meat market was a dress store, the creamery a complex of sushi, cappuccino, and moccasin shops. La Graciosa hadn't turned precious yet, but it was fighting the battle. With costs up and prices down, the influence of the old cattle ranch families had waned. Auctioneers already had carved up one grand 20,000-acre spread and offered 40-acre parcels at fire-sale prices. Onetime ranchers now took "day jobs" in town, or grew kiwi and grapes, or raised purebred Arabians. Searching La Graciosa's storefronts, it was easier to find a lawyer or accountant than a blacksmith.

Jimmy circled the plaza, lingering, not ready yet for JB's. Near the steps of the *asistencia*, a woman was strumming a guitar. Beside the creek, a small boy laughed at two ducks fighting over his crumbs. Alone on a bench, a man wrapped in a navy blue peacoat sat hunched over, deep in thought. So what if you had to close your eyes sometimes to make La Graciosa what it should be? Jimmy didn't object to dreams, as long as you understood clearly what they were transforming, what they were transcending. *This is not, I say, the dead Ireland of my youth, but an Ireland the poets have imagined, terrible and gay.* They ragged him at JB's about Yeats, but what the hell. They could learn a couple things from poets.

Not until he reached the plaza's far side, and gained a more direct view, did Jimmy realize that the man in the peacoat was Greg Monarch. He started toward him, then stopped. Greg wasn't just lost in his thoughts. Like the children, he was feeding the ducks, although with whole slabs of bread rather than crumbs. He wasn't sprinkling the water, he was slapping it, startling the swimming birds with the food he hurled their way.

So typical of Greg, Jimmy thought. Always fuming or hungering for something ineffable. Jimmy savored Greg's agitation. He didn't wish equanimity on his friend; rather, he worried over the ebbing of his spirit. He'd seen too much of that in his time. Everywhere he turned, people had lost heart. *The best lack all conviction, while the worst are full of passionate intensity.*

When he had filed his story about Greg taking over as Ira Sullivan's attorney, there'd been a few raised eyebrows at the *News-Times* among the more vinegary copy editors. Even those on the desk most appreciative of Greg speculated openly over his willingness to counter Dennis Taylor. Jimmy had finally glared the desk into silence. He cheered Greg's decision. Cheered it even though, knowing Taylor's ways, he also felt it wise to pray fervently to God for Ira's deliverance.

Full of such thoughts, Jimmy stepped toward his friend, then stopped. Greg's creekside bench was empty. Jimmy hadn't noticed his leaving. He scanned the plaza without success. He'd lost him.

Greg walked up Carmel Avenue, pretending he was wandering aimlessly. At the corner of Cerros Street, he stopped. Here was one lingering treasure from La Graciosa's past. The Shilling Brothers Building still stood where it always had, and looked much as it did when built in 1884.

It was a two-story affair with a prominent cast-iron facade, Venetian Renaissance style, fabricated by the City Iron Works of San Francisco and shipped in sections by steamer. From the day it opened until well into the 1950s, Shilling's had been the finest dry goods store and clothing emporium in Chumash County. Housewives, farmers, and ranchers flocked there daily for supplies and provisions—everything from clothes and fabrics to furnishings, groceries, and farm machinery. You could also talk to La Graciosa's mayor there; Lawrence Shilling held that post for a good twenty years.

Times change, of course. First Shilling's sons had been obliged to drop groceries and farm machinery. Then they'd been forced to give up entirely. A realtor bought the store in the late 1970s and resold it to an investment group three years later. Standing before the building now, Greg peered into a cavernous gift shop full of T-shirts, coffee cups, and postcard stands.

He walked inside. Alison Davana stood behind the main counter, blessing a customer with her well-practiced, if slightly bored, look of understanding. Whatever the man was talking about, however vain or pigheaded or grasping his intent, Alison surely would make him feel appreciated. She was good at that.

They had never been as close as they'd imagined, but, off and on, they'd been companions of a sort. Then they'd drifted apart entirely in the months after he left the D.A.'s job. The split had not surprised Greg.

"Aren't you off soon?" he asked after she'd dispatched her customer. He absorbed her sour gaze, knowing it meant little.

"Okay," she said. "But not JB's."

They sat by the creek, at a small round table on the patio of Stella's Café. Alison chain-smoked Marlboros and stirred a Diet Coke. They'd met at JB's, and had played out much of their relationship there. Greg had always insisted Dylan was on the jukebox that first night. *Come in, she said, I'll give you shelter from the storm*. Maybe not, though. Maybe he imagined that. Shelter surely wasn't Alison's strong suit, at any rate. She was better at looking you directly in the eye, her manner openly carnal when she was in the mood. "I didn't think you'd noticed," she'd sighed that first night, after he settled on the stool next to her.

"Tell me about Dennis Taylor," Greg said now, frowning over his black coffee.

Alison rolled her eyes. They'd always avoided talk of her time with Taylor. It had seemed to Greg so unlikely a pairing. "What part do you want to know about?" she asked.

It was almost a taunt. An image of Alison in bed flashed involuntarily across Greg's mind. Alison with her long, thin skirt hitched up to her waist, so urgent and shameless, her slender, curving body wrapped around his, her mouth slightly parted, her hands expertly roaming. Greg had never known another woman so full of daring and abandon.

She was more exotic-looking than pretty, with her deep green almond-shaped eyes and thick jet-black hair and smooth olive skin. She knew well that she drew men's attention. Their glances neither annoyed nor flattered her; she tended to look back, but in a diffuse manner, rarely direct or intimate, more acknowledging an admirer than reciprocating. Power was Alison's subtext.

"What was the deal between the two of you?" Greg asked. "You can spare me the details. I just need you to explain him."

"Nothing really to explain," Alison said. "It was quite simple, really. I liked coke in those days. He always had coke around. He wasn't the D.A. then, remember, just another young Hoover-nosed lawyer."

"What else?"

Alison sucked on her Marlboro and gave him a funny look. "I thought you didn't want the details," she said.

Her brazen acceptance of herself had always attracted Greg. For a while, she'd felt like home to him, or at least almost home. She needed nothing from him, though. She wanted nothing.

Greg beckoned with an open palm. "I need to understand Taylor," he said. "So bring on the details."

Alison blinked her bawdy eyes. "Well, okay then, let's see. He liked to do it standing up. Right there in the corner of his office. That what you're after?"

Greg said nothing.

"It was kind of exciting," Alison continued. "The way his secretary could have walked in and all. Also convenient. Considering I couldn't afford to pay for coke in those days."

Greg studied his coffee. Alison reached out, took his hand. "He can be a charming guy, Greg. I was young."

Greg forced himself not to think of her in Taylor's office. With anyone else, the notion might excite him. Not with Dennis, though. "Where did he get his drugs?" he asked. "Was he dealing large-scale, or what?"

Alison held up a hand. "Whoa, whoa, down boy. You're jumping to conclusions. I don't know that he was dealing at all. It struck me as mainly recreational. He was a party-hearty consumer, though. Used to scoop my little gram out of a nice-sized bucket. Don't know where it came from."

"Try to remember, Alison. Who came to visit him? Where was he getting it from?"

Alison watched a duck that, distracted from its paddling

by all the creekside attention, was being swept downstream. "I'm not sure, but I think maybe it had something to do with someone out at Pirate's Beach," she said. "He was always driving out that way."

"Did he use anything else?"

Alison cocked her head, arched her back, grinned slyly. He'd seen that look before. "I do know he kept some amyl nitrate around," she said. "He liked to pop an amyl when he was coming. I always worried he was going to have a heart attack."

After Alison, Greg headed for JB's, but when he reached the tavern's door, he hesitated. Through the window, he could see Jimmy holding forth in one corner, Shirley sitting by herself in another. To his surprise, it did not look inviting. He didn't think he could sit at the bar this night. It wouldn't work.

He backed away, found his car, started driving. Halfway to the sea, at the southern mouth of the valley, he turned off at Los Osos Lake. Ira's fishing spot, Greg's swimming hole. He welcomed the chill water of spring and swam here often, sometimes for an hour or more without stopping, across and back, across and back. *Could I but have my wish, colder and dumber and deafer than a fish*. Jimmy had taught him that line. Greg stripped and dove in. Loons called, and frogs. Greg plunged toward the lake bottom, floated, let himself rise, stroked toward the far shore. The notion of living underwater appealed to him. Everything moved slowly there, everything was muted. Back and forth he swam, his mind still, his muscles stretching. Kick, stroke, dive, kick, stroke, dive. All in silence. *Colder and dumber and deafer than a fish*.

It took a while for Greg to hear his name being called, and a little longer to realize someone was throwing small stones at him from the shoreline. He stroked toward shallow ground, found a footing, stood still, listened.

"Goddammit, Greg, I know you're out there," a voice

shouted from shore. "Will you please get your friggin' ass over here? I'm not about to swim out there to get you."

Through the fog, Greg could see Jimmy O'Brien tottering at the edge of the water. As lure, the newspaper reporter held a half-gallon jug of Black Bush high over his head. Greg took the bait.

They sat on the shore under a spreading oak, perhaps the very one Ira daydreamed under years before. Greg rubbed the water from his hair with a dirty towel as they passed the bottle back and forth.

I will arise and go now, and go to Innisfree, and a small cabin build there, of clay and wattles made. Jimmy recited quietly. *And live alone in the bee-loud glade. And I shall have some peace there . . .*

Greg interrupted. "What I don't get is how a blue-collar, white-cracker grease monkey knows poetry."

The wide gap in their backgrounds always provided them something to spar about. That Greg grew up amid cultured comfort, the only child of a venerable country doctor, irked Jimmy almost as much as his own bleak upbringing in a car mechanic's home intrigued Greg. Each suspected the other knew something he didn't.

Jimmy took a swallow of the Black Bush. "I saw you start to come into JB's, then back out," he said. "I thought I'd keep you company."

"Company was what I backed away from, Jimmy."

Jimmy ignored that. "Why don't we compare notes," he suggested. "We've both been working on the same thing, after all."

Greg considered and shrugged. He'd shared with Jimmy for years. The truth was, he usually came out ahead on the deal.

"You first," Greg said.

"Okay," Jimmy offered. "Here's what I have. It's a little blurry, but it seems Sandy Polson and Ira were both doing what they could to make ends meet."

"Cocaine?"

"Meth."

So that was it. Methamphetamine. Speed, crank.

"Why deal meth?" Greg asked.

Jimmy snorted. "Meth is what's circulating, that's why. For those on top, it's a nice, easy, multimillion-dollar bonanza. You set up a lab in any old farmhouse out in the Valley, surround it with some kids, chicken coops, maybe a lawn, it all fits right in. No smell, no signals, no red flags. Inside, all you need is a bunch of flasks and burners, and a couple of farmworkers to do the cooking. Your merchandise is out the door within hours."

Greg feigned ignorance. "How do they make it?"

"All you need basically is ephedrine and hydriodic acid. Getting the ephedrine's no problem. Swiss pharmaceutical brokers ship tons of the stuff to Mexico. From there it's smuggled in along the regular coke, grass, and heroin routes. Except without the usual heat; the feds' dogs aren't trained to smell ephedrine. You don't even need to smuggle it, though. You can buy pseudoephedrine anywhere, perfectly legal, and it's easily converted to meth."

"Pseudoephedrine?"

"That's your basic over-the-counter decongestant. Sudafed, all of them. Hell, you can order it in bulk from East Coast outlets, no questions asked."

"And hydriodic acid?"

"Used primarily as a dairy disinfectant, so there's plenty around here. It can be smuggled in from Mexico or bought on the black market or made from scratch."

"How big a market?"

"That's what's so nice. It's a growth business. Meth used to be mainly for long-haul truckers and college kids pulling all-nighters. Now everyone's injecting, snorting, or smoking. Partying teenagers, housewives who want to lose weight, tired ranch hands, hotshot professionals on the fast track, bedroom cowboys out to perform. You get a coke high, but it lasts longer and is much cheaper."

Greg waved off the whiskey bottle in Jimmy's hand. Hitler was a meth addict, he knew. John Kennedy got injections before important meetings. No wonder Ira succumbed. They said the high was great at the start. Euphoria, energy, confidence, just what Ira needed after Jeffrey. Trouble was, eventually the great buzz turned into depression, then paranoia, bad nerves, giant waves of anxiety. In the late stages, any stimulus—someone's twisted smile, the wink of an eye—could trigger rage and violence. Lots of snarling, crazy killers were meth freaks. Greg tried to imagine Ira in such a lethal drug's grip.

"Who's in charge?" he asked Jimmy.

"Years ago, bikers ran the central California meth labs. But the Mexican gangs have edged them out. They're mean and tough, I tell you. More than a few bodies turn up on those country roads in the Valley. Ira's been playing in a risky game."

"Why?"

"As I understand it, he just sort of fell into it. Owed a dealer some money, I think. Got an offer he couldn't refuse. This was a way out, fronting on the local level for a distributor. Small-time stuff, way down on the feeding chain. Sandy Polson stood on the same rung, more or less, paying off debts. Except, Ira couldn't handle it like she could. Walked away from it nine months ago. Resigned."

Greg labored to connect the dots. "I've been told Dennis Taylor has a recreational drug habit. Anything there?"

Jimmy shrugged. "Not that I know. I have nothing on Taylor. I will say this. I don't believe anyone shot the postmaster for three hundred thirty hundred-dollar bills."

"What, then?"

"Think about those private mailboxes in the wall there. You know there's no home delivery up in Crocker. Everyone comes to the post office, picks up their mail. Only Wilson's hands touch whatever goes into those boxes. They'd be a nifty way to swap drugs and money. No physical contact, no eyes watching. Just eighty-year-old Wilson as the unwitting mule."

Jimmy grinned at the thought. He had a bent for weaving

plots, that was clear. He'd make a fine mystery novelist, Greg thought.

"What if this wasn't a simple robbery, what if Wilson had discovered what was in his P.O. boxes?" Jimmy continued. "What if this wasn't about a lousy thirty-three thousand dollars at all? What if the cash were a decoy, to draw attention away from the boxes? What if—"

Greg stopped him with a raised hand. "You're getting a little fevered out here, Jimmy. Calm down, think. It doesn't make sense. It doesn't explain what Taylor is up to. With Sandy Polson in possession of thirty-three thousand dollars cash and the probable murder weapon, why is Dennis so determined to see Ira as the postmaster's killer?"

Jimmy chewed on that awhile before answering. "Hard to say," he finally offered. "But Taylor doesn't do anything without thinking of his career. He's been spending even more time than usual in Sacramento. Probably measuring the A.G.'s office, seeing if his furniture will fit. He's also been dining out with big donors. Don't think there's a corporation in California that hasn't bought him a steak these past few months—"

"Okay, okay, we know Taylor is ambitious," Greg interrupted. "But what does that have to do with Ira's case?"

"Don't know," Jimmy allowed. "Sure it's something ugly, though."

It was Greg's turn to grin. "Welcome to Jimmy's world. Evil everywhere."

A jagged flash of lightning, then the rumble of thunder interrupted them. A spring storm had blown in on the wind without warning. Before they could get to their feet, the downpour began. Greg grabbed his coat, started for his car, but Jimmy didn't move. He just watched the storm, his face turned to the sky. Electric bolts cracked in the hills almost directly above them, followed by the thunder's roar. The rain deepened and pummeled them, feeling as if dumped from a giant bucket. Finally Jimmy jumped to his feet, ran to the lake's edge, lifted the Black Bush bottle to the sky. "Owwww," he yelled, wolf-howling to the moon. "Owwwww, owwwwww, owwwwww."

The next lightning bolt appeared to lunge directly at Jimmy. Greg ran to his side, started pulling at his arm. "Jimmy, Jimmy," he pled, "this is dangerous, you could get hit, we have to get out of here."

Jimmy cackled, shook off Greg's hand, lifted both arms to the sky, danced a jig. "Maybe so, maybe so," he shouted. "But what a way to die, Greg. . . . Yeeha! . . . What a way to die."

The look in Jimmy's eye alarmed Greg. He backed away, shook his head, turned toward his car. "Jesus, Jimmy," he said. "You're nuts. You're a goddamn madman."

SIX

Sandy Polson, wiping her brow, sighed at the ancient steam radiator rattling away in the far corner of the sheriff's interrogation room. Somebody had given it a good head of steam, too much. The humid, oppressive heat it produced made her feel ill. So did the whole room, for that matter.

The *asistencia* showed its age in this wing, particularly under the bank of fluorescent lights they'd hung from the cracked and splintered rafters. The painted walls, a sickly green hue, were peeling. The solitary table and four chairs were scuffed and rusted. A film of dirt and mildew clouded a window that otherwise would offer at least a passing glimpse of the outside world. Sandy felt forlorn. Forlorn, and overwhelmingly bored.

If only she were home right now, she thought. Home, sitting on her deck in the oak-thick woods of Apple Canyon. Listening to the owls hoot, watching the falcons soar. Maybe practicing the saxophone she'd bought but never learned to play.

"Mr. Taylor," Sandy said. "I don't think Detective Kandle believes a word I'm saying."

They were sitting across from her, all of them. The D.A., Buzz Johnson, Roger Kandle. What a trio. Roger with his soft, fat belly, Buzz with the hair growing out of his nose, Dennis with all those horribly banal lines of patter. At least Dennis and Buzz had been listening in a manner familiar to Sandy. Something in their expressions told her they accepted her story. That's how it usually worked. She could convince people of just about anything. Even if they'd heard bad reports about her, once people spent time with her, they always came around.

Not Roger Kandle, though. He just sat there with a dull, vacant cow face. She wasn't affecting him at all. This made Sandy feel uneasy. She couldn't help wondering what Kandle thought about her, what Kandle knew about her. His manner stirred so many unpleasant memories. It had been long ago, but there'd been plenty of times when no one believed her.

That day when she shot her little half brother, for example. It was only buckshot, he wasn't hurt badly, and besides, it was an accident, something that happened when she tried to wrestle the rifle from the silly boy's scrawny arms. Everyone had acted so coolly to her, though. No one had behaved as if they truly believed her. Her family, classmates, teachers, counselors—they all looked at her funny, as if she'd actually tried to harm her half brother. No one saw that she'd been trying to protect him. Him, and well, yes, herself also. He might have shot her if left to wave that rifle around. No one understood that, no one thought about that one bit.

At least she endured the experience with no worse than a roomful of suspicion. How had the rifle ended up pointed at her brother? Why did the trigger get pulled that second time? Wasn't that an argument the nanny heard just before the shots? Sandy still shuddered a little when she thought of those questions, but she'd handled them easily enough. Yes, of course, she had been angry at her half brother. Who wouldn't be, with such a noisy, snotty brat? She hadn't tried to kill him, though, goodness no. She'd approached him meaning only to quiet him down. If he'd only not resisted, everything would have been okay. Instead, they had an accident. Thank God the bullets only grazed his arm.

The episode in Costa Rica had been an accident too, though once again not everyone saw it her way. Traveling alone there that summer, she'd met some Americans. They all dined one night at a cliff-top restaurant overlooking the stormy Caribbean, just south of Limón. The surf wildly pounding on pale pink coral reefs, lavish rain forests crowding almost to the sea's edge—everything felt so wonderfully exotic there on the Caribbean coast, so much dense flavor compared to the broad spotless resorts of the Pacific. Such a sense of delicious danger, too. All those dark, lithe, brooding waiters, silently watching the Americans as they cracked local lobsters and washed down the rich white meat with frosty bottles of Chilean chardonnay. The feel of obeisant resentment in that restaurant fueled Sandy's hunger. She waved her arm and ordered a platter of grilled prawns.

It was raining hard when they finally left. The seven of them—four women, three men—climbed into three rental cars, one Sandy's. The narrow dirt roads were riddled with rocks and potholes. Sandy still remembered the deluge, pounding first on the café's tin roof, then on their caravan. She remembered, too, that strange film clinging insistently to their windshields. It looked like vapor, it looked like something you could wipe or blow away, but you couldn't. Twice, they all stopped their cars and stood in the driving rain at gas stations, furiously scrubbing grimy glass with buckets of soapy water. Finally they surrendered, accepting the vague, milky view their windshields offered. Feet on accelerators, they plunged deeper into Costa Rica's dense tropical interior, heading for the guest house of a vast banana plantation in the remote Valle de Estrella, its use offered by a gracious Castle & Cooke foreman they'd met at the restaurant just as they were finishing the last of their wine.

Chávez was his name. Short, burly, with exceptional hooded eyes that broadcast both menace and wisdom, he was celebrating his sixty-fifth birthday that evening. He told stories as Sandy drove, his voice sonorous and rhythmic. He talked of catching the local trains as a youth by riding alongside them on his horse, then jumping on and pulling himself up and waving his horse home. He talked of happily waiting three hours on a Limón highway during the annual March of Crabs, not minding the delay because the slow, thick crustaceans were heading to the beach "to make love." He talked of pitching tents as a boy in lost, hidden forests, of riding bicycles on Limón streets empty of automobiles, of scrambling through chocolate-tree plantations grown so wild they looked abandoned. Sandy loved it when Chávez forced them all to detour ten miles down a back road so he could proudly show them a wild, untamed coastal park. Standing under an umbrella in the deep, wet sand, the rain pummeling her shoulders, the surf breaking on the reef a mile out, she particularly enjoyed watching one of her more irksome traveling companions squirm in discomfort as her penny loafers filled with water.

Was that why some in their group turned on Sandy later? Just because she smirked at one of them in the rain? Whatever the reason, it was true, later not all of them sided with her. Not all of them agreed that they'd left the second gas station with filmy windshields. Some insisted they could see clearly after that stop. Even Chávez made this claim, though how he knew for sure—waving his arms, yammering his ceaseless nonsense—Sandy never understood. It didn't really matter, of course. Even if she could see clearly through her windshield, it still remained indisputable: At the moment she came upon that woman sprawled facedown, smack in the center of a narrow, twisting road, she was driving through a dark, storm-whipped rain forest.

In such a setting, who could not understand Sandy's conduct? Why assume that woman in the road was sick? Why assume she needed help? Could it not just as easily have been a trick? The rain forests were thick with *bandidos*, after all. They'd been warned about just this type of ploy. Someone sprawls on an isolated road, faking injury; the bandits leap from the dense roadside brush when the concerned motorists stop and get out.

It was a trick, anyone could see as much. Anyone could see that's why Sandy chose not to slow and stop and get out. Anyone could see that's why she chose instead to accelerate. She'd meant to swerve, too, of course. She'd meant to steer to the side of the road as she gunned her car past this decoy. The road was so narrow, though, so close to the thick brush that harbored the bandits.

Why couldn't everyone see that's why she ended up driving over the woman? It had been a dreadful mistake; a fatal mistake, as it turned out. She certainly hadn't meant to kill anyone, though. It seemed so unfair for people to treat her as they did. All those questions, all those funny looks. It wasn't right, not after she'd been trying to protect them. They all could have been murdered but for her quick thinking. Yes, it was true, it turned out that the poor wretched woman was just a drunk who'd fallen on the road halfway between the local bar and her home. Who knew that at the time, though? Surely not Chávez, no matter what he was calling out from the backseat. *Stop, she's drunk, she's hurt,* he kept saying. How did he know? That woman could have been a bandit's decoy. That woman could have been danger.

Sandy, at any rate, had managed to survive the Costa Rica nastiness almost as easily as her half brother's shooting. You could call it fabulous luck if you wanted to, the way she swiftly negotiated her way through all those foreign authorities and made it back home. It wasn't really luck, though. It finally came down to talent—an ability to convince. She hadn't always had it; back in junior high, certain counselors and doctors had disregarded the stories she told about her stepfather. That had enraged her, but as time went by, she'd learned how to win people to her side. Being agreeable and deferential helped. So, too, did controlling your temper. Hold your tongue, maintain equanimity, and soon enough the others would erupt in anger or anxiety or some such messy emotion. Sandy had to laugh, thinking of all the men she'd watched roar and sputter and wave their hands before her. They were so utterly amusing.

You looked at them through lowered eyelids, though not too seductively. You hung on their every word, then spoke earnestly when it was your turn. If you spoke at all, that is. Sometimes a quiet bearing worked best. At the least, you took your time answering a question, letting the other person know he'd asked something weighty indeed. Above all, you paid attention to responses, you anticipated emotions, you watched and listened until you understood what people expected from you.

Sandy found it terribly easy to copy those around her. Lovers strolling arm in arm, parents swinging children over their heads, teenagers laughing at private jokes—examples of how to act, how to feel, were everywhere. Appearing joyful was easy; you threw your head back, you opened your mouth, you laughed and tossed your head. Desire? You looked straight into their eyes, boldly. If they took your hand, you squeezed back, held theirs. Concern? A different kind of look, softer. You held their hand, but didn't squeeze. Sincerity? Easy, a natural. Just be yourself. If you believed it, they would.

Everyone was like her inside; Sandy felt sure of that. Even if they didn't admit it. Everyone pretended. They must. How else could they know what to do?

"Come on, Sandy," Dennis Taylor was saying, waving her concerns away as if they were cigar smoke. "It doesn't matter what Detective Kandle thinks about you. Or what any of us in this room think. All that matters is what the jury thinks. The jury has to believe you."

"Do you think they will?" Roger Kandle asked. Those were the first words he'd spoken all morning.

Taylor kept his eyes on Sandy. She was busy rearranging two bracelets, switching the wide silver Zuni cuff to her left wrist, the narrow turquoise and coral piece to her right. "Oh, I'm sure they'll believe her," he said. "Sandy just has to practice telling her story. Polish up her choice of words a little."

Behind them, the radiator hissed. Kandle cleared his throat. "And what about Paul Platt?"

Taylor smiled at Sandy. "Yes," he said. "Paul, too."

When he came through the pass this time, Greg barely noticed the allure of Pirate's Beach. He wasn't there to sightsee.

What was he after, though? Greg couldn't help wondering. Not the truth, exactly. His and Ira's grandest law professor, the much-celebrated Oscar P. Hammilberg, had disabused them of that notion long ago. Or at least, had tried to. It was a forty-year-long tradition at Chumash State. Hammilberg sitting in his great padded brown leather armchair, his law students almost at his knees, some bent into rickety straight-backed chairs, others with legs crossed on the thick taupe carpet of the professor's office suite. Before them, a Reed & Barton silver tray bearing delicate sherry glasses and a bottle of Tio Pepe wrapped in a napkin. Hammilberg had been playing the English don for so long, he sometimes slipped into a British accent.

"Just what would you say the legal system delivers?" Hammilberg always asked the third-year students at these gatherings, a sort of final test before sending them out into the real world. Someone invariably blurted out, "The truth," while everyone else rolled their eyes and elbowed their neighbors in the ribs. At Ira's and Greg's session, a stalwart few promoted "justice" as a possibility. The majority dismissed that notion too, then split fine hairs, debating on and on as the sherry bottle slowly emptied. Finally Hammilberg reached for a biscuit, studied it, let show his amusement. "Ladies and gentlemen," he proclaimed with a smirk, "what the legal system delivers is a verdict."

His goal, Greg reminded himself as he strode the Pirate's Beach boardwalk, was not the truth but a story. A story to tell the jury. A story that sounded better than the district attorney's, and Sandy Polson's, and Paul Platt's.

In that careful *pas de deux* between defense attorney and client, Greg had sketched their needs and Ira had provided such a story. *Polson and Platt say you all met at six* P.M.*, were together until past midnight. If you could account for those hours . . . ? If you had people you were with? If you could deny having a green Dodge van? If you could deny owning a gun?* Ira's tale, though not complete, had ended up fitting their requirements well enough.

He didn't own a gun, he didn't own a Dodge van. He'd spent the early evening at the Foghorn, the late evening in the dunes with two friends. Where he blacked out. Even if he couldn't account for his whereabouts after eleven or so, his was an alternative story, a seed for reasonable doubt. There'd surely be people at the Foghorn who saw him, maybe even someone in the dunes. Most important, there'd be his two friends, his companions under the stars.

That was the problem: his two friends. If Ira's story fit well enough, his pals did not. Jurors don't listen to facts and details; they watch the witnesses on the stand and make intuitive judgments. That was another lesson Professor Hammilberg had gleefully expounded as he brushed biscuit crumbs off his ample belly. "Ladies and gentlemen, a good story is only half of what you need," he declared. "You must also have a good storyteller. If the jurors don't trust your witness, it doesn't matter how good a story he is telling." Here Hammilberg would out-and-out smirk. "Or how true."

Planet. Moose. Those were the unfortunate names of Ira's friends. They were legendary figures on the Pirate's Beach scene, familiar even to Greg. Reaching the north end of the boardwalk, he crossed the street and entered the Foghorn Beach Pub. Ira's pals would likely be in there.

Not that they were beer drinkers or bikers, or even liked to play pool. Reflecting the odd, uneasy mix in Pirate's Beach, one corner of the Foghorn more closely resembled a Greenwich Village coffeehouse than a beach bar. At a few round tables nearest the entrance, the central California coast's lingering version of post-1960s bohemia gathered most afternoons, nursing the pots of chamomile tea that the Foghorn bartender had grudgingly agreed to stock.

Planet and Moose were at their usual spot, just inside the Foghorn door, closer to the ocean than to the pub's swirling smoke and pulsing jukebox. Greg ordered a Graciosa Brew and joined them. "I thought I'd find you here," he began.

Planet considered him tentatively, as if trying to recall who he was. Moose ignored him.

With his flowing white hair and beard, Planet suggested a biblical prophet. In his mid-sixties, his sun-bronzed physique hardened by diet and exercise, he remained handsome in a dramatic, weathered fashion. Even young women found him exciting. Worldly pleasures, however, were not Planet's interest. Seeking purity of spirit, he'd long ago taken a vow of chastity. As the story went, a lusty lady once tested his resolve by stripping naked and lying in the sand at his hut's front porch, moaning and writhing. Those passing by that day swore Planet had sat for hours before this demonstration, stoically gazing straight ahead, munching on wheat cakes, apparently happy to absorb the sky's cosmic energy.

Moose presented another story entirely. He was a big sixty-year-old Dutchman with short, bristly white hair, fiercely hooded eyes, a deep, rumbling voice, and a permanent scowl. The Hermit, they called him around Pirate's Beach, although through voracious reading—from Einstein and Nietzsche to the classical Greeks and Omar Khayyám—he knew the world well. Moose's scowl was misleading. He had a temper, he couldn't suffer fools, but he also laughed easily and often.

Relics of the Dunites—that's how Greg regarded Planet and Moose. The last vestiges of an imagined utopia. Ira, he knew, would have appreciated them, despite their strange feel of homeless decline and New Age babble. There was something ineffably touching about their eccentric individuality. Greg couldn't imagine any more colorful antidote to the creeping homogenization and vulgarity he saw everywhere. He also, however, couldn't imagine any worse candidates for the witness stand at Ira's murder trial.

"The mating of many small animals has been disrupted in the dunes," Planet intoned, gazing blankly at Greg. "Do not become attached to the beauty of the dunes. Remember that basically everything is just an illusion."

Planet paused to sip his tea. Beside him, Moose frowned.

"Do you know who I am?" Greg asked.

Planet's eyes came into focus. He studied Greg. "I don't know, do I?"

"I'm a lawyer. I'm defending Ira Sullivan. You may know he's been charged with a murder. He says he was with you two that night. Here at the Foghorn, then out in the dunes."

Planet and Moose glanced at each other. "The dunes are a state of mind," Planet reminded.

Greg took a pull on his beer. "I'm simply asking whether you were with Ira that night."

Planet didn't answer. Finally, Moose leaned forward. "It would not be a good idea for us to get involved," he said.

"I understand," Greg replied. "But I can protect you on the witness stand. We just walk through the evening, establish that Ira was with you out in the dunes."

Moose's scowl deepened. "I have spent my entire life avoiding things like courtrooms and lawyers."

"What about Ira? You know him. You sat under the stars with him. Ira didn't do this, Ira didn't kill anyone. This just isn't right."

Greg, searching for signs that he'd had an effect, detected none. Planet and Moose sat rooted in their own private world. Apparently not even Dunite utopian relics responded to talk of justice and moral obligations.

"You two have seen what the law does, what the government does," Greg said. "You must have had the law after you in your lives. You want Dennis Taylor to win? You want our D.A. to come after you next?"

Planet waved off that anemic argument. "We are left alone because we leave others alone."

Greg slapped the table hard enough to upset Planet's teacup. "Is that what it comes down to?" he asked. "Are there not things in this universe that we finally must say are flat-out wrong? Can everything be shrugged off? Is it all endless equivocation? Are there no moral imperatives?"

Moose still scowled, but Planet looked troubled, as if recalling certain moments in his past. He closed his eyes, sat still. "Man finally transcends the pull of things by the love of primary abstractions," he murmured. Then he reached for Greg's hand. "Are your motives pure?" he asked.

Greg was almost hissing now. "Tell me about that night."

Planet nodded, sipped his tea, appeared to be listening to a private voice. "Yes, okay, I will tell you," he said at last. "But there is not much to say. We were here, Ira was here. He was drinking that night, as usual. Ira was in pain. The more he drank, the sadder he became. It has always been that way, since he first started coming here after his boy died. We took him out to the dunes. We thought the stars and sky might help him more than the whiskey."

"But you brought a bottle with you," Greg reminded him.

Planet looked mildly chagrined. "Ira brought the bottle."

"When?" Greg asked. "What time did you go into the dunes?"

Planet shrugged. "Maybe ten?"

"What about Sandy Polson? And Paul Platt?"

Moose joined in now. "They were here. Sandy was dancing with Ira and everyone else. But then we left. They didn't follow, they weren't with us."

"Did you see anyone else that night?"

Planet and Moose glanced at each other, didn't answer

at first. Then Planet sighed. "Yes, yes we did. June joined us. June Blossom."

"Who is June Blossom?"

Moose tried to wave off the question. "Just a lady," he snapped. "A strange lady."

"What kind of strange lady?" Greg inquired. "Who is she, where is she?"

They didn't really know. That much was clear after a few more questions. She lived here and there around the dunes was all they could say. Kind of a drifter, she kept mainly to herself. She had long gray-black hair, she wore shawls, she dug for crabs, she listened to music, she painted. Sometimes she came around trying to sell her paintings.

"I think she truly could not handle talking to a policeman or a lawyer," Planet offered.

"I need to hear more," Greg said.

"No," Moose snarled. "Leave it be."

Planet put a hand on Moose's arm, nodded at Greg. "Yes, you do need to hear more. You need to see how it happened, how it ended."

They came into the dunes that night off a bumpy dirt road that threaded through the cabbage fields down near the county line. They hiked past Venano Gordo Lake; they followed a trail that wound through dense stands of willow, then south along the beach, then back up into the dunes. They sat down finally at the foot of a vast golden hill, a dune blanketed by tall, wiry plants in full bloom. Eight-foot-high daisies they looked like, a brilliant yellow-orange. The hill so spectacular; a shimmering gold dune lit by the stars.

Lost in the memory, Planet fell silent for a moment.

"Please," Greg urged. "Go on."

June just appeared, Planet continued. They were sitting and talking, then June, as she sometimes did, suddenly turned up. Ira was crying, drinking whiskey. They tried to talk about an afterlife, but couldn't console him. Finally

June took Ira in her arms, held him, wrapped him in her shawl.

"Then the siren started," Planet said.

It took a moment for Greg to digest that last note. Finally, he remembered. The Devil's Peak power plant, of course. Its siren sounded that night. How could he have forgotten?

"The siren upset us," Planet continued. "It always does. The noise, where it's coming from. It is not conducive to a natural state of consciousness. We wanted to leave, Ira wanted to stay. June was helping him better than we could, anyway. So after a while, Moose and I hiked back out."

Greg leaned forward. Midnight, that's when the postmaster was murdered, around midnight. "What time?" he asked. "When did you leave Ira?"

Plainly, Planet didn't know. He wore no watch, paid little attention to such matters. "Maybe eleven?" he offered.

Greg turned to Moose, who shrugged. "All I can say is, we left Ira and June alone in the dunes. We left her holding him wrapped in her shawl."

Greg fought off the image of Ira sobbing in a stranger's arms. "Help me," he implored. "Tell me where I can find June Blossom."

Planet and Moose exchanged glances. "Try the motels on the cliff above Clam Beach," Planet said finally. "She moves around, but she sometimes stays at one of them."

Greg drained his beer, rose to leave. A strange woman, they'd called June. Greg tried to imagine what it took for a woman to seem strange to Planet and Moose. He tried also to imagine how he could possibly find her.

Just south of Pirate's Beach, before the shore widened into the Chumash Dunes, a jagged, eroded wall of cliffs rose sharply from the water's edge. Atop the cliffs, cut off from Clam Beach below, sat a faded mix of motels, curio shops, and saltwater taffy stands. Two hours after his conversation with Planet and Moose, Greg pulled into the empty parking lot of Day's Rest Motel & Apts, the tenth complex along these cliffs he'd visited since leaving the Foghorn.

At this one, a peeling, white single-story horseshoe of connected units faced the cliff's edge. A strong odor of disinfectant hadn't quite obscured the even stronger smell of mildew. Greg walked across a browned patch of lawn toward the office. Before he reached it, a woman bounded out to greet him. She wore what looked to be a flapper's outfit from the 1920s—a short skirt, an overblouse, oxfords, rolled-up stockings, a beret, and an incongruous turkey feather boa. The woman wearing it, by Greg's estimate, would have been a teenager when her outfit was in fashion.

"I'm Miss Elaine," she offered, full of hope. "Can I help you? We do have rooms available just now."

"Thanks, I'm just looking for someone I was told is staying here," Greg apologized. "A lady named June Blossom?"

Miss Elaine's attitude changed. She pulled out a pair of spectacles, set them on her nose, stared hard at Greg.

"Who wants to know? You a relative?"

"No, just a friend of a friend."

Miss Elaine considered that for a while, then decided not to extend the scene. "Well, whoever you are, you're too late. Miss June Blossom packed up and left a week ago."

He had her scent now, at least.

"Do you know where she was moving to? Did she leave a forwarding address?"

Miss Elaine whooped. "A forwarding address? My dear, she crept out in the middle of the night. Owed me two months' back rent, that's why." A thought occurred to her. "If you're a friend, maybe you're good for her debts?"

"Do you have any sense why she'd leave so quickly? Did you talk to her in the days before she disappeared?"

Miss Elaine frowned. "No, I didn't. But someone did. A gentleman came by, her very last evening here. They visited for a while. I took notice, because we have rules about overnight visitors."

"Did this one stay overnight?"

"No, no. They were together half an hour, I'd say. Then he left."

"Did you get a look at him?"

Miss Elaine blushed. "I must say he was a charming young man. So very nice. Why, he even kissed my hand when he left. They don't come like that anymore. Yes, he was a real charmer."

Downtown La Graciosa normally was fifteen minutes from the Day's Rest Motel, but Greg made it in ten. The Chumash County probation department closed sharply at five, and by his reckoning he'd need an hour there. Thirty minutes to cajole Sandy Polson's confidential file from his old college pal Cindy Seaman, thirty minutes to read it. If such a file existed, that is. Greg figured it did. Since Sandy Polson dealt drugs, she'd probably had some brushes with the law. So there'd probably be a presentencing investigative report on her. A sealed PSI.

Cindy met Greg in the department's lobby, grabbed his arm, pulled him down a hallway. "I don't want to be seen in public with you," she explained, grinning. "I don't care about this job, but my reputation matters." Cindy had cut her brown hair short and wore culottes almost every day, choices that Greg regretted. She also was unceasingly bubbly, which got on his nerves. Cindy truly liked people. She made a terrific probation officer.

"Sandy Polson," Greg said. "What do you have?"

Cindy whistled. "Now, that one I remember. That one was quite a number."

"You've done a report on her?"

"Nothing big. She got caught once selling a little meth, I wrote her up, she drew rehab and probation."

"What was your impression?"

"My impression?" Cindy thought out her answer before continuing. "My impression is, this gal just flat-out doesn't care. That's the only way I can explain how poised she is, how unfazed. It never occurs to her she's ever done anything wrong. Every time I caught her in a lie, she just shrugged and gave me a big, gracious smile. Sort of laughed it off, rather than defend or correct herself. Like she was terribly amused."

"You caught her in lies often?"

"Nothing but lies. I don't think you can believe a word she says. We went through her whole history, I took pages of notes. She was as sweet and sincere and contrite as could be. Talked so wisely about her regrets, her mistakes, her confusion. Greg, I'm used to hustles, but I believed her absolutely. She scammed me from start to finish. Not until I started digging did I realize she'd told the most outlandish lies with the straightest of faces."

"Such as?"

"Well, for one thing, she'd gone on and on about how her stepfather raped her and made her pregnant when she was fourteen. No one believed her, she said, no one even listened. But it turned out they hadn't ignored her at all. They just hadn't found any evidence, not a shred. A doctor's exam showed no sign of penetration, let alone conception. The shrinks saw nothing in the family dynamics. The parents were horrified, embarrassed, perplexed beyond words. When I confronted her with all this, your Ms. Polson just sort of rolled her eyes. Acted perfectly at ease. Didn't seem to feel that the facts conflicted with what she'd told me. It was amazing."

Greg labored to imagine this woman. "Could there possibly be something to her story?"

Cindy chewed on that, then shook her head vigorously. "I'll tell you what I think," she said. "I don't think you're going to get anywhere searching for some terrible childhood trauma that shaped this lady. I've dealt with plenty of victims of broken homes, child abuse, incest, alcoholism, everything you can imagine. Hell, without them, I wouldn't have a job. I know that type. They're angry, they're depressed, they're driven by some mighty bitter passions.

Not Ms. Sandy Polson, though. She doesn't strike me as exactly angry at all. That's too hot an emotion for her. I think there's something colder and stranger going on inside your pal. Gives me the creeps, to tell you the truth. I found her kind of spooky."

"Sounds like you're getting soft, Cindy."

"Nope, no sirree. At least I can take some comfort there. It wasn't just me. As you will see, she's been scamming folks since she was a little kid. Scamming them, and scaring them."

Cindy brought the file and guided Greg into a small conference room. "You've got thirty minutes," she warned. "Then this turns back into a sealed document."

He read quickly. Cindy was right. Sandy's record of psychiatric care began when she was ten. The doctors and counselors who made notes back then sounded as baffled and frustrated as did Cindy. Polson came from an educated, well-off family, her stepfather a respected music professor. They'd started in Virginia, but moved around. By adolescence, Sandy was really falling apart. One report from a church counselor described her habit of telling "false, peculiar stories." A school psychologist warned that although Sandy always "gave the 'right' answers, one must constantly keep in mind that she is an extremely effective manipulator." She "never presents enough evidence to actually get in trouble, typical of a sociopathic orientation toward life."

Greg flipped through the pages. Sandy certainly managed to get her siblings in trouble, if not herself; she'd goad them quietly, then look innocent when they started shoving her. Once she pushed a sister down a flight of stairs. Another time, she accidentally shot her half brother. Eventually her parents sent her to a special facility for troubled adolescents. Then, for a while in her twenties, she'd apparently regained her footing. It seemed as if she'd suddenly learned how to behave, learned how to handle herself in the world. A bachelor's in literature from the University of Virginia; a part-time museum job; halfway to a master's in fine arts. Then she dropped out. Why, the record didn't say.

"Closing time," Cindy announced, sticking her head in the doorway. "Gimme my file back."

Greg handed it over. There were more pages to read, but he'd seen enough for now.

With amusement, Sandy Polson studied the small hole cut at the bottom center of the thick oak door leading from her jail cell into the adjacent one. These rooms, she knew from her reading, were once a dormitory for young Indian girls. What of these holes, though? It was said that each mission kept two cats to control the mice. Perhaps that was it, Sandy decided. Perhaps the hole was a cat door. On the other hand, maybe it was just a drain hole.

"Paul," she called softly. "Paul Platt, can you hear me?"

She lay prone on the floor of her cell, her mouth close to the hole in her door. Whatever its initial use, she'd found another one. She didn't even have to raise her voice to be heard. She could whisper.

"Paul, I feel lonely. Come sit down here and talk to me some more."

Sandy could hear Platt rising and shuffling obediently toward their mutual wall. This pleased but did not surprise her. Paul was such a dear, witless boy. Not really a boy, actually, but he acted and looked like one, even if he was nearly forty. Or maybe he acted more like a scared girl, what with all that trembling and hand-wringing. Even his silly mustache looked like a girl's, so thin and sparse and futile. Sandy had to force back a guffaw at the thought of Paul. So eager to please, so eager to be her pal.

"What's going to happen to us, Ms. Polson? Everybody's telling me things I don't understand. Everybody's coming at me. I told them some things just to get them to stop coming at me . . . I didn't mean them . . . What should I do now?"

Paul's voice quavered as it floated through his side of

the hole. Sandy suspected he was curled up on the floor, crying.

"You must listen to me, Paul. I'll help you. You just have to pay close attention to what I've been telling you."

"But . . . but . . ."

"But what, Paul?"

"But, Ms. Polson, I didn't do anything. I did nothing wrong."

"Paul!" Sandy hissed, her voice a hoarse whisper. "We've gone over that now quite a bit, haven't we? If you keep talking like that, they're going to put you away forever."

"But, Ms. Polson . . . I . . . We . . . I wasn't even there . . ."

"Paul!" This time Sandy barked his name loudly. "Come on now, let's not start that again. They found our fingerprints there. They've got us nailed but good. Only way we save ourselves is if we tell them the truth about Ira."

"Ira . . . he was there?"

Sandy pulled herself halfway off the *asistencia* floor as she mulled that question. Was Ira Sullivan there? Sitting and leaning now against her cell's thick plaster wall, Sandy summoned from memory an image of Ira Sullivan.

He was standing in the Foghorn Pub, billiard cue in hand, an uncombed forelock hanging over what once must have been vibrant blue eyes. Ira looked a little shaky on this particular night. He'd been buying meth from her, just a bit here and there. This evening, he'd asked for more, lots more. He was buying for friends, he explained. She'd tried to oblige, but something went wrong. Her contact got ripped off. She'd taken the call, then gone to tell Ira.

Sandy had never forgotten his response when she told him the bad news. *No way,* he insisted. *No way.*

Why had Ira said those words? Did that mean Ira thought she was lying? Did that mean Ira thought she'd ripped him off?

No way . . . No way.

What a truly disagreeable thing for him to say. She'd

imagined that Ira thought well of her; she'd imagined he was on her side. Instead, he was like all the others. He didn't believe her. After that night he pulled away from her, looked funny at her, stopped talking to her.

No way . . . No way.

She'd not entirely expected the detectives to go along when she first named Ira Sullivan as the postmaster's killer. The whole thing had started out as a game, as a way to get even. Ira Sullivan had been annoying to her, so she'd be annoying to him. It was simply an amusing notion. That unctuous prosecutor Dennis Taylor had believed her, though. Swallowed her story whole. Especially after she threw in Paul Platt as an accomplice. She'd sensed Taylor wanted a corroborating witness, so she'd given him the simplest man in the Foghorn, a man she imagined would be fun to sway. Taylor had looked so delighted after that; Taylor clearly thought he'd worked her, but good. So who was she to disabuse him of his little victory? The thought of Ira Sullivan not being believed, the thought of Ira Sullivan struggling to convince people he was telling the truth—it made Sandy laugh out loud.

"Oh yes, Paul," she murmured, lowering her mouth again to the hole in their door. "Oh yes, Ira was there. Paul, we have to face up to everything, you know. We have to tell the truth."

"I . . . I am. I didn't do nothing."

"You've got a short memory, Paul. When you drink, you forget. You were drinking that night."

"I was drinking?"

"Paul, I can't lie to people for you or anyone. I have to tell them the truth."

"About what . . . ?"

"You don't remember driving up to Crocker, going to the postmaster's with Ira? Come on, Paul, when you drink you black out . . ."

"I went with Ira up there . . . ?"

"You don't even remember, see."

"You were there, too?"

"Of course I was, Paul. How do you think I know what happened?"

"Oh, man . . ."

"You were there, Paul. You and me, we saw Ira shoot the postmaster."

"Oh God . . ."

"Paul, they're going to put us both on Death Row unless we tell about Ira. There's no way to get out of it. We've already confessed. They won't believe us if we try to change our stories now. That'll just make them angrier. They'll be really mad at us then."

Paul blew his nose, shifted his body. It sounded to Sandy as if he was sitting up now. What a good, brave boy. No more scared, curled-up ball. She'd figured right; this was fun.

"Okay, Ms. Polson, you tell me what I'm supposed to say. You tell me what to say so they won't get mad at me."

Sandy slid both bracelets off her wrists. No matter how she arranged them, neither the wide Zuni cuff nor the narrow turquoise piece much pleased her. If only she had her jewelry box. What a bother jail was proving to be.

"Don't you worry, Paul," she whispered. "Don't you worry."

From the Chumash County probation office, Greg walked two blocks to the east. He had one more stop to make before JB's. Doc Lewis was just finishing for the day when Greg reached the steps of the white clapboard house that he used as an office.

"What you want, Monarch?" Doc grumbled. "I'm on my way to JB's. You're blocking my damn path."

"Need just a couple minutes, Doc, if that's okay. I've got a record to ask you about."

"Greg, come on. Working day's over."

"It involves Ira Sullivan's murder case."

Doc, looking puzzled but intrigued, waved Greg into his waiting room. Greg settled on a couch, weighing how to frame his question.

Just before Cindy kicked him out of the probation department, he'd noticed a handwritten item, scribbled near the bottom of Polson's record. Sandy had come in one day and reported an incident to a probation officer. She'd been to Doc Lewis for stomach pains, she said. Doc Lewis had touched her. Rubbed her high up between her thighs, cupped her breasts, pressed hard against her. She'd pulled her clothes on, she said, and run out of his office. Wanted to file a complaint.

That was all, just a notation. No indication of how it was resolved.

"I have to ask you this, Doc," Greg finally said. "Do you know a Sandy Polson?"

Doc flushed, looked as if he was going to break something. "Now look, Monarch—" he began. Then he stopped, took a breath, rose, disappeared inside his reception area. When he returned, he was carrying a small bucket of ice and a fifth of Johnnie Walker Black. "If we're going to talk about Sandy Polson, I damn well need a drink," he snorted.

Greg flipped open a small notebook.

"Sandy Polson," Doc began. "Sandy Polson appears late one day complaining of stomach pains. Never saw her before, not a patient of mine, my nurse had gone home. But she seemed okay. Came off as a truly lovely lady, actually. Can't stand talking to most women of your generation, Greg. They're all so damn consumed with trashing men and flexing their muscles. It was a pleasure talking to Ms. Polson for a change."

"You talked at length?"

Doc glared. "It was the end of the day. I had no other patients coming."

Greg nodded his absolution.

"When I mentioned that I gardened," Doc continued, "she went on about soil conditions, alkaline balance, coastal fog. When I started talking alternative medicine, she wondered whether hepar or pulsatilla was better for sinus infections. When I complained about HMOs, she pointed out that Medicare had started the whole health-cost spiral. It was really something. Thoughtful comments, natural taste, wide interests. Nothing posed or silly. She even likes Ben Webster, for Chrissakes. If I were thirty years younger—"

"So, what happened?"

Doc slammed the table. "Goddamn it, Monarch, nothing happened. I examined her, could find nothing wrong. Gave her a Zantac prescription just in case. She left, I locked up, went to JB's. That was it."

"Then?"

"Then, next thing I know I'm being paid a visit by a goddamn lynching party. Three of them, one from probation, one from the D.A., one from the county medical association. We have this complaint from a Sandy Polson, blah, blah, blah. I was sort of flattered at first, that she'd had sexual fantasies about me. Truth is, I had them about her. But my lynching party wasn't treating this as fantasy. No."

"The record I saw didn't indicate any resolution. What came of this?"

Doc studied his whiskey in the soft light of dusk. "What happened is, I handed off to my lawyer and insurer, who tripped all over themselves in their haste to pay hush money to Ms. Sandy Polson. Don't ask me how much, because I don't know, refused to learn. It wasn't my money, so it shouldn't matter, I guess. But hell, this was a classic scam, Greg, a really polished hustle. Wonder how many other times she's pulled this. Or what she's up to now."

As he walked beside Doc on the creekside path, heading toward JB's, Greg considered just that question. He'd yet even to see Sandy Polson, but she'd nonetheless become a dominant figure in his life.

False, peculiar stories . . . An extremely effective manipulator . . . Typical of a sociopathic orientation toward life. Was that really true? Was Polson the central architect here, or yet another pawn of Dennis Taylor's?

Greg could not say. Of only one matter was he utterly

certain: The prosecutor had a better storyteller than he did. Greg shuddered at the notion of a jury weighing Planet's and Moose's testimony against Sandy Polson's. It looked as if Ira Sullivan was right. Sandy Polson sounded like the perfect witness.

SEVEN

Greg Monarch paled as he drove the winding, climbing single-lane road that threaded through the coastal hills north of Pirate's Beach. Each hairpin turn brought him face-to-face with the limitless sky or the pulsing ocean, both vast swatches of blue without a horizon. Few tried to negotiate this passage, not even the four-wheeler enthusiasts who dove readily into Chumash County's remote wooded canyons. It wasn't just that the road appeared often to plunge into open space. It was also that the road led nowhere. Nowhere but to the high-security Devil's Peak Nuclear Power Plant.

Until Planet and Moose mentioned it, Greg had forgotten about the power plant's siren. He'd forgotten that it had gone off three times on the night of the postmaster's murder. Even after being reminded, it had taken Greg a while to realize what that meant.

If there were a siren, there also would have been a security team out patrolling the surrounding environs. When the siren blew, the plant's crisis specialists always fanned out, reaching as far south as Pirate's Beach and the Chumash Dunes. Even when it was just a test, one or two showed up; during real accidents, many more came, their numbers signaling to old hands just how serious the event had been. "Environmental protection," they called it; Greg always assumed they were looking for saboteurs. The Central Coast had its share of treehuggers and earth-first zealots.

To the general public, Devil's Peak was generally referred to as a commercial power plant, for that was its visible role in central California. Only those with a long, astute memory recalled that Devil's Peak for years had also been a compact and little-noticed link in the nation's system of nuclear bomb factories. The feds had arrived at Devil's Peak in the mid-1950s, during the height of the Cold War. The big, well-known central bomb factories were already up and running by then, spurred on by the Manhattan Project and a public focused on conquering the enemy. What the feds needed at Devil's Peak was something smaller, more refined and private—a specialized laboratory where they could design and test experimental plutonium triggers.

Most in Chumash County either weren't aware of or didn't care about the facility's arrival, but it had been a hotly disputed topic in Greg's home. For weeks on end as a boy, he listened to his father rail against the coming laboratory's threat to his beloved Pecho Rancho state wilderness preserve. Rising directly to the north of Devil's Peak, Pecho Rancho was a spectacular 8,000-acre expanse of wooded stream canyons, golden poppy fields, teeming tide pools, and winding hiking trails. "This will all be ruined one day," Greg's father would mutter as they scrambled down perilous Pecho slopes to hidden coves. "This will all be gone."

Pecho Rancho in the end had survived the arrival of the Devil's Peak lab, but barely. There'd been two explosive fires at the plant, two that became public knowledge, in any event. One, in 1957, spread unfiltered plutonium into the air, precisely how much no one really knew. Another, two years later, was kept so secret after the first day, the press never did manage to determine its full impact. Those monitoring Devil's Peak from the outside were certain only that plutonium-contaminated oil had leached into the soil in the early 1960s, and toxic beryllium into the groundwater in 1965. Much later, there'd been the familiar flurry of lawsuits and settlements, against both the Department of Energy and Rolfson Industries, the giant

California conglomerate hired by the feds to operate Devil's Peak. The furor had finally died down in the late 1980s, what with the end of the Cold War and the dismantling of the bomb plants. As far as most citizens knew, Devil's Peak functioned only as a power plant now, still under Rolfson's management. The special bomb lab sat dormant, manned only by a cleanup crew. No one had use any longer for plutonium triggers.

That didn't mean Devil's Peak stood unguarded. Rounding a bend, turning onto the plant's long, private approach road, Greg could see as much. The entire Devil's Peak site—10,000 acres, including fourteen miles of coastline—was still a high-security fortress surrounded by motion detectors and a barbed-wire fence. In the distant mist, the plant's twin reactors rose like an apparition, two great, white, 215-foot-tall concrete cones. At the main entrance stood a half dozen armed guards who looked as if they had permission to shoot at will. On their shoulders hung what appeared to be semiautomatic M-16 rifles. Greg eased off his accelerator pedal.

His phone calls to Devil's Peak had accomplished little. The Rolfson crowd didn't know what to make of a criminal defense attorney asking what the plant's security patrols might have seen in the dunes on a certain night several weeks before. They'd handed Greg around, but he'd never penetrated beyond the first layer of administrative assistants. Greg finally had decided he might have better luck in person. The worst that could happen was, he'd end up in the plant security office, which was precisely where he wanted to be. They could interrogate him as much as they wanted, as long as he could ask one question in return: Had their people seen Ira and June in the dunes on the night their siren sounded?

Three of the six guards approached him now, their rifles lowered, pointed at him. Greg braked to a halt, rolled down his window.

"Identification, please," the tallest of the guards commanded. With his broad chest and thick neck, he looked like Buzz Johnson's cousin.

"I'm an attorney," Greg began. "I'm here to—"

"Identification, please." This time the guard clapped his rifle's barrel on Greg's windshield.

Greg stopped talking, reached for his wallet, handed it out the window. Mr. Riflebanger walked it back to the guardhouse at the entrance, picked up a phone. A moment later he returned.

"Mr. Monarch, do you have an appointment with someone out here?"

"No, I don't, I found it hard to—"

Again an M-16 slapped his windshield. "This is a private, secured facility," Riflebanger instructed. "You can't just come out here. If you will, what we need you to do now is back up over there, turn your car around, and drive away."

Greg tried to look agreeable. He even reached for his gearshift. Then he stopped. "One question. How do I go about getting in here?"

Riflebanger almost looked amused. "Don't know that you can. Our orders right now are to keep this place sealed tight to everyone who's not authorized to be here."

It took Greg a moment to digest those words, to realize three guards were following not their usual dance, but special directives.

"Okay, I'll get authorized," Greg proposed. "Whom do I call?"

Riflebanger stared silently, but now appeared to be weighing something.

"Come on," Greg pressed. "At least tell me who I should go crawling to."

At that, the guard softened. In his time, Greg imagined, old Riflebanger has probably done a fair amount of crawling.

"What I'd suggest you do, Mr. Monarch," he finally said, "is call the U.S. Attorney's office."

"The U.S. Attorney? Why? What do the feds have to do with a state-regulated power plant?"

Riflebanger adjusted his cap, shifted his rifle. "All I know is, that's who you need to see for authorization."

"Which one? Whom do I call?"

"Call the assistant U.S. Attorney for the central district branch office," Riflebanger said. "Call Miss Kimberly Rosen."

The wind in her face, bareback on a whiskey-brown thoroughbred, she flew across an open field. The memory of that day stirred her, warmed her. Then, abruptly, it was interrupted by the insistent intercom buzzer sounding on her desk. Kim Rosen frowned at the gray metal box, and for the moment ignored it.

She enjoyed her job; she appreciated the order and meaning imposed by the legal system. In recent months, though, she'd had a major case fall apart on her. That, combined with her posting to the U.S. Attorney's dismal branch office in Chumash County, had set her on edge. More than once, she'd found herself staring out her window at the distant mountains, much as she'd done in law school. On late afternoons and weekends back then, she regularly dropped her books and took off for long, meandering hikes in the alpine forests ringing Santa Cruz. She found she had a genuine passion for the backwoods wilderness. Sometimes with men friends, sometimes with women, sometimes alone, she rafted and camped and traipsed, forgetting her textbooks for days on end. Always, though, they required her return.

The intercom buzzer rang again. Rosen forced herself to punch the button, although she could not abide the bored, sullen voice of Julie Chapman, the office's twenty-two-year-old receptionist.

"Some lawyer's been calling every hour," Julie advised, openly irritated. "I keep writing you messages, but you don't answer them, and he keeps calling."

Rosen pawed across her desk, but it was pointless. Pink

message slips were scattered everywhere. "Who is he?" she asked. "What's he want?"

"Greg something," Julie replied. "Greg Monarch. Keeps mentioning Devil's Peak. That's all I know."

Rosen stiffened, stopped fiddling. "Devil's Peak?" she asked.

"Yeah, that's what he said. Needs to talk to you real bad, sounds like."

Rosen clicked off the intercom and sat thinking. In her mind, she scanned through all the names connected with Devil's Peak. Then, turning to her computer, she called up a more formal list. To no avail, she tried cross-references and alternative spellings. Who was this guy? What was he after? Above all, why now?

Rosen rose and paced back and forth across her office. She thought she was at long last done with Devil's Peak. Now this, whatever it was. She wished she could ignore it, but knew she could not. Standing at the edge of her desk, she picked up the red phone that provided her a direct line to the U.S. Attorney's regional office in San Francisco. "Give me Curtis," she snapped into the mouthpiece.

Ushered into Kim Rosen's office, Greg had to remind himself he was being introduced to an assistant U.S. Attorney. Rosen looked more like the young women Greg had studied with at Chumash State, only more self-possessed. She had feathered bangs and dark curly hair spilling to her shoulders; she wore a long floral skirt and an embroidered denim jacket. The echoes of a dreamy flower child ended there, though.

Kim Rosen's eyes were cool and direct; her handshake firm, brief, dry. "Mr. Monarch," she asked, "how can I help you?"

They were always like that, Greg thought. To believe themselves real prosecutors, they had to act so grown up. So tough and humorless and contained.

Rosen's office undercut her effort at authority. Outside the magisterial corridors of the U.S. Justice Department's headquarters in Washington, federal prosecutors toiled in more mundane surroundings. Most could be found ensconced in the dreary cubbyholes of aging office buildings, sitting behind battered metal desks under dim fluorescent lights, their views obscured by dirty windows and torn shades. The central California branch office in Chumash County was particularly dispiriting. A tiny waiting room, a hallway clogged with stacks of cardboard boxes, Kim Rosen's cluttered mess. Depositions, transcripts, and briefs spilled everywhere, rising in piles from a grimy linoleum floor.

Rosen hadn't even bothered to hang anything on her pale green walls. Behind her, Greg saw only a solitary photo. It was of Kim herself, romping on a beach with a jubilant black Lab puppy. Greg glanced at the prosecutor's fingers. They were free of rings.

"Black Labs are wonderful dogs," Greg said, nodding at her photo. "You must have fun with him."

"It's a her," Rosen replied, a hint of a smile at the corners of her mouth. "Her name is Pepper." She tossed the bangs out of her eyes and started to say something more, but then stopped. The hint of a smile disappeared. "Mr. Monarch," she resumed, "I don't want to be rude, but there are many matters pressing in this office. What can I do for you?"

"I'm trying to open a small door at the Devil's Peak power plant. I'm told you have the key."

Rosen displayed nothing at the mention of Devil's Peak, but the manner in which she now looked straight at him struck Greg as uncommonly arch. There was a challenge in her unblinking gaze. Her lips had a natural pucker to them. Whoever hired her, Greg decided, had good taste. He couldn't help it, he found this tough-lawyer-in-a-floral-skirt business quite stirring. What was she, thirty, maybe thirty-five?

"I don't know what you're talking about," Rosen said evenly.

"Neither do I," Greg offered. "All I know is, I can't get

anyone to answer the phone, and when I drive out there, I can't even get to the front gate. I have to be 'authorized,' and for that I was told to call you. Why the U.S. Attorney's office is involved, I wouldn't know."

"Nor would I, Mr. Monarch." The arch look remained, but behind it, Greg now sensed something veiled and stony.

Suddenly, there was nowhere to take the conversation. Kim Rosen was playing this so close to the chest, he had nowhere to turn. He wondered why she'd even agreed to see him.

"I take it you're not going to tell me anything?" Greg asked. "Or help open that door?"

"There's nothing for me to do. Devil's Peak is a quasi-public utility, I believe. Power plants are regulated by state boards, not U.S. Attorneys."

"Why was I told to call you?"

"I wouldn't know."

Greg couldn't read what was going on, and also couldn't read Kim Rosen. Her rigid, stony manner suggested a certain resolve, and feel for power. Greg didn't entirely believe it, though. He sensed vulnerability in her. No doubt that was why she needed to keep such command over herself. Vulnerability would not get you very far in the U.S. Attorney's office.

"An innocent man is facing an almost certain murder conviction," Greg said. "Maybe a death sentence."

Rosen thought that over for a minute. Greg imagined her elsewhere, at the beach in shorts, in her bed wrapped in a sheet.

"Is that why you're trying to get inside Devil's Peak?" she asked finally. "I don't understand what a murder case has to do with this power plant. Just what kind of small door are you trying to open?"

Seizing the opportunity, Greg explained his situation. The murder, the arrests, Ira and Sandy, Planet and Moose, Ira and June, Dennis and Buzz. As he spoke, he watched Rosen. She appeared to be listening; she even looked concerned. "The siren went off that night," he concluded. "The Devil's Peak patrol must have gone into the dunes. What did they see? Did they write a report? That's all I'm wondering."

Rosen tapped the eraser end of a pencil on her desk. "So you are just assuming the plant patrol was in the dunes that night?"

"They always are when the siren goes off."

"Do you know why the siren sounded that night?"

Greg hesitated. He didn't like her asking the questions. "Aren't we drifting off the point here?"

"Depends what your point is."

Then again, only by following Rosen could he learn where she was heading. "No," he said, "no, I don't know why the siren sounded."

"You've just arrived here on a chance, hoping to track down a witness to help your client?"

"That's about it."

"That's your entire interest in Devil's Peak? That's why you went out there to the plant?"

Greg rubbed his jaw. "I'm slow-witted, I'm afraid. I thought we already covered this ground. Asked and answered, Counselor."

At that, Rosen rolled her eyes and flashed a look of sheepish apology. "I'm sorry, Mr. Monarch, I'm just so used to interrogating people. Even when I'm simply curious, I do it. Please forgive me."

He would have, but by then, Kim Rosen had stood and walked halfway to the door. Apparently, she was escorting him out. The appointment was over.

With regret, Greg realized he'd just been debriefed. That's why Rosen had received him so readily. Apparently she'd heard whatever she was after, so now had no further use for him.

"The problem," she said as she guided him toward the hallway, "is you are talking to me about a murder in Chumash County that is none of the U.S. Attorney's business. I agreed to meet out of courtesy to a local attorney, but I frankly can't help you. This is a waste of time for both of us."

Greg stopped at the door. "Ms. Rosen," he asked, nodding at the photo behind her, "isn't that Pirate's Beach where you're running with your dog?"

The prosecutor, startled, looked back. "Why, yes," she stammered. "Yes, it is."

Rosen stared at the empty doorway as Greg disappeared down the hallway. "You can come out now, Larsen," she murmured finally. "He's gone."

From a small storage room at the rear of Rosen's office stepped a short, egg-shaped man with suspenders and frizzy red hair. Rosen could never look at James Larsen without feeling the urge to laugh. Larsen appeared nothing like her image of an FBI agent. His dumpy build wasn't in the least helped by his dismal taste in clothes. From his yellow polyester sport coat to his drooping, checked socks, Larsen suggested the class boor more than a crack investigator. Yet Larsen had a great nose for public corruption. He'd been lead agent in a half-dozen federal environmental cases, including two of Rosen's biggest coups.

"Your visitor didn't sound like he knew his ass from his elbow," Larsen suggested. "Nothing much to worry about there."

Rosen frowned. "You really think so? Why does he just happen to be representing Ira Sullivan, of all people? Come on. Tell me that. He must know about Sullivan's connection to Devil's Peak."

Larsen slumped into a chair and picked at a wart that had recently erupted high on his forehead, just below the hairline. "No, don't think so," he grunted. "He's just fishing."

"Maybe you're right," Rosen allowed. "He certainly didn't have a clue why those sirens went off that night."

Of course, Rosen reminded herself, neither did she. Not really. An "accidental explosion," that's what Rolfson Industries had called it. To this day, the precise details remained fuzzy. Rolfson had played it cute and careful. A scientific experiment gone awry, they'd explained. Two engineers, testing the overpressure waves emitted when different chemical mixtures explode. Two engineers, inadvertently mixing chemicals the wrong way.

Scientific experiment my ass, Larsen in turn called it. Nothing more than a bucket test. A goddamn bucket test. That, Rosen knew, was Devil's Peak slang for tests of no scientific value. For "tests" designed merely to get rid of hazardous wastes. Rolfson, though, flatly denied the explosion even involved waste materials. It was chemicals, they insisted, "supplementary chemical inventories." Rosen had to admit, Rolfson at least hired sharp lawyers: Burning hazardous wastes would be illegal without a special permit, but not chemicals. They could do what they wanted with chemicals.

"It sure would have been nice to get to talk to those two engineers," Larsen muttered.

Rosen labored to ignore Larsen's tone. After Main Justice closed down their whole Devil's Peak investigation, the notion of chasing after those two engineers just hadn't seemed worthwhile to her. "Knock it off, Larsen. You know I tried. But they disappeared, and we were finished anyway."

Larsen had drawn blood now, worrying his wart. A dark red drop glistened on his forehead. "I'll say they disappeared," he replied. "But good. In the explosion, way I hear. We should have checked on the regional hospitals. Maybe even a few funeral homes."

Rosen stomped back to her desk. They complemented each other nicely: She was smarter; he knew more. Still, Larsen got on her nerves sometimes. "Larsen, that day you said 'Let's do Devil's Peak,' I wish I'd kicked your ass out of here."

Larsen tugged at his suspenders, trying to stuff a loose shirttail back into his trousers. "We had the evidence. You said so yourself. Then they pull me off the case. Phone call from Washington, out of the blue. You could have argued a little longer with them. Instead, what was that you told me? 'I know it's hard, but this is the best we can do.' "

"Come on, James," Rosen sighed. "They came down on me. I was outvoted."

Larsen, relenting, forced some warmth into his expression. She had tried, at least. "Okay, Kim, okay, I know, I understand. But maybe, just maybe, this whole thing isn't over yet."

Rosen studied him. "What do you mean?"

"I mean, maybe it isn't just coincidence that a lawyer representing Ira Sullivan shows up in your office."

"I thought you decided Greg Monarch was just fishing."

"I still think that. But I'm also wondering how Sullivan ends up the defendant in a murder trial. I'm wondering what's going on now."

"All this has made you paranoid, James. Ira Sullivan has been on the skids for years. We weren't even sure he'd hold up, remember?"

Larsen dabbed at his forehead with a soiled handkerchief. "He did hold up, though, didn't he? That's my point. He did hold up."

An unease suddenly seized Kim Rosen and wouldn't let go. It wasn't just Larsen's suspicion that tugged at her. Something about this Monarch fellow also had thrown her off stride. Something about his eyes. He hadn't stopped looking at her, examining her; his gaze had felt so intimate.

Rosen turned away from Larsen, stuck a pencil into her electric sharpener, tapped it on the edge of her desk. When the point broke off, she sharpened it again. Then she picked up the red phone. "Looks like a false alarm," she reported. "Just a guy on a fishing expedition. Nothing to worry about."

Jimmy O'Brien was reaching for his second Black Bush when Greg Monarch took the stool next to him at JB's. He reluctantly turned away from the piano, where Shirley was moaning into the microphone about her evil man. *I'm like an oven that's crying for heat, he treats me awful each time that we meet* . . . There was obviously something weighing on Greg. "Okay, Monarch," he asked, "what you been up to?"

Greg didn't answer at first. He'd been thinking of how Ira would feel about his futile encounter with the federal prosecutor. Only slowly did he turn to Jimmy and begin to recount his experience. He started with the Devil's Peak siren, then moved on to Mr. Riflebanger. Halfway through his description of Kim Rosen's cramped office, Greg abruptly stopped. Something about her quarters, he now realized, had been nagging at him all day. There'd been an awful lot of boxes lining her hallways. RCRA-DP-SGJ. Half the boxes had those letters scrawled on them.

"There's something going on," Greg said. "Riflebanger at Devil's Peak directs me to the U.S. Attorney's office, where Kim Rosen trips over boxes while she pumps me. I wonder—"

"Of course something is going on," Jimmy interrupted, impatiently slapping Greg on the back. "There's always something going on at Devil's Peak. I don't know what this time, but they never stop investigating stuff out there. Probably going to nail them again for peeing in the water or killing off egrets. Who cares? Hell, if I went out to Devil's Peak every time I heard a rumor about toxic discharges or accidental leaks, I'd be living on their damn driveway. Nobody cares about egrets anyway. Nobody even knows what egrets are."

Jimmy turned back to Shirley, still swaying at the piano. This time he joined her, howling the lyrics from his bar stool. *I'm like an oven that's crying for heat* . . . Greg tentatively tasted the glass of Black Bush in his hand. Someone cares, he thought. Ira surely cares.

Greg looked up just in time to see Alison Davana walk into JB's. She was laughing and holding hands with a man Greg didn't know, a broad-shouldered, swarthy fellow with the weathered, callused look of a cowboy. Or a lumberjack. Or a fisherman. Anything but a lawyer. Alison, so lost in her mountain man's spell, didn't notice Greg. The amorous couple, laughing and touching, retreated to a corner table near the piano. As Greg watched, Alison nuzzled Mountain Man's ear. This one he didn't mind. So long as it wasn't Taylor, he could enjoy the show.

Alison did not long hold his attention, though. His mind drifted to an image of Ira sitting in his bare, damp cell. That triggered a memory. Despite himself—it was not an event anyone would voluntarily recall—Greg began again to relive the moment when Joe Hilliard met his maker.

The encounter was not a natural one. They'd strapped Hilliard into the electric chair at 6:19 A.M. Hilliard never blamed Greg, not even in those last hours. He'd never in his life expected fair treatment, never for a moment thought he lived in a benevolent world. He'd neither received nor dealt much kindness over the years, and would have frowned with puzzlement if such a stranger had suddenly made an appearance now. In the electric chair, Hilliard looked straight ahead, proud and unbent, befitting the innocent man he was. In the end, though, a malfunction deprived him of his dignity. After the first jolt of electricity, sparks and flames erupted from the electrode attached to his leg. The electrode then burst from the strap holding it in place and caught on fire. A doctor entered the chamber and found a heartbeat, so they had to reattach the electrode. More smoke and flames followed, and again, the doctor found a heartbeat. A third jolt finally did the job, leaving Hilliard's body charred and smoldering. Being Joe's lawyer, Greg felt obliged to watch the entire sixteen-minute exhibition without once turning away.

He treats me awful each time we meet . . . Jimmy, having fled the bar stool next to Greg, stood now with one arm around Shirley's shoulders, joining her in a duet. At his seat, Greg tried to sway with the music, tried to smile and tap out the beat on JB's ancient mahogany bar. Jimmy didn't think Greg was making a terribly good show of it.

EIGHT

It was almost dusk when the phone rang on Greg's desk. He winced at the intrusion. "Yes," he snapped into the receiver.

"Mr. Monarch?" The voice sounded timid.

"Speaking."

"Mr. Monarch, this is Paul Platt. I'm calling you from the jail."

Greg stiffened and picked up a pen. "Yes?" he said.

"I guess you know I'm being charged with that murder? Along with Ms. Polson and Mr. Sullivan? Except if I testify against your client I get off easy?"

"Yes," Greg agreed. "So I've heard."

With help from his pal Cindy in the county probation office, he'd been able to piece together a brief dossier on Platt. Ira had been right, he was none too bright. Borderline retarded, in fact, IQ around 70, special-ed classes, never got past the tenth grade. Came out of a four-year army stint an alcoholic, worked at gas stations when he needed money, pled guilty to a couple of two-bit burglaries. If Greg recalled correctly, his take in the last one was $24. Ira really knew how to pick his gofers.

"What is it you want with me, Mr. Platt?"

"I need to talk with you; I need your help."

"What kind of help?"

"Help getting out of here. I don't belong here. I wasn't even up in Crocker that night."

Greg hesitated. He should hang up, he should notify Platt's lawyer. The state canon of ethics prohibited him from speaking with a person he knew to be represented by counsel. He couldn't talk to another lawyer's client.

Greg forced himself. "You need to speak to your own lawyer, Paul."

"Please. He doesn't believe me. I need your help."

Again, Greg hesitated. Platt's approach left him with no easy course. No way could he counsel Paul Platt. He was Ira's advocate, he represented Ira's interests alone. He couldn't give Platt the slightest sense that he'd help him. He was obliged to escort Platt to the executioner if that would free Ira. And yet—talking to Platt might be exactly what was needed to gain Ira's release.

Greg wondered suddenly if Dennis Taylor had a hand in this call. He listened for the distinctive click of a tap on his line.

"Will you help me get out of jail, Mr. Monarch?"

Greg snapped his ballpoint open and shut. "You have a lawyer, Paul. He's there to help you. I represent Ira Sullivan. I suggest you ask your lawyer to file an affidavit with the court."

"My lawyer believes everything I told the cops. He thinks I did it. I need a new lawyer. Will you help me? Please, will you get me out?"

What would other lawyers do? What would Ira Sullivan do? Greg picked his words carefully. "Paul, the truth will exonerate you. I suggest you write the judge a letter on your own, asking for a new lawyer. Tell the judge what happened."

"Please, Mr. Monarch—"

"Paul, I can't even talk with you like this. I have to hang up."

An hour later, sitting on a bench beside La Graciosa's central plaza, Jimmy O'Brien hooted when Greg tried to explain how he'd handled the Platt phone call.

"You did what?" Jimmy demanded.

"I had no choice, Jimmy."

"Doesn't make sense," Jimmy sputtered. "No one else is playing by the rules."

"So I'm a loner."

Off to one side, a small boy was scrambling down the creek's bank, chasing a duck toward the water. A stiff, chilly breeze had kicked up.

"Jesus, Paul Platt is the key," Jimmy said. "Sandy Polson has a big reason to lie. She's caught with the cash and a gun. She needs to hang this on Ira and cut a deal with Taylor. Platt's a different story. He has no reason to say he was there if he wasn't. He's the key, he's the case."

"But he's a moron, Jimmy. He couldn't pull his pants on without someone telling him which leg first."

Jimmy glared. "Exactly. That's the whole point."

"There are ethics involved, Jimmy. Believe it or not, there are things you just can't do." Greg turned to watch the boy at the creek. His feet were in the water now, his mom after him.

"What about Platt's lawyer?" Jimmy asked. "Would he cooperate?"

"Not likely. Platt drew Jerry Belson. Ex-cop. Went to law school at night, thought it would change his life. Must be making less now than when he was in uniform. Takes these court assignments to make a living, then realizes he only comes out ahead if he pleads them. Maybe he even convinces himself that's the thing to do. Platt told me his lawyer thinks he's guilty. Hard to believe that."

Jimmy slapped the bench. "Stop looking at everything through your own eyes, Greg. Not everyone sees it like you. Haven't you noticed?"

Greg kept watching the boy in the creek. "Yes, Jimmy," he said. "I have noticed."

Leaving the plaza, Greg turned toward the *asistencia* rather than his house. "All right, come this way," the deputy on duty grunted irritably at the jailhouse entrance. Their heels clacking on the concrete floor resounded in the late-night still.

Greg found Ira stretched out on his cot, eyes half-closed, one arm hanging to the floor. He studied the silhouette before speaking. He didn't want to tell Ira about Paul Platt. No point getting him worked up about something that likely wouldn't amount to much. Also no point getting drawn into a debate over legal ethics. They'd traveled that road often enough as law partners.

"Ira," he began, "when you went into the dunes with Planet and Moose, do you remember anyone else being there with the three of you?"

Silence.

"A woman, Ira. A woman named June Blossom. Who held you, who wrapped her shawl around you."

Ira lifted his head, turned toward Greg. Yes, that he remembered. Not the particulars, but the warm embrace, the succor it provided. As if there were nothing wrong, as if he were a young boy again, his mother shielding him, watching over him, making everything okay. "I remember long gray hair in my face," he said. "Someone humming and rocking."

"Planet and Moose say they left you with her. They hiked out, left you alone with June Blossom."

Ira dropped his head back to the pillow. What a foolish memory. Truth was, his mother never once watched over him.

"Don't know about a June Blossom," Ira said. "Like I told you, I blacked out. Last I remember, I was with Planet and Moose in the dunes."

Greg watched his ex-partner. He suspected Ira had been crying. "I've heard a little about your meth dealing."

Ira at first didn't acknowledge the comment. Then he clapped his hands. "Well, aren't you the clever gumshoe, Greg."

Greg sat down next to Ira on the edge of his cot. "Come on, now," he said carefully. "Whatever happened, we need to talk about it."

Ira's voice was husky. "Just like old days, huh, Greg?"

"Yes, like old days."

"Before events?"

"Yes."

Ira rose from the cot and drifted toward the far corner, running a palm across his cell's rough plaster wall. Then he turned to the small barred window that provided a glimpse of the *asistencia*'s inner courtyard. He wrapped both hands around the iron rods.

"Before you backed off?" Ira asked. He kept his eyes on the courtyard.

Greg swallowed hard. "Before we both backed off."

Ira squeezed the bars. "I stood by you after Florida. After Hilliard."

"Yes, you did."

"What, then?"

What then, indeed, Greg wondered. He couldn't answer.

Ira turned to face him. "I tried," he said. "After Jeffrey died, I tried to keep going. Come into the office each day, open the files, get to work. Defend the helpless, fight the bastards, play by the rules. Even if it all was a stinking game. Couldn't keep it going, though. Couldn't keep pretending."

"Yes," Greg offered. He nodded. "I understand."

Ira rubbed his eyes. "I didn't care anymore. It's terrifying how quickly it can all fall apart. I couldn't move. That's how the meth started."

Greg spoke softly. "I know the feeling, Ira. That's why I had to keep my distance."

The two fell silent. Greg stared at Ira's face as if he'd never seen it before. Although rudely dimmed, hope still flickered there.

"The dealing, Ira. How did you get into that?"

Ira hesitated. For a moment, he could barely remember. Then it came to him. Sandy Polson, the five grand lost when her contact got ripped off. He hadn't felt right blaming her; it was he who'd asked for the meth, he who'd taken his friends' money. That's how he'd started dealing—in order to pay back what he owed those friends.

"They had me pinned to the mat," Ira explained. "Lousy

few bucks really, but it was the principle of the thing. A friend of mine lost the inventory, I had to pay for it. Rules of the game."

Greg leaned forward. "What else, Ira? I'll ask again. What is driving Dennis Taylor? What makes Dennis want you to be the killer, not Sandy Polson?"

Ira started pacing back and forth. He could imagine nothing that might place him in Taylor's line of sight. It had been years since he'd stood side by side with Greg, fighting the D.A.'s office on behalf of the weak and deviant of Chumash County. It had been years, for that matter, since he'd done much of any lawyering. There'd been just that one case, that one poor gal from the Foghorn who begged him for help. Labor law it was, a wrongful dismissal claim against her employer. Jenny Branson was a good old soul, a Foghorn regular, so he'd tried his best, he'd made a foolish pass at resurrecting the past. For a time, it had looked as if he might pull it off. Soon after, though, Jenny went and drove herself drunk off a Clam Beach cliff. It had amounted to nothing, nothing at all.

"I truly don't know why Taylor's after me," Ira said. "Hell, I don't know our district attorney, Greg. You've been a greater source of displeasure to him than I have. Something happened in those first hours of the case, I think. Taylor disappeared for a while, then came back beaming. Bastard was just about breathless. Why, I couldn't say."

Now Greg paced across the cell. This had been their way as law partners, wearing out the cheap office carpet as they prepared for a case. "Sandy gets caught with Wilson's cash, not you. Sandy's got the gun, not you. What is going on here, Ira? Why does Taylor think you're guilty?"

Ira chuckled sourly. "Why do you assume he does?"

Greg started to respond, then stopped himself. He believed Ira incapable of murder. But he could imagine Ira, depressed and not giving a hoot, getting caught up in something. He could imagine him trailing along, finding himself at the postmaster's that night. He couldn't bring himself to ask Ira directly. *Don't ask, don't tell*. But he couldn't help wonder: Was Ira somehow involved?

"The money you needed for that debt, Ira?" Greg said. "You could have come to me."

Ira had the good grace not to say anything.

The next morning, Greg punched in the number for Jerry Belson. He dreaded the prospect of talking to Paul Platt's attorney, both because he despised the man and because he knew already the call's outcome. He had no choice, though. He felt like an actor, mouthing lines written by someone else.

He'd visited Belson's office once on a case. It was like entering an animal's cage. Mountains of tottering documents climbing the walls, the top pages spilling into adjacent piles. Empty coffee cups, cigarette butts, shards of greasy pizza. The phone ringing, no one answering it. Belson collapsed in his chair, uninterested in Greg's words, probably uncertain which case they were discussing. The law didn't suit him any better than it did Greg, but for different reasons. To Greg that day, Belson looked lazy and overwhelmed. The swarthy, thick-necked ex-cop had made the wrong career move.

"Belson Law Offices." Greg recognized Belson's indolent, disconnected drawl. Probably couldn't afford his receptionist any longer, he guessed. The state paid only a few bucks for the type of court-appointed cases that came Belson's way. Holdups, spousal batterings, car thefts. He had to handle dozens a month to make a living. The lousy couple thousand for this murder case was probably Belson's biggest take of the year.

"Jerry, this is Greg Monarch."

A pause. Belson trying to concentrate, trying to recollect. "Ah yes, Greg. Yes. Yes."

Greg offered his help. "We both have clients charged with the murder of Bob Wilson?"

A shuffling of papers, something being knocked over.

Belson probably was searching for the file in the debris on his desk. "Paul Platt, yes, Paul Platt," Belson finally offered. "We're going to plead him out, I believe. He's already confessed. D.A.'s offering a deal. Not too bad. Best we can do, I'm sure. Paul was there, what can I say. Though it was your guy who did the shooting. Yes. Well, hell. Paul will be testifying against him. Only way out for him."

"Paul wants to talk to me." Greg could imagine Belson, at that news, making the effort to lift himself from the depths of his overstuffed chair.

"How do you know?"

"Paul called me from jail late yesterday."

From the sound of it, Belson had summoned the energy to stand up. "What?" he sputtered. "You can't talk to him, you know that. I'll have you before the ethics board if you do, Monarch. Just exactly what was said?"

"He wanted me to come visit. I told him I couldn't. But I'd like to. He says he's innocent, he says he wasn't there. Which, of course, calls into question the notion that Ira Sullivan was there."

Belson's cop instincts were rising to the fore. "Shit, you believe every damn thing these creeps say, you'll never finish a case. I'm sorry, Monarch, but your client's interests and my client's do not coincide. We are not kindred souls. So no, you cannot talk to Paul. I forbid you to talk to Paul."

Guessing what was probably the case, Greg took a chance. "Little different policy than for the D.A., Mr. Belson? I understand he's got an open door. Visits your client whenever he pleases, without you there."

"My client does best by cooperating with the D.A."

"Without you there?"

Belson sounded as if he were strangling. His thick neck would be a pulsing red by now, Greg imagined.

"Now, look," Belson finally managed to get out. "I've got dozens of cases piled up here. The state pays me shit. I cannot spend all day down there holding Paul's hand."

"How about if I hold it?"

"Goddamn it, Monarch, you can't talk to my client," Belson barked. Greg wondered if he broke his phone, slamming it down so hard.

At the end of the day, just as Greg was locking up, Paul Platt called again. He sounded even shakier than he had the day before.

"Mr. Monarch, I know you said you couldn't talk to me, but you should know. This afternoon, my lawyer came to see me. So did Mr. Taylor. They knew that I'd called you. Mr. Belson was very angry. He said I was making a big mistake, trying to change my story now. And, Mr. Taylor, he said if I didn't stick to my original statement, I would spend the rest of my life in jail."

Greg picked up a pen, grabbed for a pad of paper. "What did you say back?"

"I told them my whole story was made up. I told them it wasn't the truth. But they didn't believe me."

"Anything else?"

"I told them I wanted to talk to you. That's when Mr. Taylor really got mad. He pounded the table and hollered. He said not to trust Greg Monarch. He said you couldn't help me, that you cared only about Ira Sullivan."

Greg put his pen down. Taylor's advice wasn't in the least inaccurate, of course. "Write to the judge, Paul."

"I'm scared. I don't know how to say things right. If you'll come to the jail, I'll talk into your tape recorder, I'll take back my whole story."

He'd possibly been wrong about the canon of ethics. Greg understood that now, after spending the afternoon researching the question. As he read it, the canon didn't prohibit him from speaking with any person represented by counsel. The wording was more precise than that. The canon prohibited him from talking to an "adverse party" who is represented by an attorney.

"Adverse" could mean a number of things. Bad, evil, hostile, harmful. But in the law, it generally meant the opposition, the adversary. Paul Platt was not, it seemed to Greg, an adverse party to Ira Sullivan. He was just a witness. This reading was a stretch, maybe, but the law allowed stretches.

"Will you tell me the absolute truth if I come down there, Paul?"

"Mr. Monarch, I promise. The absolute truth."

Stretches, of course, could catapult you over dangerous precipices.

"Will you stick to your story, Paul? No going back to what you first told the cops?"

"Yes, sir, Mr. Monarch. I'll stick to it till hell freezes over."

Ethics, Greg told himself, would be easy if you didn't have to make choices. Ethics would be easy if Ira weren't inching toward Death Row.

"I'll be down to the jail in an hour," he said.

Sheriff Dan Wizen was standing outside the *asistencia*'s entrance when Greg arrived. He had his arms crossed, and was trying to look stern.

"Where you going, Greg?" he inquired.

"Have an appointment to see a prisoner of yours, Sheriff."

"Ira's sleeping, I believe."

"Not Ira. Paul Platt."

Wizen pushed his hat back off his forehead, rubbed his chin, pretended to be puzzled. "Well now, Greg, Paul Platt is not your client. I can't let you in to see him. Wouldn't be proper."

"You let the district attorney in to see him all the time, Dan. Paul's not his client. Nor is Sandy Polson."

Wizen whinnied with amusement. "Life isn't fair, Greg. You keep forgetting."

Greg moved toward the entrance. Wizen took a step toward him. Greg brushed past him, reached for the door. Wizen grabbed his shoulder, spun him around, placed a Colt .38 next to his ear. "You want I arrest you, Greg?"

Greg looked sideways at the gun. Wizen was such a fool. "Why don't you just shoot me?" he suggested.

For a moment, it looked as if Wizen were contemplating that option. Then a noise, the crack of a twig off to the south, distracted him. Detective Roger Kandle stepped out of the mist and signaled to the sheriff. The two met halfway, started whispering. Kandle did most of the talking, Wizen the listening.

Greg, watching, tried to imagine Roger's life. Working for someone like the sheriff, carrying his water, then going home to a house full of adoring kids. Going home to hug them, guide them, help them grow up. Maybe Kandle was telling off the sheriff right now. More likely, ever methodical, he was reminding Wizen that there was no law keeping Greg out of the jail, and no basis for arresting him. Or perhaps—it suddenly occurred to Greg—they were setting a trap.

Whatever was going on, in the end, after a round of shrugs and kicks at the dirt by Wizen, they let him in. Kandle led the way, impassive as ever, winding through the *asistencia*'s corridors toward the interview room facing the inner courtyard. There he left Greg, then returned a minute later with Paul Platt at his side. As Platt stepped into the room, the door closed behind him.

Platt jumped, he was that spooked. Then he froze, unable to bring himself to take a step further into the room. Greg studied him.

At thirty-eight, Platt looked a dozen years older. He had rough, wizened skin, a crew cut, a sparse mustache, and a wasted, lanky build. From the records, Greg knew that a school psychologist twenty years ago had thought him a "rather nice boy" who "tries hard" but "is always bewildered." Whether or not his father had actually beaten him as a child, the counselors weren't sure. But Paul had come from a household "full of tension and anger."

It showed. Platt was cringing, and they hadn't even started talking yet. What a perfect candidate, Greg thought, for a coerced false confession.

It happened more than people realized. A dim-witted teenager from a squalid trailer park outside Naples, down on Florida's steamy Gulf Coast, gets convinced by cops that he'd killed three eight-year-old boys. A fundamentalist father up in Idaho decides he molested his daughters. After sixteen hours of questioning, a Kentucky groundskeeper believes he killed his neighbor.

Modern interrogation tactics gave even well-meaning investigators the power to convince certain vulnerable types that they'd committed the most heinous crimes. Sometimes innocent suspects admitted guilt simply to escape the stress of interrogation; sometimes they actually came to believe they'd committed the crimes. It was hard for most people to believe it possible, but then again, most people didn't often find themselves alone in a small, windowless room for six or ten uninterrupted hours, face-to-face with a master of psychological coercion. A master who starts by asking you to "assist" with his investigation, maybe provide your own hypothetical murder scenario. Who then starts shaping your responses with leading questions, and tossing your answers back as evidence of guilt. Who then bluffs you with claims about witnesses or physical evidence. *We found lots of hairs and fibers on her body . . . We have your hair . . .* Who then leans forward, violates your personal space, gets closer and closer, nose to nose. Not yelling or bullying, but genial. *Come on now, that last story wasn't true, was it? Let's not even go into that again.* Then maybe one short outburst. *Hey now, let's get back to the subject!* Still smiling though, still amiable.

After that, lots of folks would feel like confessing to something.

"Hello, Paul," Greg began. "I'm Mr. Monarch. Why don't you come sit down over here, across from me?" He tried to make his voice soft and soothing, but wasn't sure he'd succeeded. It had sounded to him more like a gruff command.

"I did nothing wrong," Platt said.

"What's that?"

"I did nothing wrong, Mr. Monarch."

"Okay then, come sit down, you can talk into the tape recorder." Greg didn't want an off-the-record conversation; he wanted this meeting documented.

Platt took a couple of steps toward him, stopped. He wrapped his arms around his thin chest, rocked back on his heels. "They said I was making a big mistake, they said if I didn't stick to my story, I'd have to stay in jail a long time."

"They're trying to scare you, Paul."

"Well, what's going to happen? Can you help me? Can you get me out of jail if I give you this statement?"

Greg thought of Ira, just down the hallway, lying on a cot. Was he staring at the ceiling? Sleeping? Dreaming?

"Paul, I will try to help you," he said. "I will do whatever I can to see that the truth comes out. If the truth comes out, you will be exonerated."

That wasn't quite enough for Platt. "If I make this statement, you can get me out?"

Greg found it hard to draw a breath. "Paul," he said. "Your story might be putting Ira Sullivan in the gas chamber."

Still not good enough. "You will help me?" Platt repeated. "You can get me out?"

Joe Hilliard asked Greg that once. When they first met, when the prospect still seemed quite likely.

"Yes," Greg promised Paul Platt. "I will help you, I will try my best to get you out."

With that, Platt stepped to the table and sat down. Greg punched his tape recorder. "Okay, Paul, tell me what happened as best you remember. From the day of the murder to the time of your arrest."

Paul Platt frowned, rubbed his whisper of a mustache, appeared stymied by the notion of narrating a sequence. Here, Greg marveled, was the person it all turned on. The integrity of the legal system, Ira Sullivan's life, the state's case, his own—his own what?

Platt began to talk, straining, but managing to line up his sentences.

He was over at the Foghorn Pub that night, drinking beers. So was Ira, which was good, because Ira owed him money. He started not feeling well, his head hurt real bad. So he went home around ten, took some pills, went to bed. That was his night, nothing more. Until around four A.M., when the banging started on his front door. An awful racket. He woke up, looked out, saw a big, tall fella. Detective Buzz Johnson, who told him to get dressed. Paul was dazed, drugged up, half-asleep. He hardly knew it when Buzz led him out to the police car, put him in the backseat. Couldn't believe it when Buzz told him he was under arrest for murder. No way, he told the detective, there's got to be something wrong. Buzz just grinned at him. Sorry, Buzz said, that's what we got.

Greg interrupted, fighting to hide his irritation. "Why did you give the sheriff a taped confession if they had the wrong man, Paul? What happened at the sheriff's station?"

Platt wrapped his arms around his chest. "They started just coming at me," he stuttered. "Getting all over me. Buzz Johnson, he got right in my face and told me, 'Mr. Platt, if you don't tell us the truth we are going to put you away for life.' It scared me, I just couldn't believe it. I was, like, in shock."

"Then what?"

"Well, after I kept saying I didn't know what was going on, then they stopped threatening, did more kind of trying to convince me. That Buzz Johnson left the room, another officer came, talked calm to me, asked me questions, nice and soft."

"Do you remember that officer's name?"

"No, don't think so, but he was a calm guy—a nice, strong, calm guy."

That wasn't a bad description at all, Greg thought. He couldn't have done better himself. "Does the name Roger

Kandle sound familiar?" he asked. "Was it Detective Roger Kandle?"

"Yes, that's it, right, Roger Kandle."

"What went on with Roger?"

"Well, when he came in, he made me less scared. He just said, well, could you make a taped statement, this will help you, you won't be in such trouble then. Then that Buzz Johnson comes back in, starts getting in my face again, saying we're going to put you away for life. That, well, that got me to the point where I was just so tired of him, you know, I just wanted him to get the hell out of my face."

"Go on."

"So I gave them the taped statement."

Noticing Greg's expression, Platt's voice climbed to a whine. "To get them off my back, don't you see? I had no choice, no choice at all. What could I do? What could I do?"

"How did you come up with all the details? The bracelet, the number of shots?"

The crux of the matter, the key to the case. And, Greg could see now, the biggest problem. For Paul was frowning, trying to remember, faltering. He had not a clue. The simpleton flat-out didn't know where he'd gotten the crucial details in his story.

"Well, someone told me, didn't they? Didn't someone give me all that stuff?" Paul nodded to himself. "Yeah, that's it. They told me everything. That must be it, sure, that's what happened."

Greg could hear Platt on the witness stand. *Didn't they tell me, didn't they?* He could also see Dennis Taylor standing before Platt, grinning at the jurors and rocking back on his heels.

"Now, Paul, what about the district attorney, Dennis Taylor? Did he talk to you after he learned you'd called me?"

"Sure did. Got real angry at me. He made me feel it would be my fault if the murderer gets off. That really spooked me bad."

"So what did you say?"

"Well, I didn't say nothing, 'cause he didn't give me a chance. He just kept saying how he wanted Ira Sullivan really bad, and needed me to get him. Said that over and over."

"Do you know why the D.A. wants Ira so badly?"

"No, sir. Doesn't make sense to me, not at all. Ira's real nice, gives me work, never hollers at me. I can't see how Ira might kill anybody. Just doesn't seem possible. No way."

"Paul, after everything the D.A. told you, you still called me. How come?"

Paul looked as if he were trying to remember. "Mr. Monarch, we had nothing to do with this," he said finally. "It's just not right. Ira charged with murder and all. That's not right."

Not bad, Greg thought. Not bad at all. Even Ira will appreciate this.

Paul kept talking. "It's the God's honest truth, Mr. Monarch. That can't hurt me, can it?"

Greg beat back the image of Professor Hammilberg. "No, Paul," he promised. "The truth can never hurt you."

When she saw Ira Sullivan's attorney in the *asistencia* corridor, walking away from the jail's interview room, Sandy Polson pulled on a pair of shoes. Then she studied them. Dirty white leather flats, scuffed gray at the toe. They looked so dreary, so unbearably boring. Sandy longed for the closet full of clothes that sat untouched in her Apple Canyon home. They allowed her only a few items in here, just a scattering of blouses and pants and skirts. She didn't even have her full makeup kit. It was so terribly unfair. A crime really, a violation of her rights.

Sandy turned to the small mirror above her cell's chipped porcelain sink. She preferred minimal makeup—just a dab of blusher, a hint of black mascara, a touch of natural lip gloss, maybe a little taupe eye shadow. Finished applying those, she ran a brush through her tousled hair, then a hand. She put the hairbrush down next to a large, shallow bowl full of white daisies. They looked so forlorn, Sandy thought. She gently plucked off brown, withered leaves. These few sorry blossoms were all the garden they allowed her in here. So different from the abundant field behind her home, thick with sycamores and manzanita and wild lilac. Sandy wondered if any of her neighbors had thought to care for the broccoli, lettuce, and snap peas she'd so carefully planted in the sheltered plot just outside her kitchen. An image of those vegetables poking through rich coastal valley soil inspired Sandy to reach for the sketchbook and pastels she kept under the cot's mattress. Sitting down on the bed, leaning against the wall, she started drawing a garden. Not hers exactly, but a grander one, the sort she'd always fancied having. Row after row—big, sugary Sequoia strawberries; plump, juicy Crimson Cushion beefsteak tomatoes; long, thick Caserta zucchini; huge Green Globe artichokes the size of basketballs—each precisely marked with written descriptions and planting histories. Raised beds, well-aged compost, a narrow, winding creek, redwood benches—

Footsteps interrupted Sandy's sketching. Finally, the guards were bringing Paul Platt back to his cell. By her calculation, he'd been with Ira's lawyer for a full hour. Sandy waited until the guard retreated before summoning Paul.

"Hey there," she murmured into the small arched hole between their cells. "Where have you been? Tell me all about it."

Platt did not appear to hear. Either that, or he was ignoring her. The notion bothered Sandy. She did not think it possible.

"Paul, come sit down here next to me."

Now she could hear Paul stirring. It sounded as if Platt was moving a little more slowly than normal toward their meeting spot, but at least he was moving.

"Paul, what's going on? I need to know, Paul. Remember, we're in this together. We must always have the same stories."

"How can we have the same stories, Ms. Polson? I didn't do anything. I wasn't there."

Sandy made sure her voice sounded soothing. "Now, Paul, are you forgetting all over again? That happens, I understand. It's too late, though. We can't change our stories now. They'll just get madder at us. It'll make things worse for us."

"That . . . that's not what this lawyer said. This lawyer, he said he could get me out. This lawyer . . . he said if I told the truth, he could get me out."

Sandy pushed herself off the floor. A pay phone hung on a wall at the end of the hallway, only yards away. Sandy's good behavior had earned her the full range of Sheriff Wizen's jailhouse privileges; she could move about her secured corridor at will. She started out of her cell, then, staring at her feet, turned back. She kicked off her scuffed white flats and reached under the cot for the black ankle-high lace-up boots, her only other option. She pulled them on, then headed for the door.

"It's me," Sandy said into the phone. "If you want to save your case, you better get yourself down here right now."

At JB's two hours later, Greg celebrated by asking Shirley to dance. As usual, the piano player's wife obliged, swaying to the music her husband Dave so obligingly provided. As she moved she hummed, her eyes half-closed. Greg couldn't imagine what she was thinking. Shirley seemed more a part of the natural world than the one forged by men and women. It would not be a surprise to stumble upon her while hiking the thickly wooded canyons above La Graciosa. The notion of such a moment aroused Greg. He tightened his grip on Shirley's waist.

Just then a hand fell on his shoulder. For a second, he thought Dave was finally claiming his wife. Turning, he saw instead Jimmy O'Brien. "There you are," Greg said.

"Been looking for you." Then he noticed Jimmy's pallor. His skin was ashen. He'd never known Jimmy could look so distraught.

"Greg, come sit over here," Jimmy said, tugging toward the potbellied stove.

"Followed your advice," Greg said. "Taped Paul Platt's statement couple hours ago. He recanted. Says Buzz and his pals threatened him, fed him the story. Got it on tape—"

Jimmy held up a hand to stop him. "I know, I know," he said. "I've heard. But I've heard more, Greg. Thirty minutes after you left the jail, the sheriff and the D.A. paid your friend Paul a visit. Spent almost an hour with him. When Taylor and Wizen came out, they had their own taped statement. Paul Platt took it all back, flopped again. Retracted his recantation."

Greg's throat went dry. The God's honest truth sure had a short run. "Hell, doesn't matter," he insisted. "I have Platt on tape, I can use it, no matter what he's saying now."

Jimmy shook his head, placed his hand on Greg's arm. "There's more. Paul Platt is now saying you bamboozled him. He's saying you promised you'd be his lawyer. He's saying you promised you'd get him out of jail if he told that story for your tape recorder."

Greg looked around for a drink. "Jesus—"

Jimmy squeezed his arm. "Greg, Dennis Taylor is preparing an ethics complaint against you. He's taking this to the State Bar. He's going after your license to practice law."

NINE

The weasel approached as he always did, sauntering as if he had no purpose at all. Then he stopped at Jimmy O'Brien's desk, still feigning indifference. Jimmy returned his editor's artificial smile.

How such a man could come to run a newspaper, even one as sorry as the *News-Times*, was beyond Jimmy. Horace Alan Macauley's grasp of public affairs was almost as puny as his command of the English language. He'd started out at the paper monitoring weekend police logs, a task that appeared to overwhelm him, but he had nonetheless managed to survive. The gardening column had proved his salvation. Through it, he'd curried abiding favor with the publisher's wife, who he soon discovered harbored a fanatic interest in grafting obscure ornamental succulents. By the time Macauley had written his eighth column on how to create the multihued *Sulcorebutia glomerseta* hybrid, he was taking lunch in the publisher's private dining room. It was about then, as Jimmy recalled, that Horace added a middle name to his byline.

"Got something for you," Macauley announced. "Sort of came in over the transom, if you know what I mean. Why don't you take a look." The fat envelope in Horace's hand made a slapping noise when he tossed it on Jimmy's desk. Although Jimmy was sitting, the two men were almost at eye level with each other. Even with elevator shoes, Macauley stood no more than five feet two inches.

"What's this about?" Jimmy asked.

Macauley shrugged. "Not sure, really. Just sort of

glanced at it. Why don't you read it over, see what it's worth." The editor placed his narrow, bony face next to Jimmy's, an act that required only a slight bend of his waist. "But let's not take all month on this, O'Brien. I'll give you a couple of days."

Watching Horace march off on his two-inch heels, Jimmy resisted the impulse to bark out an inquiry about the latest in succulent propagation techniques. He needed this job, after all, despite its paltry paycheck. Even living as he did, alone in a one-bedroom shack on the seedier side of Clam Beach, involved certain unavoidable expenses, not least JB's monthly tab. So Jimmy turned to the envelope sitting on his desk. From it, he pulled out an inch-thick document, stapled in the top left-hand corner. CALIFORNIA FEDERAL DISTRICT COURT read the uppercase, boldface words centered at the top of the cover page. "Report of the Special Grand Jury 29-8. Confidential Document. Not for public disclosure without prior court order." Jimmy looked up, searching the newsroom for Macauley, but the editor had disappeared. Horace probably hadn't even opened the envelope, Jimmy surmised. He turned back to the document, flipping over the cover sheet. "Grand Jury Report: Introduction," read the first line on the next page. Jimmy's eyes widened as he scanned what followed.

> The Department of Energy, its contractor Rolfson Industries, and many of their respective employees have engaged in an ongoing criminal enterprise at the Devil's Peak Plant, which has violated federal environmental laws. This criminal enterprise continues to operate today at the Devil's Peak Plant, and it promises to continue operating into the future unless our government and Rolfson Industries are made subject to the law . . .

"Wooha," Jimmy muttered to himself. "Got more than dead egrets here." He reached for his phone and hit the "send all calls" button. This mother was 125 pages long.

Might take him the rest of the afternoon. Hell with Horace, this might take all week. Jimmy began typing notes into his computer as he turned the pages.

In places, the catalog of environmental abuses sagged into technical jargon. Effluents, pondcrete, parts per million, oxygen levels—Jimmy had little patience for such detail. It wasn't all so mind-numbing, though. The legacy of the bomb plant days at Devil's Peak screamed from almost every page. Building weapons was dirty work; you ended up with all manner of radioactive trash. Which, Jimmy could see, still saturated the place, mainly because they had nowhere to put the stuff. Jimmy laughed out loud at their quandary: Legally, they couldn't burn or ship or bury the waste, but by law, they also couldn't keep it.

They had no choice, in other words, but to break the law. As far as Jimmy could tell, they'd been doing so not reluctantly but with vigor. Burning radioactive waste in an incinerator, discharging effluents into Pecho Creek, leaching toxic liquids into the ground, filling the skies over Chumash County with all sorts of gases and particles. Everything done in secret; no permits, no telling anyone.

Jimmy loved it. Not because he particularly cared about environmental crimes; what he relished was the grand jury's outraged rebellion. After ranting on for a hundred pages or so in their report, the grand jurors had actually started naming names and indicting people. Three from Rolfson, two from the DOE. They'd never released this report, though. There'd been no indictments, nothing. Now the report was being leaked to the *News-Times*. What was going on?

Jimmy vaguely recalled reading something months before about a plea-bargained settlement involving Rolfson and Devil's Peak. It hadn't mattered to him, just the usual murky federal waste-disposal charges. There'd been the expected flurry of complaints from the treehuggers about the size of the fines, but it hadn't lasted long or commanded much attention. Until now. Obviously this grand jury had gotten its head cut off. It wasn't hard to imagine that at least some of the jurors were mighty annoyed. Which no doubt was why Jimmy now held this fat document in his hands.

A name in the report caught Jimmy's attention. Assistant U.S. Attorney Kimberly Rosen, the lead prosecutor presenting the Devil's Peak case to the grand jurors. It sounded familiar to Jimmy. Wasn't that the gal Greg Monarch visited?

Jimmy shrugged off the question. He had no time to dwell on such matters just now. Ira Sullivan's prosecution, Greg's State Bar problems, all that would have to take a backseat. Jimmy had no choice. He had a runaway federal grand jury to deal with.

Kim Rosen, studying the newspaper spread across her desk, tried to tune out the commotion rising from the parking lot just beyond her office window. This reporter Jimmy O'Brien had certainly stirred the pot well. Satellite vans, helicopters, floodlights—it looked as if the whole rolling national media circus had descended on La Graciosa.

No wonder. The feds had plea-bargained with Rolfson even though a grand jury wanted to indict people—that's what O'Brien's *News-Times* article revealed. The *News-Times* had splashed the grand jurors' secret, unreleased report across four full pages. It had also quoted at length the jury's colorful foreman, a hayseed rancher from Chumash County's backcountry. *Runaway grand jury . . . cowboy foreman . . . sinister cover-up . . . radioactive clouds . . .* It must be hard for the poor out-of-town journalists to know which angle to fix on.

Right now, Rosen had little desire to deal with the news media, no matter how hungry they were. Less than six hours before, she'd been standing before the federal district judge who'd overseen the Devil's Peak inquiry, getting reamed royally and publicly. The spectacle of grand jurors speaking openly to the news media had sent U.S. District Judge Horton Q. Archer into sputtering paroxysms. That the cowboy foreman Mac McCasson had included the venerable judge in his dry-witted ridicule didn't help at all. Sitting on the bench in his nearly empty courtroom, tearing into the lawyers he'd summoned for an emergency hearing, Archer looked as if he were about to suffer a stroke. Grand jurors just did not do things like that. Grand jurors didn't violate their oaths of secrecy; grand jurors didn't snigger at judges.

"Ms. Rosen," Judge Archer thundered, "do you quite understand that secrecy is vital to how grand juries work? Do you understand that we just can't *have* grand juries unless they're secret? Do you understand that if you violate their secrecy, you're in contempt of court? Do you understand if you're in contempt, you go to jail?"

Kim Rosen bit her lip and adjusted her reading glasses as the judge scowled down at her. Horndog Archer, the women lawyers in Chumash County called him. He'd once backed Rosen against the bookcase in his chambers, wrinkling his broad, pink, veiny nose at her in a look meant to suggest warm generosity. Before she could slip away, she felt something hard pressing insistently against her upper thigh. Rosen, recalling that moment now, wondered if Judge Archer was doing the same.

"Your Honor," she said. "I have no idea who leaked the special grand jury report to the newspaper. It certainly wasn't the U.S. Attorney's office. I am as dismayed as you are at what has transpired."

Rosen turned away from the judge then and leaned over the prosecutor's table to consult a loose-leaf notebook. It took her a moment to realize Archer was avidly absorbing her from that angle. It took her another moment to turn slowly and again face the bench. "Your Honor," she said. "If it may please the court, I'd suggest looking elsewhere than at the U.S. Attorney's office. This leak obviously came from the grand jurors themselves. As you know, they wanted to release a report. Apparently, they've done so."

Archer peered over his glasses at the prosecutor. He was still frowning, but Rosen sensed the old coot had been distracted a little. "Okay, Ms. Rosen, okay," he muttered. "Here's what I want. I want an appropriate and immediate investigation, that's what I want. An investigation into this outrageous breach of grand jury secrecy."

An investigation. Sitting in her office now, listening to the muted rumble of the media vans outside her window, Rosen tried to calculate how to begin. Just what should she investigate? The leak obviously came from the grand jurors, but they weren't truly culpable. Who really was responsible for the situation so gleefully described in the *News-Times* pages? That's who deserved an investigation.

Perhaps, Rosen reasoned, she should pin it on Jim Larsen. If that runty bulldog FBI agent hadn't found a wildly incriminating memo penned by a top DOE manager—"Everything is grossly deficient at Devil's Peak, we have serious contamination"—they wouldn't have taken on the plant in the first place. Or perhaps she should blame the Rolfson managers who blindfolded EPA inspectors before allowing them into Devil's Peak. Or maybe she should nail the DOE supervisors who regularly looked the other way.

No, Kim Rosen thought. She'd rather aim her first shot at the pompous infrared expert hired by the FBI to analyze the pictures they took while flying over Devil's Peak in fancy high-tech spy planes. "The white stuff signifies elevated temps," he'd declared, pointing knowingly at fuzzy contact sheets full of oddly shaped plumes. "Devil's Peak is hot as Hades." He didn't flip-flop on them until he'd worked the federal expense account for two months of dinners and, Rosen imagined, received a few phone calls. Whatever the impetus, one morning just before his scheduled grand jury appearance the FBI expert decided he couldn't really say precisely what all those white plumes meant.

Not long after, Rosen discovered that certain renegade lawyers in Main Justice were secretly serving as consulting counsel for the DOE. In which capacity, they'd actually written legal briefs supporting Rolfson's claim that federal statutes exempted Devil's Peak waste from regulation. Before she could even holler in protest, Rosen found herself instead listening to her bosses' elevated voices. What the hell is going on? they demanded. We thought you had bombshells and smoking guns. Now it's a major investigation into illegal toilet-flushing. The clock is ticking, Rosen. This is costing money. What's the point? What's the fucking point?

Rosen sighed and rubbed her temples. Then, because she was alone, she wrapped her arms around her body and hugged herself. The scariest moment for her had not been her bosses' blustering. She knew how to respond to that. What had most unnerved her was the pile of documents she found herself poring over one afternoon. She'd been trying for weeks to get them out of Rolfson through a series of increasingly bitter discovery motions. Leafing through them finally, she came across a single page marked, in the upper-right corner, HOT. Thinking that odd, she walked down the hall to James Larsen. At first glance, the FBI agent blanched. Then he jerked the sheet out of her hand, stuffed it into a rubber bag, and bolted from the office. Just as he had predicted, the lab report came back positive: Kim Rosen had been sent radioactive documents. Some 800 disintegrations per minute of alpha radiation. In a letter faxed to her the next day, Rolfson lawyers promptly apologized for the error, saying the radiation levels were "very low, quite safe, but above the limit for releasing records off site."

Kim Rosen refused to believe anyone had purposefully tried to harm her. She refused, as well, to believe that her own government harbored a sinister collaboration with Rolfson. Certain bullies and ideological blowhards did run loose in Main Justice, but Rosen didn't for a second believe the Department was her enemy. Rosen had too complex a perception of the law, and of human nature, to regard matters so simply. This wasn't black and white. The case had fallen apart on them; the case hadn't panned out the way she'd initially billed it. Why, you could fairly argue that Main Justice had done the best it could against Rolfson, given the fuzziness of the regulations. You had to admit—at least they'd tried.

All the same, Kim Rosen felt rattled and uncertain. After everything that had transpired, she could see why the grand jurors might be just a little bit suspicious. She understood why they might feel compelled to speak out. She could even grasp why they might want to leak their unreleased secret report.

Rosen glanced toward the window. Outside, the media vans awaited her statement, their satellite uplinks blinking impatiently. What to tell them?

Sitting on a stool at JB's, Greg watched the television that hung in a corner behind the bar. On the local news, a scraggly cowboy was riding his mare across the barren eastern plains of Chumash County. The camera couldn't get enough of him; his floppy mustache and red bandanna and dirty white hat filled the small screen. Mac McCasson, they said his name was. Mac McCasson, foreman of the Devil's Peak grand jury.

"Little guys and little companies sure get prosecuted for environmental crimes," McCasson was telling the TV reporter now. "Our judge's instructions said no one is above the law. If that's not true, let's go tell America, let's tell 'em what the deal is. Or let's change it. Let's not throw small guys in jail and not prosecute big companies . . ."

Greg couldn't help but chuckle. He welcomed the distractions brought by this Devil's Peak grand jury affair. For several blessed weeks now, hardly anyone in town had asked him about Ira's trial. All eyes were on this cowboy foreman. McCasson played his role to the hilt, happily obliging all comers. He pushed his big white hat back, rubbed his chin, talked plain and simple. "It seems kind of funny, coming after the average Joe while letting the real criminals go," he informed one TV reporter. To another, he shrugged when asked if the judge's threats troubled him. "I'd rather face the judge than face myself and know

I didn't do my duty. Hell, they call for an investigation of us, we'll call for an investigation of them . . ."

Finally, the camera pulled back from McCasson and pivoted to a new image: Kim Rosen. Watching her replace McCasson on JB's television screen, the best Greg could say was that she came off earnest and genuine. The federal prosecutor was listening carefully to the reporters' questions, mulling them over before answering. In this setting, she intrigued Greg as much as she had in her office. She sat before the camera as if it weren't there, straddling a bench outside her office building, her back arched, her chin propped on her fist. She scrunched up her nose and, seemingly unaware, puckered her lips. When her bangs fell across her eyes, she blew them away.

The grand jurors were good, honest people, Rosen was explaining. But the grand jurors have ignored certain facts. They've ignored that key environmental laws didn't even exist until a dozen years ago. They've ignored that certain statutes just didn't apply to Devil's Peak. The jurors were calling things crimes that weren't crimes. They were failing to distinguish between what's bad and what's a crime. She felt outraged too, Rosen declared. But you can get outraged at lots of things that aren't illegal.

Listening, Greg couldn't work up much resentment. Kim Rosen had deceived him when they met, but he could see why. She must have thought he was gunning for her troubled grand jury investigation. All those boxes piled up, not yet even stored. RCRA-DP-SGJ. Of course. RCRA was the operative federal environmental law; DP was Devil's Peak; SGJ stood for special grand jury.

"It's not that simple," she was telling the TV reporter. "Your questions require more than an eight-second sound bite . . ."

Raucous laughter at Greg's side drowned out Rosen's words. Jimmy O'Brien, sliding onto the adjoining stool, pointed at the TV.

"Not going to work," Jimmy announced. "She's not going to match McCasson that way."

Greg nodded. Jimmy was right, of course. Still, he couldn't quite share Jimmy's delight over Kim Rosen's predicament. The sight of a lawyer mired in subtle complexities aroused in him a mix of feelings. Sympathy, for one. Maybe a little disdain. Above all, recognition.

"You reporters have been sort of hard on Rosen, don't you think?" Greg asked. "Maybe she's got a point?"

Jimmy started to respond, but checked himself. He peered at Greg with curiosity. He hadn't exactly abandoned Greg in recent weeks, while he chased the grand jury story. But he had left him on his own.

"What point?" Jimmy asked. "The feds folded, caved."

"Anyway," Greg continued, "McCasson is irresistible. Have to give you that."

Jimmy scowled. "Where's your head at, Monarch? Identify with this prosecutor, do you?"

"No, not exactly identify with her."

Jimmy stared wildly. He'd clearly left Monarch alone too long. "You going to cop a plea with Ira? Is that it, Greg? Is that it?"

Greg turned back to the TV. Kim Rosen was still trying to explain subtleties and complexities. "It's hard to make your way and still keep a clear conscience, Jimmy. Maybe that's what she's trying to do."

Jimmy shook his head. "It's hard to make your way no matter what," he said slowly.

"That is true," Greg agreed.

The Devil's Peak siren once again sounded as Greg walked the creekside path toward the *asistencia*, and a meeting with the district attorney. The siren had been going off more often than usual in recent weeks, sounding almost like a taunt. Each one sent the visiting journalists scrambling, although none signified anything. Tests and false alarms, that's all Devil's Peak delivered these days.

After his exchange with Jimmy, Greg couldn't help but think of his father. How to make your way, that had always been his dad's topic. Growing up, Greg had watched his father wrestle daily with that question.

Dr. Philip A. Monarch believed in prevailing, but he would have sooner shot his foot off than do something he thought unethical or immoral. That stance worked well enough, at least until a giant HMO from Southern California established a beachhead on the Central Coast. There came a day when, if you were a doctor and wanted to see patients, you had to sign up with Health Shield. Phil Monarch resisted until his waiting room had grown empty most afternoons. Then, ten months after he reluctantly enrolled, Health Shield sent a notice saying he was "overutilizing" the system. He needed to think about the "financial implications" of his "practice habits." Emphasis needed to be placed on "the judicious utilization of services" and "not just the philosophical goals of the traditional primary-care physician." On the day he found himself sending a possible pneumonia patient home with antibiotics rather than order a chest X ray and blood tests, Phil Monarch quit. Within a year, he had to close his practice. Soon after, late one winter night, he suffered a devastating stroke. Greg sat by his bed, hour after hour, during his last week.

Where the creek path ended, Greg turned toward the plaza, and the matters facing him.

The first official notification from the State Bar's Office of Attorney Discipline had arrived days after his jailhouse visit with Paul Platt. Then came notice that the initial inquiry had convinced the State Bar to file an informal complaint against him. Next would be a hearing, which, if unfavorable, would lead to a formal complaint in state district court. Greg's prospects ranged from reprimand to probation, suspension, or disbarment.

Before all that loomed Ira's trial. It was due to start in two weeks. Greg had fixed on a concise, sharply defined defense: Sandy Polson's and Paul Platt's statements, full of exactly the same inaccuracies, simply made no sense. That much was utterly undeniable, but was it enough? No matter which way he twisted things, after all, it would still come down to Sandy and Paul for the state, Planet and Moose for the defense. That they were going to base Ira's murder trial on these four witnesses confounded Greg.

He had reached the *asistencia* entrance. He stood still for a moment, gathering himself before entering. Just then the door swung open. Detective Roger Kandle, about to step outside, blinked.

"Hey, there," he grunted.

"Hey, there," Greg replied.

Kandle looked as if he was searching for something else to say. "I think Taylor's waiting for you," he finally offered. "I'll take you back."

Greg fell in beside him. The silence stretched on as they wound through the *asistencia*'s hallways. "Still an open-and-shut case?" Greg finally asked.

Kandle stiffened, hitched up his belt. "Taylor's waiting," he replied.

The D.A. appeared harried and preoccupied as he ushered Greg into his office. A panel of lights blinked on his telephone console; dozens of court dates covered the master calendar taped to a wall. Here, in private, at his desk, Dennis Taylor looked more like a working lawyer than a public politician.

"Goddamn," he groaned to Greg, pointing to a chair. "Just got back from a hearing. Got smacked hard on a Proposition Eleven, no more than ten minutes ago. Hold on just a sec, okay? One call I've got to make."

Greg sat down as Taylor punched a button. Proposition Eleven was the state's mandatory sentencing statute, passed by voters fed up with softhearted judges. "Mike," the D.A. barked into his phone. "You won't believe this. That damn Judge Rendell just threw me out on an Eleven. . . . No, didn't rule it unconstitutional, just said it didn't apply to my guy. . . . No, not that one, the fella who's been sticking knives in folks under the downtown bridge. No priors, so Rendell says Eleven doesn't apply, gives him straight probation. . . . What we gonna do? Appeal, file a writ, what? Look into it, will you, let me know. We have to decide by tomorrow."

Taylor hung up the phone, but his mind remained in the courtroom he'd just left. He turned to his computer, started punching the keyboard. "Sticking people with knives," he muttered. "But we haven't caught him before, so he walks."

Greg tried to look sympathetic. He knew some citizens truly appreciated Taylor. "It's a tough area. Those mandatory sentencing laws give everyone trouble."

Taylor swung around to face Greg, finally focused on his visitor. "So, Greg, how can I help you? Is this a pretrial negotiation?"

"You could call it that."

"What do you propose?"

"That you drop this prosecution."

Taylor studied Greg for a moment, then shook his head. "You are always a surprise."

"You don't have a case against my client. You have a case against your star witness. Sandy Polson had the gun, Sandy Polson had the money. Why don't you put her on trial? You wouldn't have to work as hard."

Taylor's face twisted with irritation. "Sandy Polson's a very believable witness," he said. "I believe her. We'll see if the jury does also."

"Juries make mistakes."

Taylor rubbed his temples. "There'd never be any trials in Chumash County if I worried about that prospect. Someone's got to make the call, Greg. Someone's got to decide."

Greg pulled an envelope from his inside coat pocket, tapped it in the palm of his hand. "I've received notice from the State Bar on your complaint."

Taylor suddenly found something demanding his attention on the computer screen. He turned away from Greg, began striking the keys again. "I'm sorry, Greg," he said over his shoulder. "We're adversaries now. You're in a battle."

Greg nodded agreeably. "I've been told that before."

Taylor started to answer, then stopped himself. Glancing at his watch, he rose and motioned Greg to the door. "I just don't have time to philosophize with you right now, Greg. Sorry. Please understand. I've got six cases about to roll, plus that damn Proposition Eleven appeal. See you in court."

Greg felt eyes on him as he retraced his steps down the *asistencia* corridor. He wondered where they had Sandy Polson right now. It wasn't Sandy watching him, though. From a corner alcove, it was Roger Kandle examining Greg's retreating back.

TEN

A second, even more savage spring storm slammed into La Graciosa in the hours before Ira Sullivan's trial was to begin. Lying on the cot in his damp, cold cell, Ira listened to the rain hammer the *asistencia*'s roof. Back in high school, he sometimes trained for the track team in such deluges. Jogging five or ten miles along flooded country roads, the downpour slapping his back, the water whipping into his face—he always found the experience intoxicating. Merely running wasn't enough of a challenge. Facing a storm, that he considered an accomplishment.

When Ira returned home after such runs, though, he met only disdain from his parents. Ira knew they resented him, or at least found him irksome in a way he didn't quite understand. *You are such a peculiar boy, such a fanatic*. That, in various forms, was the message he always heard from them. It was, Ira eventually came to understand, a way of venting their own disappointment at life. This insight into his parents did not rid his memory of their scornful voices.

Greg Monarch, whatever his moods and impulses, had never made Ira feel foolish. Nor had Greg ever showered him with mindless adulation, as had so many of their classmates and teachers. Greg always acted as if he truly enjoyed him. Greg would just shake his head in amusement at his various excesses. "Whatever it takes," he'd mutter.

It took nothing now. At least, that's what Ira tried to tell himself, lying on his jailhouse cot. He struggled to numb his mind, to purge the sharp terror gripping his chest. As hard as he tried, though, he couldn't do it; he couldn't embrace oblivion. Letting go scared him too much, scared him even more than the forces now gathering against him. He wished the rain pounding on the *asistencia* roof could lull him back to sleep. Instead, the deluge roused him. He longed for a flooded country road; he longed for the water once again to whip into his face.

Lying in his bed, Greg also listened to the storm, and to the creek rushing toward the sea. He imagined what it would feel like to be on a raft, riding those roiled waters all the way to Pirate's Beach. Greg forced his attention to the day's coming events. He wondered if Chumash County Circuit Judge Martin G. Hedgespeth would disqualify him from the trial, even though its preliminary motions were due to start in two hours. That did not seem likely, he decided.

Ethics didn't much interest Judge Hedgespeth, after all. "I wish I could sit here and tell you I've studied at length the Code of Professional Responsibility," the judge liked to inform attorneys who were arguing in his courtroom about arcane points of lawyerly behavior. "But I can't do that. I know it exists. And I know the bottom line of it is, if you can make money at it, it's unethical. Other than that, I am not too familiar with it."

Hedgespeth would be more interested in the practical impact of Paul Platt's flip-flops and accusations than in orations about high-minded principles. How was this going to affect Ira Sullivan's murder trial? Hedgespeth prided himself on rarely being overturned by appellate judges. That's what this morning's hearing would really be about. Hedgespeth, knowing they'd chew on it for months, would let the State Bar bureaucracy in Sacramento deal with Taylor's ethics complaint.

Greg finally climbed out of bed at 8:00. Shaving and showering, mulling legal tactics, he found odd memories intruding. His sixteenth birthday in San Francisco, hanging on the strap in a cable car, a laughing, dark-haired girl he didn't know feeding him cookies from across the aisle. Ira rising with an eager, lopsided grin to argue their first-ever case before a La Graciosa jury. Jimmy, eyes on a Vancouver car ferry's rising access ramp, punching his accelerator, soaring across a bright blue sliver of air.

At 9:00, wrapped in a hooded slicker, Greg stepped outside. He studied the rising water as he followed the creek-side path toward the *asistencia*. It looked to him as if the stream would jump its banks by afternoon.

Chumash County's solitary courtroom occupied what had been, a century before, the *asistencia's* modest church. It had a high vaulted and beamed ceiling, but was compact and narrow, only twenty-five feet in width, with seats for just 150 in twelve rows. Entering it from the town plaza, through the two-story-high oak double door, Greg imagined he was coming to pray.

"Ready to start?" Dennis Taylor stood impatiently at the rear of the courtroom. He looked neither pleasant nor hostile this morning, just in a hurry. Together they approached the front of the courtroom, and settled on opposite sides of a single table placed perpendicular to Judge Hedgespeth's bench. The chamber was too narrow for separate attorney stations.

"No hard feelings, Greg," Taylor offered. "I've just got to protect my case here."

"No hard feelings," Greg agreed.

Judge Hedgespeth entered from a door behind his bench and quickly sat down before the clerk could cry out, "All rise." Although they were dealing only with preliminary motions and procedural matters this morning, spectators already filled many of the courtroom's seats. Taylor approached the bench, handed the judge a document, then turned and gave Greg a copy.

"Oh no, not a written motion," the judge groaned.

Hedgespeth was like that. He didn't welcome much formality in his courtroom, although he could wield a firm hand when necessary. At sixty-six he was a wiry, compact five-foot seven-inch man with a partiality for Copenhagen snuff and tam-o'-shanter caps. He willingly stared down lawyers when necessary, but usually acted genial, and sometimes downright playful. He'd been reelected by Chumash County voters every two years for the past three decades; it was a point of pride to him that he'd carried every precinct in the last five elections. He took the public's support as a validation of the judicial system, at least as administered in his courtroom.

"Your Honor," Dennis Taylor explained, "the reason I'm submitting this now is because Mr. Monarch might be planning to dispute Paul Platt's testimony. If so, he might have to testify. I don't know how he's going to handle that."

Greg and the judge leafed through the D.A.'s petition. It was a motion *in limine*, a pretrial effort to exclude evidence. It charged Greg with rank misconduct in obtaining Paul Platt's recantation. The D.A. wanted the judge to bar that statement from the trial. If he didn't, Taylor warned, then he'd challenge it; he'd put Platt on the stand, have him describe Greg's coercion. Greg's only possible defense would be to take the stand himself and give his version of what happened. If he did that, though, he'd have to withdraw as Ira's lawyer. By law, he couldn't be both witness and defense counsel at Ira Sullivan's trial.

Greg fumed as he read the D.A.'s words. "What Mr. Taylor ignores," he told the judge, "is that there are also questions about his talks with Paul Platt. He might have to be a witness, too. He also has a problem."

Taylor pivoted toward the judge. "Your Honor, I'm not planning to dispute anything Paul Platt says on the stand. So I won't have to testify."

Greg approached the bench, his shoulder almost touching Taylor's. "Your Honor, Mr. Taylor has been talking to Platt almost daily, and he's never disclosed to me what they talk about. I have a right to know how Mr. Taylor got Platt to change his story after my visit. . . . Besides, Platt is a witness, not an adversary. I would have failed my client if I hadn't gone to talk with him."

Taylor stepped away from Greg. "I don't agree. Paul Platt gave a statement against Ira Sullivan, so surely he's an adversary. Mr. Monarch must know he can't talk to another lawyer's client. To be honest, I'm quite astonished at what has happened in this case."

Greg stared at the D.A. "You are astonished, Mr. Taylor? You are astonished?"

Taylor nodded toward the judge. "Your Honor, we're supposed to argue a motion by talking to the court, not to each other. That's what I'm doing. Mr. Monarch should also."

Greg circled back around the attorney's table. "I would like Mr. Taylor to disclose what he told Paul Platt," he said. "He's talked to Platt far more than I have."

Taylor turned to Greg. "Telling the truth," he said. "That's what Paul Platt and I have talked about. Telling the truth."

Judge Hedgespeth finally stopped them. With a weary, distracted wave of his arm, he directed both lawyers to their seats. He just wasn't going to get drawn into this debate; in fact, he'd barely been following it. "While you gentlemen have been so genteelly communicating," the judge said, "I've been thumbing through my unused copy of the Code of Professional Ethics. This is what I can tell you. Number one, we're not going to decide here whether Mr. Monarch has violated the code, whether Mr. Monarch's license is in danger. That's for another body, another time. Number two, for the purposes of this trial, Paul Platt is a witness, not a codefendant. So it's my judgment that Mr. Monarch has a right to talk to Mr. Platt, as does Mr. Taylor. Mr. Monarch is required by the rules to represent his client as vigorously as possible. Mr. Taylor is to prosecute Mr. Sullivan as vigorously as possible. That's what's going on here."

The judge leaned forward, peered over his glasses at the two lawyers. "What say we let the jury sort all this out, gentlemen? Apparently Mr. Platt is not going to deny he made the statement to Greg; he's just going to deny its truthfulness. So it won't be necessary for Greg to testify. Greg can use the statement, and Mr. Platt can deny its truth, and Dennis can introduce Platt's other statement. Who knows what the jury will make of all that?" The judge tapped his gavel. "The state's motion *in limine* is denied."

Greg was still savoring his small victory when Dennis produced another piece of paper. It was the prosecution's updated witness list. Greg could never pick up such a document without thinking of Joe Hilliard's trial. He remembered still the moment he first received Bill Lasorda's witness list. He'd read it carefully. He'd made a point of making sure it contained the name of the FBI ballistics expert.

"Mr. Monarch," Judge Hedgespeth said, "do you see any problems?"

Greg would not be rushed, not this morning. "Your Honor, I'd like to look this over a bit before I respond, if that is okay."

The judge nodded as he surveyed the spectators in his courtroom. "No point keeping everyone in their seats," Hedgespeth declared. "I'll adjourn this hearing. You two come to my chambers when you're ready."

Examining Taylor's sheet, Greg saw all the expected names. The postmaster's two grown daughters. The coroner, the sheriff, the county forensics technician. Detectives Buzz Johnson and Roger Kandle. Sandy Polson, of course, and Paul Platt.

When he reached the last name, a pathologist, Greg stared at it, then scanned back up the list, searching in vain. Nowhere did he see the names of the two men who said they'd driven Sandy Polson to Crocker.

Greg turned to Taylor, who was packing his papers into a briefcase. "As you're not inclined to call Simon Hutch and Rob Linter, then I will." He spoke softly, shielding his voice from the spectators. "I'm going to subpoena them."

Taylor also spoke in a lowered tone. "I'm afraid that won't get them to the stand, Greg. They're both claiming Fifth Amendment privilege against testifying. They can't be forced to incriminate themselves."

"Fifth Amendment? They're just witnesses. What are they afraid of?"

"We take drug abuse very seriously in this county, Greg. They were smoking pot that night, they admitted as much in their statements. We have reason to believe they had a big stash in the car. Enough to stock a small store. We've charged them with possession with intent to sell."

Greg raised an eyebrow. "Why, Dennis, if I didn't know you, I'd think you were trying to keep them from testifying."

Taylor grinned and held up his hands, but said nothing. Several spectators were studying them now.

Greg imagined how it would feel to slam Taylor's face into the table. "Grant them limited immunity, Dennis. Agree that you won't use their testimony against them."

Taylor snapped his briefcase shut. "That's exactly what they asked for. But I refused. We have a policy in the D.A.'s office. No immunity on drug charges, ever. We're very proud of that policy. We think the citizens of Chumash County appreciate it greatly."

In Judge Hedgespeth's chambers minutes later, Greg explained the situation as best he could, then asked the judge himself to grant immunity. It was, he knew, a futile request. For the same reason Hedgespeth had declined to intervene over Paul Platt's taped statements, he would demur now. Let the adversaries duel, that was his creed. Then let the jury choose the victor. Hedgespeth believed passionately in the legal system. It had been his universe for some thirty years.

"I'm sorry, Greg," the judge said. "But I can't force the state to grant immunity. And no, I don't feel it's in my power to grant it myself. That's the prosecutor's province."

Greg turned to Taylor. "I trust I can at least introduce the written statements Hutch and Linter gave the police? And refer to them on cross? Mr. Taylor has not figured out a way to keep them out of the trial?"

Taylor nodded. "Of course you can, Greg. The rules of evidence allow that. And we would never violate the rules of evidence."

The judge looked from lawyer to lawyer. "Gentlemen, are we ready to go to trial?"

The creek had jumped its banks by the time Greg, with Jimmy O'Brien at his heels, started walking back to the courthouse after lunch. JB's patio was half-underwater, as were those of most creekside cafés. Under a pounding downpour, customers were stacking sandbags, waiters nailing up plywood barriers. Here and there along the pathway, chunks of earthen bank and concrete had collapsed into the raging torrent. Halfway to the courthouse, Greg and Jimmy found it necessary to abandon the pathway and scramble for higher ground.

"So what do you think?" Jimmy asked, breathing heavily, shivering and perspiring at once. "How is Taylor going to make Sandy's and Paul's stories fit with Hutch and Linter? How is he going to explain the gun and cash?"

Greg answered, but in the roar from the creek and the storm, Jimmy couldn't hear him. "What's that?" Jimmy hollered.

Greg repeated himself, fighting the wind. "He's going to tell a story," he shouted.

They were inside the courthouse now, standing in the rear, behind the twelve rows of seats. Off to his right, Greg noticed two plump, middle-aged women huddled together. In their hands, each clutched a small photo. With a start, Greg realized these must be the postmaster's daughters; the photos were of their father. They'd refused all defense requests for interviews. Greg fought an impulse to corner them now and ask his questions. He finally turned from the women, just in time to see Ira Sullivan being led into the courtroom.

They'd fixed him up, as Greg had insisted. They'd put him into a new blue suit, they'd brushed back the untamed forelock, they'd shaved the perpetual stubble. It wasn't the prison staff, though, that had altered Ira's worn, troubled eyes. Ira had managed that himself. He winked at Greg as if they were sharing a private joke.

Greg approached, put his hand on Ira's elbow, guided him to a seat on their side of the table. Dennis Taylor settled across from them, not more than four feet away. A door swung open, and the jury filed in.

Picking the jurors in Chumash County had not involved the type of prolonged arm wrestling and psyche-probing that went on in certain reaches of the country. Just as some lawyers consulted marketing firms to test their stories, some now also hired specialists to help identify those jurors most likely to embrace their side. The pool of potential jurors in Chumash County, however, wasn't large or varied enough for such tactics. What's more, Judge Hedgespeth wasn't inclined to tie up the county's single courtroom with hours of what he considered tomfoolery. His faith in the citizens of Chumash County was such that he believed any of them would do a good and honorable job, or at least a job equal to his peers'. Win your case in the telling of it, he liked to say, not by handpicking your listeners.

Of course, that didn't mean Hedgespeth didn't weed out some jurors during the *voir dire* questioning, which he largely conducted himself. It's just that when he dismissed a prospective juror, he did so not to help either side's case, but rather, to accommodate the prospective juror. All those in a Chumash County jurors' pool, after all, were potential voters. Hedgespeth found it unnatural to displease a voter. If you owned a salvage yard and were self-employed, you were excused. If you worked at a lumberyard and it was the busy season, you were excused. If you had a son in kindergarten and no baby-sitter, you were excused. If you were eight months pregnant, "Come back in six years," the judge was likely to advise with a broad, warm smile. "Your baby will be in school then."

Beyond that, just about everyone landed in the pool, and eventually on a jury. The foolish, the prejudiced, the indolent, the crazy. One legendary Chumash County jury, in a sexual assault case just three years before, had ended up including a woman with an IQ of 66. As usual, Judge Hedgespeth's screening of potential jurors in that case had consisted largely of general questions directed to the whole pool. In a brief individual exchange, the 66-IQ juror told Hedgespeth that no, she'd never been to court before, and yes, she was single. When the judge asked the group if anything might affect their ability to serve, she'd remained silent.

So had Dennis Taylor, who was prosecuting the case. Taylor remained silent even after he received a phone call, on day two of the four-day trial, from a nurse at the juror's group home for the mentally retarded. The nurse rather sharply objected to her patient being on a jury. Taylor did not share the nurse's concern. "What the hell, we're winning the case," Taylor told one deputy.

The D.A. was right. He won his conviction, and a twelve-year prison sentence. The public defender eventually caught on, and filed for a retrial based on his client's being denied a mentally competent jury. At a hearing, a clinical psychologist called the juror in question "gravely disabled," but Taylor argued that only people under conservatorship are considered mentally incompetent for jury duty. Judge Hedgespeth apparently agreed, for he let the verdict stand.

Have you been unduly influenced by publicity? Have you read about Postmaster Wilson's murder in the newspaper? Those were the sort of questions Hedgespeth had asked potential jurors for Ira's trial. Those—and questions about their attitudes toward the death penalty. By declaring the state's intention to make Ira's a capital case,

Dennis Taylor had gained the right to exclude any potential jurors who said they were unwilling to impose a death penalty. The result—a "death-qualified jury"—was a prosecutor's ideal for every murder case.

What is your opinion of the death penalty? If you found someone guilty of murder, could you sentence that person to death? Would you automatically be for the death penalty? Would you automatically be against it? The first twelve citizens who avoided extreme answers made Ira Sullivan's jury. They sat now, some looking at the judge, others at Ira. They were, undeniably, an honest cross section of Chumash County. Shopkeepers, cowhands, housewives, a mechanic, a carpenter, a realtor. They'd all grown up together in this pocket of the central California coast. Their faces were familiar to Greg, as were their earnest, artless attitudes.

At 2:17 P.M., Dennis Taylor rose before a packed courtroom to give his opening argument. Agitation showed in the faces of many spectators; their concern about this case had only deepened in the wake of certain recent public comments by the Chumash County D.A. It was upsetting enough that Postmaster Wilson had been killed; that his death might be linked to drug dealing, as Taylor now was suggesting to reporters, alarmed Chumash County citizens beyond words.

"Good morning, ladies and gentlemen of the jury," the D.A. began. "As the judge previously mentioned, what I will present here this afternoon is a kind of overview of what we are going to offer."

Greg listened with growing fascination to the story Taylor now wove. It bore little resemblance to the one the D.A. initially bought from Sandy Polson on the night of Ira's arrest and subsequently sold to a Chumash County grand jury. Taylor was spinning something entirely new. New, but also familiar.

No longer had Sandy Polson driven up to Crocker with Ira and Paul in a green Dodge van. Now, as Taylor told it, she'd driven there with Simon Hutch and Rob Linter. Just as those two young men had always said. You will hear testimony, the D.A. promised the jurors, that Sandy Polson left Hutch and Linter at the Pozo Tavern, borrowed Simon's white Plymouth Fury, met Ira and Paul at the postmaster's house. You will hear that there she found the defendant standing over the postmaster's body, a .22 pistol in his hand. You will hear that the defendant placed the gun and other articles into a paper sack, and the sack into the white Plymouth. You will hear that the defendant put $33,000 cash in Ms. Polson's purse, begging her to keep it for him. You will hear that Mr. Hutch and Mr. Linter drove Ms. Polson back to her house. You will hear that she carried the sack into her house. You will hear that she didn't look in the sack, didn't know what it contained . . .

Greg couldn't help but marvel at Dennis Taylor's outrageous nerve. It wasn't just that Sandy Polson's story now fit consistently with Hutch's and Linter's. Polson's story also now protected her, by having her arrive on the scene after the murder. Most important, most remarkable, Polson's story resolved the troublesome fact that the murder weapon had been found in her house. However improbable, this account fit the evidence. No matter if it also was outlandish. They'd all seen too many juries act foolishly to assume they wouldn't buy this story. After years of watching mindless television shows and extravagant movies, jurors thought irrational plots and impossible motives verily mirrored the human condition.

After less than an hour, the D.A. finished talking. Judge Hedgespeth pointed toward the defense attorney.

Greg rose, looking as if lost in thought. He approached the jurors slowly, nodding at those willing to meet his gaze. For an instant, he looked back at Ira. Then he began.

"May it please the court, Mr. Taylor, ladies and gentlemen. My name is Greg Monarch. I practice law here in La Graciosa. I represent Ira Sullivan. You have just heard Mr. Taylor summarize what he plans to present to you. You have just heard Mr. Taylor say he will prove that Ira Sullivan, with his accomplice Paul Platt, killed the postmaster, Bob Wilson. I am going to tell you something else. I think if you listen to all of the evidence throughout the trial, at the end you will decide that one person committed this crime, not two. One woman, to be precise. Sandy Polson, the state's star witness. Sandy Polson, and no one else."

Greg waited for the jurors to absorb those words before he continued. Behind him, he could hear spectators' confused murmuring.

"Why do you think you will decide this? Well, Mr. Taylor did his best during his opening statement, but he didn't give you the whole picture. Perhaps he didn't have time, perhaps he simply forgot, but Mr. Taylor failed to mention certain facts that you may find of some importance. As the trial unfolds, for example, you will find that the murder weapon Mr. Taylor alluded to, a .22-caliber gun, has never been linked to Ira Sullivan in any way. You will find that Ms. Polson never told detectives a word about this gun until it was discovered in her living room. You will find that the sheriff and D.A. ordered Ira Sullivan's arrest based entirely on Sandy Polson's statement. You will find that Sandy Polson's statement conflicted utterly with that of the two men who drove her up to Crocker . . . And yet, after you find out about all that, Mr. Taylor is still going to ask you to believe Sandy Polson. He is going to ask you to convict Ira Sullivan, based upon Sandy Polson's testimony. Sandy Polson, who had possession of the gun. Sandy Polson, who hid the gun . . ."

Composing his statement late the night before, Greg had felt certain he would prevail, felt certain he'd chosen the right words. Now, though, standing at the edge of the jury box, he began to harbor doubts. Something did not feel right to him. He tried to make eye contact with the jurors, but most were looking elsewhere. It would only get worse when Sandy took the stand. The lovely, composed, guileless Sandy Polson as killer? The focus-group consultants who tested jury responses for lawyers surely would frown. So would the jurors.

He'd been fooling himself. His was not, Greg suddenly realized, the story the jury wanted to hear.

ELEVEN

Witness by witness over two and a half days, Dennis Taylor spelled out the basic foundation of his case. The postmaster's daughters, Buzz Johnson, Roger Kandle, the coroner, the pathologist, the forensics technician—through them the D.A. methodically established the obvious: Postmaster Bob Wilson in fact had been found shot in the head, after an apparent struggle.

Jimmy O'Brien, yanked off the Devil's Peak story for this trial, sat in the press section tapping on his notebook with mounting irritation. There were no critical physical facts in dispute, as far as he could see. If Taylor was going to send Ira to Death Row, he was going to do so by means of Sandy Polson's and Paul Platt's testimony. That was the absolute sum of the state's case. So that was all Jimmy wished to hear.

The two sheriff's detectives would be worth listening to under other circumstances, but not in this courtroom. Both were practiced and unmovable on the witness stand. *No, we didn't coach; no, we didn't coerce; no, we didn't threaten. We hardly did anything. Mr. Platt started talking on his own. Mr. Platt wanted to talk.*

The forensics technician, Matt Thomas, proved equally articulate. *There were indentations to study, and clumps of crumbled plaster. Possible ricochets. I made no conclusions that first night. We determined the number of shots late the next day. . . . That's when we advised the detectives . . .*

Even the postmaster's eldest daughter spoke without

equivocation. *We realized the emerald bracelet was missing the next day, that's when we told the detective . . .*

As the witnesses talked on, Jimmy shifted in his seat, glared at the courtroom's ancient hissing radiators, wiped the sweat off the back of his neck. His thoughts drifted. He could never sit in this courthouse—any courtroom, really—without thinking about Chumash County's legendary Committee of Vigilance.

They'd all learned about the committee, growing up in La Graciosa, for it was a source of eternal local pride. Any schoolchild could talk of how it began. Of how five deserters from a British man-of-war one night in October 1848 massacred an entire pioneer family that had unwisely offered hospitality, then displayed the bulging bag of gold dust they'd mined from the Sierra Nevada. Of how the next day, a dozen Chumash County citizens began relentlessly pursuing the killers south down the coast. Of how those citizens found their quarry on a beach below Santa Barbara, and executed them on the spot, and left the bodies where they fell.

After that, lawlessness and vigilantes both mushroomed in Chumash County. California, taken from Mexico in 1848, made a state in 1850, was in transition. Tension flared between Americans and Mexicans and native *Californios*. Since most of the legal citizens were *Californios*, they made up the juries, and weren't overly eager to convict a fellow countryman. Thus trials became futile endeavors, and bandits roamed freely; just about every month a traveler would disappear in Chumash County, or a skeleton turn up under the brush.

Worst among the Central Coast highwaymen was the feared duo of Pio Linares and Jack Powers. Jimmy cackled whenever he reflected on how these two managed to retain the esteemed Anglo-Scottish lawyer Walter Murray to defend an associate charged with murder in 1853. As it happened, Walter Murray abhorred Jack Powers, and recognized that Chumash County would never prosper while crime was rampant. Yet Murray also ardently admired the legal system; he believed in a committed defense for all accused. Which is what he apparently provided Powers's associate, for he won the accused murderer an acquittal.

Thus emboldened, Powers and Linares escalated their villainous ways, outraging more and more of the populace. Matters came to a head in 1857, when one of the duo's companions was arrested for the ambush murder of two cattle drivers. Arrested—and promptly acquitted, an outcome no doubt helped by the fact that the jury included one of the defendant's accomplices, as well as a fugitive from another murder charge. Chumash County citizens had seen enough.

Formed in 1858, led by none other than the onetime defense attorney Walter Murray, the Committee of Vigilance eventually counted 148 men on its rolls. The justice it delivered for several years thereafter was swift and violent. The committee invaded jails to execute some they were after, and for others, built a makeshift outdoor gallows at the corner of Cerros and Carmel in La Graciosa. One of the committee's first official acts was to hang the associate of Jack Powers whom Murray had defended so effectively against murder charges. The result of all this, according to what they'd learned in school, was "a county in which men walk about unarmed, transact their business, and feel at ease."

Nothing but distant history, Jimmy liked to say whenever they were recalling the Committee of Vigilance at JB's. No longer any need for vigilantes, of course. We all feel at ease, don't we? Right? Right?

It wasn't until late in the morning on the third day that Dennis Taylor finally called Sandy Polson to the stand. Greg turned to the rear of the courtroom. They'd be bringing her from the jail; she would enter from the anteroom.

Greg felt a chill pass through him as soon as he saw her. Negotiating the courtroom aisle toward the witness stand, clad in a simple white dress and black lace-up boots, Sandy appeared to be floating. She scanned the room with an open curiosity. Greg could sense no nerves, no anxiety, no self-consciousness—no anything. Tilting her head, eyeing the jurors and spectators and lawyers, she plainly was enjoying herself.

So, it seemed, was Dennis Taylor. He turned first to Sandy, then the jury, drawing them into a joined circle. Then he perched one foot on the witness-box, as if he and Sandy were simply going to chat. "Ms. Polson," he suggested, "why don't you just tell the jurors about that evening."

Sandy, nodding agreeably, began her story in a voice rich with calm certitude. She went to the Foghorn Pub, she explained, because she could walk there from her Apple Canyon home. That was important, because she didn't like to drive after drinking. There she talked to several people, but mainly Ira Sullivan. His was a familiar face; they'd spent time together before. Then Ira's friend Paul Platt came by. Those two started talking between themselves. She thought they were talking about a party up in Crocker. That caught her attention.

"Why did it catch your attention, Ms. Polson?"

Sandy sighed, and looked at Ira now for the first time. "I was lonely . . . And I was attracted to Ira. He seemed so sad that night. I'm afraid I have a weakness for lost souls."

Ira turned to Greg in agitation. "What's she talking about?" he whispered.

Dennis Taylor offered a reassuring nod. "Go on, Ms. Polson. What happened next?"

Sandy resumed her story. Ira wouldn't take her with them, but an hour later called her at the Foghorn. He needed her help, he said, right away, up in Crocker, in the post office parking lot. She didn't have her car, so she asked Simon Hutch and Rob Linter for a ride. They agreed, Crocker being only ten minutes away. Once in Crocker, she left them at the Pozo Tavern, borrowed Simon Hutch's Plymouth, drove to the post office. Paul Platt met her in the post office parking lot, led her toward a small house . . .

The courtroom by now had settled into utter silence. Through the thick adobe walls, Greg could hear the roar of the storm still pounding La Graciosa. It was amazing, he thought. She told this story as convincingly as she did her first one, although they were entirely different. Sandy Polson was so good, Greg halfway believed her himself.

"Ira was standing over the bloody body of an old man, holding the gun and—well, I don't know how to explain this, he was sort of grinning. I started screaming. Ira came toward me. I stopped screaming . . ."

Greg had to give it to Dennis. The Ira-grinning business was a particularly nice touch. That was new, that wasn't in any of the previous statements. Until now, Dennis really didn't have a capital case. But the grinning could put Ira on Death Row.

She was so upset, Sandy continued. So sick, so cold, so woozy from drinking at the Foghorn. She dropped her shawl; her navy beret got knocked off. She stood at the door, unbelieving, facing outside, while Ira and Paul moved about behind her. She could hear drawers being pulled out. Then they led her toward the parking lot. As they walked, Ira stuck her shawl and beret into a paper sack.

Sandy looked again at Ira, this time with profound regret. "Only later did I realize Ira put more in that sack than my own belongings. All I knew then was that Ira placed the sack into the car I was driving, then stuffed something into my purse. When I saw it was a bundle of cash wrapped in a kitchen towel, I tried to give it back. But Ira begged me to hold it for him. He looked so desperate, so terrible, I finally agreed. Then he and Paul drove away in a green Dodge van."

At the defense side of the table, Ira was squeezing Greg's arm. *What is going on?* he scribbled on a pad.

Dropped off at her house an hour later by Simon and Rob, Sandy continued, she picked up the sack, climbed out of the car, walked inside, put the sack down. She was too nervous to sleep, too upset. So she left again, in her own car. She meant to find Ira at the Foghorn, meant to give him back the cash. That's where she was headed when she ran off the road.

"When did you learn what was in the paper sack?"

"When the sheriff told me, two days after they arrested me. His detectives had searched my house and looked in the sack."

"That was the first time you realized Ira had left you with the murder weapon?"

"Yes, it was."

Taylor started to close his direct. "Now, Ms. Polson, the person you've mentioned throughout your testimony as one Ira Sullivan, is that person present in the courtroom here today?"

"Yes, he is."

"And could you please identify him for the record?"

"He's sitting at the defense table next to Mr. Monarch."

Greg straightened in his chair; he hadn't realized she knew his name.

"In a blue suit?"

"Yes."

Taylor turned to the judge. "Could the record reflect that the witness has identified the defendant, Ira Sullivan?"

Hedgespeth nodded. "The record will so indicate."

Taylor half bowed to Sandy, then the jury. "I don't have any further questions."

Judge Hedgespeth cleared his throat. "That's enough for today, I think. Adjourned until tomorrow, nine A.M."

So many times before, Sandy Polson had fielded questions from strutting, self-important people. Sitting in her darkened jail cell late at night, hours after her turn on the witness stand, she recollected. Teachers, principals, doctors, counselors, detectives, prosecutors. Each utterly certain they were in control. Then there'd been the schoolboys. Slack-jawed and inarticulate, awkward and uncertain, yet determined to act like autonomous creatures. She'd let them all feel powerful. Why not? It was so amusing, studying their misguided faces.

Sandy sketched as she mused over the day's events. She'd put aside images of gardens; in recent days, she'd started drawing the people around her. Dennis Taylor, Roger Kandle, Buzz Johnson, Paul Platt, Sheriff Wizen—each had merited his own page. Sandy couldn't help it, she favored caricatures to realistic representations. Fat lips, ponderous noses, fevered eyes—whatever made these people even passably interesting.

At least she was having a good time in Judge Hedgespeth's courtroom. All those spectators sitting on the edges of their chairs, studying her with such obvious curiosity, hanging breathlessly on her every word. Best of all, they were believing her. Sandy could tell—she'd convinced this crowd.

It was funny, in a way. She'd started out meaning only to annoy Ira Sullivan, but she certainly couldn't stop things now. Poor Ira, sitting there at the defense table, believed by nobody. She'd studied him there in the courtroom. Once, for a split second, their eyes had even met. She could tell, in just that passing moment—Ira's opinion of her hadn't changed one bit from that night in the Foghorn. *No way . . . no way.* It was such a dreadful thing for Ira to say, so unfair. Why had he sneered at her like that? Did he know about Sandy's half brother? Did he know about the accident in Costa Rica?

Sandy turned to a fresh page and began to sketch Ira's face. The angular features, the graying forelock hanging over careworn blue eyes, the gentle, tentative smile . . . Sandy couldn't think of a way to caricature Ira. Nor did she want to; Ira needed no alterations to make him interesting. He needed something, though. Placing her pen at the top of Ira's jaw, Sandy drew a jagged scar across his neck from ear to ear. Then she closed her sketchbook and prepared for bed.

First, she picked up the clothing scattered about her cell, arranging the items neatly on a shelf by her cot. Then, turning to the sink, she brushed her teeth and flossed with the special waxed mint string she'd persuaded Sheriff Wizen to provide. Finally, she slipped out of her thin white dress and pulled on the pink silk pajamas the sheriff had also so nicely furnished.

Never been here before, Sandy mused as she crawled between the sheets of her cot. New turf, this murder trial. She could feel the *asistencia*'s chronic dampness; she could hear strange, distant sounds. They didn't bother her one bit, though. Sandy pulled the sheets tightly around her and slept soundly.

Rising to begin his cross-examination, Greg Monarch stared hard at Sandy Polson. She smiled faintly, tilted her head, held his gaze. In her eyes, he searched for a sign of madness, for evidence of where she'd been, where she now dwelled. He saw nothing.

If only the jurors could know her as he did. That was not possible, though. He'd been shown her confidential presentencing report on the sly. There was no chance he could introduce something so remote in time, involving a witness's minor years. Hedgespeth had snorted when Greg tested that issue in chambers. Her drug-dealing conviction he could get in, but nothing more. If she was to be further revealed, it would have to be by her present conduct in this courtroom.

How to bring that about? How to unnerve a witness who had no nerves? As Greg mulled that question, the spectators in the courtroom leaned forward with anticipation.

"Ms. Polson," Greg began. "You are still being held in the Chumash County Jail, facing charges related to the murder of Bob Wilson, are you not?"

"Yes, I am."

"And you have been in the Chumash County Jail awaiting trial since the day of your arrest?"

"Yes, that's true."

"And you still are negotiating what you finally will be charged with?"

"Yes, I am."

Greg was thinking again of Joe Hilliard's trial. Frankie, testifying against Hilliard, insisted he'd cut no deals with the prosecutor. Only later, when Hilliard was sitting on Death Row, did Greg find a confidential memo in the case file. *Detective Bobo has requested the sentence on Frankie Frazier be postponed until after Joe Hilliard's murder trial.*

"And is it true," Greg asked Sandy, "that your case has been continued from time to time to allow you to testify against Ira Sullivan?"

Dennis Taylor jumped up. "Objection, as to why the case was continued."

Hedgespeth waved him down. "Overruled."

Sandy Polson looked almost as if she were going to reach out and place a calming hand on Greg's arm. "Yes, it has been continued for that reason."

"Are you expecting any benefits in your case from your testimony?"

"I haven't been promised anything, no."

"So will you tell us why you're testifying here today?"

Sandy regarded him gently. "Because I don't feel anyone should get away with murder, Mr. Monarch."

As the day unfolded, it became clear to Jimmy just how trying a task Greg faced. Sandy Polson could explain everything, and always in a light that left her appearing not just innocent, but admirable. She cared about Ira. She didn't realize what he was doing up in Crocker. She fell into this situation unwittingly. Sandy routinely expanded on Greg's questions, appending rationale to what could be answered with a simple yes or no. Their exchange became a struggle of wills.

"The murder weapon was found at your house?" Greg asked.

"I didn't know Ira had put it in that paper sack."

"The answer is yes, it was found in your house?"

"I had no idea what was in that sack."

"After the murder, the weapon was found in a sack in your house?"

"Yes, that's when we all found it. I didn't know it was there until then."

"Ms. Polson," Greg instructed, "I'd appreciate your just answering my questions, okay?"

Sandy looked sorrowful. "I'm sorry, I thought I did, sir."

"Well, no, you didn't."

Taylor intervened. "I think she did, Your Honor. I think he's badgering the witness."

On the bench, Hedgespeth frowned as he scribbled a note. He wanted the jurors to hear as much as possible without his editing. He finally looked up, nodded at Sandy. "Just answer the questions, please, Ms. Polson."

The witness held the judge's gaze a beat longer than required. "Of course, Your Honor."

Greg closed in. "Now, Ms. Polson, you haven't always told the same story that you just told here, have you?"

"No, I have not."

"The first thing you said to Sheriff Wizen on the day of your arrest was that you didn't know the postmaster was even dead?"

"That's right."

"Then did the sheriff mention something about fingerprints? And tell you that you'd better come up with who killed Mr. Wilson, or else you would fry?"

"Actually, Mr. Monarch, I think it was Buzz Johnson who made that suggestion." Sandy sounded amused at the memory.

"Okay, when Detective Johnson made his suggestion, that's when you mentioned Ira Sullivan and Paul Platt?"

"Yes. I was scared, but I had to tell the truth."

"Just yes or no, Ms. Polson. No elaboration."

"I'm sorry, Mr. Monarch."

Greg leaned even closer to her. "In your first version of the truth, you told them you'd not been there, you only heard about the postmaster's murder from Ira, who gave you the thirty-three thousand dollars to hold?"

"That's right."

"Then you admitted you drove up to Crocker with Ira Sullivan and Paul Platt, but claimed you hadn't seen anything, hadn't gone inside the postmaster's home?"

"That's right."

"Then you made yourself an eyewitness? Then you stated you saw Ira shoot the postmaster?"

"That's right."

"And now you're telling us an entirely different story?"

"Yes I am, Mr. Monarch."

"Why, Ms. Polson? How can you explain all this?"

"Well, Mr. Monarch, I think it's obvious. I was scared, I was flustered, everything was a blur in my mind. I was afraid I'd get blamed for the murder. Wouldn't most people?"

Greg turned to Hedgespeth. "Judge, I think the witness needs to be advised again."

This time, Hedgespeth kept his eyes fixed on his notepad. "Ms. Polson, once more I remind you, just answer the question."

Sandy dipped her head. "Yes, Your Honor."

"Ms. Polson," Greg continued, "when you told your story today under oath, you said you rode up to Crocker with Rob Linter and Simon Hutch."

"Yes, I did."

"That wasn't what you told the sheriff back on the evening of your arrest, was it?"

In the press section, Jimmy sat on the edge of his seat. If ever Greg was going to trip her up, it would be over this point. Yet Sandy didn't look the least perturbed.

"No, I told him I came up in a green Dodge van with Ira and Paul."

"So when you told the sheriff you'd ridden to Crocker with Ira and Paul, you were lying?"

"Yes I was, Mr. Monarch."

"Why did you lie to the sheriff, Ms. Polson?"

Sandy didn't hesitate. "Because, Mr. Monarch, I wanted to keep Simon Hutch and Rob Linter from being involved. They were nice, sweet young men who'd given me a ride. I'd gotten them connected with some trouble. I wanted to protect them. I'm sure you can understand."

Greg moved to the witness's side. "Ms. Polson, isn't it true that you didn't switch your story about whom you rode up with until after Hutch and Linter gave their statements to the detectives?"

"Yes, that's true."

"Ms. Polson, isn't it true that you changed your story to conform to the facts that the detectives had discovered? Isn't that the truth?"

Sandy took her time. She reached for a glass of water, sipped, replaced the glass. "I'm sorry, Mr. Monarch," she said finally. "No, that's not true. I changed my story because once Simon and Rob talked to the sheriff, there was no reason to protect them anymore. They'd told the truth. So then I could tell the truth."

"The truth, Ms. Polson? The truth?"

"Yes," Sandy breathed, "the truth."

Greg and Jimmy ate ham and cheese sandwiches as they sat on the porch of the *asistencia*, watching La Graciosa's plaza. The rain had dwindled to a drizzle, but the engorged creek still swamped the stores and cafés along its bank. His mind on Sandy Polson, Greg gazed vacantly, not noticing that dozens of volunteers were frenetically piling sandbags. At his side, Jimmy shifted impatiently, unable to fathom Greg's distracted bearing.

"Could have been worse," Jimmy said.

"That is certainly true."

"The jury won't be fooled by her."

"Ah, yes," Greg said. "The jury."

Judge Hedgespeth, determined not to let this or any other trial in Chumash County drag on forever, had pressed them past the dinner hour. The half-hour recess he'd granted allowed time only for this vending machine meal.

On the far end of the *asistencia* porch, Greg noticed Detectives Roger Kandle and Buzz Johnson sitting over steaming paper cups of coffee. As Buzz talked, Roger's eyes roamed the plaza. For a moment, they locked on Greg's.

"Besides," Jimmy was saying, "Platt's the key witness. Polson has plenty of reason to lie. But not Paul."

"No," Greg agreed. "Not Paul."

Following Sandy Polson to the witness stand, Platt corroborated her account, detail for detail. As Taylor led him through his testimony, Greg turned to look at the spectators who'd filled the rear of the courtroom for the evening session. Most were frowning, or rubbing the stubble on their chins, or clutching each other's hands. The revelations at Ira Sullivan's trial by now had kindled much turmoil in La Graciosa; even citizens who didn't usually think about meth rings or the Foghorn Pub found themselves unable, at least for the moment, to ignore such elements in their community.

Were they all La Graciosa citizens, though? Scanning the rows of seats, Greg suddenly noticed two unfamiliar men in the far back corner. Maybe they were strangers only to him, maybe they were locals he didn't know, but Greg thought that unlikely. If the cut of their gray flannel suits didn't give them away, their manner did. They sat as if alone, recognizing no one about them. Their eyes remained fixed on Dennis Taylor, who, as Greg watched, appeared now to meet their gaze for a passing moment as he turned from his interrogation of Paul Platt. Perhaps not, Greg told himself. Perhaps he imagined the contact. At any rate, what did it matter if the D.A. knew someone among the spectators? So did he, after all. In another corner, Greg now realized, sat Alison Davana, making a face at him.

"Yes, I met Ira in the Foghorn," Platt was saying. "He told me, come on, let's go up to Crocker. Then Sandy showed up, she wanted to come, too . . . Ira said no. He and I drove up alone . . . Then Sandy met us in the post office parking lot. She was driving a white Plymouth . . ."

The chief difference between Sandy's and Paul's tales remained the two crucial details Platt provided. Dennis Taylor made sure the jury understood that the number of shots, and the diamond and emerald bracelet, were particulars that neither Sandy nor the investigators had known about. How could Paul, unless he was there?

Dennis Taylor ended his direct examination by playing the taped statement Platt gave the sheriff's deputies on the morning of his arrest. *This statement is of your own free will?* had been Buzz Johnson's final question. *Yes, my own free will,* Platt had replied.

With that, it was the defense attorney's turn.

Approaching the witness stand, Greg could see he was inspiring fear in Paul's eyes. He was a danger to Paul now; he was the enemy. This slight nervous wreck of a man wasn't so dim that he didn't understand people were yanking him around. He just couldn't say for sure which ones.

Dennis Taylor hadn't tried Platt for the postmaster's murder, and never would. Greg was sure of that. Paul's defense attorney, Jerry Belson, would eventually plead him out on a lesser charge. It simply hadn't happened yet. Dennis would never cut a deal before Ira's trial.

"Hello, Paul," Greg began. "Let's talk about the day you were arrested. What happened when you first got to the jail?"

Paul spoke haltingly, but he remembered his lines. He talked to Detective Buzz Johnson. He gave him a taped statement. No, Buzz didn't discuss details of the murder before he gave his statement. He just gave the statement on his own.

"Now, Paul, you've just testified today that you drove up to Crocker alone with Ira Sullivan, but that's not what you said in your taped statement, is it?"

"No, sir."

"What did you say then?"

"That Sandy Polson drove up with us."

"Paul, can you tell us how you managed to get that so wrong?"

Paul frowned. "I just got confused. I was tired and groggy. I forgot how we went there."

"You got confused. Well, that's understandable. But did you know Sandy Polson got confused the very same way in her first statement?"

"No, I didn't know what Ms. Polson said. I just happened to get mixed up."

"Didn't Detective Buzz Johnson relay to you what Sandy Polson had just told them?"

"No, sir. He never did. I just got confused."

There truly was no way Greg could avoid the course he now chose. That much even his most unforgiving critics would later agree upon. Monarch certainly had to confront Platt about their visit together, everyone conceded. Monarch had to get Platt's statement to him in the record, even if Paul had later retracted it.

"Now, Paul," Greg began. "Did you call me just before the start of this trial?"

"Yes, sir. That was because—"

"Just yes or no, Paul. You have to wait until I ask you a question before you answer. Please. Did you tell me on the phone that your entire statement to the police was a lie?"

"Yes I did, but that was because you—"

Greg stopped him again. "Yes or no, Paul. Please just answer the question."

"Yes, sir, I did say that."

"Okay. Now. Didn't I tell you I couldn't talk to you, you should call your own lawyer?"

"Yes, but then you told me—"

"Paul, stop. Just answer the question. Now. Didn't you call me again the next day? Did you tell me you didn't want the D.A. to know you were calling, but you wanted me to come visit you right away?"

"I didn't say that to you."

"Isn't it true—"

"I said it was all right if you wanted to come talk to me."

The further he led Platt down this road, the more uneasy Greg felt. It was not he cornering the witness, he sensed, but rather the district attorney cornering him. There was no way out, though. He could travel in only one direction, stepping carefully.

"Your Honor, at this time I would ask leave to play for the jury the taped statement Mr. Platt gave to me at the Chumash County Jail."

Dennis Taylor rose to object, but Hedgespeth waved him away. "Go ahead," the judge said. "Play the tape. Let the jurors listen."

The morning I was arrested, I tried to explain I didn't do anything. The detective was hassling me and telling me stuff about the murder . . . Mr. Taylor said I would get life if I didn't help him get Ira Sullivan. What else could I have done? . . .

As the tape unwound, Greg watched the jurors, trying to imagine what they were thinking. That here Paul was telling the truth? Or that Paul would never place himself at the postmaster's if he hadn't been there?

One more question, Greg had said to Platt at the end of his statement. *Tell me why you called me, why you gave this statement.* Paul's answer now rumbled through the courtroom. *Because, Mr. Monarch, I'm tired of the things that are happening. I cannot see myself going to prison and Ira Sullivan to the gas chamber for something we didn't do. It isn't right. It isn't fair . . .*

Greg clicked off the tape recorder and turned to the witness.

"Okay now, Paul. After you gave this taped statement to me, you decided that it wasn't true?"

"That's right, Mr. Monarch, it isn't true."

Before Greg could form his next question, Platt rose from his chair, his hands clenching the sides of the witness-box. "Mr. Monarch," he cried, "you promised me, didn't you? You said you'd get me out of this mess. You told me if I made this statement you'd represent me. You promised you'd help me get free. You told me all that. Didn't you, Mr. Monarch—"

"Paul, Paul, Paul." Greg wanted to clap his hand over the witness's mouth. These words sounded rehearsed. "Paul, I haven't asked you a question."

"Well, I'm asking you one."

"Isn't it true, Paul, that I told you the truth would—"

"No, no, that's not right. You didn't tell me that. You're lying. You said you'd get me freed if I made that statement. You're a lawyer. You said you'd help me—"

"Paul, I'm sorry, you must wait for a question—"

"You didn't want to help me, you were only trying to save your client—"

"Your Honor," Greg implored. "Judge, please . . ."

"Mr. Platt," Hedgespeth murmured without expression. "You are here to answer questions put to you."

It was too late, of course. Everyone in the courtroom could see the jurors muttering to each other, their eyes wide, their hands to their mouths. Everyone could see Dennis Taylor rising, a tight, triumphant grin pasted on his face.

"Your Honor, this is the problem I expected," the D.A. pointed out. "If Mr. Monarch wants to dispute this testimony, he's going to have to testify. And if he testifies, he will have to withdraw as Mr. Sullivan's lawyer."

At Greg's elbow, Ira moaned and clutched his arm. "Please," he whispered. "I need you."

TWELVE

A concealed, little-used tunnel connected the Chumash County Courthouse with a small adobe building to the rear of the *asistencia*. Legend had it that Father Abel Ramona, the last regular Franciscan assigned to the La Graciosa outpost, ordered the tunnel built out of desperation in the summer of 1834. In some versions of the story, insistent black bears inspired Father Ramona's desire for safe passage between the church and what was then his private living quarters. Other versions blamed it on the unusually savage human characters who just then were drifting through the region. Many were homeless immigrants from Sonora and Sinaloa, dislocated and directionless. They lingered at the *asistencia*, they stole the outpost's horses and mules, they sold liquor to the neophytes. For a time, they carried on at will, unchecked. Father Ramona had a trying sojourn in La Graciosa.

Now, in more civilized times, his private quarters behind the *asistencia* housed a modest county law library. Without black bears or overtly savage humans on the prowl, most who used the library approached it aboveground, on a brick path that crossed the *asistencia*'s courtyard. Judge Hedgespeth, however, preferred the tunnel, particularly when he didn't want to encounter grasping, combative lawyers.

As dawn broke the morning after Paul Platt's "excited utterance" on the witness stand, as such outbursts are officially called in the law, the judge moved carefully through the damp tunnel. He was heading toward the library, in search of a possible solution to the legal problems that had suddenly consumed his courtroom. The surface pathway would surely be empty at this hour, but Hedgespeth still preferred the tunnel's dark insulation. He was not in a happy mood. Signs of imperfection or disarray in the legal system unsettled him, particularly when they occurred in his own courtroom, before the watchful eyes of anxious Chumash County citizens. Walking, he listened to the echoing clack of his heels on concrete, and thought of poor Father Ramona hiding from the savages, human or otherwise. Thus occupied, he never noticed the figure approaching in the gloom. Not until Greg Monarch was upon him did he realize he wasn't alone.

"Good morning, Greg," the judge said. "Up early, I see."

"Yes, Your Honor. I have a few legal quandaries to research."

"I do too," Hedgespeth brooded. "I see we also share a liking for this tunnel."

"It's a mighty fine hiding place," Greg said.

Hedgespeth let himself smile at that. Protected against the early chill, the diminutive judge was wearing his customary tam-o'-shanter and a heavy blue wool overcoat. Without his robes he looked less like a judge than a friendly neighborhood ward heeler. Marty Hedgespeth really wasn't cut out for the bench, despite his many honorable years on it. He would have been happier as a city councilman or state legislator, pulling strings and finding patronage jobs for his constituents. It wasn't all that uncommon for him to drop by JB's for a Bombay gin martini on the way home. He never stayed long, though, for his family beckoned. He had six grandchildren, and was forever showing strangers their pictures. Greg couldn't help but like the judge, at least partly because of their differences. Hedgespeth wasn't a private man, and didn't much appreciate silence.

"It's too early and dank in here for that 'Your Honor' business, Greg," the judge finally said. "We'll have plenty of that in the courtroom."

Greg rocked back on his heels, stuffed his hands in the pockets of his sport jacket. It was utterly forbidden to have an *ex parte* exchange like this with the judge, private and alone, without opposing counsel present. If Dennis Taylor knew, he'd demand sanctions, he'd scream to the state supreme court. Still, Greg thought, what did it matter? How much worse could things get? He already faced losing his seat at this trial, not to mention his license to practice law.

"Judge, may I ask you something?"

Hedgespeth started to hold him off with a raised palm, then let his hand drop. The judge never had been able to resist back-channel conversation; there were few Chumash County lawyers who hadn't swapped gossip and theories with Hedgespeth in his chambers. The judge said nothing now, just raised his eyebrows in inquiry.

"Why are you letting this happen?" Greg began.

"This?"

"You must know there's no evidence against Ira. There's just Sandy and Paul's word. One of them is a master liar, the other a scared dimwit—"

The judge started to interrupt, but Greg didn't notice.

"Listen to Sandy's tape, then her testimony. Two utterly different stories. But could you tell when she was lying? Could you hear any difference in tone? Dennis gets a grand jury indictment based on her first story, then switches to her second for the trial. It's a hall of mirrors, Judge. A hall of mirrors."

Hedgespeth grimaced and shifted his weight off his right foot. His gout was flaring up again. Above them, the judge could hear signs of life as the courthouse staff reported to work. For the moment, he preferred Monarch's company.

"Nothing makes sense," Greg continued. "Platt and

Polson give exactly the same false statement when arrested. Platt says he got confused, Polson says she got confused, Taylor thinks that's just fine, and I can't seem to convince anyone otherwise. So maybe it's only me, Judge. Maybe that's it. Maybe I'm crazy."

Still Hedgespeth stood wordless, but now his eyes glinted, as if he'd heard a good joke. Greg noticed.

"Am I amusing you, Judge? I suppose you're right. I suppose we should think of this as a comedy."

Hedgespeth placed a hand on Greg's shoulder. It was a kindly gesture, not a dismissal. The judge couldn't help it, he regarded Greg with affection. He'd known him since he was a boy, since the days when the judge and Greg's dad served jointly on several Chumash County betterment committees. Phil Monarch and Marty Hedgespeth occasionally had lifted a glass together in those days, talking grandly of the region's future. Phil Monarch had wanted the county to prosper as much as any of them, but that hadn't stopped him from raising objections to some of their more brazen plans.

"You remind me of your old man," Hedgespeth told Greg gently. "I much admired your old man."

"Yes," Greg said. "Just about everybody did."

A silence took hold between them and lingered. Finally, the judge spoke. "No, Greg," Hedgespeth said. "You're not crazy."

Although he wouldn't admit it to anyone, the judge found both of the state's witnesses unconvincing. Sandy Polson knew all too well what she was saying, Paul Platt not enough. But what he thought didn't matter to him. The second instruction he always gave the jury was "You are the sole judges of the believability of witnesses." Witnesses were for the jury to fathom; the jury was the finder of fact. If the jurors chose to believe Sandy Polson and Paul Platt, then he did too.

"You aren't crazy," the judge continued. "But there's no point arguing your case to me. It's the jury you want to convince."

Greg bit off his words. "I see. I must have lost touch with the ever-evolving legal system. When I attended law school, judges could still direct verdicts, judges could still overturn verdicts. 'Custodians of the system,' we called them."

Hedgespeth resisted the impulse to react. There was little he could say, after all, to one who actually aspired after something immutable and knowable called truth. Hedgespeth wished he could share Monarch's lofty ambition. He could not, however.

"Overriding juries is a dangerous path to start down," the judge said. "Juries carry the banner for democracy. Juries are the great defense against abuses of power, including my own. Would you rather I assemble the evidence, question the witnesses, deliver the verdict? Do citizens really want to give this much power to me?"

Hedgespeth started to chortle at that notion, but his amusement dissolved into a hacking cough. Consumption along with gout; that's what Greg had to look forward to in the coming years. It took a moment before the judge could continue.

"God knows, we love the good king," Hedgespeth finally gasped. "But we fear the bad king. If you want a king, you must take everything that comes with it. You know when I'm a good judge? When I agree with you."

Greg shivered and tugged at his sport coat. Ira's cell, he imagined, must feel like this. "There are things that are either true or not true," he said. "Either Ira killed or didn't kill the postmaster. That's not something that hinges on a jury's decision."

Hedgespeth nodded. "No it doesn't, Greg. But you and I have no way of truly knowing the truth. We're not graced with divine inspiration. We can only know what the jury thinks after listening to the evidence and witnesses."

Greg turned, started to pass by the judge. Hedgespeth stepped in his way.

"Greg, if you will, recall your Chumash County history

for a moment. Remember the Committee of Vigilance? Is that what you'd have me do? Take the law in my own hands?"

The judge's question stopped Greg. Indeed he did remember the Committee of Vigilance. He'd remember it even without Jimmy O'Brien's occasional reminders.

"I think what I like best," Greg said, "is how Walter Murray first wins Jack Powers's buddy an acquittal, then arranges the man's death at the hands of his vigilante gang. A lovely paradigm of the lawyer's ways, wouldn't you say? Relativism at its finest. You've got to give it to Murray. He could really see things from all sides. He understood that truth is a mutable thing."

Hedgespeth shook his head, coughed, leaned off his throbbing toe. "That's not what I meant, not how I see it. My point was, there are dangers there. We can't just ignore the jury and twist the system whatever way we want it to go."

"Oh, I don't know," Greg said. "Trials were more or less pointless back then. You could fairly argue that it was necessary to organize a little extrajudicial action. Your hallowed legal system wasn't working."

Hedgespeth, at last, bristled. "Vigilantes, Greg? Is that your idea of justice? You want I just decide who should hang, and string them up at Cerros and Carmel?"

Greg enjoyed the effect he was having on Hedgespeth. "What do our county historians say?" he asked. "Because of the Committee of Vigilance, Chumash is now 'a fit county to raise an American family.' Isn't that what they say?"

Hedgespeth started to object, but Greg interrupted. "Another thing. Walter Murray emerged from it quite nicely, didn't he?"

The judge looked puzzled.

"Murray went on to serve many honored years as the county district judge," Greg reminded him. "The very position you now occupy."

Hedgespeth glowered at his throbbing toe. He turned toward the end of the tunnel. "Time to go up into the real world. They'll be sending a search party for us soon." Then the judge hesitated.

"Greg, I've figured out a way to let you stay on this case," he said. "I'm going to let you make an allocution before the jury. You know, a statement not under oath, at the end of the trial, about your contact with Platt. That way you're not a witness. Allocutions aren't common, but they've been used. Hell, maybe I won't even get overturned on this one."

Greg started to say something, but Hedgespeth stopped him, summoning the sternest, most imperial look he could. "Of course, you understand, Monarch. This conversation did not occur. I will see you for the first time this morning in my courtroom."

Jimmy O'Brien glanced anxiously at his watch, then relaxed. It was still early, still a half hour to go before the morning courtroom session. There was no need yet to leave his creekside table at Stella's Café. The rain had ended, and sandbags held back the raging creek. He could nurse his cup of coffee for almost twenty minutes.

In truth, Jimmy wished for a much longer respite from Ira Sullivan's trial. He didn't look forward to the coming days. The notion of chronicling yet another Dennis Taylor victory appalled him. Yet that, he feared, was what loomed.

Not until Jimmy pivoted to wave for another cup of coffee did he notice the woman sitting at a table on the far side of the patio. She was hunched over a pile of papers, sipping a glass of grapefruit juice, brushing the bangs out of her eyes. Jimmy started to look away, then stopped. He squinted and studied her. Damn if that wasn't Kim Rosen. Ms. Assistant U.S. Attorney herself, in person.

Jimmy rose and approached her table. Rosen didn't see

him until he was standing by her side. Looking up, she gave him no more than a glance. During the Devil's Peak exposures, their paths had crossed.

"O'Brien, I've got a court appearance this morning over in San Luis," she said quickly. "No time to talk with journalists."

Jimmy chuckled. "You're probably sick of reporters by now, I imagine."

Rosen arched an eyebrow. "Well, now that you mention it."

"Come on," Jimmy said, slipping into the chair next to her. "You know how these media events play. Runaway grand jury, cowboy foreman, sinister cover-up. It's irresistible. And there's gotta be a villain, you know that. So you were the villain. So what? It all blows over in days. Evaporates soon as the next circus rolls by. I'm not even writing about Devil's Peak anymore."

"What is today's story?"

"Ira Sullivan's murder trial."

Rosen started at those words. Jimmy noticed, but didn't understand how he had affected her. The investigation into the grand jury leak appeared to be petering out without resolution, so she couldn't still be antsy about that. Was there something else brewing?

"You guys simplify everything," Rosen said. "That's what I can't stand. You and the grand jurors, you glossed over all the hairy legal issues I have to face daily."

Jimmy shrugged. "Public wants a simplified view. Public wants cowboys and Indians."

Her eyes stayed on him, but she'd lost interest. "Please leave, O'Brien. I'm busy. Haven't we exhausted your attention span, anyway?"

"It's got a couple more minutes to go, I think."

Rosen slid back in her chair. Her expression softened; this was consuming too much energy. Besides, Jimmy was right, the grand jury stuff was already starting to blow over. "I thought I was doing good to tackle Devil's Peak," she said. "How have I turned out to be the bad guy? I have as much moral outrage as anyone. I just have to work within the law. It would be easy to play the hero if I didn't have to mind the legal system."

Jimmy had no answer. He wished Greg were here to argue about the law. Surely Greg would have a good response. The thought of Greg suddenly jarred him. He stared at his watch. It was 8:55 A.M. Court would be convening in five minutes. Jimmy jumped up, almost knocking over Rosen's juice. "Sorry," he gasped. "I'm late. Gotta get to Sullivan's murder trial."

Rosen stopped him with a hand on his arm. It wasn't a gentle touch; she was clutching his wrist. "How is that trial going?" she asked. "How is that defense attorney handling things?"

Jimmy shrugged. "Not very well, things are going pretty badly," he said. He started to walk away, then turned back. "Why do you ask?"

Rosen, already absorbed in the pile of documents before her, waved off the question. "No reason," she said, sounding distracted. "I just like to follow murder trials."

Walking down the *asistencia* hallway, Roger Kandle steeled himself. It was his job this morning to bring Sandy Polson to the holding area adjacent to the courtroom. She'd already testified, but the lawyers might recall her, so they wanted her nearby. Roger had delayed facing her as long as he could. Now it was 8:57 A.M. He was late, he had to hurry.

"Morning, Sandy," he said, unlocking the door to her cell. "We better get moving. Judge Hedgespeth doesn't like stragglers."

Sandy smiled and kept her gaze on him until he finally met her eyes. She'd never figured out how to handle Detective Kandle, even how to speak with him. He always appeared so uncertain, so soft and mixed-up. Right now, he was frowning. Why couldn't she win him over, why couldn't she convince him? It hurt her in a way, Roger thinking so ill of her. Maybe he'd read certain accounts about her half brother and Costa Rica. Sandy knew those reports didn't look good, but no laws had been broken, or charges filed. If only she could explain that to Roger Kandle. It was dismaying to have unfortunate accidents tarnish the way people regarded you. Particularly since so many others truly deserved Roger's poor opinion.

"You look a little tired this morning, Detective," Sandy said. "Haven't you been sleeping well?"

Roger frowned, scratched his head. "Hard to sleep with three young daughters in the house," he mumbled. "Hard even to think."

Sandy laughed. "I bet. How old are they?"

Roger hesitated, feeling odd discussing his family with Sandy Polson. He didn't want to appear rude, though. "Let's see," he said. "Nine, seven, five."

Sandy sighed with longing, as if lost in a memory. She tried to imagine being the parent of three young daughters. If she could only watch Roger at home, she'd understand how to behave around him. It was hard knowing how to act without a model to observe and copy.

"Oh my, what delights they must be to you right now," she said, as Kandle started guiding her down the hallway.

Roger's unease deepened. "Yes . . . Yes, they are."

When they reached the holding room, the judge's bailiff was waiting to take Sandy. He reached for her arm, but she pulled away and swung around to face Kandle. She looked at him frankly. She couldn't resist asking a final question. "Detective," Sandy said. "Tell me the truth. How did I do out there in the courtroom?"

Kandle backed off, shaking his head. "Not for me to say, ma'am. You'll want to ask the jurors."

No need to do that, Sandy thought as Roger retraced his steps along the *asistencia* corridor. She already knew how she'd fared. Yes, she found that courtroom quite amusing indeed. Watching Greg Monarch fume and flush and stomp about was particularly entertaining. Didn't anyone ever teach him to control his emotions? Sandy laughed out loud. She felt brilliant. The world was not so boring a place after all.

THIRTEEN

At least Planet wasn't wearing his breechcloth in the courtroom. That was the most positive thought Greg could summon as he rose to open the defense's case. Planet had arrived in a pair of khaki pants and a real shirt with buttons. He'd strapped sandals on his feet and tied his mane of white hair into a long ponytail. If still far from conventional in appearance, Planet now resembled a certain recognizable type of Central Coast habitué.

Greg entertained no illusions regarding what he was about to offer. From the trial's start, his central plan had been to create reasonable doubt by attacking the state's case. The screaming inconsistencies in Sandy's and Paul's statements provided reason enough for such a strategy. But Greg had another motive as well: a mighty thin case for the defense.

Planet and Moose would be their only two witnesses. That was it, except for the written statements of Simon Hutch and Rob Linter. Greg couldn't call those two to the stand because of Taylor's refusal to give them immunity. Nor could he call Ira, because Ira couldn't account for his whereabouts at the time of the murder. The critical witness for the defense should have been June Blossom, but even after hiring an investigator, they'd never been able to find a trace of that mysterious lady of the dunes.

"Your Honor," Greg began. "If the court pleases, the defense would like first to introduce the transcribed statements of Mr. Hutch and Mr. Linter."

As these documents were being marked into evidence,

Greg placed blown-up versions on an easel before the jurors. He watched their eyes follow the words as he read them. Here certainly was the heart of the defense, Greg believed. As he feared, though, the jurors' attention appeared to drift. Shifting accounts, multiple accounts, they all blurred in the end. Greg couldn't overcome the empty witness chair. Sandy and Paul in flesh and blood were simply more compelling storytellers than a typed transcript.

Not until Greg finally put Planet on the witness stand did the jurors appear to focus fully. Planet did well enough. He even responded to his real name, much to Greg's relief. Planet had started life as Grant Ellsworth and now grudgingly took the oath as that person. Asking Planet to state his address at the start did create something of a problem, though. *I live in the dunes under the stars and skies* was not quite precise enough for the Chumash County district court. Finally, Planet offered a description of a hut on a street that abutted the dunes, and Judge Hedgespeth decided that sufficed as his place of residence.

Greg then began carefully leading Planet through his story, making sure to head him off whenever his answers started touching on things like "primary abstractions" and "harmonic convergence." The story Planet offered sounded much the same as the one he'd shared weeks before at Pirate's Beach. Ira so sad, Ira gulping down whiskey, Ira dancing with Sandy Polson. Ira leaving with Planet and Moose, Ira drinking and crying in the dunes.

Only one thing was missing: June Blossom. Planet mentioned her not at all.

"And then the siren blasted," Planet concluded his story. "Which disturbed us, which is not conducive to a natural state of consciousness. A little later, Moose and I decided to leave. Ira did not want to come with us. So we left him there in the dunes."

Greg spoke cautiously. He didn't want to impeach his own witness. "Were others in the dunes with you that night, Mr. Ellsworth?"

Planet's eyes remained opaque. "Of course," he said.

"The dunes are teeming with life. There were deer with us, and rabbits. Foxes, skunks, songbirds, ravens, herons—"

"Mr. Ellsworth," Greg interrupted, "I meant other people."

Planet shook his head. "No," he said. "I saw only Moose and Ira."

Oh well, Greg told himself as he sat down. We can't find June Blossom anyway.

The courtroom spectators watched with growing amusement as Dennis Taylor dismantled Planet on cross. The issue of time had always been the soft spot in Planet's story. Specifically, what time they'd left Ira in the dunes. *A little after eleven,* Planet had said weeks before at Pirate's Beach. *Around midnight,* Planet had answered vaguely when Greg asked him on the stand. This was a valuable if unexpected difference, placing Ira in the dunes at the time of the murder. Greg had left it alone, though, hadn't milked it, for he knew Planet didn't really know. The D.A. wasn't so obliging; he aimed straight for the weakness.

He did it artfully. Now, what time did you get to the Foghorn? When did Ira arrive? How late was it when you left the Foghorn? What time was it when you left Ira alone in the dunes? The last, of course, was all Taylor truly cared about. The other questions hardly mattered, except to show that Planet essentially never knew what time it was.

"I would say it was near midnight," Planet answered again. "Yes, midnight when we left the dunes."

It occurred to Greg that Planet was trying to help Ira, in his way. He wouldn't serve up June Blossom; he'd decided to keep her out of this. So instead he was trying to give Ira an alibi that covered the time of the murder.

It was no use. Taylor could see Planet wasn't wearing a watch, Taylor could figure out that Planet didn't own a watch. Hell, Planet probably didn't believe in watches, or, for that matter, in mortal time.

Taylor paced slowly across the courtroom, his arms

crossed, his chin cupped in one hand. "How can you know what time it was when you left the dunes, Mr. Ellsworth?"

"I am a student of the stars and the sky," Planet intoned. "I can tell by the position of the moon."

"I see," Taylor said, smiling as he walked to the prosecutor's side of the attorneys' table. Perhaps he'd anticipated Planet's response; more likely he'd heard its sort before at one trial or another. Certainly, he knew the story of how a young Abraham Lincoln discredited the sole witness in a murder case by citing the 1857 *Farmer's Almanac*; the witness couldn't have seen the slaying by the light of the moon, Lincoln showed, because the moon then was in its first quarter, riding low on the horizon. From his briefcase, Taylor now removed his own tattered *Farmer's Almanac*. He offered it into evidence, opened it to April 28, then handed it to Planet.

"Mr. Ellsworth, can you tell me what stage the moon was at on the evening of the postmaster's murder?"

Planet frowned, studied the page. "It says here there was a new moon that night." He closed the book, handed it back to the D.A., looked at him defiantly. "I was mistaken about the moon, then. But I can still read the sky. It was midnight, maybe later."

Taylor nodded thoughtfully. Back at his briefcase, he pulled out a single sheet of paper, a letter from the Devil's Peak operations manager. The D.A. offered it into evidence as another state exhibit.

As Taylor did so, Greg slumped in his chair. This was why he'd wanted to avoid dissecting the time issue. The Devil's Peak siren located the time too precisely. It was public record when the siren sounded. It went off at 11:00. Everyone knew that, everyone who remembered, or listened to the radio, or looked at a newspaper. Everyone, in other words, but Planet, the great improviser on the witness stand. If Planet had stuck to 11:00, it wouldn't have provided Ira a full alibi, but it would at least have been a believable one.

Taylor approached the witness stand, handed the letter to Planet. "Could you read what it says?"

Planet squinted at the letter. *In response to your inquiry, this is to inform you that as part of a test of our warning systems, we set off the Devil's Peak siren three times on the night of April 28. The first test occurred at 6:30 P.M., the second at 11:00 P.M., the third at 1:15 A.M. Attached please find a certified copy of our alarm log.*

Taylor leaned against the jury box. "Now, Mr. Ellsworth. You say you heard the siren blast, then you and your companion departed, leaving the defendant alone in the dunes?"

Planet frowned. "Yes, yes, that's right."

"Then is it fair to say you can only account for the defendant's whereabouts until eleven P.M.?"

Planet looked truly sad. "Yes," he allowed. "That is fair to say."

It was comforting, Greg mused. It was comforting to know that the Devil's Peak managers weren't so rude as to ignore absolutely everyone who knocked on their door.

A murmur rolled through Judge Hedgespeth's courtroom when Dennis Taylor rose, at the close of the defense's case, to say he had one additional witness to call. Jerry Belson, Paul Platt's attorney, hadn't been available earlier. Now he was.

Greg wasn't nearly as surprised or puzzled as the spectators. It was obvious to him why Belson would willingly testify for the state; he wanted to protect his client's pending plea bargain. Greg suspected a more self-serving motive as well. He studied the witness with barely disguised contempt.

If anything, Belson had grown even more unsavory-looking since Greg had last seen him. His stomach hung out over his belt, sweat glistened on his thick neck, what looked like a coffee stain discolored his wrinkled white shirt. The man was unraveling. Taylor, on direct, approached him as a colleague.

"Did you have a conversation with Mr. Monarch about his talking to Paul?" the D.A. asked.

"I surely did," Belson replied.

"And what did you say to him?"

"I told him that he couldn't talk with Paul. I told him to stay away from my client."

"Were you there in the room when Paul Platt gave a taped statement to Mr. Monarch?"

"Absolutely not."

"Did you ever change your mind? Did you ever tell Mr. Monarch he could talk to your client?"

"Definitely not."

After twenty minutes of such queries, it was Greg's turn. He approached Belson with distaste. Lawyers made mistakes, lawyers weren't all brilliant, but Belson was something else. His failure to challenge Platt's confession smacked of utter sloth; his insistence now on a plea bargain screamed self-protection. Platt had to have been at the postmaster's house, or else Belson had committed legal malpractice.

"Mr. Belson," Greg began. "Have you ever made any attempt to deny the statements that Paul Platt made in his initial taped statement to sheriff's deputies?"

Belson had an odor, Greg realized. Now that he was standing next to him, it was unavoidably apparent. Whether metabolic in nature or the result of a failure to wash, this man reeked.

"No, I did not," Belson replied.

"Mr. Belson," Greg continued. "Have you ever heard Paul Platt tell a story different from the one he gave initially?"

Belson smirked. "Well, I've heard the story he told you."

"I meant another one in which he still is confessing."

Belson hesitated. "I have no personal knowledge, no."

"Indirectly, Mr. Belson. Have you been made aware of what Paul Platt testified to at this trial?"

"I've been given a summary, yes."

"Is it the same story he initially told police?"

Belson resisted. "In its essence, I believe so."

Greg leaned toward him, trying not to inhale through his nose. The tenor of this trial had weighed on him from the start, but now felt unbearable. Greg longed to yank Belson from the witness stand, to shake the truth out of him.

"In its essence, Mr. Belson? In its essence?"

"Yes, I would say."

"Except, Mr. Belson, for how he got to the deceased's home? And with whom he went? And in what car? Isn't that so, Mr. Belson? Isn't that the truth?"

Belson shifted in his chair. "Those details don't change the story. The basic story is that he was present at the murder scene but didn't do anything to make him accountable for the killing of Postmaster Wilson."

If only he could reveal this man for what he was. If only he could strip him bare.

"Mr. Belson, you told me I couldn't talk to Paul Platt, that you absolutely wouldn't allow it. Is that correct?"

"Yes, that is correct."

In the press section, Jimmy squirmed nervously at Greg's obvious ire.

"Okay, Mr. Belson," Greg continued. "Tell me this. Did you also forbid the prosecutor to talk to Paul Platt?"

"No, I did not."

Greg hung his face in front of Belson's. "Would you tell us, please," he invited. "Tell us why you didn't want me talking to Paul Platt but you let the prosecutor talk to Paul Platt."

It was a dangerous question, shaped by indignation. Greg realized as much, even as he asked it. So did the witness. Belson grinned hungrily at the opportunity. Greg saw him coming, but couldn't stop him.

"Okay," Belson replied. "Since you asked, Mr. Monarch, I'll tell you. As his attorney, it's my job to decide what's in Paul Platt's best interests. I happen to believe that Paul was there at the murder scene. I happen to know—"

Greg spun toward Hedgespeth. "Your Honor, I object to that response. Your Honor, I ask that it be stricken from the record."

The judge started to respond, but Belson kept talking, his voice rising. "It's not in my client's best interests to lie, Mr. Monarch. He hasn't been sentenced yet. He can still help himself. You may think this outrageous, Mr. Monarch, but I believe—"

"That's enough," Hedgespeth finally snapped. "All that is stricken. All that the jury is to disregard."

Fat chance, Jimmy thought as he looked at the jurors. They sat perched on the edges of their seats, gaping in wonder, avidly studying the scene before them.

"When all is said and done," Greg said, "I'd like to go to heaven. But if I don't, I truly hope it won't be because of anything I've done in this trial."

Jimmy didn't reply. They were sitting in Greg's office during the lunch-hour recess. Lines he'd learned long ago filled his mind. *How can you compete, being honor bred, with one who, were it proved he lies, were neither shamed in his own nor in his neighbors' eyes . . .*

"I'm on the right side here," Greg continued. "I may not be playing the game right, but I'm on the right side."

Jimmy grunted. "Not sure that's enough, Greg."

Outside his window, Greg could see the first wisps of afternoon fog rolling in from the sea. He thought of an image from long ago. His father's waiting room, empty on just such an afternoon. His father, staring at a tower of cardboard boxes stacked against his wall, full of former patients' files.

"We're going to lose," Greg said.

Jimmy flushed. "Jesus, Monarch, this isn't over yet."

"I should never have agreed to defend Ira."

"You did agree, though, damn it. Now you've got a job. You've got to do whatever it takes for your client."

Greg stared out his window. "Whatever it takes?"

Jimmy smacked Greg's desk. "Yes, damn it. For God's sake. This is the real world. Detesting the jerks isn't enough. You can't assume you'll prevail just because you're more honorable than them. You have to respond with an equal force of your own. You don't, you lose. You want to lose, Greg? Is that what you want?"

Greg rose, walked to his window. His father hated losing, but his father hated also those who would have him forsake his patients in order to prevail. By resigning, instead of waiting to be "discontinued" by Health Shield, he'd chosen something other than defeat.

"No, Jimmy," Greg replied. "I don't want to lose. But there are boundaries. You want justice, you act just. I see no other choice."

Jimmy looked stricken. "Your job is to be Ira's son-of-a-bitch advocate, Greg. Against the terrible might of the state, Ira needs someone fighting back with whatever is required. Plain and simple, Greg. Plain and simple."

Greg turned to Jimmy. "Is it?" he asked.

By the time Hedgespeth reconvened court after lunch, Greg had decided he couldn't give an allocution before the jury about his contacts with Paul Platt. Couldn't, even though the judge had offered him the chance. To make it work, he'd have to dissemble, but he lacked Sandy Polson's talent. He couldn't so easily conceal facts, motives, intentions, feelings. It wasn't just a matter of ethics; even if he were willing, he couldn't pull it off. Sandy could look you in the eye and lie without a tremor. He'd give himself away in an instant.

Just what had he told Paul Platt to get him to recant his confession? *The truth will exonerate you. Stick to the truth, the truth will exonerate you.* Yes, he'd said that. There'd been more, though. *I'll do whatever I can to see that the truth comes out.*

There was no avoiding it. He'd gone still further. There was no transcript, there was no tape recording of his words. But he'd promised Paul something. He surely had. *Yes, I will help you, I will try my best to get you out*. The prosecutor was not the only one to cross lines.

What would Dr. Paul Monarch do in this situation? A silly question, of course. Dr. Monarch would never be in this situation. Dr. Monarch would never have crossed this line.

He wouldn't be under oath, but he'd have to look those jurors in the eye and flat-out lie. It was a position Greg couldn't endure. Ira certainly would understand; Ira certainly would see theirs was the better course. Rather than lie, they'd use their closing argument to attack the state's case. Then they'd ask the jury for something more than a mere verdict.

First it was Dennis Taylor's turn, though.

The D.A.'s closing argument began shortly after 1:30 P.M.

Taylor approached the jury with a certitude as genuine, and as limited, as the human mind permitted. He neither expected nor required a stronger sense of conviction than that. He'd listened to the testimony, he knew he had the better witnesses. He believed he also had the truth. That was enough for him: to believe. What more was possible?

With vigor the D.A. laid out for the jurors his understanding of what happened the night of Postmaster Wilson's murder. Ira Sullivan's need for money to pay off a drug supplier, Ira Sullivan revved up on meth, Ira pulling Paul and Sandy into his web. The drive to Crocker, the struggle, the cash stuffed into Sandy's purse. Detail by detail, moment by moment, Taylor wove his portrait. Finally he stepped back and invited the jurors to study it whole.

Yes, there were inconsistencies in this case, Taylor allowed. They weren't terribly important, though. What was important? That Paul Platt and Sandy Polson, who hardly knew each other, who had no connection, both happened to say Ira Sullivan shot the postmaster.

Do you not believe Sandy Polson? Taylor asked the jurors. Do you not believe Paul Platt? The D.A. approached the jury box, studied each juror for a moment. If he believed Sandy and Paul, surely they would, too. "Here is the central truth, ladies and gentlemen. If you believe the story of Paul Platt, if you believe the testimony of Sandy Polson, then you have to believe this was a cold-blooded murder."

Taylor turned and pointed to Ira. As he did so, his eyes once again appeared to meet those of two gray-suited men watching from the courtroom's far corner. "A cold-blooded murder," the D.A. concluded, "committed by the gentleman sitting over there."

Greg rose slowly when it was his turn. He rested a hand on Ira's shoulder for a moment before he approached the jury. In the packed gallery, dozens of spectators shifted in their seats, leaned forward, adjusted their glasses. They studied the defense attorney with curious eyes. Prowling the courtroom floor, seething at hostile witnesses, hewing to an inner voice, Greg had behaved as no lawyer they'd ever seen.

"May it please the court and Mr. Taylor," he began. "Ladies and gentlemen of the jury, I must start by complimenting Mr. Taylor. I must compliment him because he has done a very good job." Greg paused and turned toward the district attorney. "A very good job of confusing all of us."

Taylor started to rise in protest, but Hedgespeth waved him down. Greg turned back to the jury and continued.

"There is absolutely no legitimate evidence in this case that connects Mr. Sullivan to the postmaster's murder, but this does not daunt Mr. Taylor. He asks you to convict my client of first degree murder based on the inconsistent, illogical statements of Sandy Polson and Paul Platt. He asks you to convict my client even though all available evidence suggests clearly that Sandy Polson alone killed the postmaster. Ms. Polson had the murder weapon, Ms. Polson had the postmaster's cash. Her stories kept changing, and Paul Platt kept telling the same wrong stories.

Amazing coincidences, truly amazing. So why is Ira Sullivan on trial? There is only one reason—Sandy Polson is a very effective storyteller. Sandy Polson is a master con artist. Sandy Polson is trying to perpetrate a hoax and fraud upon everyone in this courtroom."

Greg circled back toward the attorneys' table and stood by his client. "There is another reason why Ira Sullivan sits here today. He sits here because Sandy Polson is being assisted. She is being assisted by a poor, pathetic man named Paul Platt. And she is also, I regret to say, being assisted by the awesome might of the state, by the far-reaching power of the district attorney's office. Please, I beg of you. Do not let Sandy Polson succeed. Please, do not let any of them succeed."

Greg once again approached the jurors. Their eyes remained fixed on him. It was clear they wanted to hear about his contact with Paul Platt; it was clear they wanted to know why Platt rose and denounced him in the open courtroom. Greg longed for an answer both honest and favorable to Ira's cause. He stood silent for a moment, imagining the possibilities. Then he cleared his throat.

"Ladies and gentlemen," he said, "that's all I have for you. I hope and pray I've been able to present what really happened in this case. It's scary, what happened. It's scary that somebody can be arrested and charged with first degree murder based on a statement like Sandy Polson's. I don't know why they're doing this to Ira Sullivan. I truly don't know why. It shouldn't be happening, though. People shouldn't lie, people should be just. Please stop this thing that has happened. Ladies and gentlemen, please don't let them do this to Ira Sullivan."

Judge Hedgespeth studied Greg for a long moment, then tapped his gavel. "Let's take a recess," he said.

In the end, after the judge's instructions, after an early break for dinner, the jury stayed out only two hours. At 8:23 P.M., the bailiff announced that court was reconvening, then ushered the jurors into the courtroom. Judge

Hedgespeth watched them walk to their seats. They were, he thought, one dozen citizens of Chumash County, no more, no less. Neither wise people nor dullards; simply folks taken off the street to hear this case.

"Have you arrived at a verdict?" Hedgespeth asked the foreman, Thomas Henderson. Tom worked at the hardware store when he wasn't running his few head of cattle up in the hills.

"Yes, Your Honor, we have," Henderson said.

During *voir dire*, Henderson had said that he read newspapers "hardly at all," that he belonged to "no organizations whatsoever," that he believed in the death penalty only if "the evidence was overwhelming." All those answers had satisfied; in fact, all had painted Tom as an ideal juror.

"May I have it, please?" the judge asked.

Hedgespeth looked directly at the defendant after reading the single sheet. Ira trembled beneath a mask of steely resolve.

"Mr. Sullivan," the judge said. "The verdict of the jury is as follows. 'We, the jury, find the defendant, Ira Sullivan, guilty of the offense of first degree murder.' "

Whether a man should live or die, that was not the type of decision Judge Hedgespeth enjoyed making. Yet that was the one he faced in the wake of Ira Sullivan's conviction. As he feared, the defense chose to leave Ira Sullivan's fate up to him, instead of to the twelve citizens who had so quickly found Ira guilty. Hedgespeth wished Greg had asked the good citizens of Chumash County to decide. He trusted their judgment more than his own.

Early on the morning of the sentencing hearing, Hedgespeth sat alone in his chambers, trying to ignore the gout flaring up yet again in his big toe. Before him rose three piles of papers. The state's arguments, the defense brief, the presentencing probation department report. The judge eyed them with dread. He imagined what was to come in his courtroom. Pleas, citations, prayers, all in service of one point of view or another, all voiced before the watchful eyes of Chumash County citizens. *If I were in your shoes, hearing the evidence that I have in this case, I could not impose the highest, most severe penalty,* Greg Monarch would advise. To which Dennis Taylor would rise indignantly. *I think it's time for the defense to realize that a jury has ruled in this case.*

That was the problem for Hedgespeth. The jurors had ruled. And it wasn't as if they'd taken a long time. This jury of twelve Chumash County citizens had taken a very short time. They believed the witnesses for the state were telling the truth. Their easy willingness to trust Polson and Platt had surprised the judge. What could he do, though? That was the whole point of a jury trial. Witnesses get up and testify while jurors watch and evaluate. The justice system had spoken, and the notion of defying it sent anxious pangs through Hedgespeth. Regardless of personal feelings, he had to follow the dictates of the law, or else there would be no law. Which to Hedgespeth seemed unthinkable. Only the thin skin of the law held back unruly chaos.

Wincing in pain as he rose, Hedgespeth pulled on his judicial robes and limped toward the courtroom.

Both lawyers at the sentencing hearing argued valiantly. Greg Monarch made all sorts of offers of mitigating evidence: Ira's past life, military career, tragic loss of a young son. Dennis Taylor focused on Sullivan's more current record: his drug dealing, his barroom assaults, his unsavory ways. Hedgespeth listened unhappily, knowing where it was headed.

Murder during the commission of a felony. Drug busts and assaults in Ira's past. By law, Ira's was what they called a "special-circumstances" or "death-qualifying" conviction. As Hedgespeth read the statutes, when aggravating circumstances overwhelmed the mitigating ones in this fashion, he had no choice really. The death penalty was the mandated punishment. He felt the law spoke quite clearly on this question, and the law reflected the will of the people. He was not a particularly enthusiastic believer in capital punishment, but he was an ardent believer in reading statutes as they were written. He was also an ardent subscriber to the will of the people. He didn't carry each and every precinct on five straight election days by ignoring Chumash County sentiment.

When the lawyers were finished, the judge offered Ira the opportunity to speak. "Mr. Sullivan, as I understand the law, you are free to say anything at this moment, on any topic you wish."

Ira found his mind roaming wildly. Fishing at Los Osos Lake with Jeffrey; playing pool until dawn with Greg; dancing drunkenly with Sandy Polson at the Foghorn. He longed to reverse time, he longed to be sitting once again in the Monarch & Sullivan law offices. More than anything, he longed to be holding Jeffrey on his lap. Holding him, hugging him, never letting him go.

"What can a man in my position say?" Ira finally whispered. "What can I say?"

Judge Hedgespeth nodded, looked away, cleared his throat, sat up straight. "Okay, then, okay," he declared, his voice husky. "It is the judgment of this court that this defendant be hereby sentenced to death."

Greg tried to make eye contact with Hedgespeth, but the judge, already heading toward his chambers, refused to look at him. Greg next turned to Ira. For a moment, Ira met his glance. "Tell me, Greg," he said. "Just whose job is it to see that justice is done?" Then Ira, too, pivoted away, offering his wrists for the bailiff's handcuffs.

PART TWO

FOURTEEN

Dusk had fallen. Looking out Greg's office window, Jimmy watched wistfully as couples headed toward the plaza and the creekside cafés. It was Thursday, almost time for the start of the weekly La Graciosa farmer's market. Jimmy relished these evenings. The town closed Carmel Street to cars, converting its main artery into a mile-long extension of the plaza. On both sides of the blockaded roadway, farmers opened pickup trucks and card tables laden with the region's fresh produce, flowers, and nuts. Local restaurants joined them, manning enormous oakwood barbecues full of ribs, chicken, sausage, and tri-tips. Street musicians, puppeteers, jugglers, magicians, belly dancers—anyone who could perform, or thought they could, set up shop at the La Graciosa farmer's market.

Not them, though. Not Greg and Jimmy. They had work to do.

Jimmy turned from the window to survey Greg's office. Tottering stacks of law books, files, transcripts, and briefs filled the room, covering desks and counters, spilling onto the floor, creeping into the hallway. Greg sat at his desk, sleeves rolled up to his elbows, thumbing through a report as he scratched a four-day-old beard. He'd taken to sleeping on an office sofa rather than go home. He'd been laboring over his latest petition for a week now.

Jimmy regarded Greg with unease. Watching him these past difficult months, watching his relentless but fruitless struggle, Jimmy had started to regret ever having pushed him into Ira Sullivan's case. He still believed in Greg, he still rooted for him. Perhaps, though, he'd miscalculated. Maybe Greg had been right, maybe he just wasn't suited for this game. He'd lost another capital case, that much was undeniable; Ira sat on Death Row now. Jimmy felt responsible.

"Greg," he said gently. "None of the appeals you've filed have worked. You keep getting turned down. Maybe it's time to let the state public defenders handle this. Maybe it's time to let go."

Greg did not appear to hear him. He reached for a thick law book, began turning pages. "People just don't get *Herrera v. Collins*," he said. "It isn't as bad as they think. The Supreme Court didn't really say innocence isn't enough to get your guy out. Rehnquist did, I'll give you that. But the majority didn't go along with all his reasoning. Look at O'Connor's opinion, you'll see that. She didn't close the door on everyone else. We can do this, Jimmy. We just have to figure this out—"

Jimmy interrupted. "It's not working, Greg. You're not helping Ira. You're just getting yourself into trouble now. More and more trouble."

The latest letter from the State Bar sat somewhere under the debris on Greg's desk. They had scheduled a hearing to consider a formal complaint against him. *You have a right to present evidence,* the notice advised. *You have a right to counsel.* The amended complaint charged him with violations of rules concerning "competence, diligence, and misconduct." Meaning that besides unethically coercing Paul Platt, he'd grievously injured Ira Sullivan by failing to withdraw from the case, or give an allocution to the jury.

"There's something I still don't understand," Greg insisted. "Something missing. Something that explains why this happened."

Jimmy did not know how to respond. They'd drifted apart, there was no helping that. While Greg rehashed and researched and obsessed, Jimmy by necessity had moved on. As soon as the Sullivan trial and Devil's Peak became old news, Horace Macauley once more had slouched over to his desk with a fat file. This time it involved funny business at the county hospital. Puzzling deaths, going back two decades. Uncertain causes, murky explanations. Off and on, Jimmy had been chasing it for weeks. Taking so much time drove Macauley nuts, which only encouraged Jimmy to drag it out longer. Maybe they'd lead Horace away in a straitjacket before it got finished.

"Greg, it's over," Jimmy urged. "Give it to the state public defenders."

"No," Greg said. "It's not over. I've got a job, whatever it takes; this is the real world. Remember, Jimmy?"

Jimmy remembered. He'd meant those words; back then, it had somehow seemed so important to keep Greg swinging from the heels. What else could a person do? Acts of will, plain and simple, untempered by epiphanies or divine inspiration—that's what kept you going. That's what kept Jimmy going, at least. Acts of will about which Jimmy felt proud—but not overly satisfied. Where had he landed, after all? The La Graciosa *News-Times*, doing Horace Alan Macauley's bidding, while the vainglorious and mendacious still reigned. A dreary rented shack, a grimy busted dishwasher, a monthly alimony check sent to a woman whose face he could no longer even remember. Jimmy wondered where his path led. Acts of will demanded such vigilance.

"Greg, you're just getting hurt now," Jimmy said. "You tried. At least you tried."

Greg slapped shut the book before him. "Trying isn't good enough. I have to win."

Sandy sat in a wooden straight-backed chair, facing them all once again. On impulse, she'd pulled her tousled locks into a half-pony this morning, deciding it became her. She'd eschewed even a hint of black mascara, having concluded it was unnecessary. From her limited options she with some regret had chosen a simple blue skirt and white blouse; since she regarded this gathering in the D.A.'s office as a victory celebration, she would have preferred wearing something more jubilant. No matter, though. It was a day to relish. With Ira's trial over, Sandy looked forward to her reward. She'd given Dennis Taylor what he needed; now it was time for the D.A. to return the favor.

Sandy expected considerable leniency. Although they'd charged her with second degree murder, she assumed, from her many private conversations with Taylor, that they'd let her plead to something minor. Something they could dispatch with time already served, plus probation, of course. Sandy had not even brought her court-appointed lawyer with her today. What need did she have of that sorry fellow? She and Dennis had an understanding. He was on her side, he didn't think badly of her. He believed her.

At least, that's how Sandy understood matters until Taylor started to talk. Not his words but his tone was the first clue that she had it wrong. Right off, Taylor began in his boring, pompous courtroom voice. Lots of legalese, mixed with flights of rhetoric. *The rule of law must prevail . . . Consequences of our actions . . . Fairness dictates equitable punishment.* It took a while for the essence of his message to emerge. Being there at the scene, being present at a burglary in which a man was killed, second degree murder was the best Sandy could expect. He just couldn't downgrade that charge. Best he could do was deal on the sentence. If she'd plead, he'd make it no more than fifteen years . . .

Sandy listened without expression. When the D.A. finally stopped talking, she smiled sweetly. "Mr. Taylor," she said, "I thought we had an understanding."

Taylor moved to the front of his desk and stood right before her. "That's not how you testified at Sullivan's trial, Sandy. Remember? When Monarch asked, you said no, there'd been no deal. No arrangement."

Sandy ran a hand through her tousled locks. "That's what I was supposed to say. That's what you wanted me to say."

Dennis shook his head. "I never told you that, Sandy. I wanted only the truth from you."

Sandy tried to look puzzled, but in truth, she understood perfectly well. Dennis must feel so amused, so very powerful. That was natural. Perhaps one day she'd get her turn. Not today, though. Sandy dipped her head in surrender. "Of course," she said. "Of course, you're right, Mr. Taylor. You never did tell me, did you? My mistake. How awful of me. I should have known."

Dennis settled in behind his desk, looking enormously pleased. "Yes, you should have, Sandy. At least you understand now. At least there's no confusion now."

Watching this exchange, Roger Kandle rubbed his jaw. What exactly it all meant, he had no idea. It was clear, though, that Taylor had somehow gamed Sandy. He'd worked a master, and he'd won.

This thought provided Roger an odd sort of comfort. Whatever his doubts about the D.A., it was clear he'd chosen the right footsteps to follow. Better Dennis Taylor's path than Greg Monarch's. At least Dennis knew what he was doing.

Greg walked slowly up Carmel Street, watching the farmer's market come to life. The crowd—a mix of families with toddlers stuffed in strollers, Chumash State students looking for dates, and San Francisco–bound tourists who'd lost their way—was already starting to thicken. Threading his way among them, Greg studied the overflowing piles of avocados, tomatoes, apples, and sweet corn. At one corner, he watched a man appear to swallow a flaming sword. At another, he watched Chumash County matrons display the results of their belly dancing lessons.

Go back home, they'd told him in Sacramento. Go back to Chumash County. His trip to the state capital had been pointless, as he knew it would be, but it had given him satisfaction. *Confess error,* he'd urged the attorney general. Tell the state supreme court you've made a mistake. Do not write a brief opposing my appeal. The law did allow that; the law allowed the state in effect to say we won, but we're not in the right. Few prosecutors, of course, had ever shown themselves inclined to do so. Certainly not the California attorney general. Ronald Burgan had climbed to his high post by winning, not admitting mistakes and freeing convicted murderers. Yet Greg had wanted to offer him that option. He'd also wanted to hear just how the A.G. would turn him down. He'd wanted to hear Burgan say flatly that he cared not a whit whether Ira Sullivan actually killed Postmaster Wilson.

In the end, Greg realized all his goals.

Sitting in the A.G.'s small private office one crisp fall morning, he spelled out his case. Then he leaned back and stared at Ronald Burgan's florid, self-satisfied face, at his three obeisant aides ready with whispered prompts, at his bare desk bearing only a single typed sheet of talking points. Burgan eventually started to recite. *It's not my job . . . We all play different roles in the system . . . I can't substitute my judgment for the jury's . . . It's not up to me . . . That's our system . . .* The meeting didn't last long; Burgan never even glanced at the fat stack of files carted in by Greg. "You filed an appeal," the A.G. declared after thirty strained minutes together. "Now I'm going to respond and the courts will rule."

Only after Greg started packing up his briefcase did the others in the room relinquish their assigned roles a little. By nature more a backslapping politico than a lawyer, Burgan approached Greg. Their paths had crossed before; Burgan had started as a county prosecutor in the suburbs south of San Francisco. He made up in ambition what he lacked in acumen. "I'll give you this, Monarch," he said, his voice a hearty boom. "The boys down there in Chumash tell me this was one hell of a case."

"It was that," Greg agreed. "From the very first night."

Burgan's expression turned wistful. "I was skiing that night up at Tahoe. Squaw Valley. Just wonderful. Packed powder on a ten-foot base. Wish I could get away like that more often."

"A man in your position must have many obligations."

"Too many, Greg, too many."

Driving home later that day, heading south from the state capital through Stockton, then west across the vast, brown San Joaquin Valley, Greg's mind stayed on Burgan's parting comment. It didn't make sense, of course. Why would the state attorney general know precisely where he was on the night of the postmaster's murder? Why, for that matter, would the A.G. even know when the postmaster had been murdered?

Greg surveyed the flat, tilled fields reaching for miles beyond his windshield. He'd often traveled this state route 46 with his father, on their way to campsites in the Sierra Nevada. He'd also, more recently, traveled it to visit Ira Sullivan at the California Men's Colony in the northeast corner of Chumash County. Different eras, different destinations.

He'd misunderstood the stakes. Greg saw that now. Somehow, the playing field stretched well beyond Chumash County. The realization shook him, but also brought clarity. Bygone mores simply would not do in this strange world. He would have to find another way to save Ira. He would have to choose another course, wherever it led.

Greg stepped carefully, threading his way through the dense farmer's market crowd that now filled Carmel Street. Lines had sprouted beside the sizzling outdoor barbecues; fathers lifted toddlers to their shoulders to watch a puppet show.

Perhaps the State Bar had been right to censure him, Greg thought. Surely he had injured Ira, that much was clear. Ira looked thinner and paler each time he visited. Alternating between despair and rage, Ira often refused to eat or leave his cell for exercise. The state public defender's office, overwhelmed as usual, so far had done little. Eventually the country's elite coterie of expert Death Row lawyers would focus on Ira, but not until he was much closer to the gas chamber. By then, Greg feared, Ira would be barely alive.

"Hey, mister, careful, willya?"

Someone was yelling at Greg. Not watching where he was walking, he'd stumbled into a canvas-walled booth, almost knocking over a corner post. It was, he saw, the Chumash County Historical Society's display, one of his favorites at the farmer's market. Greg stepped back and studied this week's exhibits.

One featured a replica of the granite, twenty-five-foot-tall Dorn Pyramid, built in 1905 at the edge of town by a local attorney distraught over the deaths in childbirth of his wife and newborn son. Another told the story of Tambo, an Irish minstrel turned La Graciosa hotelier who got tarred, feathered, and marched out of town for providing weary travelers with "special conveniences" more intimate than certain citizens thought tolerable.

At a third exhibit, Greg froze. Here, once again, was the Committee of Vigilance story. *So man can walk at ease . . . A fit place to raise a family.* Greg kicked at the curb.

You want another Committee of Vigilance, Greg? You want I just decide who should hang, and string them up at Cerros and Carmel? The truth was, Greg shared Judge Hedgespeth's sentiments in some ways. There was danger in giving anyone too much power to decide right from wrong, truth from deceit. So much was ambiguous, so much depended on perspective. Take the widely reviled *bandido* Pio Linares, for instance. What if people knew his background? What if people knew that when Mexico began dispensing sprawling land grants to *Californio* families, his father, Victor Linares, received the vast Rancho Cañada de Los Osos in 1842—only to have it stripped from him the next year, and re-granted to one John Wilson, native of Dundee, Scotland. John Wilson, whose eligibility for land derived from his marriage to Ramona Carillo de Pacheco, the young widow of a fallen lieutenant. The Mexican land grants enriched many early

California families, made them prosperous land barons for generations after, but Victor Linares, father of six, didn't do as well as many of his Hispanic—and all of his Anglo—neighbors. Was it so surprising that Victor Linares's son Pio would become the most feared *bandido* on the Central Coast a decade later? Who could say that Pio was not, in his own eyes at least, a righteous vigilante?

Committee of Vigilance. Yes, Greg had to admit, it would be foolish to pretend the matter wasn't complicated. You couldn't just let someone impose his will or vision. The notion of a judge or attorney general playing superjury scared Greg.

Yet that's just what he'd wanted them to do. He'd begged them. *Confess error.* Overrule twelve Chumash County citizens. Take the law in your own hands.

Greg walked on down Carmel. He watched the puppeteer's show; he threw a dollar into the hat of a solitary musician coaxing "Gee, Baby, Ain't I Good to You?" from his saxophone. For half a block, he followed behind a clown waving a six-foot-long plastic zucchini. He started at the sound of a siren wailing before realizing it was a fire truck, not Devil's Peak.

Then he saw her. At first, Greg didn't realize he knew her. He was admiring a stranger, he thought. A stranger who stared back at him with alert, unblinking eyes. The denim jacket finally informed him, the denim jacket and the feathered bangs and the mane of dark curly hair. Kim Rosen, assistant U.S. Attorney. With her black Lab puppy on a leash beside her.

Greg watched with appreciation as she walked toward him. There was something irreverent in how she moved. The smoked-glass streetlight gave her face a faint sheen. What to make of this woman? Now that everyone had basically dropped the Devil's Peak probe, it was hard to say. Had Kim Rosen bailed on Devil's Peak, folded under the pressure? Certainly, Greg thought, she'd let him twist in the wind when he came seeking the plant's security logs. Whether that affected Ira Sullivan's fate, he did not know.

"Greg Monarch, isn't it?" Kim Rosen paused, raised an eyebrow. "Remember me?"

"I do, indeed."

The puppy rose on its hind legs, leaned against Greg, licked his hand. Greg knelt; now the puppy licked his face. "What a nurturing dog you have, Ms. Rosen. Pepper, isn't that her name?"

Kim Rosen pulled Pepper off Greg. "Very good memory," she said. She looked at him steadily, saying nothing more. Greg held her gaze, feeling the heat rising to his face. He wondered if she looked at all men like that. "And my name is Kim," she said finally. "Enough with the Ms. Rosen business."

Greg nodded agreeably. "Okay, Kim," he said. "Now that we're friends, maybe you can tell me what happened back when I needed your help."

Kim lowered her eyes. "I was sorry to hear you lost that murder trial."

"So was I."

"And I'm sorry I wasn't able to help you."

Greg's words came out harsher than he intended. "Yes, well, we now know why, don't we?"

"It was a touchy situation."

"I understand."

"Were you ever able to find out about those patrols in the dunes?"

Was he being debriefed again? Greg couldn't tell. It didn't seem so; he didn't want it to be so. "No, never did. Just one of several frustrations about that trial."

Kim looked up, and stared at him now as if trying to read his mind. "You told me something when you visited my office. You said an innocent man was facing conviction, maybe a death sentence."

"Yes, I recall."

"Was that true? Do you truly believe Ira Sullivan is innocent? Don't defense attorneys always say their clients are innocent?"

"You're right, they do," Greg allowed. "But I meant it."

Kim, stroking Pepper, looked away again. Greg missed her scrutiny. "There are things I still don't understand," he said. "Things about Ira's prosecution."

Kim did not appear to hear him. She was fussing over a sore she'd just noticed behind Pepper's right ear. She pulled a small tube from her purse and began spreading ointment on her puppy. Then she rose, tugging at the leash in her hand. "It's late," she said. "I'd better be going."

JB's was packed when Greg finally got there, its usual state after a farmer's market. With no stool available at the bar, he leaned against a wall. He saw Jimmy O'Brien in the crowd, and Doc Lewis, but stayed where he was. At the piano, Dave Murphy backed Shirley as she caressed the microphone.

When Shirley sat down, Greg joined her at the small table where she customarily awaited her cue to sing. "How's my dirty blues singer?" he asked, over the din.

Shirley arched her eyebrows, offering him a languid smile. That was good enough for Greg, that was all he needed. No conversation, just Shirley's smile. "Don't leave me," he murmured. "Don't ever leave me. Let's grow old together."

When he felt a hand on his shoulder, he thought for sure it was Dave this time, reclaiming his wife. Once again, though, it was Jimmy. He looked agitated. "Let's go over to the corner," Jimmy suggested. "Got something to talk about."

They settled near the potbellied stove. At first Jimmy said nothing. He sighed, and frowned, and ran a hand through his hair. When he finally spoke, his voice quavered.

"Something I guess I should tell you, Greg. I wasn't going to. Figured it was nothing, figured you'd just go chasing your tail. But hell, if you're really not going to let this thing drop, you might as well know. I got a call a week ago. From Mac McCasson."

Greg squinted. "Who is Mac McCasson?"

"You don't remember?"

Greg forced himself to focus. "Oh yeah. Devil's Peak. Our cowboy grand jury foreman."

"Exactly right. McCasson wants to talk, Greg. Says he has something to tell us."

Greg looked around the tavern, searching for Shirley. "Devil's Peak is your story, not mine."

Jimmy pulled his chair closer to Greg. "Not about Devil's Peak. McCasson wants to talk about Ira Sullivan. Says he thinks he might know why Ira got in all this trouble."

Something in the way Jimmy spoke commanded Greg's interest. He tried to blink back the excitement he suddenly felt. A vision of Ira walking free through the *asistencia* doorway rose in his mind.

"Tell me about Mac McCasson," Greg said. "Tell me everything you know."

FIFTEEN

Together, Greg and Jimmy drove out Dollar Canyon Road, heading northeast from La Graciosa into the rich, verdant section of Chumash County called North Region. Here was land Greg had always savored, land full of rolling hills and towering oaks, vineyards and orchards, farms and fishing lakes. North Region wasn't their destination, though. By midday they'd reached the dusty, barren high plains called East Region. Here was Mac McCasson's domain: a few sleepy hamlets, lizards and snakes everywhere, a blazing sun in summer, bitter frost on winter mornings. To the fifth-generation descendants of East Region pioneers, it was home; to others, a place to pass through quickly.

Mac McCasson had not told Jimmy much when he called him at the *News-Times*. Only that he'd read in the newspaper about Ira Sullivan's death sentence, and had been thinking on it ever since. There was something important to talk about, he'd finally decided. That, of course, had been enough to get Jimmy's attention. That, and the way McCasson spoke. Direct, independent, self-assured, he sounded like the undiluted East Region rancher he was.

He ran a few head of cattle, McCasson had explained to Jimmy when the Devil's Peak story first broke. Ran a few head on the land his daddy worked before him for five decades. Jimmy had never come out to his ranch, since his readers wouldn't be as impressed as the national audience by a cowboy on a horse. McCasson instead had come to him, and to the steps of the *asistencia* courthouse, to declare the grand jury's revolt. So Jimmy now found it necessary to frown over a map of Chumash County.

Were they in Panza? What with the twists and turns and all the miles of dirt road, McCasson had warned, you'll never find my place. I'll meet you at the Conoco station down on route 14, outside a little town called Panza. Little, indeed; Panza appeared to be nothing more than a café, a ramshackle wooden water tower, and a weed-clogged, long-closed gas station. An empty gas station with a broken Conoco sign out front.

"Hell, this couldn't be what he meant," Jimmy said.

"He said on the road *outside* Panza," Greg pointed out. "I think we're *in* Panza. Keep on going down the road."

Two miles further on route 14, they saw an Arco gas station off to the right. Inside the office, they found a small, wizened woman sitting behind the counter, sipping a Coke and flipping through a *National Enquirer*. Beyond the station's windows, the brown, empty plains reached to the horizon. It was midday, with not another car or person in sight. They were half an hour late.

"Ma'am," Jimmy said, "we're supposed to be meeting Mac McCasson. Would you know if he's been around?"

Without looking up from her tabloid, the woman handed Jimmy a slip of paper that had been sitting on the counter next to her Coke. "I reckon this note's for you," she said.

Together, Greg and Jimmy read the single handwritten sentence: "Patience is characteristic of a wise man."

Jimmy scratched his head. "Now, what the hell does this mean?"

"I think it means we ought to sit down and wait for Mac McCasson," Greg said. "If we're wise."

A half hour later, a battered brown pickup bounced its way up to the gas station in a cloud of dust, pulling behind it a rickety wooden trailer. Between the slats, Greg could see a dozen or more head of cattle jostling for position and air. From the pickup's cab stepped a man who looked as much like a cowboy as anyone Greg had ever seen in Chumash County. The floppy mustache, the week-old stubble, the dusty blue jeans, the muddy boots with spurs, the red bandanna, the dirty white hat—combined, they suggested someone who spent a good deal more of his time around livestock than people. Reaching out to shake Greg's hand, Mac McCasson stopped first to wipe his palms.

"Well, I guess you made it okay," he said. "Sorry to be late. We're moving cattle from the pasture to the corral for grain feeding. Those that are going backwards, that is."

Jimmy didn't understand. "Going backwards?"

McCasson peered at him with surprise. "Why, doing poorly. You know, in need of a little tender loving care." He made sure that was clear before continuing. "Anyway, we also had some flat tires to change. First on my pal's trailer, then mine. These damn seventy-five-dollar Texas tires last only fifty miles, I swear."

Greg looked at the trailer's tires. He didn't want to tell Mac, but another one appeared to be mighty low. "No problem," Greg said. "We got your note. We've been trying to be wise."

McCasson laughed out loud at that. "Work's not done yet this afternoon," he said. "How about you boys ride out with me to get the rest of the cattle? Then we can go over to my house and have us a talk."

Jimmy turned pale at the thought of getting on top of a horse, but Greg didn't give him a chance to respond. "That sounds fine," he said. "Glad to help."

Squeezed three into the cab, they bumped along route 14 in Mac's pickup for five miles, then turned onto a dirt path and drove another four miles before reaching a corral. Three cowhands greeted them with nods and waves. Two were working cattle through the chutes while the third was readying the horses.

For his ride out across the plains, in pursuit of a wayward herd of steers, McCasson chose a nervous colt not yet overly familiar with saddles or riders. It was, he explained, a chance to see if he could ride him. When

Mac mounted, the colt tossed his head, whinnied, and reared up.

Greg and Jimmy watched with concern, but the three cowhands started laughing. "He's hee-hawing on you, Mac, he's hee-hawing on you," one of them called. McCasson shortened his grip on the reins and pulled the colt around in tight circles until he had control. Then he kicked him lightly and headed out. Greg and Jimmy, atop a pair of docile mares, followed behind the cowhands.

As they rode, McCasson and his men swapped stories. In the wind, Greg couldn't hear much. The punch line to one tale had something to do with a pair of red panties found in the back of someone's pickup; another involved a drunk driver unable to decide which was worse, thirty days in jail or joining Alcoholics Anonymous. Halfway out, they stopped at a water tank, where they pulled a rope tied to a dripping six-pack of Graciosa Brew out of the water. "Boys like to keep their beer cold," McCasson explained.

Sitting and sipping, McCasson scanned the horizon. "You want to make sure the calves are with the mommas," he explained to Greg. "You watch for upset cows at the road's edge who might have lost a calf when they got weeded out. You want to see a content bunch of cows, that's what you want."

When they reached the wayward herd, McCasson and the three hands started circling them, swinging their ropes, yipyeeing, heading the cattle around and driving them back home. Watching them work, with the sun low in the sky behind them, the light turning the soft pink-gray of dusk, Greg felt happier than he had in months. He could not imagine, though, what Mac McCasson had to do with Ira Sullivan's murder trial.

Even when they got to McCasson's home, that wasn't made clear right away. It turned out to be Mac's birthday, his forty-seventh. Jimmy and Greg found themselves at a party of McCasson's extended family. His parents, a brother and sister, nieces and nephews, his own three children, his wife Suzanne. "My wife of twenty-four years" was how he introduced her, proudly. They all sat outside at a redwood table eating barbecued hamburgers and sweet yellow corn, then cut a chocolate cake and sang. After supper, McCasson, amid much cheering and many huzzahs, lifted his giggling seventeen-year-old daughter high over his head like a barbell, holding her horizontal in his two hands. "A family tradition," he explained. "On my birthday every year, to show I can still do it."

McCasson's home rose alone on the bare plains, eighteen miles down an unpaved road. It looked as if his family had built it themselves. An open central space contained the kitchen, dining area, and living room, all circling around a big cast-iron wood-burning stove. Small bedrooms sprouted directly from this hub. So did a compact office, where McCasson apparently handled the ranch's business. It was to this office that he finally led Greg and Jimmy, after the dinner dishes were cleared.

McCasson sat in his desk chair, Jimmy and Greg on a small sofa opposite him. "Well," Mac said, "I might as well start at the beginning."

Much to Jimmy's dismay, that's precisely what he proceeded to do. McCasson had grown fond of all those microphones in his face. For a passing moment, he'd been a hero. He wanted to tell his story once more, even though the camera crews had packed up long ago.

On and on he spun his tale. The postcard in his mailbox, summoning him to grand jury duty. His confusion over what a grand jury was, what Devil's Peak was. His love for the pledge of allegiance, his willingness to serve. His dismay at what they'd learned in the grand jury, his anger over what they'd been doing out there with all that radioactive stuff.

Listening, Jimmy started shifting in his seat, anxiously flipping his reporter's notebook open and shut. He'd felt impatient all day, having no bent for horses or cattle or cowboy birthday parties. Now he was beside himself.

"Mac," he said. "I know all this. Could you get to what this is about? How does this tie in to Ira Sullivan?"

McCasson looked disappointed. "Getting to that, Jimmy, now just don't get your britches on fire."

Greg found McCasson intriguing. Spinning yarns must be as central to his life as herding cattle. There was about this rancher a bit of theater. He knew how to play the rube cowboy and enjoyed doing so. On the office wall, though, Greg couldn't help noticing McCasson's framed college degree. A bachelor's in math and physics from a small four-year college north of San Francisco.

Mac continued his narrative. How many sessions they held, who came to testify, what they said. Kim Rosen's smart-as-a-whip comments, the judge's instructions, their plans to indict. Finally, Jimmy jumped to his feet.

"For Chrissake, Mac," he hissed. "Where's Ira in this? What's the point of this story?"

McCasson barely acknowledged Jimmy. "Yep, hold on, getting to that right now. As I was saying, we were ready to indict them all—the Rolfson crowd and the DOE managers. Indict them and write a special report." McCasson tapped his cowboy hat back on his head, put a boot up on his desk, grinned at Jimmy. "That's when Ira Sullivan showed up in the grand jury room."

Greg and Jimmy looked at each other, then at Mac. "Let me get this straight," Greg said. "Ira Sullivan testified before the Devil's Peak grand jury?"

Just then, Mac's wife, Suzanne, poked her head into the office. "You fellas want anything? Coffee, maybe?"

"Whiskey?" McCasson added.

"No," Jimmy said. "No."

"So where was I?" McCasson continued, after Suzanne closed the door. "Oh yes, Ira Sullivan shows up to testify. An interesting fellow. Very soft-spoken, not a wild man, not a tree-hugger. But sharp as can be."

Greg held up both hands. "Wait a second, back up. Ira Sullivan? A witness before the Devil's Peak grand jury?"

McCasson looked at him strangely. "That's what I just said, son. Wasn't it?"

Mac rose, turned back to his file cabinet, pulled out a sheaf of papers. "Some notes I took, so I can remember," he said. "It seems Mr. Sullivan got involved in this as a lawyer. He was representing a lady who worked at Devil's Peak, around the plant's incinerator. Jenny Branson, a mechanical operator. She'd gotten suspicious about the incinerator, she'd decided they were running it in the middle of the night, burning stuff they shouldn't. First she talked to her supervisors, then went to an FBI agent. That's how this whole investigation began, I take it. Anyway, she got fired for her trouble. Fired, followed around, called crazy, everything. Mr. Sullivan tried to help her. He put up a mighty fight, far as I can tell. Hollered plenty, filed a wrongful dismissal claim, finally got Rolfson to pay a pretty penny."

Jenny Branson. For a moment, Greg couldn't place the name. Then he remembered. Jenny Branson, the gal who'd driven her car off a Clam Beach cliff.

"Not long after they settled, Ms. Branson died in an accident," McCasson continued. "So Ms. Kimberly Rosen put Mr. Sullivan on the stand to tell the grand jury her story. To tell his story, actually. What he knew, what he'd learned from representing her. He knew a lot, I'll say that."

Greg wished he'd taken that offer of whiskey. Despite the Foghorn and the meth, Ira had still been trying. More than any of them, really. Ira hadn't folded his hand. Ira hadn't backed off.

"What did Sullivan know?" Jimmy asked.

"Mainly about the late-night burns of radioactive waste. When Jenny came in some mornings, she could tell they'd been running the incinerator all night. She'd see big overnight drops in the oxygen logs, and only the incinerator uses oxygen. Sullivan had copies of the logs, lots of other stuff. But what bothered him most was how the

Rolfson managers treated Jenny. After she raised questions, they assigned her to a contaminated workstation. Knew it was hot, sent her there anyway. Acted surprised when she came out triggering the alarms."

Jimmy interrupted. "That was it? A little dirty air, a labor dispute, people tiptoeing around at midnight? Didn't lots of others tell you stories just like his?"

McCasson pushed his cowboy hat even further toward the back of his head. "Yep, they did, more or less. That's true. So maybe I'm seeing too much here. But when I heard that Ira Sullivan had gotten himself into all that trouble, I just thought it sort of interesting."

"Why?" Greg asked. "Was there anything particular about Ira's appearance before the grand jury?"

"Well, yes sir," McCasson said. "Guess I forgot to mention. Ira Sullivan, he was the last witness we heard. They pulled the plug on us right after Sullivan testified. Right after him, they shut us down." McCasson frowned, rubbed the graying bristles on his jaw. "I just thought that was funny. Seems to me that means something."

Greg and Jimmy drove out of the high plains in stunned silence, under a silent night sky crowded with stars.

"It's hard to believe," Greg said finally.

"Oh, I don't know," Jimmy replied. "I can believe it."

Greg looked sideways at Jimmy. "You'd believe anything about your fellow man, Jimmy. But this doesn't tie together. You're talking about a federal investigation into environmental crimes on the one hand, and a Chumash County murder case on the other. How do they connect?"

"Phone lines, that's all you need to connect," Jimmy offered.

"What are you saying has happened here?"

"I'm not saying anything happened," Jimmy pointed out. "I'm not even going to write one of my sensationalized news stories yet. I'm just saying anything could have happened."

Greg reflected. What puzzled him most was Ira's silence all these months about Devil's Peak. Over and over, he'd asked Ira for reasons why the D.A. might want to get him. Ira had appeared genuinely mystified. Why hadn't he mentioned the grand jury and Devil's Peak? Had his addled mind just forgotten? Or was he hiding something? Was he purposefully keeping from Greg what he felt his defense attorney shouldn't know?

Maybe the attorney was at fault. *Control the client's dialogue*. Had Greg too resolutely honored that adage? Had he too directly constructed Ira's story? Had he insisted on casting Ira simply as a forlorn drunk and druggie, lost in the dunes, nothing more?

They'd descended now out of the North Region, and were driving through López Valley, heading southwest to La Graciosa. The stars had disappeared, lost in the fog rolling in from the distant ocean. The obvious suddenly occurred to Greg. Ira never mentioned the Devil's Peak grand jury because he didn't think it had anything to do with his murder prosecution. Which, of course, was an utterly sensible judgment. Why would Ira see a connection between the postmaster's murder and his appearance before a Devil's Peak grand jury?

"Ira doesn't know," Greg told Jimmy as they pulled into La Graciosa. "Ira doesn't know."

SIXTEEN

Out of habit and instinct, Kim Rosen kept Greg waiting twenty minutes before punching the receptionist's button. "Mr. Monarch," Julie Chapman finally called out, not bothering to look up from where she sat behind a translucent window. "You can go in now. Ms. Rosen is off the phone."

This time the hallway held no cardboard boxes. RCRA-DP-SGJ was a thing of the past. Kim Rosen greeted Greg with a tentative smile. She'd wrapped herself in a baggy cable-knit sweater today, as if to ward off a coming chill.

"Well, Counselor," she asked, "what mission are you on now?"

"All those boxes in the hallway," Greg observed. "I see they're gone."

A shadow crossed Kim's face. She forced her expression into the semblance of a smile. She wasn't accustomed to losing her bearings with men. Every time she bumped into Greg Monarch, though, she felt uncertain. He always seemed so watchful. Kim knew few guys like him. Those who populated the U.S. Attorney's office were full of polish and eager energy, but whenever one cornered her for drinks, she soon tired of his raucous anecdotes and self-serving plans. That they preferred boasting to intimacy, and power to sex, baffled her. So did Greg Monarch, but for other reasons.

"Yes," Kim said slowly. "We cleaned up. Managed to get a little organized around here finally."

"You must be glad to be done with Devil's Peak."

Kim showed her back, walking toward a window. "You know the law," she said. "Even after all the media hoopla, even after that cowboy foreman just about hog-tied me on TV, I can't talk about a secret grand jury proceeding."

She wanted to, though. It struck her that Greg Monarch would listen; Greg Monarch might even understand. There was that promise in the way he looked at her. She stood still, saying nothing.

"It's hard, isn't it?" Greg said. "To do the right thing and still win?"

Kim's lips puckered. "Now, that one I can answer, Counselor. Yes, it is hard."

They stood as they were, studying each other, unwilling to turn away. Then a boisterous exchange in the hallway interrupted them. Two cocksure assistant U.S. Attorneys, bolting for the exit at the noon hour, were celebrating. One of them tapped on Kim's door, stuck his head in. "Oh, excuse me, Kim, didn't know you had someone with you," he apologized. "We were just heading out to lunch, wondered if you wanted to join us."

Kim hesitated, looking down and to the side. Then she raised her eyes to Greg's. "No, thanks, Brian, I'm tied up just now," she said. "I'll get something at the vending machine later."

Greg stepped toward her. "What do you say we get out of here?" he suggested. "It will be so much easier to talk without these four walls around us."

They rode out into the Chumash Dunes on sturdy broad-shouldered roans rented at a stable just behind the sand, amid the cabbage fields ten miles south of Pirate's Beach. The trail from the stable followed Arroyo Flaco Creek, where, in the blue-green, algae-rich water, they saw a snowy egret standing utterly still, waiting for minnows. They passed three ducks combing the creek for worms, then a ramshackle cottage ringed with black poplar and willow. A vestige of the Dunites? Greg wondered.

Kim rode with ease, firming her grip and sitting heavy

in the saddle when it came time to cross a stream. "They'll want to sit down in that water," she advised. "Don't let them or we'll never get out." Then they were in the secondary dunes. Beach grass, ice plant, verbena, and dune buckwheat held the sandy knolls together, giving them a riot of color. They rode through rolling hillocks, past bygone Indian campsites full of bleached shells. The trail to the ocean threaded through a grove of willow and poplar, then opened onto the beach. There Greg and Kim kicked their roans into a gallop and flew across the hard sand at the surf's edge. Fifteen miles of wide-open beach stretched before them. Watching Kim lead the way, her hair wild and loose in the wind, Greg felt as if he could ride forever.

Their horses could not, however. When they tired, glistening with sweat and heaving for breath, Greg and Kim dismounted and tied them to a driftwood log. The two lawyers settled in the sand, their backs against the timber.

The dunes were silent, but bursting with life. All about them, plants abounded. Wildflowers, bush lupine, California sagebrush, sand verbena. Some grew only in the dunes, nowhere else in the world. Nipomo lupine, crisp monardella, surf thistle, La Graciosa thistle.

Animals, too. Opossums, weasels, coyotes, kangaroo rats, beaver. There were butterflies of all sorts, crabs, urchins, sand dollars, limpets. Resident and migratory birds teemed. Waterfowl, shorebirds, raptors, herons, sandpipers, curlews, willets, gulls, loons, coots, cormorants.

"I wanted to be a hero." Kim, staring out to sea, her legs pulled up, her arms around her knees, spoke so softly that Greg barely heard her. Then she turned toward him and repeated the words. "I wanted so much to be a hero."

Greg studied the sky. "So do we all," he said.

Silence then. Kim considered, debated with herself.

"I want to tell you a story," she said finally. "It's only a story, though, okay? A made-up story."

"Okay."

"It's about a young, idealistic lady lawyer who grows

tired of corporate law, of moving big amounts of money from one pocket to another. Who decides there's more important things to do, so goes to work for the U.S. Attorney. Who means to right wrongs, prosecute the bad guys, make the world a better place."

"Ah," Greg said. "My favorite type of character."

They shared a faint smile.

"One day, an FBI agent comes to her office," Kim continued. " 'Let's do Devil's Peak,' he proposes. The lady lawyer laughs, treats it first as a wacky joke. Prosecuting Devil's Peak is a wild idea, after all. First, because Washington and Sacramento both jump through hoops for Rolfson Industries. Second, because the bomb lab is owned by the DOE. The Department of Justice would be prosecuting the Department of Energy."

Greg chuckled. "Imagine the President's Cabinet meetings. The Attorney General sitting next to the Secretary of Energy."

"Right," Kim said absently, lost now in her story. "On the other hand, there's something awful going on out there. Not just to egrets and creeks, but to hundreds of thousands of people today, future generations later. The lady lawyer thinks it over. She has studied a little moral philosophy in between her torts and contracts classes. She's interested in how the legal system forms social values."

Greg stretched out on the sand. "So she decides to do Devil's Peak."

"Yes," Kim said. "She decides to do Devil's Peak. After convincing her bosses, of course. Which is not easy. Lots of skeptical faces stare at her, but she prevails. They give her a search warrant, they give her a special grand jury."

"Wow," Greg said. "A very persuasive lady lawyer."

"She's a hero, remember?" Kim arched her eyebrows. "In this story, there's a hero."

The early fall day had grown warm, as it often did on the Central Coast, in those months when the fog stayed away. Greg unbuttoned his shirt halfway and kicked off his boots; Kim rolled up her sleeves.

"For a while," she continued, "the lady lawyer feels on a roll. The FBI flies over Devil's Peak with infrared gadgets, then shows up at the Devil's Peak gates with a search warrant. Carts away hundreds of boxes of documents."

"Which," Greg interrupted, "get piled up in the lady lawyer's hallways."

Kim made a face. "She convenes her special grand jury, starts running in the witnesses and documents. Dozens of witnesses, mountains of documents. Too many, she starts to realize, and too detailed. She's losing the grand jurors. Then she loses the evidence, too. An infrared expert flip-flops about seeing hot spots. As if he's been persuaded to reconsider. Which creates just enough confusion to queer the interest of Main Justice."

"They want clandestine skulking," Greg said. "Not just a public policy debacle."

"Exactly," Kim agreed. "So Main Justice steps in. Starts negotiating directly with Rolfson, pushing for a plea bargain. Rolfson won't deal unless there's no charges at all against individuals. Technical violations only, for which the corporation pays a fine. No person is culpable, no person is even named. To this, the lady lawyer objects, but Main Justice keeps negotiating, week by week ceding more to Rolfson's lawyers."

The next plot turn, Greg realized, the whole world already knew. "The lady lawyer has a problem now," he said. "She's been too good at her job. She's managed to wake up those dozing grand jurors."

"Yes," Kim said. "The grand jurors are angry. When they hear about the bomb lab at Devil's Peak, they go ballistic." She paused, looked at him oddly. "God knows what they would have done if they'd heard about the missing plutonium."

Greg tried not to show anything, but Kim noticed his confusion. "You did know about the missing plutonium," she asked. "Didn't you?"

Greg held his palms up. "How could I know? This is a made-up story."

"Right. Of course it is. Anyway, it's just *maybe* missing plutonium. Could be lousy record-keeping, believe it or not. But an incinerator operator out there thinks something like twenty-five pounds are gone, based on what she's seen and heard. Enough to make dozens of bombs, or possibly contaminate half of Europe's groundwater supply. Who knows, maybe terrorists or a rogue government have it, maybe it's just lost somewhere at Devil's Peak. Frightening, but there isn't nearly enough solid about that to give the grand jury."

Greg made it sound casual. "This incinerator operator? She still around?"

Kim looked at him sharply. "No," she said. "The incinerator operator gets drunk, drives off a cliff. Instead, her lawyer testifies before the grand jury. In fact, her lawyer is the last witness the grand jury hears before it disbands."

Greg studied the waves. "This lawyer, he have a name?"

Kim had been longing to tell him for so long now. She'd always wondered whether it somehow might have helped at the trial. The rule of law, though, had stopped her from identifying grand jury witnesses. The sacred rule of law.

She searched Greg's face. Sprawled on the sand, he for once looked utterly at peace. "For the purposes of this story," she said, "let's call him . . . Ira."

"Okay," Greg agreed. "Ira it is."

"Ira has seen all his dead client's records, he's talked to her colleagues, he's rooted around so much he's an expert. So he tells the grand jury what he knows. Except for the missing plutonium angle. We don't let him get into that, not a word. What he testifies about is enough. The grand jury leaves enraged that day."

It was noon now, the sun directly overhead. Kim pushed her bangs out of her eyes, rolled her sleeves higher, undid the two top buttons of her flannel shirt. "Next day," she continued, "the lady lawyer is ordered to Washington. For two meetings at Main Justice. The first is in the conference room at the Environment and Natural Resources Division. At one end of a long table sit two senior partners from Rolfson's big-shot Washington law firm. At the other end, Main Justice's division head, his lieutenants, the lady lawyer. Except for her, everyone in the room is over fifty, everyone has silver hair, everyone has a penis."

Kim was smiling, so Greg smiled back.

"For twenty minutes," she continued, "one of the big-shot senior partners talks. Rolfson has done no wrong, he says. Rolfson was just adhering to forty years of public policy. The country wanted to make bombs, not worry about the environment. The country didn't adopt tough environmental laws until a decade ago, the country even then didn't clearly apply them to bomb plants. Do you now punish Rolfson because you've suddenly decided public policy priorities were misguided? Is that right? Is that fair?"

"And the lady lawyer's response?" Greg inquired.

Kim sighed, and kicked the sand. "For one thing, the lady lawyer marvels at how Rolfson even got this meeting with Main Justice. The lady lawyer wonders how many letters it took, how many phone calls, how many pulled strings. But the lady lawyer also has to admit she can't entirely deny Rolfson's point. She can't ignore the ambiguities, not after dragging through the Devil's Peak case for months. It's true, she concedes. Rolfson is as much a symptom as a cause. A symptom of a gung-ho bomb-production culture. A culture encouraged by Congress, allowed by the regulatory agencies. How do you prosecute what's wrong and evil, but not illegal? How do you indict a culture? That's what the lady lawyer asks herself."

Greg shrugged, uncertain what to say. It was paralyzing, he knew, to see every side of an issue. Or, for that matter, to understand others too much. You became hostage to your rampant sympathies.

"The second meeting is in the office of the Criminal Division's chief," Kim continued, her voice quavering now.

"It is a somber palace. Twenty-foot-high ceilings, wainscoting, oil paintings, dark walnut walls. Again, except for her, all silver-haired men. The lady lawyer argues for tougher settlement terms and a grand jury report. But the silver-haired men shake their grand, noble heads. 'You guys don't get it,' the lady lawyer says. 'The grand jurors are going to do a report whether you want one or not. What we have here is a runaway grand jury.' The silver-haired men don't care. Main Justice cuts a deal with Rolfson, Main Justice instructs the lady lawyer to disband the grand jury. Which is what she does. She obeys her bosses, to her everlasting shame."

Kim pondered, then revised a little. "Actually, she's not entirely ashamed. She's also proud of what she's done at Devil's Peak. The two feelings being not mutually exclusive. She feels both at the same time."

Greg moved closer to Kim's side. He could smell her now, a musky mix of horse and sweat. "We all have to make our way in the world," he said.

"Yes," Kim agreed.

He longed to touch her, but did not. "Tell me," he asked. "What's the meaning of Ira being the last witness? Did he affect your silver-haired men in Main Justice? Did his appearance somehow convince them to pull the plug?"

Kim shrugged. "I can't answer that," she said. "I simply don't know."

"What did he have to say? What did he tell the grand jury?"

Even now, this far down the road, Kim hesitated. Revealing the testimony of a grand jury witness could bring severe sanctions.

"He had certain particular details," she said finally. "Technical stuff mainly, but nothing outrageous. What made him special to the jurors was his manner. Centered, direct, certain of his facts."

Greg turned away. Kim started doodling in the sand.

"I recognized your name," she said. "That first day you came to my office asking about the Devil's Peak security patrol. I would have agreed to see you anyway, just to find out why you were nosing around the plant. But when I recalled who you were, I had to meet you."

"Who I was?"

"In law school, one of my professors came from Florida. He'd followed the Hilliard case, watched them execute Joe Hilliard. He taught it to us as a lesson in the adversarial process. He'd even copied the important public documents for everyone. He wanted us to see what to expect, to understand that it was all a ferocious battle. Never trust the other side, he lectured. You must be unbridled advocates, you must fight as if in a war."

Now it was Greg's turn to feel ashamed. "Jesus. I was offered as the model for what not to do?"

"Yes, that's how he taught it. But that's not how I learned it. I always imagined what it must have been like for you. Trying that case, making that mistake, fighting the appeals, watching your client die."

His client. Greg tensed, imagining for a moment they were talking of Ira. "What I still don't understand," he said, "is how the Devil's Peak story ties to Sullivan's murder prosecution. If it does at all. Why does it matter that Ira testified before your grand jury?"

Kim glanced up at the bright sun, wiped the back of her neck, stood up. "Would you mind terribly if I ran into the ocean for a minute?" she asked. "I feel so grimy and hot, and it looks so cool out there."

Greg, his thoughts still on Ira, simply nodded.

Kim's eyes danced. "Well, then, do you think you could discreetly look away for a moment?"

Studying the dunes behind them, he listened to her pull off her jeans, then her flannel shirt. At the sound of her splash into the water, he turned to see her long bare legs kicking through the waves. Just what, he wondered, would Ira feel about this? In a moment, his jeans were off too, and he was dashing for the surf.

* * *

Maybe she should have kept drifting after law school, maybe she shouldn't have become a lawyer. At least she wasn't still moving wads of money around for monster corporations. She'd left that job to help a tree-hugger crowd. Then she'd realized they preferred booby-trapping redwoods to circulating petitions. Way too many rooms she feared, and beds she regretted. She'd started feeling the urge to rejoin the real world. When the U.S. Attorney called, she jumped.

Kim told her story as they lay in the sand, their shirts clinging damply to their still-wet bodies. She looked so young with her hair plastered to her head. So untarnished, so undamaged. Kim's shirt reached only to her hips. Greg couldn't avoid noticing a tiny red heart tattoo high on her right inner thigh. Nor could he avoid noticing the swell of her breasts and the outline of her nipples.

Glancing up, Kim caught him admiring her. Rather than admonish, she looked at him frankly. Then she took his hand and pulled him toward her. He felt her body soften into the bend of his arm. She wrapped herself around him, raised her mouth to his. She tasted like the sea. It had been years since Greg felt so afire. He reached for the buttons of her shirt. She caught his hand.

"I honestly don't know," Kim said, her voice thick. "I don't know whether there's any connection between Ira's murder trial and Devil's Peak. I've held nothing back now, Greg. Ira Sullivan testified before the grand jury, Ira was our last witness. That's all I know."

"I need more," Greg said.

Kim's fingers roamed down his back. "Someone will call you," she promised.

SEVENTEEN

Sandy Polson ran a hand through her tousled, tawny mane. She crossed, then uncrossed her legs, tapping the floor with her black lace-up boots. She dabbed at her reddened eyes with a tissue pulled from a small box sitting at her side. Look at them, she thought. They're so absurd. Yet again they sat around her in a semicircle, watching and asking questions, sounding so utterly foolish.

"Sandy, you can't just walk free on this, you're gonna do some time."

"Sandy, this plea deal is in your best interests . . ."

"No, Sandy, I never said that, that's just not true . . ."

That prosecutor, Dennis Taylor. Those detectives, Buzz Johnson and Roger Kandle. Roger frowning, Buzz breathing heavily through an open mouth, Dennis smiling in that way that didn't look like a smile at all.

Oh, was she tired of such smiles. How long ago they had started. She'd had her fill by the ninth grade. Everyone back then pretending to be concerned, pretending to be her friend, while really embracing her family. Her horrid brother and sister, her strung-out mother, her stuffy, unbearable stepfather. Him above all they believed, the eminent composer and music professor. Whatever she claimed he did to her, it didn't matter. They'd nod, examine, take notes, then go talk to the grand professor. After a while, she didn't much care. She did what she wanted; she stayed out all night with boys, played pinball, rode motorcycles.

Not that she was a wild girl. Kissing and making out

with boys, she'd felt only a vague pleasure, a mild arousal. True, one night, she'd ended up in a hotel room three hundred miles from home, with a middle-aged traveling salesman she'd met downstairs in the dining room. She'd not planned that, though, really wasn't sure how it happened. He hadn't provided her any pleasure, that much she knew. Nor had all the other men she'd started spending nights with back at home. She apologized regularly to her parents for her ways, but she never really felt sorry. After all, she'd never done anything wrong.

Only later did Sandy decide it was just as well her family exiled her. Getting sent to a special home, at least she escaped her dreary relatives. She couldn't escape everyone, though. Not at that home, not at the university, not in Costa Rica. Always there were doubters, always there were those quick to suspect the worst. So what if she told everyone a school counselor seduced her? So what if she sold meth in her college classrooms? So what if she stopped at the Bar La Guaria three hours after that accident in Costa Rica?

It was almost dawn by then, and she was hungry. Quite ravenous, actually. After all those horrible questions, she needed nourishment, she needed to settle down. It so happened that the Bar La Guaria offered an excellent *pinto gallo*. Just what she craved, especially when washed down by a cold Bohemia. As for why she took to the dance floor after her meal, well, why not? She'd survived a terrible accident; that certainly was something to celebrate. If there were people who looked askance, if there were people who thought ill of her, that was their problem.

At least everyone believed her here in La Graciosa. Everyone believed her about Ira Sullivan. For good reason, too. Sandy could still see the image in her mind: Ira Sullivan smacking the postmaster with the barrel of the gun, swinging his arm back and forth, back and forth. Then Ira Sullivan pulling the trigger, shooting a bullet into the postmaster's head. She'd seen that moment, oh, how she'd seen that moment. Just as clearly as she'd heard Ira say, *no way . . . no way . . .*

Of course, some of the details were hard to remember now. In fact, some of the details had always been a little fuzzy. She'd had to work them out as the D.A. and the detectives questioned her. She wasn't quite sure how she'd reached the final version. It was a true story, though. Dennis Taylor had declared it so. So had the jury.

Now the D.A. was trying to welsh on their deal.

"The best we can do," Taylor was saying, "is second degree murder, fifteen years. Behave yourself in there, you're out in ten."

Sandy crossed her legs again and pushed away the tissue box. She'd dismissed her court-appointed attorney weeks ago, after watching him cave to Taylor once too often in these negotiations. Cave to Taylor, and tell her the D.A.'s offers were "worth considering." She could consider well enough without a lawyer at her elbow.

"Actually, Mr. Taylor, I can't go along with that," Sandy said. "In fact, I can't go along with any plea arrangement you might offer."

Taylor stood, paced, rubbed the bald spot in his thinning hair. It appeared to Sandy that his salt-and-pepper beard had a bit more salt in it these days. "Why not?" the D.A. asked. "Why risk a trial? You could end up with Sullivan on Death Row."

Sandy let a faint smile color her grave expression. "Because I'm not guilty of murder," she said evenly. "Neither, for that matter, is Ira Sullivan or Paul Platt. Nothing I've ever told you is true. Ira was never there at the postmaster's. Paul was never there. I was never there. Everything was a lie. All I'm guilty of is lying."

At first, Taylor said nothing in response. Despite himself, though, his body reacted. His hands jerked, his eyes widened, his elbows flared. "No way," he finally choked out. "No way is this true."

Those words again. *No way . . . no way.*

"Is what true, Mr. Taylor?" Sandy's smile deepened with that question.

Taylor glared at her. "What you're saying right now, in this room. What you just said is not true."

Sandy sat perfectly still, her hands folded in her lap. "How do you know what's true or not, Mr. Taylor?"

The D.A. loosened his collar. "Ira Sullivan's jury," he gasped. "They decided what's true. They decided that Sandy Polson spoke the truth in the courtroom. No one can alter that fact now. Not even Sandy Polson."

"All the same, Mr. Taylor, that's what I'm doing."

Taylor flung himself at his computer, punching the keyboard, frowning over the monitor. Minutes passed. Buzz Johnson and Roger Kandle exchanged glances, shifted in their chairs. Finally, Taylor swung around to face Sandy.

"You were following Ira around," he said. "You didn't realize where it was taking you. You ended up where you didn't want to be. You saw something you wished you hadn't. You thought it was wrong. You told us. End of story."

"I made it all up, Mr. Taylor."

"No," the D.A. insisted. "Why would you do that? Why would you put yourself at a murder scene? Why in God's name would you implicate yourself?"

Sandy shrugged. "I wanted the detectives to believe me. I didn't think they did. I thought if I put myself there, at the murder scene, they'd believe me."

Taylor clawed at his beard. "It doesn't make sense, Sandy. Why would you want them to believe you if there was nothing to believe? Why not just say you knew nothing about this murder?"

"I had that cash on me. I'd found it at the Foghorn, hidden in the bathroom behind the toilet. Someone's drug money, waiting to be picked up. But I knew you wouldn't believe that. I didn't want to get blamed for stealing it. I had to explain it somehow."

Taylor was sputtering now. "So you made yourself party to a murder?"

Sandy looked down at her pale, bare arms. She regretted leaving her two bracelets in the jail cell, even if she had grown tired of them. "I was terribly disturbed at the time, Mr. Taylor. I didn't care if I lived or died."

Taylor nodded. "I see. And what about Ira? You didn't care if Sullivan lived or died?"

Sandy reached for another tissue, dabbed again at the tears in her eyes. "You wanted a suspect, so I gave you him. I gave you what you wanted. I have this terrible habit of trying to please people."

Taylor opened his mouth, then closed it. A calm suddenly settled over the D.A. He stopped arguing, stopped resisting. His was the look of a man who'd just spotted an opportunity. "Okay, Sandy," he said. "You play it that way, we're going to trial."

For a moment, as they were leading her out of the room, Sandy's eye met Roger Kandle's. He tried to appear stern, but it didn't work. That poor man, she thought. He looks so puzzled.

It required much more effort for Greg to visit Ira Sullivan at the California Men's Colony in northern Chumash County than at the La Graciosa *asistencia.* Greg had to pave the way with phone calls, then submit to an identification check at the main gate before even gaining access to the modern, three-story complex.

It was a medium-security facility, with long, white stucco buildings set in a landscape of lawns and paths. Turning from a narrow rural road onto the prison grounds, Greg thought the place looked more like a college campus than a penitentiary. The entry area didn't match the prison's exterior, though. Here the walls were a dirty white, the floor cracked cement. A dozen wooden benches ringed the perimeter. Long fluorescent bulbs provided a pale yellow light. "Do not bang on this," advised a handwritten sign on a candy vending machine. "If you do, your visit will be canceled."

When his turn came, a sullen clerk with a wispy mustache shoved paperwork at him while a burly sheriff's deputy patted him down with little subtlety. Then a guard sitting in an elevated bulletproof cubicle, eyeing him as if he were a new inmate, pressed a hidden button. Iron gates at one end of the reception area slid open. As Greg stepped past them, they slammed shut. A second iron gate now rose in front of him, imprisoning him in a ten-square-foot cell. The guard pressed another button, and that gate slid open. Greg stepped forward, into the penitentiary.

The woman guard leading him down hallways to the attorney interview rooms sounded pleasant after all that. "You been in here before?" she asked.

"A handful of times," Greg replied. "Not recently. Don't do much criminal work anymore."

"Your client is really swinging up and down and all around, I tell you that."

Greg started paying attention. "What do you mean?"

"One day he's ranting at the guards, one day he's in the law library helping everyone with their appeals, one day he won't talk. They were going to take him to the prison hospital, but something happened, I don't know. I heard he refused to go."

"Death Row must not suit my client," Greg said.

The guard installed Greg in an interview room, then left to get Ira. Greg looked about. The room was empty but for a plain linoleum-topped table, two chairs, and a window giving onto a larger communal visiting area. Inmates out there sat huddled with families at small tables, fidgety young children on their laps, tearful mothers at their shoulders. From vending machines, relatives bought candy, chips, soft drinks. Grandmothers carried babies in backpacks while young men with ponytails inspected their beepers. "How come Daddy can't come home tonight?" one little girl asked her mother.

"Hello, Greg." Ira, standing at the door, alarmed Greg. He was rail-thin now, and startlingly sallow. They began to shake hands, but Greg pulled Ira's arm forward and embraced him. They'd hugged once like this on a playing field, Greg recalled. They'd just won a football game, and Ira was pretending Greg had been the star who'd saved them.

"I dreamt of Jeffrey last night," Ira said.

This was new. Ira never talked about his son, not voluntarily at least.

"He came to me in my cell like he was lost," Ira continued. "Like he didn't know where he was going. But when he saw me, he smiled. He had something to show me, marbles in his pocket, green and purple marbles. He climbed on my lap and turned them in the light. Then he told me it was okay. That's what he kept saying. 'It's okay, Daddy. It's okay, Daddy.' "

Greg waited a moment before speaking. "How you doing, Ira?"

Ira forced a small smile. The embrace from Greg had roused a memory for him, too. Of being at Greg's home one night in high school, of watching Greg's father impulsively hug his son. The sight had startled him. "It's Death Row," he replied. "What can I say? A nine-foot-by-six-foot cell, twenty-two hours a day. Not too much of a social life. How to put it? People are under sort of a strain where I live."

"They tell me you're acting kind of moody."

Ira shrugged. "Hell, that was me even before I got in here."

For a time, neither man said anything. Then Greg spoke. "There is much I'm sorry for, Ira."

Ira ran a hand through his hair. "No sense looking back."

"Sometimes it helps."

"I'd rather figure out where we're going."

Greg leaned toward him across the table. "Okay, then," he said. "Tell me about Devil's Peak."

For a moment, the question stopped Ira. He didn't know what Greg was talking about. Then he realized. The recollection gave him uncommon satisfaction. For once he didn't have to wince at a memory.

"Gal I knew from the Foghorn used to work there," Ira offered. "Foulmouthed old broad, a regular at the bar. Ran their incinerator. At least, she once did. Got fired. Blew the whistle on them. Hazardous-waste violations, stuff like that. Got her into lots of trouble. Asked me to help her. I was the only lawyer she knew, I guess. Didn't want to tell her I wasn't really practicing anymore. What the hell, I figured. Rolfson, wasn't it? They run Devil's Peak?"

Greg nodded.

"Yes," Ira continued. "I told Jenny I'd help. Figured it would be easy. Just file a lawsuit, then rattle their cage until they settled. Make some waves, get them more inclined to negotiate. I poked around for ammunition, then met with some Rolfson lawyers. They ended up paying her a fair amount. Not that it helped much. She ended up getting drunk and driving off a cliff a couple months later."

Ira said nothing more.

"What about the grand jury?" Greg asked. "I'm told you testified to the grand jury."

Ira labored now. So much had happened since then. He recalled a pretty young woman and a big empty courtroom.

"That's right, almost forgot," he said. "They called me one day after Jenny died. I went up to San Luis. Talked about what Jenny knew about the plant, how she'd been treated, how they spooked her and fired her."

"Who called you? Kimberly Rosen?"

"Yeah, that's it, Kim Rosen."

"Anything else on this, Ira? Think, think. What else can you remember? Any connection to the postmaster? Dennis Taylor? Anything?"

Ira turned away. He wished he could talk more about Jeffrey's visit to his cell. A memory from long ago tugged at him. He'd stopped at a roadside diner, expecting only a sandwich and a beer. What he'd found was a scrawny, saucer-eyed woman, sitting on a stool, plucking a battered guitar. *Oh will they come back home someday,* she sang, her voice a haunting *a cappella. I'm lonesome for my precious children. They live so far away . . . I hope and pray we'll live together, in that great land hereafter lie . . .*

"I'm sorry, Greg," Ira said. "What are you after? All that happened long before the murder. Why are you asking about Devil's Peak? What does that have to do with anything?"

"I don't know," Greg admitted. "I'm just trying to figure something out."

Ira said nothing. He was thinking now of the homes where he and Greg grew up, of the home where he raised Jeffrey for six years, of the lake where a father and son went fishing one sunny morning. He tried to remember what it felt like in that meadow with the low, soft spring sun in your face, the purple lupine and golden poppies at your feet. Then he stopped himself. It was madness to dwell on all that, just as it was madness to entertain the notion that Greg could prevail. Better to seal himself off from such thoughts; better to escape from such cruel false promise.

Greg clutched Ira's shoulder. "We can fix things. We can alter what we've done."

Ira didn't hear him. "I told Jeffrey I'd see him soon," he said. " 'I'm coming,' I told him. 'We'll live together.' "

That evening, the phone rang in Greg's house as he sat on his deck, staring out over the creek. The noise startled him.

"Greg Monarch?" The man's voice sounded gruff, impatient.

"Yes, speaking."

"This is James Larsen."

Greg searched his memory. The name was vaguely familiar, but he couldn't make the connection. "Do I know you?"

"No, I guess not," Larsen said. "But we have a mutual friend. She told you that you'd be getting a call."

Kim had meant it, Greg realized; Kim had come through. Then he grasped why Larsen's name sounded familiar. Of course. In the Devil's Peak documents he'd been studying. James Larsen. The FBI agent who started it all, who brought the charges to Kim.

"I was just going out for dinner," Greg said. "If you're nearby, join me."

They sat on the creekside patio at Stella's Café, Greg poking at a salad, Larsen tearing into a double bacon cheeseburger. Greg couldn't stop staring at this man. It was hard to imagine him as an FBI agent. With his funny round body and head of tight red curls, Larsen reminded Greg more of the boy who sat next to him in tenth-grade math, furiously rushing through their tests in half the allotted time.

"They pulled me off the case just when we were starting to really nail them," Larsen complained. "Headquarters told me to back off, said there was no point, they were going to cut a deal. I objected, they told me to stop whining. Damn thing was, we had enough evidence already. Workers out there were telling me the wildest things. Foremen ordering leaking blocks of waste capped with concrete so they'd look okay to inspectors. Chemists pumping so-called medical waste from so-called research labs into ponds and streams. Supervisors dicking with documents, throwing up fences, 'defining access.' " Larsen slammed the table. "Damn. We could have indicted people. They didn't have to fold their hand, they didn't have to plea-bargain like that."

Kim's world would be a lot easier, Greg thought, if she could see things as Larsen did.

"Our mutual friend felt you might be able to help me understand the connection between Devil's Peak and Ira Sullivan's murder trial," Greg said. "That is, if there is one."

Larsen shook his head. "Our mutual friend assumes I know more than I do. It's true, I have been suspicious, I have wondered how your man ended up charged with homicide one. But I have no answers for you. I know nothing at all about your murder trial." He paused, leered at Greg. "She seemed mighty motivated to help you out, I'll say that. Our lady friend, she's not usually so concerned about criminal defense attorneys."

Greg hoped Larsen couldn't see him flush in the twilight. "Okay," he said. "Let's leave aside the murder trial. What about Ira and Devil's Peak?"

Larsen washed down the last of his burger with a big swig of beer. A trickle of the brew ran down his chin, then mixed with the crumbs on his collar. "All I know is, he certainly did irritate the boys at Rolfson. Spooked them, actually."

"Why do you say that?"

"The diaries of the Devil's Peak plant manager."

Greg waited, but Larsen said no more. Apparently the agent wanted to be prodded.

"What about the diaries?" Greg asked.

"We found them when we raided the plant."

Greg had an idea. *Tell me about yourself, tell me about your work*—those, he and Jimmy both knew from their trades, were some of the most seductive words in the English language. You didn't have to pump and cajole. You just appealed to vanity, then sat back.

"That must have been quite a day," Greg said. "The day you raided Devil's Peak."

Larsen belched, wiped his mouth, patted his stomach. Then he leaned forward, eyes gleaming.

"Yessir, that was quite a day," he said. "Got through the gates by saying we needed to talk about Earth First! saboteurs on the prowl. Once in, we slapped a copy of the search warrant into Dan Cowling's hand. Cowling was Rolfson's manager out there. Jowly, balding old guy, three different types of college degrees on the wall in his office, lots of awards. Real veteran of these places. He couldn't believe it. 'You gotta be kidding,' he sputters. Then we start poking around. Four hours into the search, I'm looking in a cabinet in Cowling's office. Under a big pile of documents, I find some steno pads. I start leafing through them. My eyes bug out. It's Cowling's diary. A diary of events at Devil's Peak."

Greg put down his fork. "Anything interesting?"

"Lots of the stuff is just boring detail," Larsen offered. "Hard to understand. But every few pages, something just jumps up at me. *Environment becoming a big deal, hazardous waste can destroy us,* reads one note. *Don't tell press, tie mind-mouth-asshole together,* reads another. *No one follows the law,* goes a third."

Larsen gave Greg his best sly, knowing look. "I guess the diary entry you'd most appreciate was the one I saw right near the end. Not long after that incinerator gal Jenny Branson came to me, and I'd gone to Kim Rosen."

Greg waited, let Larsen follow his own pace. The FBI agent rehearsed first to himself, checking his memory, then recited the diary entry out loud: *Asshole Sullivan has a big mouth. Asshole Sullivan has to close his mouth.*

"Yep, that was it," Larsen repeated. " 'Asshole Sullivan has to close his mouth.' "

Greg already knew the answer to his next question. "What happened with those diaries? What was ever done with them?"

Larsen spat onto the creek's bank. "Nothing, that's what. They shut down the grand jury before we could introduce them. No one ever saw them. Stored away in a box somewhere now. Unless, of course, they've gone missing on us."

From the sky, the Devil's Peak plant resembled nothing so much as a small industrial foundry. Greg was sitting next to Larsen, who occupied the pilot's seat in the FBI's single-engine prop. After dinner, Larsen had suggested they take her up, so Greg could see what all the shouting was about.

"It's still dirty out there," Larsen hollered now over the plane's straining rumble. "They still have no place to put the crap. Still can't ship it or store it or treat it."

In the cockpit, they were surrounded by a mass of cables, scanners, and blinking lights. Greg studied a monitor connected to an infrared camera. On it, he could see white streams snaking toward a body of water, and several big oval white blotches.

"On the infrared, white indicates a hot spot," Larsen explained. "Thermal activity. Those big white things are holding ponds, full of waste. Holding ponds that leak into the groundwater and spill over onto the hillside. That white stream is running from the treatment plant to Pecho Creek."

It was so strange, Greg thought. Like they were on a spy mission, deep over the old Soviet Union. Except they were on the central California coast, flying over a commercial power plant with ties to the U.S. government. A power plant whose operators Ira had ticked off. Why, though? Just because he negotiated Jenny Branson a nice settlement?

"One thing I guess I didn't tell you about," Larsen said, as he banked the plane in the direction of La Graciosa's airstrip. "One thing that might help."

Greg watched the horizon stand up, go diagonal on him. Turning sharply like this in small planes, he always thought they were flipping over. "What's that?" he said.

"During the raid, we picked up the Devil's Peak patrol logs. When they go out, what they do, the warning siren record. All that. I looked through them, but they didn't mean much to us. No use for our case."

They'd straightened out now, had reconciled with the horizon, were heading home.

"One report," Larsen continued. "Maybe it would mean something to you. There was a night the siren went off three times. Radio bulletins called it a test, but they were really burning hazardous wastes. Stuff exploded on them. Sprayed crap everywhere, badly injured two engineers. Maybe worse. That happens, the sirens go off on their own, security guys start scrambling. Out in the dunes, their patrol saw something. Man and a woman, staggering around. Patrol guys stopped, checked them out, decided they were just drunks. Helped them to the lady's car, let them go. Later, noted the incident in their report log."

Such meticulous Good Samaritans, Greg thought. "You wouldn't recall the date?" he asked.

"Not offhand, but it would have been in the spring, sometime around late April."

"What about the time? The time of night?"

Larsen was lining the plane up with the runway now, bringing her down. Almost home, Greg thought. Almost home, Ira.

"The time is definite," Larsen said. "Half past midnight. Those guys clock everything. Time-stamp their toilet breaks, I swear. There's no question. The man and the woman came out of the dunes at exactly half past midnight."

Just about when the forensics unit was dusting for fingerprints at the postmaster's home, Greg imagined. Also just about when Buzz and Roger first spotted Sandy Polson sitting dazed in her banged-up Volkswagen, a purse full of cash at her side, waiting for help on a lonely Apple Canyon road.

EIGHTEEN

Walking through the La Graciosa farmer's market, Greg savored the smells—sizzling ribs, homemade sausages, barbecued tri-tips—and enjoyed the children. They sat wide-eyed in a semicircle before the puppeteer's booth, they shook and jiggled to the street musicians, they gawked at the belly dancers. "Belly button dancer?" Greg overheard one slight, incredulous little blond girl ask her daddy, she not quite hearing his words clearly. Balloons, face-painting, bright-colored handmade bracelets—everything tantalized, everything beckoned to young, eager eyes.

Greg was watching a magic show when he felt a squeeze on his elbow, and turned to find Alison Davana at his side. "It's nice to see you haven't changed," she said. "Still expecting bunnies to jump out of hats."

Alison looked as striking as ever. With appreciation, Greg surveyed the deep green eyes, the olive skin, the cocky awareness of her own allure. "How's your cowboy?" he asked.

Alison snorted with disgust. "That got old real fast. How about you? You still fighting for Ira?"

Greg wondered how to answer that.

The Devil's Peak security patrol logs were nowhere to be found, of course. "Gone bye-bye," the FBI agent had declared the night before, after he kissed the runway with his little prop and started rolling toward the hangar. "Had no use for them with the grand jury, so just tossed them in a box. Next time I looked, no box. Lost, thrown out, who knows? Bottom line is, they're gone."

No logs, and as Greg now well understood, no cooperation from the Rolfson managers running Devil's Peak. If only they could find June Blossom, that lady of the dunes who helped a drunken Ira, then disappeared off the face of the earth.

"I'm still fighting," Greg said. "Hard to say where it's getting us, though."

Looking down Carmel Street at the festive crowd, Greg and Alison both saw him at once. The Chumash County district attorney, with a red balloon in one hand, a young boy in the other. Dennis Taylor had spotted them first, and was now fast approaching, a broad smile spread across his face.

"Alison, Greg. What a pleasure to see you out here." Taylor leaned over, gave Alison a peck on the cheek.

Greg felt the blood rushing to his head. If there was anything that aggravated him about Taylor more than his lawyering, it was his past relationship with Alison. However passing it had been. An image of them together in Taylor's office involuntarily rose in Greg's mind. If only Taylor had dropped dead popping that amyl.

"Greg was just saying that he's still fighting for Ira," Alison remarked, looking back and forth at them, hands on her hips, a Marlboro hanging from her lips. She wasn't sure which of them she was trying most to annoy. She was having fun, though. It was always exciting, standing between two men she'd slept with.

Taylor easily maintained. "Well he should. That's what the legal process is all about. First at the trial, then in the appeals, we argue our sides. From that comes justice, what we all want in Chumash County."

Greg knelt on the street, next to the little boy holding Taylor's hand. Since Dennis hadn't thought to introduce him, or include him in the conversation, Greg figured he might. Now that he was on his level, he could see the boy had acquired several purple and orange tattoos. A dinosaur, a pirate, a soldier. "You sure look like you're having fun tonight," Greg said. "Where did you get those?"

The boy stretched out his arms proudly. "Face-painting lady," he announced. "She rolled them on. Don't worry, they'll wash off."

Dennis finally remembered his charge. "Let me introduce you. My nephew, Billy. My sister's son. They're visiting from Los Angeles. Billy, this is Mr. Monarch and Ms. Davana. They're friends of mine."

Billy shook their hands gravely. "I'm seven," he declared. "First grade."

"I'm thirty-two," Alison said. "You can call me Alison."

Greg wondered how old he looked. Whatever the answer, he didn't feel old. "You can call me Greg," he said.

In the distance, a church bell tolled. Taylor looked at his watch, shook his head. "Damn, didn't realize it was so late. I promised to get Billy back to his mom by nine. Sorry to rush, but we've got to get going."

The D.A. reached over, offered Greg his hand to shake. Greg accepted it reluctantly. Then Dennis turned to Alison. He took her hand in his, pulling her a little closer to him. With a theatrical flourish, he leaned down and kissed the back of her hand. "My lady," he intoned, waving his free hand in the air. "Always a delight to see you."

Greg fumed as he watched Taylor retreat down the street with Billy. What an utterly corny gesture, he thought. Only Dennis Taylor would pull a stunt like that. Only Taylor.

Something nagged at Greg, though, something that had nothing to do with jealous rivalry. A scrap of an image, on the edge of his memory. A moment, a story told. In an instant, Greg realized what it was.

On the cliff's edge, the sorry little motel south of Pirate's Beach. The proprietor, Miss Elaine, in her flapper's outfit, explaining June Blossom's sudden disappearance. A gentleman came by on June's last night there, Miss Elaine recalled. A charming gentleman with a big smile. A gentleman so nice, he kissed Miss Elaine's hand when he left.

* * *

"Goddamn it, Greg, wait up, we're going to do this together." Jimmy O'Brien again was lagging behind, perspiring and breathing heavily. He and Greg had plunged into the dunes five hours before; now it was well past noon, the sun high in the sky. Jimmy had not in the least welcomed the idea of an all-day hike, but he couldn't resist Greg's obvious fire. Nor did he wish to; he'd given up all thoughts of diverting Monarch. So what if Greg wasn't suited for this game? So what if he was getting into more trouble? So what if he was chasing his tail? Jimmy felt gleeful. It wasn't over yet.

Not unwillingly, Greg slowed down. Hiking the stark, wind-sculpted dunes was a lot harder than riding through them on horseback. The paths down the slopes were as treacherous as the paths up were trying. A misstep sent you tumbling down sheer slipfaces, and missteps were easy in the shifting sand.

It was hours after Greg's fateful encounter with Dennis Taylor at the farmer's market. Jimmy had beamed when Greg told him the hand-kissing story, for on his own, working Pirate's Beach contacts, he'd been after June Blossom's trail. He'd picked up a scent in recent days. A faint scent, but better than nothing.

The old abandoned Dunite shacks, he'd heard, weren't all uninhabited. Two or three had squatters living in them even now. No one knew exactly which shacks, for they were hidden deep in the vast wilderness preserve of sand and wetlands. It was easy to stay lost, if you wanted, in 22,000 acres of dunes and marshes. But on certain silent, starry nights, Jimmy was told, you sometimes could see thin strands of smoke, and even hear music. As if the Dunites were still gathering by an open fire, dancing to a wind-up Victrola. Occasionally, it was said, early-morning horseback riders had seen a woman on her knees in the surf, digging for clams and crabs. A barefoot woman in a shawl, with long gray-black hair hanging loosely to her shoulders. A woman not unlike Planet and Moose's description of June Blossom.

" 'All we need to do is find her,' " Jimmy gasped now, as he caught up with Greg atop a dune. "That's what you said last night. Jeez. This is turning out to be as easy as flying to the moon in your FBI pal's rubber-band plane."

Looking at the vista before them, Greg felt forced to agree. The desolate dunes spread for miles, an epic landscape of immaculate sand bordered by pounding, foam-capped surf. They'd seen so much this morning. Hidden valleys, misty wetlands, trails decorated with gray fox and mule deer tracks, dune lakes teeming with migrating mallards and teals. They'd even come across a midden of Chumash Indian artifacts—shells, tools, pieces of bone, ornaments, all piled in a large mound. The only thing they hadn't spotted was a sign of June Blossom. Of June Blossom, or any other human being living in the dunes.

Turning, shading his eyes with a hand at his forehead, Greg surveyed what now surrounded them. Inland to the north, off in the middle distance, he spotted a round body of water sparkling in the sunlight. Venano Gordo Lake, Greg surmised, based on where he thought they were. That haunting oasis where sixty-three tired, hungry Spanish explorers—the Gaspar de Portolá expedition—camped more than two centuries ago, en route to Monterey. Looking due east, Greg spotted a large dune covered with giant green plants. Six feet high those plants were, maybe eight. They looked to Greg like brown-eyed Susans, but not exactly. Then it occurred to him: They weren't Susans; they were coreopsis.

Coreopsis, which in early spring blossom gloriously with brilliant yellow-orange flowers. Which in early spring must blanket this dune in startling, shimmering gold.

Like giant daisies, Planet had said. They'd sat with Ira before a golden hill covered with giant daisies. A shimmering golden dune, near Venano Gordo Lake.

So lost, remote, spectacular; there could be none other

like this one. Here was the hill where Planet and Moon sat with Ira one early spring night. Where June Blossom comforted Ira in her shawl, trying with tender succor to undo a moment's mistake at a dappled fishing lake.

"June Blossom lives near here," Greg announced.

He should have realized it from the start, but Planet's advice about checking Clam Beach motels had thrown him off. Why else would June simply appear that night? Moose and Planet had sat down in her front yard, that's why.

Through the willow and wax myrtle they searched, stepping back and forth across Venano Gordo Creek, following the brook into ever denser foliage. Heavy branches scratched their faces; gnats bothered their necks; submerged boulders banged their shins. Jimmy, spotting it first, put a hand on Greg's elbow. "There," he said. "In that willow thicket."

An ageless, dilapidated cabin, ten feet by eighteen feet at most, sat in the shelter of a huge dune, surrounded and almost obscured by the stand of willows. Three goats and a mangy mutt occupied the front porch, watching two Muscovy ducks waddle before them. To the north, a grassy plain had been converted into a thriving garden. To the east, through a break in the willows, high dunes reached toward the sun. What a wonderful view she has, Greg mused.

Then, suddenly, she was there, standing at her open door. Her gray-black hair loose on her shoulders, barefoot in a baggy black shift. Studying them, more with interest than alarm.

"June Blossom?" Greg asked, stepping forward.

She nodded, neither friendly nor hostile. Dark brown eyes, her face a crosshatch of wrinkles. "Who are you?"

"Friends of Ira Sullivan," Greg said.

For a time, she said nothing, lost in thought, weighing her options. "Come on in," she finally sighed.

June's paintings lay everywhere, many of the dunes, others of a smiling young girl with big brown eyes. A large table stood where June could work with the light coming from a north window. The door opened on the east side, located in typical dune fashion to avoid the ocean wind. Beneath the windows ran built-in drawers; above them, shelves. On the floor, a double mattress was folded into a couch, ready to open at night into a bed. The stove was an old washtub turned upside down, with a hole cut in the bottom for the smokestack. The cooler was an orange crate draped with a burlap sack, the sack kept damp by leaving one end of it in a coffee can of water. In a corner sat an ancient wind-up Victrola.

Playing hostess apparently was not a familiar role for June Blossom. She had neither the bent nor the practice. She stood now, arms folded, looking at her visitors as if they'd blown in with the wind. Not an unkind person, Greg imagined. Just someone who likes to be alone. Or needs to be alone.

From the cooler, June pulled two bunches of grapes, one light green, the other dark red. From a shelf, she took a bowl—actually the shell of a gaper clam—and in it put the grapes. She placed the bowl on the table by the north window. Still she said nothing.

"Looks like you've done well with your garden," Greg ventured.

June shrugged. "I get by. Garden, clamming, fishing. Milk from the goats. Track rabbits when I have to. It's a way to survive."

"Can you get out of here when you have to?" Greg asked. "Say, if you got sick?" He hoped she didn't realize the point behind his question.

"I keep an old Ford parked back behind here, way up past the high-tide line." June cocked her head. "Once, two guys tried to steal it, tow it straight away. I put my shotgun on them, marched them three miles to the nearest bar, held them till the sheriff came."

So she did have a car here, Greg thought. A car she could have used to drive Ira to his house.

"We've come to ask about that night when you helped

Ira," Greg said. "That night you sat out in the dunes with Planet and Moose, then took Ira home."

June's expression revealed nothing. "I don't know what you're talking about," she said.

Jimmy cleared his throat. "Moose and Planet say you were with them that night. They say they left you with Ira."

June looked at Jimmy afresh, as if she just realized he was there. Then back at Greg, in the same fashion. "Who are you guys, by the way? Who are the friends of Ira Sullivan?"

"I'm his lawyer," Greg said. "Greg Monarch. This is Jimmy O'Brien. He's a newspaper reporter. We're trying to save Ira, just as we think you did. He's been convicted of a murder that was committed the night you saw him in the dunes." Greg hesitated, continued. "Committed at midnight, half an hour before you left the dunes with Ira."

June moved slowly across the room, wound up the Victrola, set it to playing a record. *There ain't nothin' I can do or nothin' I can say . . . But I'm goin' to do just as I want to anyway . . .* Listening, June swayed, lost in Bessie Smith's aching declaration of autonomy. *If I just take a notion to jump into the ocean, t'aint nobody's bizness if I do . . .*

"Ira's on Death Row," Greg said. "They're going to execute him."

June moved again across the room, this time to pour goat's milk into another clam bowl. She put it on the east window ledge, where a plump brown-and-white calico appeared and started lapping. It looked as if June had dismissed Greg and Jimmy, or forgotten they were there. From her cooler she pulled a block of goat cheese, cut a slice, placed that on the north windowsill. Then, as she turned to put the cheese away, her arm knocked the jug of milk off the ledge where she'd left it. For the first time since they'd arrived, June displayed emotion and moved quickly. "Damn," she snapped, grabbing a cloth, jumping to mop up the spill. Long after the floor was dry, she kept rubbing it, her circular motions insistent, unceasing. Finally she stopped, rose, and turned to face Greg.

"Okay," she surrendered.

Greg sat down on the folded-up mattress. "That night," he asked. "What happened?"

"Planet and Moose were in the dunes, over by the golden hill," June began. "They go there often. I come out and sit with them, those nights that I feel like visiting. I felt like it that night, so hiked over. When I got there, I saw there was another man with them. Almost left, but didn't."

As she talked, June remained standing by the cooler, wiping her hands on the milk-damp dishcloth. Greg had expected someone mystic, ethereal. Instead, this woman struck him as a plain-talking realist. She spoke with little inflection, showed no feeling. Whatever illusions she'd started out with, she'd apparently discarded long ago.

"I sat with them," June continued. "Planet as usual went on about the stars, Moose did his astrology number. If I weren't really starved for company, I'd never endure them. It does get lonely, though. So I sat and listened. The third man said nothing. He had a bottle of whiskey. When he passed it to me, he almost dropped it. I realized he was drunk, way gone. Then I realized he was crying. Silently, tears running down his face."

Jimmy reached for a notebook in his back pocket, but Greg, noticing, shook his head. June followed the exchange, said nothing.

"Later, the siren went off from the power plant. The noise rattled Moose and Planet. They started saying stupid stuff about the siren ruining their celestial karma. They wanted to go, Ira didn't. By then I knew his name was Ira. I said I'd stay with him. So Moose and Planet left."

With relief, Greg saw that June wore a watch. "What time was that?" he asked.

"Siren went at eleven, they left maybe eleven-ten," June said. "After that, Ira and I talked. He talked mainly, I listened. About his son. He told me the whole story. The lake, the train. He cried, he drank whiskey. Pitiful, really.

There wasn't much I could do. I held him, I put my shawl around him."

Greg tried to imagine that, tried to imagine June with Ira, providing shelter from the storm.

"Later, I said he could stay the night at my cabin. He didn't want to, though. Kept saying, 'Home, home.' He was half out of it by then, incoherent, his eyes rolling back in his head. I tried to get him up, said I'd drive him home. Better that than have him pass out in the dunes. But he could barely walk. That's when the Devil's Peak patrol showed up. They helped me get Ira to my car. I don't know how I got him into his house, but I did. Left him on a sofa in his front room. That was it. Never saw him again."

"What time did you leave the dunes?" Greg asked.

"Half past midnight," June answered. Without hesitation.

Jimmy cleared his throat. "Why didn't you come forward with this story?" he asked. "You must have known what was happening. You could have saved Ira. You were with him when the murder took place."

June turned to Jimmy, her expression unreadable, her eyes flat brown stones. "Ira Sullivan was just someone I met one night. I didn't consider him a friend. The sheriff and D.A., they were his problem, not mine. I didn't want to be involved in it. I still don't today."

She was good at this, Greg thought, but he didn't believe her, not for a moment. "You didn't care?" he asked. "That he was arrested, convicted, sentenced to death?"

Just a flicker of something in her eyes. "No. I didn't believe he'd go to prison for that murder. I figured everything would be dropped, because I know for a fact that man was with me at midnight."

For once, it was Jimmy who couldn't stop himself. "You believed wrong, though," he snapped. "Ira did go to prison."

June turned away from both of them. "It's not my problem."

Greg rose and circled around until he faced her again.

"Tell me about Dennis Taylor, June. Tell me about your visit with Dennis Taylor at the Day's Rest Motel."

June kept her face obscured, but could not stop herself from inhaling sharply. Then her shoulders sagged. Slowly, she looked up. Her eyes were moist. "You know about that?"

"Only that he visited you before Ira's trial, then you disappeared."

"Yes," June said. "Yes, that's what happened." Suddenly she looked frail in the afternoon light. The gray hair, the crow's-feet, the long years of surviving on her own, they made her appear older than her years.

"What did Taylor say to you, June? How did he cause you to disappear?"

A tear ran down June's face. Her body looked as if it had lost all its air. She sank onto the folded mattress. When she next spoke, her voice sounded faraway.

She'd come into the dunes ten years ago. After her husband left her, after she'd decided to try a different way of life. She and her daughter, together. They put in the garden, cleaned out the well, tar-papered the leaky roof. Got a dog to keep the coyotes from the goats, a cat to fight the pack rats. They did fine, Becky and her, just fine. When it came time for Becky to start school, they talked to the county people, worked out a curriculum, got the school's textbooks, set up a study area in the cabin. In between her paintings, she tutored Becky. History, geography, writing. Becky wrote her own stories, did the drawings for them, even acted out some. They met other people in the dunes, ate meals with them sometimes, but let them have their solitude. Becky learned respect for other people's rights.

June pulled her legs up on the mattress and wrapped her arms around them. Slowly, she rocked back and forth.

Her paintings, Greg realized. The little girl with big brown eyes.

"Three years ago in early spring," she continued, "I decided to clear more of the north plain, expand the garden area. Becky and I, we chopped and cut, then piled up the leaves and brush to burn. We kept working in the smoke from the fire, kept working on our garden even when the smoke got dense. Why, I don't know, that's just what we did. A few days later, Becky started turning red, beet-red. Her eyes itched, she had a bad cough."

June wept, squeezed her legs. "I don't like doctors, don't believe their medicine. Antibiotics or surgery, that's all they know. There are better ways, more natural ways. That's what I believed. So I treated Becky myself. Vitamins, fluids, nasal irrigation. I thought she had a virus, I thought she'd get better on her own. I should have known, I should have thought back to what we'd been doing. Expanding our garden, we'd burned poison oak. Breathing poison oak smoke like that can be fatal. Not for everyone, some are immune. My Becky wasn't immune, though. My Becky was poisoned."

June buried her head in her arms, unable to continue. Greg looked at Jimmy, who'd turned ashen. No wonder she wrapped Ira in a shawl, Greg thought. They were kindred souls.

"Dennis Taylor knew about Becky?" he asked. "Is that it, June?"

She gathered herself, settled, wiped her eyes. "Yes. When Becky died, the coroner came, and the county social service people. Then the D.A.'s office. There was talk about child neglect, child endangerment. Worse even. Involuntary manslaughter, reckless something or other. 'Conscious disregard for her life.' I heard that a lot. In the end, though, they let it drop. I don't know why, but they finally left me alone."

"Until Taylor visited you at the Day's Rest Motel."

"Yes, until Taylor visited me."

"What did he talk about when he came to see you, June?"

"Becky's death. Unresolved, he called it. Undetermined. There's been cases like that around the country, he said. Cases of child abuse that authorities had ignored.

He was looking at all the old unresolved child deaths in Chumash County, just to make sure they hadn't missed anything. He didn't want to be one of those prosecutors caught with a mistake in his closet."

Greg sat down next to June on the mattress. "June, did Taylor talk about Ira Sullivan at all?"

"Not a word. Never came up."

"So you don't know if Taylor even knew you'd been there in the dunes with Ira that night?"

"No, I don't. He never talked about Ira. Later, I did wonder if there might be some connection. I didn't ask him, though, and he didn't say. Didn't matter to me, really. Wouldn't make any difference. All that mattered was not reliving Becky's death again. I didn't care about being charged, I just didn't want to relive it, especially not in front of the whole county."

"So you left?"

"That very night. Went up to Oregon, later to the San Juan Islands. For a while I was okay, but then I missed the dunes. I still don't know if the D.A.'s visit had anything to do with Ira, but with the trial over, I decided maybe I could come back. Disappear into the dunes. Which I did, until you found me."

Greg spoke softly. "Can I get an affidavit from you, June? Will you put your story down on paper, let me take it to a judge?"

June rose, went back to her cooler. From it this time she pulled out a head of cabbage, which she began to shred. Then two tomatoes, which she sliced. Green onion, mushrooms, olive oil. As she worked, June regained her composure. When she looked up at Greg, she once more appeared rooted, impassive. "I don't know," she said. "I will have to think about it."

That evening, Greg and Jimmy lay in the dunes, staring up at the stars, imagining the world the Dunites inhabited decades before. Or rather, the world the Dunites tried to inhabit. They surely hadn't managed to forge a utopia. That was undeniable. *Moy Mell*, they called it; in English, pasture of honey. After it all collapsed, a few remained in the dunes for years, alone, savoring their utter isolation. They were oddballs, though, not visionaries.

"The socially challenged," Jimmy exclaimed. "That's what they'd be called in the late twentieth century. The socially challenged."

In the distance, a mechanical whine disturbed the sable starlit still.

"Another sign of the late twentieth century," Greg said.

It was a Friday night, start of one more raucous Chumash County beach weekend. Certain reaches of the dunes now regularly drew roaring herds of off-road all-terrain vehicles. Some were factory ATV scooters—Honda 300 EX full-suspension four-strokes, Yamaha Blaster 200cc two-strokes, Suzuki 80cc electric starters—and some were stripped, homemade air-cooled VW dune buggies. All made a ferocious noise, all scarred the virgin dunes with crisscrossed tire tracks. In the most accessible areas, traffic congestion was actually a problem on weekends. At peak times it wasn't even safe to walk the dunes; an ATV or dune buggy could loom suddenly atop a hill and plunge toward you without warning. Those driving them often were drunk. When they finally retired to their inland RV camps, they got drunker. The smashing of empty bottles punctuated the late hours on many nights.

After their visit with June, Greg and Jimmy had hiked well out of her isolated preserve, heading north toward their car. They were nearer civilization now, too near. They tried to ignore the approaching din.

"Even if you get June Blossom's affidavit," Jimmy said, "what have you got? A transient hermit who skipped town over a dead daughter. You gotta hand it to Taylor, he played this nicely. Never once mentioned Ira to her."

"What about the Devil's Peak patrol guys?" Greg asked.

"Hoo ha," Jimmy exclaimed. "Rolfson Industries is not going to be Ira Sullivan's savior. I promise you that. Hundred dollars says those fellows no longer work at Devil's

Peak. Hundred dollars says they no longer live in California. Bimini, that's where they are. A suntan lotion franchise on the beach. Rolling in dough. Set for life."

The ATV roar had grown louder. Greg and Jimmy could hear laughing voices, shrieks, squeals. Cool urban cowboys giving their dates thrills by careening down sheer slipfaces. Jerks, Greg fumed. Can't thrill them any other way. So what the dunes are torn up, so what a few necks get broken?

On the hill above them, a Honda Pilot 400cc Beast of the Beach suddenly appeared at the crest. It looked like a bullet, a plump purple bullet with something monstrous astride it, waving two glaring yellow eyes. Two glaring eyes that now pitched down the dune's slope and hurtled toward them. Greg froze, mesmerized by the round, blinding flashlights closing on them. "Greg!" Jimmy shouted, but Greg couldn't make himself respond. With the ATV ten feet away, Jimmy dove for Greg, scooped him into his arms, rolled them both, entwined, out of harm's way. The ATV fishtailed as it skidded to a stop.

"Jesus H. Christ," the driver bellowed. "I didn't see you guys out there. Hell you doing lying in the sand like that?"

In the dark, Greg couldn't see the driver's face, but he could recognize that voice anywhere. That gruff, nasty, pig voice, that voice which had awakened him from a restless sleep so many months ago. Buzz Johnson climbed out of his ATV, stood over them, his face twisted into a malevolent sneer.

"Well, well," Greg gasped. "So this is how Chumash County sheriff's detectives spend their weekends."

When Greg arrived home near midnight, he pulled off his sandy clothes, then stood under a hot shower. His mind, as it often had in recent weeks, turned to Kim Rosen. She'd walked out of the ocean that day with such insouciance. Glowing in a sheath of water, slender rivulets coursing between her breasts. It surprised Greg to realize how deeply she affected him; he hadn't thought that possible.

Stepping from the shower, he walked outside, wrapped in a robe. There he sat on his deck, listening to the creek roll by.

What had just happened in the dunes? Could that have been intentional? Had Buzz really tried to kill them? It would be a perfect rubout, if you thought about it. A familiar type of accident, just another weekend hit-and-run. Greg shuddered. If only, he prayed, they all could make it through this. That surprised him, too; this urge to survive, this fear of death.

Greg forced his mind off such thoughts. Too much time around Jimmy, he told himself, Jimmy and his fevered imagination. He rose and headed inside.

Not until Greg was on his way to bed did he notice the red light blinking on his answering machine. He hoped it was Kim. It wasn't, though.

The voice on the machine sounded formal, neutral, robotic. This was the California Men's Colony calling, the voice wanted Greg to know. Calling about his client Ira Sullivan. Ira P. Sullivan. Something unfortunate has happened, the voice explained. Something regrettable. Ira P. Sullivan was in the prison hospital's intensive care unit. Ira P. Sullivan was in critical condition. Ira P. Sullivan had tried to kill himself.

NINETEEN

Greg always tried to avoid visits to the northwest fringe of La Graciosa, for it was a section of town that jarred him. Here the venerable structures of adobe, tile, and timber gave way to flavorless shopping malls and tract developments. Here stood bare, walled compounds of oversized two-story homes, jammed side by side as if space were unobtainable, although they overlooked just that—wide-open space, rolling countryside, verdant pastures. Cows still grazed feet from where this modern stucco suburbia began, but each time Greg came this way, it looked as if the developers had advanced further into their territory.

As much as he disliked this area, Greg understood why Roger Kandle lived out here. With three young children, Roger wanted a big house, a backyard swing set, safe streets, maybe a swimming pool. On a Chumash County deputy sheriff's salary, you couldn't buy all that anywhere but in the suburban tracts.

Kandle would have to see him, Greg reasoned. Or rather, he had to see Kandle. Even if it meant forcing himself through the detective's front door.

It was Saturday afternoon, less than a day after Ira's suicide attempt. Less than a day after Ira swallowed the pharmaceutical cornucopia readily available to prisoners on the California Men's Colony black market. They'd found him in time, it looked like, his pupils dilated, his breathing labored. Pumped his stomach, flushed him and rehydrated him, then tied him to his bed.

"I've decided to end all the pain and suffering the only way I know how," read the note Ira had left. "Greg, please forgive me, but I just can't take it anymore. I can't bear hoping and longing while knowing in my gut there's no point. I just can't see what the purpose is to all this. All I want is to join Jeffrey. That's all I really desire."

They'd let Greg visit Ira for only a moment this morning. With so little time together, Greg hadn't bothered with grief or dismay or exhortations, and also hadn't bothered dwelling on how terrible Ira looked, pinned down as he was by a jumble of needles and tubes. He had more pressing concerns. Awake all night, Greg had used the long, empty hours to review matters. To review, for instance, Ira's account of his labor negotiations on behalf of Jenny Branson.

You didn't need vast conspiracies or fevered imaginations to understand what had happened; you needed only human nature. Ira's among others'. Ira, longing still to be a ferocious adversary, a valiant advocate, a stellar attorney. Ira, who'd "poked around, gathered a little ammunition" for his poor, needy client. Ira, the unwitting agent of his own travail.

One question, that was all Greg posed when he visited Ira in his hospital bed. Your client, he asked Ira. Your incinerator operator Jenny Branson. How was it you managed to negotiate for her such a nice settlement? What exactly did you say? What did you bring to the negotiating table?

Ira, bleary as he was, understood the question. He'd buried that matter away, like so much else, but he knew where he'd hidden it. "Just the usual," he said, his voice a slow, drugged drawl. "Wrongful dismissal. Contrary to all promises and representations. Gender discrimination. Whistle-blower protections. All the standard labor lingo."

The standard labor lingo, and the standard lawyer's machinations.

"There was more," Greg said. "Wasn't there, Ira?"

Ira winced; whether in pain or regret, Greg couldn't tell. For a moment, it wasn't clear whether Ira would answer.

"Yes," he finally whispered. "Missing plutonium. Jenny thought she had evidence about missing plutonium at Devil's Peak. Lots of it, many pounds."

"You raised that at the bargaining table?"

A hint of defiance colored Ira's eyes. "Anything to get Jenny a better deal," he said. "I was just bluffing, didn't even know whether it was true. But hell, Greg. One little lady against a giant corporation. They had their S.O.B. lawyers, she needed hers. They threatened her. So I threatened them."

The nurses approached then, signaled for Greg to leave, but he leaned closer to Ira, just to make sure. "You told them you were going public about missing plutonium if they didn't settle? You told them that?"

Ira offered a faint grin. "Goosed them good, too. Right after that, they settled."

Settled but did not sit down, Greg thought. Settled, and kept playing.

Greg wondered how much time he had left. Rolfson's relentless executives, doing whatever they needed to avoid their own downfall. Ira Sullivan, dreaming of his eternal release. The State Bar, aiming to derail an objectionable La Graciosa lawyer. Who would get what they wanted first?

Sky Ranch Estates, they called Roger Kandle's development. Greg drove through the ersatz sculpted gates, then past rows of identical-looking houses, right down to the plastic Little Tykes Treehouses on the front lawns. Another form of imagined utopia, dashed in the end. Roger's was at the end of a cul-de-sac, a sky-blue structure with big picture windows, a huge deck, and a built-in Char-Broil barbecue. Greg had been here twice before, during his short tenure in the D.A.'s office. Once for a sheriff's department picnic, once when he and Roger were working to upend old man Bowser's manslaughter charge. Greg parked and walked up the sloping driveway.

Roger looked startled to find Greg at his front door. At work, Kandle never broke, never appeared anything but steadfast and impassive. But he was home now, dressed in frayed khakis and a T-shirt, his official identity shed for the weekend. In the background, Greg could hear music and the clamor of young children playing.

"What is it you want, Greg?" The surprise in Roger's soft, round face had quickly darkened into aversion. He kept the door half-closed and stood blocking the way. He did not invite Greg inside.

"We need to talk, Roger."

"If you have business with the sheriff's office, go there."

"My business is with you."

Mixed with the aversion was something else now. For a moment, Roger's eyes showed the anxiety of a cornered animal. Then a protective veil dropped.

"Not now it isn't," he insisted. "I'm with my family. You need to talk to me, find me at the sheriff's office next week."

Roger had started to close the door when a young girl's voice interrupted. "Daddy, who is that man? Do we know him? Is he a friend?" She was standing at Roger's side, tugging at his arm, curious and insistent. Greg thought fast. Kandle had three daughters. This one, blond and blue-eyed and delicate, must be the middle one. Greg knelt to her level. "Hi, Sofia, my name's Greg. You do know me, but I'm sure you don't remember. I came here for a picnic. You were just a peanut then. Two years old. How old are you now?"

Sofia exulted in the attention. "I'm seven. And I do too remember you. I remember when I was two."

Roger moved to block Greg's foray. "Come on, sweetheart, we're talking some business here. I'll come play with you in a minute."

Sofia didn't take him seriously. She started whistling through her missing two front teeth and rolling her eyes at her daddy, playing a private game with him only the two of them understood. Roger tried to look stern, but couldn't pull it off. Thus empowered, Sofia didn't hesitate. She reached for Greg's hand and pulled him past Kandle into the house. "We just got a new puppy," she said. "Do you want to come see her?"

Now the other two daughters appeared, one five, the other nine. Erica and Kelly, Greg recalled. Kelly, the older one with thick, dark hair and watchful eyes; Erica, the youngest, all scrambling energy. Together they tugged him into a family room where a twelve-week-old golden retriever slept in a box. "Daddy's going to teach us how to train her," Sofia said, on her knees, her nose two inches from the puppy's face.

"What's her name?" Greg asked.

"Goldy," Sofia said.

"No it isn't, it's Lily," Erica insisted.

"Garbo," Kelly declared.

As if planned, the three girls turned and assaulted Roger, grabbing his arms, knocking at his legs, jumping on his back. Kandle couldn't help himself, despite Greg's presence. He looked awkward and embarrassed, but still, he sank to the ground with his girls. He wrapped his arms around all three and squeezed until they squealed. Slipping from his grasp, they circled around and started climbing on his shoulders from behind. In a moment, they had him pinned, Erica around his neck, Sofia and Kelly on each arm.

"Three puppies, Daddy," Sofia urged. "We need three puppies."

"We're not letting go till you say yes," Erica said, laughing.

Then Roger was tickling them in the ribs and they were spinning off him, shrieking with glee. Somehow, rising, he scooped up all three, and now stood holding them in his arms. The puppy, awakened by the noise, rose on her hind legs against Kandle, jumping for the girls.

Greg watched it all in wonder. Roger, staggering about

with three exasperating, insistent burdens in his arms, looked more satisfied than anyone he knew.

"I see we've got company." Roger's wife, Miriam, emerging from the kitchen, offered her hand. "Greg Monarch, isn't it? You were here some time ago for a picnic, right?"

There were women like Miriam, Greg knew, but he hadn't met many of them. Direct, thoughtful, competent women who appeared capable of keeping ships upright in storms while still singing lullabies to restless children. Centered women, both calm and warm, who understood what they wanted, what they valued. Greg could only wonder how a thick, soft guy like Kandle had won this lady's love.

"I'm afraid it's going to get a little noisy around here today," Miriam said. "My little amateur theater group is coming over to rehearse our latest grand production. If you two men are going to visit, I'd suggest you do it out on the deck. You keep out of our way, we'll keep out of yours."

Roger started to object, but surrounded by his family, didn't know what to say. Greg, seeing him hesitate, took the lead. "Good idea, Miriam," he said. "We'll go sit outside."

The view from the deck was of the farmland the developers were invading. The grazing cows were visible over a high wall at the rear of Kandle's property. Watching them, Roger held his body stiffly, turned away from Greg.

"Ira tried to commit suicide yesterday," Greg began.

"I heard."

"Innocent man on Death Row was bad enough, Roger. This is getting appalling now, don't you think?"

"Stuff it," Kandle growled. "Ira Sullivan is a convicted killer. You had your trial, the jury sent him away."

"Which is just what they would have done to poor old Bowser if he'd gone to trial."

Poor old Bowser, who almost pulled life on a manslaughter charge. Poor old Bowser, who could thank his stars that Roger Kandle years ago didn't like the smell around his case. That Roger Kandle years ago hadn't yet decided to make his way in this world.

At the mention of Bowser, Roger frowned and fell silent. "What's the point here, Greg?" he said finally. "Why have you intruded on my family?"

Greg mulled that question. Roger was forty-eight, he knew, just two years away from a good pension. He planned to retire then; he'd talked for years of becoming a fishing guide. He had a small boat on a lake up in the mountains, and a trailer on a patch of coastal land he owned way north of Pirate's Beach. With a family that adored him, he must feel blessed.

"I've been sidetracked for a long time," Greg said. "What is it, Roger? Why did this happen?"

Kandle twisted in his chair, looked back at his house. Then he shook his head. "Don't know what you're talking about."

A door burst open, and Sofia skipped outside, defying calls from her mother to leave the men alone. She climbed on her daddy's lap, holding a drawing that looked something like their new puppy. "I just did it," she said. "It's Goldy."

Miriam stuck her head out the door, calling her daughter, but Sofia wrapped her arms around Roger's arm. "My daddy likes me, he says it's okay," she sang back to her mother. Then she turned to Roger. "Who do you love most? Mommy or me? Kelly? Erica? What's the order?"

Roger cupped her face in his hand. "I'm not going to make lists," he said. "But I will say there's nothing in the world I love more than you."

That didn't quite satisfy Sofia. "But who do you love *most*? What about your parents? Grandma and Grandpa?"

Roger had forgotten Greg. "I love them, too," he told his daughter. "But there's no one I love more than you."

Sofia thought that over for a moment. "I'll always love

my parents best. When I have kids, I'll say my parents first."

Roger stroked her hair. "I don't think so," he said. "But we'll see."

Miriam's calls finally prevailed. Sofia jumped off her dad's lap and ran back inside.

"She's adorable," Greg said.

Roger started at those words; he wasn't accustomed to outsiders gaining such intimate glimpses of his family. "Yeah," he muttered, "she sure is."

It must haunt him, Greg imagined. His children, watching him every moment. If there was anyone in this sorry deal who might break, it was Kandle.

"It must be so hard being a parent," Greg said.

Kandle's eyes clouded, uncertain where they were headed.

"It must be so hard teaching your kids right from wrong."

Kandle started to answer, then stopped.

"Tell me, Roger. How do you teach your children what to be? Which way to turn?"

Kandle flushed, but still said nothing.

"By example, I imagine. Isn't that it, Roger? Better than lectures, right? You act, they absorb? Is that how it works, Roger?"

Kandle clenched his fists. Greg tensed, ready to react. Then he saw he needn't. Roger's hands were curled in pain, not belligerence. He sat bent over in his chair, drawing a long breath. A moment later, he rose, walked to the edge of his deck, keeping his back to Greg. There he bent, began rewinding a tangled garden hose. That done, he turned to a large potted geranium and started plucking withered leaves. Next, he fussed with the brackets of a loose shelf on his barbecue. He jiggled them, trying to get them to slide into their slots. Instead, one bracket popped off, bounced toward the edge of the deck. "Shit," Roger muttered to himself, reaching to catch it. When he finally turned back to Greg, he was waving a hand at his house.

"This is the only thing that matters to me," he said. "The only thing."

"I understand. But this case needs to be undone."

Roger jammed his hands into his pockets, then moved slowly back toward his chair as if he were approaching his execution. He sat down, cupped his face in his hands. "I will tell you this story," he said. "But I will deny ever doing so."

Greg nodded. "Fair enough." Promises again, so someone will talk to him.

"You're right," Roger began. "You have been side-tracked. Funny thing is, it begins way before the post-master's murder. Has nothing to do with his murder, really. Wilson's murder is almost the end of the story, not the beginning."

Roger looked relieved to be talking at last.

"It starts about a half year before the murder. Out of the blue, we begin getting inquiries about Ira Sullivan. What do we have on him, what can we get on him?"

"Inquiries? From where?"

Roger shrugged. "Taylor fields them, so I can't say exactly. Some came from Sacramento, that I eventually managed to figure out. The A.G.'s office or the governor's, I'm not sure. I'm not positive even Dennis knows who was really behind it."

Greg couldn't help thinking of his session in the A.G.'s office, and Kim's meetings at Main Justice. "Some folks just tend to get heard more than others," he said. "They get to sit in conference rooms and share their viewpoints."

Roger nodded, even though he had no idea what Greg meant.

"Right," he said. "Anyway, someone wants something on Ira this time. Not made up, mind you, not rigged. Something real, something that will discredit him. We're not told why. We are simply asked, What do you have on Sullivan?"

"What did Taylor come up with?"

"Not enough, at first. Dennis thought he'd satisfied

Sacramento. Some small-time drug dealing, couple fights in a bar, too many nights at the Foghorn. Problem was, those were all in the past, all well known about Ira. Turned out whoever was asking wanted more than a few old blemishes. Why, I don't know to this day. I'm not even sure Dennis knows."

Poor Ira, Greg thought. He'd regarded the missing plutonium as a bluff, an empty bargaining ploy. Yet he must have been right on target. Ground zero. Ira hadn't realized just how effectively he was goosing Rolfson.

"Dennis was frantic?" Greg asked.

Roger allowed a faint smile. "Yes, Dennis was frantic. So many to please. The governor, the A.G., who knows? Dennis sees this as a gorgeous opportunity. The governor making noises about running for president, the A.G. aiming for governor. Dennis imagines himself the next A.G. Except, he can't deliver what's needed. He had us tailing Ira, for Chrissake. Which meant I had to spend a lot of cold, wet nights staring at the Foghorn. Nothing, though. Just a sad, sad man."

"Then the postmaster is murdered," Greg said.

Roger punched his thick leg with a fist. "It was incredible, Greg. One minute Dennis is twisting in the wind, next minute he's a hero. Postmaster gets shot, we pick up Sandy Polson. Who on her own nominates Ira as the killer. I swear, Greg, I swear. Because she'd been with him at the Foghorn, I guess. Figured he'd fit the bill."

"Dennis really buys her story?"

"He manages to convince himself, I think he truly does. She tells it so well, you saw that in the courtroom. And Paul Platt corroborates her. Dennis obviously wants Ira to be guilty. But there's more to it than that. He's got a believable story. He's got a story a jury will buy."

"Then the flaws pop up," Greg said.

"Right, but by then, Taylor's committed, Taylor's certain. He's been talking long distance ever since Sandy first fingered Ira. He's told Sacramento he's got Ira on a murder charge. He's told them there's two eyewitnesses identifying Ira. And Sacramento has clapped him on the back, sent bouquets, talked nice about the future. Sacramento is happy, Sacramento is delighted."

"Justice will be served," Greg said, "at the same time Taylor's friends are."

"Exactly," Roger said. "Something else, though, apart from Sacramento. In the office, Dennis keeps talking about a death sentence. Cold-blooded shooting during a felony armed robbery, plus a past record—that's special circumstances. Dennis has never had a death penalty conviction. He wants that notch on his belt."

"But why not get it on Sandy?" Greg asked.

Kandle shook his head. "Come on, Greg, you're the lawyer, not me. You know how unlikely it is to get a jury to hang a woman."

Of course he did. There'd been only one woman executed in the country since the Supreme Court allowed executions to resume in 1976. Women were hard to hang. Well-spoken women with classy, convincing demeanors would be just about impossible.

To make a death penalty case, a prosecutor has to transform a defendant from one of "us," a member of the human community, to one of "them," the predators who would destroy it. Jurors are not going to condemn someone who looks or acts like them. So in deciding whether to seek death, a key factor is what prosecutors see in the faces of their communities. "The mirror theory," Professor Hammilberg called it. A theory that explains why those who end up on Death Row are disproportionately poor and black—not us, but them. A theory that also explains why Dennis Taylor figured he could never get a Death Row conviction of Sandy Polson. Sandy Polson—us, not them.

Ira Sullivan once had been an us, not a them. But years of unraveling, years of meth and booze and the Foghorn crowd, had pushed him close enough to them that Dennis Taylor could strike. Particularly since Ira didn't remember anything about the murder night. Bottom line, Ira was the better defendant; Sandy, the better witness.

"Yes," Greg said. "A jury would not hang Sandy Polson. Fundamental lesson, Hammilberg's Law. The law of our land."

Roger rose, walked to the far end of his deck, started fussing again with his barbecue brackets. "What could I have done?" he asked, not looking up. "What could I have done?"

Greg started to respond, then stopped himself. Roger had a point. What could he have done?

All that transpired was legal, after all. Skirting on the edge, but passable, allowable. No doubt Rolfson never asked anyone to cook the evidence or frame Ira. They just made inquiries among their friends in Sacramento. Who passed the matter on to Dennis. Who did nothing but play the role of prosecutor.

For all his courtroom machinations, Taylor had never broken the rules. Not even with June Blossom. Yes, he played fast and loose, skirted on the edge. But who hasn't coached some witnesses, discouraged others? That's the adversarial system, as Greg had so often been advised. That's Bob Lasorda, star Florida prosecutor, now a venerable state judge, sending his FBI expert to fish in the Gulf Stream.

It didn't matter precisely why Dennis Taylor decided to charge Ira Sullivan, for he had wide-ranging prosecutorial discretion. All that mattered was whether he'd calculated correctly. By the rule of law, he had: The jury had embraced the state's version of events; the jury had validated Taylor's judgment. That was not a crime, not an outrage. That was how things worked.

What an absolutely unassailable situation, Greg realized. In the end, there truly was no real connection between Devil's Peak and the postmaster's murder. Six months apart, different worlds, different players. No connecting lines, no paper trails, no thumbprints. Just a prosecutor, doing his job. His everyday, by-the-book, adversarial job.

Scandal isn't what's illegal, Greg reminded himself. It's what's legal. Legal and done all the time. How wildly funny. He'd solved the mystery; he'd cracked the case. And yet, there was no wrong to right.

"Never you mind, Roger," Greg said. "There's nothing you could have done."

Graciously, Miriam invited Greg to join the Kandle family for an early dinner outside on their deck. Roger barbecued chicken while Miriam tossed a salad and sautéed fresh zucchini. Greg, left to visit with the girls, found himself cajoled into being their playmate. They were shopkeepers, he a customer eyeing bracelets and key chains. They ran game booths, he tossed balls into empty milk bottles. They were teachers, he their student at story time. The stories they told dazzled Greg. Flipping the pages of the books they'd chosen—*The Secret Garden*; *Snow White*; *Alexander and the Terrible, Horrible, No Good, Very Bad Day*—they each embellished as they read. Instead of Mary Lennox's parents being too busy to pay attention and leaving her in the care of an *ayah*, Kelly had Mary lose them in a blameless windstorm. Instead of the seven dwarfs helping and protecting Snow White from her wicked stepmother, Erica had the dwarfs first die in a fire when a candle fell over, then revive when it turned out to be just Snow White's dream. Instead of Alexander getting gum in his hair and tripping over his skateboard and falling in the mud, Sofia had Alexander dwelling on a special private hill with his two best friends.

Then it was Greg's turn to read. He picked *Babushka's Doll*. As he read—*It wasn't that Natasha was a truly naughty child*—all three girls cuddled against him, heads on his shoulders, hands on his arms. He labored to keep still, so they would not move, so the moment would not end.

"I liked that," Sofia said, when Greg reached the end of the book. "Some movies we see, I don't like."

"Why not?" Greg asked.

"Too much fighting, people getting angry. Grown-ups

sometimes are, like, crazy." To illustrate her point, Sofia rolled her eyes and drew a circle in the air next to her head.

There was a fight at the table, nonetheless, over who got to sit next to the visitor. In the end, Miriam had to draw upon complicated geometry so all three girls somehow were equidistant from Greg. It was dark out, the sky filled with stars, by the time they finished eating.

Roger walked Greg down the driveway to his car. Despite the fun with the girls, it had been an awkward evening, for the two men were not friends. Roger looked as if he regretted being goaded into so much revelation.

When he spoke, though, it was still about the murder prosecution. "Taylor sure burned Sandy Polson in the end, I will say that."

Greg stopped walking. "I assumed she worked a pretty good deal with Dennis," he said. "After all she did for him."

Roger snorted with surprise. "You don't know? Their plea bargaining fell through. Taylor wouldn't make it sweet enough."

"No," Greg said. "I didn't know."

"She went to trial. Down in Santa Barbara County. Maybe that's why you didn't hear. Her lawyer got her a change of venue after Ira's trial."

"And?"

"And they convicted her. Second degree murder. Jury didn't buy that she was just an innocent tagalong."

"When?"

"Two weeks ago."

Greg wanted to dance, to howl at the moon. Finally, Dennis Taylor had made a mistake. In Florida, in Hilliard's case, Bob Lasorda knew enough to give Frankie paper. You make sure your star witness walks, you make sure he stays happy with his lot. Taylor had overreached. Not satisfied with putting Ira on Death Row, he'd wanted to get Sandy, too.

Sandy, who now must be raging at the Chumash County

district attorney. Sandy, who now must be filled with venom toward Dennis Taylor.

Greg had always focused on Paul Platt, believing he was the one who'd flip. He'd steered clear of Sandy Polson, steered clear of her cool, bottomless gaze. No longer, though. He saw his way plainly.

Sandy Polson had been the perfect witness for the prosecution. Now Sandy Polson would be the perfect witness for the defense.

TWENTY

She was keeping him waiting a good long while, Greg finally realized. He'd been lost in his thoughts for half an hour, sitting in an attorneys' interview room at the Santa Lucia Women's Correctional Center. This state prison was far less forbidding than the one nearby where Ira dwelled. Rather than dirty walls and a concrete floor, Greg had found in the reception area a cathedral ceiling and a glossily polished vinyl-tile floor. He'd been greeted by a cheerful young guard in coat and tie, who led him to the interview room as if they were touring a hospital. Now, watching the main visiting area through a window, Greg could see women inmates mingling casually with their families. They wore slacks and blouses, not prison garb.

Sandy Polson had agreed readily to his visit. You couldn't phone in to a prisoner, only send a letter, which is what he'd done. She'd called immediately, invited him to come on up. She'd sounded plainly interested, even appreciative. She welcomed the attention, Greg guessed.

Where was she now, though? The guard had said she'd be right out. Might Sandy still be playing games from her prison cell? Greg imagined guards struggling frantically in her finely spun webs. It was so easy for those unhampered by a conscience to gain the upper hand.

He'd done what he could since his visit with Roger Kandle. He'd called Jimmy, briefed him, put him on the trail of Rolfson's Sacramento connections. They had nothing solid, and Roger Kandle of course wouldn't talk to a reporter, but Jimmy at least was working the story, ringing doorbells, yanking people's chains. Greg had also visited Kim Rosen, by mutual agreement in her office. She'd worn a navy blue suit that day, and they'd kept the conversation focused on legal matters. She'd offered to do research regarding motions for new trials. What such motions required, what arguments worked best—he'd been through it all once before with Joe Hilliard, but that was years ago, under a different state's rules. Kim's help now would be invaluable.

It wouldn't be enough, though. Greg needed Sandy Polson. He'd restudied her case file, reviewed every page back to age eight. The well-off, cultured upbringing. The false, peculiar stories, the rape charge against her stepfather, the goading of her siblings, the schemes and manipulations. He'd read her various statements to the Chumash County detectives, and her testimony at trial. He felt ready—ready as he could be.

"Here we are." The guard had opened the door. Sandy Polson stood before him, smiling. Looking quite lovely, he thought. She's been primping, he guessed. That's what delayed her. The touch of blusher and lip gloss, the powder-blue blouse that matched her eyes, the lushly tousled hair. Sandy Polson had been getting ready for a date.

"Mr. Monarch," she said, taking his hand, looking him in the eye. "I'm so glad you came to see me. I've been wanting to talk to you."

This, Greg realized, was the first time he'd been alone with her. Other than their public exchanges in Judge Hedgespeth's courtroom, they'd never spoken directly to each other.

A psychopath, the doctors called her. A sociopathic orientation toward life. An extremely effective manipulator, obscured always by a pleasant manner. Clever, evasive, expert at exploiting the sympathies of those around her. "Sugary sweet," always gives the "right" answers, but below the surface, "hostility lurks." Greg steeled himself.

As far as he knew, he'd never dealt with such a person. Never known such a person.

"Is that so?" he said.

"Yes." Polson sat down across from him, crossed her legs, brushed a strand of hair off her forehead. "You did such a valiant job at Ira's trial. I wanted to tell you that. And tell you also that I was sorry for what happened to Ira."

"Death Row happened," Greg said.

Sandy neither laughed nor flared up. She looked concerned. "Yes, Death Row."

"Where he tried to commit suicide a few days ago."

Sandy winced, raised her hand to her mouth. "Oh my," she said. "That is awful. Of course, this whole thing is awful. Ira Sullivan should never even be on Death Row."

"My thought exactly."

"Well, you are right," Sandy continued. "I can't believe Judge Hedgespeth. I would never have imagined he'd sentence Ira to death. You're the lawyer, not me. But those hardly were the worst aggravating circumstances, were they? You can't possibly call Ira a hard-core felon."

Greg watched her carefully. "You sound as if you sat next to me in Professor Hammilberg's law school class."

Sandy shrugged. "No, I just read a lot. I thought once of being a lawyer, but never managed to get to law school. What you lawyers do, I so admire."

"I can't imagine why you feel that way," Greg said.

Sandy smiled and tilted her head, showing just a whisper of mockery. Greg had seen that expression from her more than once on the witness stand.

"You lawyers bring order to chaos," Sandy explained. "That's why. You make things rational. The world out there, it's a mess, right? No rhyme or reason to who wins, who loses, who's happy. I suppose there never will be reason, but at least the law makes it a little less random. The law, and the lawyers."

"How nice of you to think so," Greg said.

"Of course, most lawyers I know are terribly depressed,"

Sandy continued. "Lots of anxious, bored insomniacs. No wonder. They start out for idealistic reasons, then discover they have to distort their personalities. Twist themselves out of shape, be nasty and aggressive. Their poor, hidden, sensitive selves can't bear that. It's so sad really. Don't you think?"

Greg shifted in his seat. "Indeed, it is sad."

On and on Sandy talked now, expansive and graceful, her manner assuming a natural camaraderie between them. From the law and lawyers, she moved to Chumash County public affairs—environmental protections, timber harvests, land subdivisions—then, after mention of a local arts program, to Hamlet's essential conflict, Ben Webster's way with a saxophone, the existential angst in Dostoyevsky. Greg listened with appreciation. Not until she started exploring structured versus progressive approaches to early education did he finally force himself to intercede.

"I came to see you because of what happened at your trial, Sandy," he said. "It seems to me that Dennis Taylor has badly double-crossed you."

Sandy offered a nonchalant shrug. "I thought I'd get off easy, maybe even avoid prison. But remember my testimony at Ira's trial. I said there were no deals, no promises from Mr. Taylor."

"Yes, I remember," Greg replied. "That is how you testified."

Their eyes met then, silently; it was Sandy who turned away first. She looked as if she was trying to remember something.

"I was following Ira around," she said finally. "I didn't realize where it was taking me. I ended up where I didn't want to be. I saw something I wished I hadn't. I thought it was wrong. I told the detectives and D.A. End of story."

Greg nodded. "Sandy, are you a meth addict like Ira?"

The question, meant to unnerve her, did not. Sandy presented only a mildly rueful grimace. "It's what ended my university days," she said. "Prison therapy has been helping me now. I've been rather self-indulgent in my life, Mr. Monarch. But now I mean to turn things around. I mean to get better, then seek parole."

Greg marveled. When she talked about turning herself around, the words made sense, but she sounded as if she were saying she needed to get her shoes polished.

"You didn't just use," he observed. "You also dealt."

Sandy tilted her head again, this time rolling her eyes. "You wouldn't believe who I sold drugs to," she said. "Very powerful people."

Greg labored to make sense of this woman. So utterly sincere, so acutely rational, but finally, so preposterous.

"Come on, Sandy. Aren't you angry with Dennis Taylor?"

She laughed, seemingly at a private joke he didn't understand. "Now, what would that get me, Mr. Monarch? Losing my temper? Indulging in such unpleasant feelings?"

"Your presentencing probation report, Sandy. It describes at length your anger with Taylor. How 'your faith and respect for officers of the law is ruined.' How 'the people in the system are just as corrupt as the people on the streets.' "

"Oh that," Sandy said. "I don't really think those are my words. Anyway, I was in shock after the trial. I was distraught."

Maybe she truly believes whatever she says, Greg reasoned. Maybe that's why she's so undisturbed, so unconflicted.

He had to admit—in a way, he envied her that state. Even if she was a sociopath. Truth was, sociopaths mesmerized him. Such aberrations of nature, like the unusual rocks Greg's dad used to identify on their camping trips. To appear normal, but to have no moral core, no regard for the consequences of your actions—what must that be like? From time to time, he'd listened to his father discuss the question, but he'd never heard an answer.

He did know that doctors no longer even called people

like Sandy Polson sociopaths. The category didn't exist as a formal diagnosis anymore. In 1949, Blakiston's *New Gould Medical Dictionary* defined *psychopath* as "a morally irresponsible person." In 1952, *psychopath* officially became known as *sociopath*. By 1968, *sociopath*—along with all manner of psychological maladies—was being called *personality disorder, antisocial type*.

It had been years now since psychiatrists sat endlessly beside people such as Sandy, seeking to observe and understand. They'd stopped the effort in part because their payment sources dried up, and in part because treatment rarely seemed to cure anyone. It was hard even to define what constituted a cure, for compared to other patients in mental institutions, sociopaths appeared utterly normal. Doctors were frequently fooled into signing their releases.

Occasionally, Greg had picked up his dad's old books from the era when psychiatrists still got paid to treat psychopaths for hours on end. Thumbing through brittle pages, he'd detected certain common themes. *Superficial charm and good intelligence . . . Absence of delusions and other signs of irrational thinking . . . Absence of nervousness or psychoneurotic manifestations . . . Never faults of logical reasoning, never verbal confusion, never technical delusion. Rather, a convincing mask of sanity . . . Perfect reproduction of a normal man.*

Reproduction? Was that it? It was difficult to imagine Sandy Polson as merely a replica. Sandy Polson could think along with him, talk to him, relate to him. Was she truly so different? Was it like looking through windows at the zoo when he was a child? Seeing the snakes then had always thrilled him, in a strange, confusing way. To see them, to be so close—but to still be separated.

"Tell me about your daughter," Greg said.

Polson flinched; tears filled her eyes. Then she blinked, smiled, and shook her head. "I'm sorry," she said. "That's off-limits."

Had he forced an opening? In her probation record, there'd been mention of a child, the result of an affair with a married man. The father had sole custody. Because she'd tried once to take the little girl for a summer—"kidnap," they called it—the father also had a restraining order keeping her away.

"Ira lost a little boy too," Greg said. "A different situation. His is lost for good. Killed in an accident. Did you know that?"

Sandy pursed her lips. "No, I didn't. How awful, how terribly awful."

Now Greg wasn't so sure about that opening. Could it be, she'd mimicked a sentiment about her own daughter? The notion clawed at him.

"Sandy, Ira is going to die for a crime he didn't commit. You know he's innocent. You know this is wrong. Tell the court what really happened. For Ira's sake, for your sake. For the sake of all the children who must live in this world."

Without expression now, Sandy shook her head. "I can't do that," she said evenly. "I've already told the truth. I can't now tell a lie."

He'd misstepped, Greg realized. Misreading the tears in her eyes, he'd projected his sentiments on her. Clutching tightly to himself, he'd failed to imagine her.

"You sound as if you're judging me," Sandy said. "You sound as if you think I'm an immoral person."

"No, no. It's just that . . ." Greg searched vainly for a response.

Sandy turned away. "I'll never change my story," she said.

Jimmy O'Brien looked back and forth at the two men sitting across from him, trying to decide which of them he more despised. Horace Macauley's weasel face inspired in him a visceral loathing, but Horace at least retained some traces of being a journalist, if not a good one. William Blankard, on the other hand, didn't even pretend to like newspapers, or, for that matter, the people who put them out. To the general counsel of the *News-Times*, all reporters were scruffy loose cannons, put on this earth to cause him problems. Whenever Blankard reviewed one of Jimmy's articles for possible legal problems, he frowned and pulled at his earlobe and looked as if he wished the whole mess of words would simply evaporate. "My daughter's college education hinges on decisions like this," he'd mutter. "Not sure we can run this piece. They might get angry at us."

They were sitting in a cramped, bare cubicle that passed as the editor's office at the *News-Times*. They'd been there for an hour now, walking sentence by sentence through what Jimmy had cobbled together on Rolfson Industries and Ira Sullivan's grand jury appearance. With an ironic tone, anonymous sources, and the strategic arrangement of paragraphs, Jimmy had tried to raise the possibility of a connection between those topics and Ira's subsequent prosecution on a murder charge.

Tried—but largely failed.

"O'Brien, you just don't have the goods," Macauley was saying, sounding not the least disappointed. "No hard proof, just insinuation. You're trying to jump from A to C. You've given us something that's unpublishable."

Blankard nodded vigorously, happy to have an ally. "We run this, by the time all the lawsuits are over, Rolfson would own this newspaper." That notion gave him pause. "Of course," he added, "don't know why they'd want to."

Jimmy couldn't summon the will to argue. As spineless and self-serving as were these two men sitting before him, he knew they were right this time. Not even the cowboy foreman, Mac McCasson, had been willing to talk on the record about Sullivan's grand jury appearance. Kim Rosen would only say things like "We're proud of what we accomplished; our settlement involved a record fine." Dennis Taylor basically sneered—"The jurors have ruled, the justice system has spoken." Rolfson passed him around to robotic public relations types. Sacramento stared blankly, as if no one in the A.G.'s or governor's office had ever heard of Rolfson or Ira Sullivan or Chumash County.

"Okay, okay," Jimmy said. "I'll keep digging some more. Maybe we can come up with something."

Macauley shook his head. "I don't think so, O'Brien. You've been on this for weeks now."

"Just a few more days."

"No." Macauley turned and pawed through a pile of files and envelopes on the counter behind him. When he faced Jimmy again, he was clutching a single piece of paper. "This came in the other day," he said. "Another nurse wants to talk about those funny deaths over at the county hospital. You've been promising me something on that for weeks. Maybe this latest kook will inspire you."

Jimmy accepted the sheet of paper without looking at it. "Come on, Horace," he tried again. "Let me stay on the Rolfson story."

Macauley already was ushering him to the door, though. The editor's narrow, bony face was at his shoulder; it looked to Jimmy as if Horace had added another inch to his elevator shoes. "I don't want to hear about Rolfson anymore," Macauley said. "Talk to me about the county hospital."

Greg labored to pay attention as Jimmy described the sorry experience with his editors. They were eating lunch on the creekside patio at Stella's Café. "Tore the mother apart," Jimmy was saying. "By the time they finished, my story was in shreds. 'Unpublishable,' Horace told me. Maybe so, but truth is, they wouldn't have printed it no matter what . . ."

Greg couldn't stay with him. His mind kept roaming back to Sandy Polson. He'd visited her several times since their first meeting. She always welcomed him, even encouraged him to come more frequently. She never wavered, though, never lost her composure, never showed anger at Dennis Taylor. She also never changed her story.

She was following Ira, she saw something she wished she hadn't, end of story.

Following Ira. Greg had eventually turned to his client for advice on how to handle Sandy Polson. Ira still resided in a special hospital ward at the California Men's Colony, but he was cogent now, nearly ready to return to the general prison population. He spent much of his time scrawling in a thick black leather journal Greg had brought him one week after his suicide attempt. Put it all down in writing, Greg had urged. Get it all on paper. Ira blinked at the journal vacantly for two days, then picked up a pen. His eyes blazed with impatience now whenever Greg visited; he wanted to get back to his writing. His brush with death appeared to have provoked him in some way. *Goddamn black-market pills,* Ira regularly growled. *Thought they'd get me to heaven. Look where they landed me. Stomachache, headache, tubes and needles. This isn't heaven, that's for sure. Goddamn pills . . .*

"Tell me about Sandy," Greg urged time and again, sitting on the edge of Ira's bed. "Help me press her buttons."

Ira always gave the question careful thought, but he couldn't help. "No buttons to push," he'd usually say. "That's just the point about her, no buttons to push."

"Her history," Greg would implore. "Something in her past. Something she talked to you about. Something that seemed to bother her."

Once or twice, Ira appeared on the edge of an answer, as if nursing a memory. Each time, though, whatever tugged at him slipped away before taking shape. Whenever Greg turned to leave, his last image was of Ira frowning and raking his hair and chewing on the end of his pen.

At a loss, one afternoon Greg turned not to the prison but to the county library, where he walked the aisles pulling down every book he could find on psychopaths. Some he remembered from his father's shelves, some were new to him. Virtually all talked of psychopaths as being mentally ill.

> Many would perhaps dismiss all this with the thought that our man might be more properly called a bad fellow and his status left at that . . . Might be called immoral, vulgar, or criminal . . . But it is confusing to interpret such a personality in terms of bad and good . . . It is necessary to postulate that the psychopath has a genuine and very serious disability. In actual living, his failure is so complete, it is hard to see how it could be achieved by anyone less defective than a downright madman. Psychopaths look normal but suffer from a grave psychiatric disorder . . .

"Bullshit," Greg said out loud. "Utter nonsense."

Jimmy blinked and paused, a meat loaf sandwich halfway to his mouth. "You talking to me?" he asked. "Or is there someone else here?"

Greg ignored the question. "Tell me, Jimmy. You think people who do evil things are sick? Do they have a disorder? Or is it just human nature?"

Jimmy took a bite of his sandwich and chewed. "What are you talking about?"

Greg waved the question away. "Nothing, sorry, just thinking out loud. What were you saying about the newspaper?"

Jimmy studied Greg. "I was saying how dumb I was. That's what I was saying. It took me a while to realize that no matter how many more facts or quotes I rounded up, they'd never run my piece."

"Why not?"

"Because guess who has just joined the board of directors of my newspaper's parent company? Who now sits on the board and plays golf with my CEO?"

A wild grin had spread across Jimmy's ample face.

"Come on, Jimmy, I give up."

"Daniel P. Bellinger."

"Okay, who is Daniel P. Bellinger?"

Jimmy chortled. "Thought you knew, Monarch. Well,

you should know, anyway. Daniel P. Bellinger is chairman and CEO of Rolfson Industries."

Greg gaped, unable to respond. Jimmy loved it.

"Way I hear," Jimmy said, "Bellinger and my CEO celebrated their new union by flying Rolfson's private jet all the way to New York City. Just to have dinner at their favorite restaurant."

At dusk, Greg walked the creekside path near his home, pondering what to tell Ira about all they faced. Jimmy's CEO story, the judiciary's deep-rooted resistance to recantations, the State Bar disciplinary panel's latest notice—each matter threatened Ira's tenuous stability.

Yet Greg could keep his mind on none of them. By now, he was thinking of little but Sandy Polson. Sandy haunted his dreams; Sandy remained as elusive to him as truth itself.

What drove this woman, what explained her? Like his pal Cindy Seaman in the probation department, Greg saw no answers in the customary childhood trauma theories. Cindy had been right—it wasn't a dark rage, but an eerie lack of something that defined this woman. Greg shuddered at the notion. He'd rather battle a ranting wild man with a smoldering core than face Sandy Polson's bloodless void. Creepy and spooky, Cindy had said. Greg believed Sandy much more terrifying than that.

Prowling now along the banks of Graciosa Creek, he thought of Melville's inscrutable, implacable White Whale. *That intangible malignity . . . that ghastly whiteness . . . such a dumb blankness, full of meaning*. Was Sandy simply a random fact of nature? If only Greg could see her anger, or fathom her injury—then he could talk of causes and reasons, of deviation and cures. He detected nothing, though. He had no means to color her appalling void. He sensed that she was pulling him to the edge of an abyss he'd long avoided. Yet he saw no choice but to inch toward that perilous rim.

Of course, he could, if he chose, turn not to certain poets

for understanding, but rather to certain doctors. Those physicians whom Greg had read would surely call Sandy's a sick mind, even if they had trouble with a precise diagnosis. They would surely say Sandy suffered from a "grave psychiatric disorder," even if they could not identify its source. Greg recognized the allure of this approach. Try as he might, though, he couldn't buy it. Sandy finally looked too familiar to him, too much a part of the natural order.

If Sandy Polson could be explained by psychological jargon, who couldn't? What about Dennis Taylor? If Sandy was sick, wasn't Dennis also? They called one a psychopath, the other a crafty prosecutor, but where was the difference? There was none, Greg believed. He thought he'd never dealt with someone like Sandy, but of course he had. Often, quite often.

Greg turned toward La Graciosa's central plaza. It had been weeks since he'd visited JB's Red Rooster Tavern. He felt thirsty.

Sitting before his computer at the *News-Times*, scanning rows of data on his monitor, Jimmy suddenly froze. He punched at his keyboard, scrolled back through the lines of names and dates. That nurse at the county hospital had slipped him a floppy disk full of interesting information indeed. He had before him summaries of every confidential action taken by the hospital's peer review committee, reaching back two decades.

Here was where the local medical community handled its dirty laundry, disciplining or rebuking colleagues privately, without the mess of public hearings, lawyers, tarnished careers. Such private self-policing had its advantages—everyone could speak openly—but the process also tended to protect bad doctors from public scrutiny. Peer review committees sometimes hesitated to identify problems, sometimes hesitated to administer more than slaps on the wrist to people they knew well.

From what Jimmy could tell, such hesitation hadn't

been uncommon at the county hospital. Three peculiar deaths involving the same surgeon. Each time, a peer review committee had basically looked the other way. Each time, the committee's chairman had signed off on this surgeon, letting him return to the operating room untarnished.

The names of the committee's chairmen over the years—that's what had claimed Jimmy's attention as he scrolled through the database. The latest one he didn't recognize, but he knew much about the chairman who'd presided over the first two inquiries. Everyone, after all, had heard of the venerable Dr. Paul A. Monarch.

Ira Sullivan paced around the attorneys' interrogation room at the California Men's Colony while Greg watched from the table where he sat. Ira had summoned him to this visit. Been thinking about your Sandy Polson questions, Ira had declared on the phone. Thinking and dreaming.

Now Ira turned to face him. "No buttons to push, that's what I said about Sandy. Maybe I was wrong. Maybe there are some."

Greg nodded, flipped open a notebook.

"Push her about drunks lying on the street," Ira said. "Something about that bothers her. Don't know what, don't know how, but maybe there's a button there."

Greg raised his eyebrows. Ira resumed his pacing. The memory was hazy, but he recalled that drunk sprawled on the boardwalk outside the Foghorn. He recalled Sandy yanking him away with great distaste, then leading him down to the distant shore.

"It was just something that happened one night," Ira explained. "Wouldn't mean much unless you knew Sandy. She showed herself a little, which wasn't the norm. That's why I remember it. Sandy opened her purse a crack."

Greg put his pen down. "Seems kind of weak, Ira. We need her exploding, not flickering."

Ira sat down across from Greg. "You're not going to

find a bloody open wound. You're looking for a sore to scratch."

Greg shook his head. "That's hardly even a sore," he said gently. "So she doesn't like drunken bums. Lots of people don't."

Ira slammed the table. "You're only going to get flickers from her, don't you see? You're not going to get a goddamn explosion, you're not going to get a goddamn parade. You're only going to get—"

Ira suddenly froze, as if he'd touched a high-voltage wire. An image had seized his mind. Sandy, approaching him after talking on a pay phone. Sandy, coolly driving the six ball into the corner pocket as she sweetly explained, "These things happen." Sandy so nonchalant, showing only the slightest passing annoyance when he impulsively blurted, "No way, no way" about a blown meth deal.

A flicker of annoyance.

"Okay, Greg, listen carefully," Ira said. "I've got something else for you."

"It's going to be in the paper," Jimmy explained. "That's why I'm telling you now."

He and Greg were sitting at Stella's, computer printouts spread on the table before them. At first, Jimmy had considered keeping this from Greg. He could spike the whole story easily enough; Macauley and Blankard certainly wouldn't mind avoiding the problems it created. Upon reflection, Jimmy had decided not to.

"It's no big deal, really," he said. "It's just how things work."

Greg nodded, feeling oddly calm. He flipped through the pages. Yes, there was his dad's name. It looked so unnatural, sitting at the bottom of those official reports full of technical jargon. He tried to imagine his father at these peer review meetings; he tried to imagine his father signing his name. He could not.

Yet his dad had signed it. There it was. *Paul Monarch, M.D.*

Greg moved his face closer to the page. He studied his father's scrawl as if it were a voice from the past. A nagging, discordant voice.

A faint, distant memory began to form. An evening long ago, late at night. He'd been put to bed. A phone ringing in the kitchen, his father answering. Greg rising, tiptoeing, softly lifting the receiver on the upstairs hallway extension. His father, talking quietly to a stranger, not sounding like himself. Greg, puzzled and scared.

Whom had his father talked to that night? What had they said? Greg couldn't recall, or never knew. He'd been nine then, maybe ten.

Had it all been illusory? Had his father forever misrepresented himself to his son? Or had Greg simply misunderstood? Such confusion, of course, would not be considered unusual in any family. So much was hidden between parent and child, however close they were.

Perhaps certain demands beyond his control obliged Dr. Paul Monarch to sign those reports. Perhaps he thought it paramount to fend off intrusion by lawyers, just as he later felt compelled to battle the insurance companies. Perhaps he deemed it necessary to choose the lesser of two evils.

"There must be an explanation," Greg said. "If only he were alive to tell us."

Jimmy cleared his throat. "Like I say, it's no big deal. It's just how things work."

Yes, of course. How things work.

Still—maybe Dr. Paul Monarch had been ill. Yes, ill. That could explain his father's conduct. In fact, that could explain everything. Maybe the doctors were right. Maybe all the morally careless folks walking the earth are ill. What an extraordinary notion. All the venal sham out there came not from bad people but poor, sick ones. In corporate boardrooms, halls of government, judges' chambers, hospital wards—everywhere, masks of sanity reigned.

Greg shoved the computer printout back toward Jimmy. "Great scoop," he muttered. "Congratulations. You've figured it all out."

Jimmy frowned as he gathered up the pile of documents. "Well, maybe not everything," he mumbled.

Greg saw clearly now what he'd been doing wrong with Sandy Polson. It was foolish to appeal to her, to reason with her, to try to break through her mask. Instead, he had to let go, give up his own protection, reach through the zoo's glass window. He had to climb into Sandy's cage.

It wouldn't be hard. After all, myriads of people had taught him well. He'd had plenty of wonderful role models.

TWENTY-ONE

"You've made Dennis Taylor's career, Sandy. He's scored big up in Sacramento. Got himself appointed chairman of a blue-ribbon crime commission. I think he's going to run for attorney general off this. Why not? Death sentence for Ira, long years for you. He's on TV every time I turn around. He really did you good."

Greg had been talking to Sandy Polson for well over an hour. They were sitting in the same interview room where they first met. For once, Sandy wasn't shaping the conversation. Greg had been going nonstop; she'd been listening with growing interest. At least, that's how it looked to Greg.

Don't be judgmental, that's what the textbooks advised. Don't moralize. Show you understand her, show you're as angry as she is. Identify with her. Be on her side. Listen. Sympathize. Empathize.

"Dennis Taylor truly did you, Sandy. Not the first time either, right? Anger would be understandable. Fury, even."

Sandy ran her tongue over her upper lip. She appeared genuinely amused at Greg's effort to taunt. "He was just doing his job, Mr. Monarch. He's a prosecutor. That's his role."

"Were all the others in your life prosecutors? All the others who betrayed you?"

Sandy shook her head. "You've been reading too many shrinks, Mr. Monarch. Especially those who write things in my file."

It's hard to do therapy with her. Therapist after therapist had observed that about Sandy. *She won't respond, won't cooperate. Continues to give "right answers" that obviously aren't her true feelings. Is frequently called down by the therapist as being fake.*

One other note in her file: *Only way can get her to express real feeling is keep pressing her until she explodes.*

"You're lying, Sandy. I know you're lying. Paul Platt has started talking. Platt says it's all made up, Platt says you fed him everything."

Sandy sat perfectly still, showing nothing. Greg leaned forward until his face was inches from hers. He kept his tone genial. "Come on now, Sandy, let's not play games. You've been gaming everybody all along, then Taylor gamed you."

Sandy pulled back, recited: "I followed Ira around . . . I saw something I wished I hadn't."

Greg kept it amiable. "Let's get back to the subject, okay?"

"The subject, Mr. Monarch?"

"Your anger. Your anger at Dennis Taylor."

Sandy chuckled. "No, I'm not angry, Mr. Monarch. Anger isn't healthy. You still need to learn that, I'm afraid. If you could only control your temper, Mr. Monarch, you'd do so much better in courtrooms."

Greg dipped his head with regret. "I'm sure you're right, I certainly have heard that advice before. But come on, Sandy, we all sometimes feel angry inside, we all rant and rage and hate, even if we keep it private. You must feel those things. After all, you have good reason to be angry." Greg put his mouth next to her ear. "I'd be angry if I were you."

This time, Sandy turned to him rather than pull away, eyes dancing. "My goodness, Mr. Monarch. I do believe you're projecting."

Greg steeled himself. *That ghastly whiteness . . .* He needed intimacy with her; he needed union with her empty soul. He kept his lips at her ear. "If nobody ever believed me," he whispered, "I'd be angry, too."

Sandy's smile glistened, cold and bright. "You are so amusing, Mr. Monarch, so very amusing."

Greg gambled. "Drunken bums," he murmured. "Drunks lying on the road. Talk about it, Sandy. Come on, Sandy, talk about it. Tell me all about it."

Sandy kept smiling, but said nothing now.

"A drunk lying on the road, Sandy. Tell me all about it."

One finger started tapping the arm of Sandy's chair. "Nothing to tell, Mr. Monarch, no matter what you might have heard. It was an accident, pure and simple, even if certain unpleasant people didn't see it that way. I can't help it if some people are so awfully disbelieving."

If only he knew what she was talking about, if only he knew what next to say. Greg took another chance. "Just like your stepfather, right, Sandy? Just like no one believed you then? Tell me about your stepfather, Sandy. Tell me about that."

Sandy still hung on to her smile, even as her fingers squeezed the arms of her chair.

So what if it never happened, Greg reasoned; it existed in her mind. "When you tried to complain about your stepfather, no one believed you, right? Everyone called you a liar, didn't they? Everyone betrayed you. Everyone scorned you."

No smile at all now.

"That's the way it has always been, Sandy, isn't that right? No one ever believes you, no one ever sees you're telling the truth."

The start of a frown. Sandy looked around her, trying to catch the eye of a guard through the interview room's window. "You are growing tiresome, Mr. Monarch. You are boring me dreadfully."

Greg kept his tone flat and cold. "No one ever believes you. No one ever sees that you're telling the truth."

Sandy bristled now with exasperation. "That's not so

at all, Mr. Monarch. People do believe me. When they get to know me, people find me quite convincing. Even your marvelous district attorney, Dennis Taylor." Sandy leaned toward Greg, gloating. "They all believed me, Mr. Monarch. Every single one of them. Every single one."

Greg looked at her steadily. "Not everyone, Sandy. You know better. Not everyone."

Sandy started to rise. "Please leave, Mr. Monarch. Our visit is over."

Not quite yet, not quite yet.

"What about Ira Sullivan?" Greg asked. "Ira Sullivan didn't believe you, isn't that right, Sandy? Ira Sullivan thought you ripped him off one night. Ira Sullivan called you a liar."

At those words, Sandy froze. Then she slowly, silently, sank back into her chair.

"Tell me about Ira Sullivan, Sandy. Tell me how he scorned you. Tell me how he didn't believe you."

"I . . . How do you . . . I . . ." Sandy blinked and squeezed her hands, no longer certain of her role in this room.

"Tell me everything, Sandy. Tell me about your half brother. Tell me about the drunk. Tell me about your stepfather. Tell me about Ira Sullivan. Tell me how they wouldn't believe you. Tell me how you convinced them. I've heard everyone else's versions, I've read all the reports and statements. All those jerks and creeps, all those revolting people, I've heard all their versions. Now tell me—"

"Their versions? Their versions?" The words came out more sharply than Sandy intended. She tried to cover them with a renewed smile. Too late for that, though. Her lips twisted with disgust. "They were all so terribly dreary," she said. "So utterly horrible. No one ever understood. No one ever believed me." Sandy surrendered finally to a welcome languor. "Yes," she said softly. "I think I will tell you."

Greg, marveling, watched the zoo window slide open.

On and on she talked now, reliving her life, revisiting every perceived betrayal and mistreatment. A dirge from a victim, a howl of indignation, a longing for retribution. A not uncommon story. Coming from Sandy, though, Greg had no idea whether a single word was true.

Her real dad disappearing when she was six. Her stepdad, the music professor; her mother, the failed, frustrated painter. Moving around a lot. Trying to report her stepdad. Junior high teachers, nurses, counselors, all disbelieving her. Everyone saying she was lying. No one even taking her to a doctor.

Maybe she was even telling the truth, Greg thought. It didn't really matter. Warranted or not, Sandy's words finally—for once—reflected rancor. Sandy's words finally provided something he could harness.

If he could only see that rancor, though: Even now, she didn't truly sound angry, not after her initial outburst. Sandy was talking with the same easy composure she'd displayed in Judge Hedgespeth's courtroom. Talking of how she rebelled, ran loose, refused to be disciplined. Of how her parents sent her to a special home. Of how the special home helped her, how she got better.

"Three years at the home, three years of therapy finally got it through my head that not everyone's a threat," Sandy said. "If I'd been left on the path I was going, I could have become a serial killer, Mr. Monarch. That is the truth. I had so much rage."

Rage? In Sandy? *A master liar and manipulator,* the therapists warned. *You must always keep that in mind. Adopted mode of adjustment is manipulating others for her own ends.*

"What about the university?" Greg asked. "What happened there?"

Tears filled Sandy's eyes. "I was on my way to a degree in art history. I was going to teach or work at a museum. I also was going to marry. I was engaged. My goodness. How fast it all fell apart."

None of this, Greg knew, appeared in her case history. "Tell me about it," he said. "Tell me about yourself."

She spoke as if she were confiding intimacies. The fiancé jilting her just weeks before their marriage. A sojourn in Costa Rica, meeting up with a fast crowd. A terrible car accident. Drifting. Another romance gone sour. Then another. Back to the university. Finally, ten years ago, Chumash County. A house in Apple Canyon, waitress jobs, a sort of life. Ira, the Foghorn crowd. Small-time dealing to pay for her own meth. That was it, Sandy said, until the night she bumped into Ira at the Foghorn. Bumped into him, and followed him. The irresistible lure of a sad, lost soul.

Sandy leaned across the table, put her hand on Greg's. It was their first physical contact. "I have a question for you, Mr. Monarch. How do you see me, now that I've told you all this? As an evil liar? Or as a victim, also?" A yearning filled her eyes.

Greg didn't hesitate. "You're clearly a victim, Sandy, clearly. But you don't have to be any longer. You can fight back, you can get even."

Sandy squeezed his hand. "Tell me how."

"There's only one way now. Get Dennis Taylor. Bring him down."

That idea didn't impress her. "Might be a little hard," she pointed out. "He being the venerable district attorney and I being a convicted killer."

"Recant, Sandy. Recant everything. Admit you made everything up. Tell them how Taylor coached you and coerced you. Blame it on Taylor."

Sandy's mind drifted. "I tried to do that once," she said. "But nobody believed me. It wasn't the right story. It wasn't the story they wanted to hear."

Where an ordinary criminal is constantly purposive, aiming consistently toward something, a psychopath seldom works to achieve particular gains. That's what the textbooks said. The textbooks also said typical psychopaths don't commit murder or violence; they're more likely to hustle you than shoot you. When they do kill, it's usually a casual act, committed not for gain or to vent rage, but for amusement. For the satisfaction of having cleverly pulled it off.

"You can do this, Sandy. You can make them believe whatever you want. You can work them, you can convince them."

"Can I?" she asked. "You really think so?"

"Sure you can. You've always been able to convince people. You've always had your way."

What had driven Sandy the night of the postmaster's murder? Greg wondered. A hustle, a scam? Then a casual shot? Which meant so little to her, she had no trouble facing Dennis Taylor with an easy equanimity?

"It's obvious Ira wasn't at the postmaster's that night, Sandy. You gave that story to the cops and they gave it to Paul. Then you coached Paul from the next jail cell over. Until your stories fit, until his matched yours. Until his matched the one you and Dennis cooked up. The one Dennis promised would get you off scot-free."

Sandy wasn't listening. "You know what Dennis said at my trial?" she asked. "He said, 'She's just as accountable, she's just as much to blame.' After all I'd done for him, that's what he said. He wanted sixty years. Sixty years."

For amusement, the books said. *For the satisfaction of having cleverly pulled it off.*

"That must have been quite a piece of work," Greg suggested. "Dealing with Paul Platt in the next cell all those months."

At that memory, Sandy's mood shifted. She giggled. "Poor Paul. Such a dear, slow man. Who so much wants to do well. I almost couldn't sleep, he kept talking to me."

So Platt was in the next cell. Confirmed.

"You must have handled him perfectly. You must have really had to play that well."

She puffed up with bravado now. "Yes, I scared the living daylights out of Paul. He's so dumb, it wasn't that hard. I told him they were going to put us on Death Row unless we went along. I told him there was no way to get out of it now. I convinced him they wouldn't believe he wasn't there."

"He tried to back out," Greg said. "He called me, he tried to recant."

Sandy made a failed effort to look contrite. "That didn't last long, though, did it? I'm afraid I'm to blame. I called Dennis right away, right after you left."

"Taylor made such a big deal at the trial about the missing emerald bracelet and the number of shots. How you didn't know those things, how no one could have given them to Paul."

This time, Sandy looked genuinely blank. "It's true, I didn't know about that. I have no idea where Paul came up with those details. He definitely didn't get them from me."

Greg tried to toss off his next question casually. "But Ira came from you, right? Ira was your idea? You decided to finger Ira?"

Sandy shrugged. "I'd seen him that night, danced with him. He fit the bill. Dennis wanted me to name someone."

"No other reason?"

Sandy's eyes darkened. She dragged out her words. "He's just a type. Ira reminds me of all the men in my life. Sweet, lost souls, who disappear on you finally."

"Disappear on you?"

Sandy stared at him as if he should know what she meant.

Which he did, of course. He wished he didn't, but there was no avoiding Sandy's staggering motive. Greg couldn't hide his dismay.

"All this," he asked, "because Ira looked funny at you?"

Sandy chuckled and preened, wordlessly.

Greg lunged toward her. "Dennis Taylor also scorned you," he taunted. "Scorned you, gamed you, disbelieved you. You got back at Ira. Now it's Taylor's turn. You can bring him down, Sandy. He betrayed you. Now you betray him. Now you bring him down."

A crack, perhaps. Through Sandy's amused gaze, nascent interest showed. She bit her lip. "He can still charge me with something," she argued. "He can still get me."

What the hell, Greg thought. The State Bar was going to fry him anyway. "No he can't, Sandy. He can't get you. It would be double jeopardy on the murder. And there's a statute of limitations on perjury. He can't get you. That's certain."

Not quite certain, of course. Double jeopardy protections were fuzzy in situations where a person's own perjury had led to her conviction. And he wasn't sure whether the statute of limitations had run out yet. Then again, nothing's certain. You could never advise a client if you always had to be certain.

"But he'll try," Sandy insisted. "Dennis will try."

"I'll represent you," Greg said. "I'll be your lawyer."

Why not promise? Empty promises are made all the time, in jailhouses and courtrooms and boardrooms and barrooms across the land.

"What would I tell them?" Sandy asked.

Control the client's dialogue. Explain your needs, wait for the client to supply a story that fits.

"Well, let's see," Greg said. "If it were to come out that you and Dennis Taylor knew each other before Ira's arrest, that would be interesting. Did you and Dennis maybe have a drug connection? Did you ever sell him drugs?"

Sandy's eyes widened; her mouth parted slightly. She said nothing, though, still wavering.

"It's just hypothetical," Greg coaxed. "What if maybe you two had this connection? What if you sold him drugs?"

Sandy floated in a private reverie. "Yes," she finally responded. "Yes, that's the way it happened. Yes, that's the truth. I . . . Yes, I met him at the county fair ten years ago, when I first moved here. The county fair over in Santa Theresa, I recall that quite specifically. In Santa

Theresa, ten years ago. After that, he sometimes came to visit me."

"Was there possibly a personal relationship, Sandy? Dennis does have a reputation with the ladies."

Sandy clutched Greg's hand. "Yes, yes, we had an affair, a brief affair. He bought coke from me, coke and meth. He even put up front money for me sometimes. We've been at parties together. I have a photo of him at a kitchen table, snorting lines. At least I did. It disappeared. Someone stole it from my house."

"Excellent, Sandy, excellent. Now we just need to talk about the postmaster's murder."

Sandy hesitated.

"You go there for money," Greg suggested. "Maybe Wilson owes you. There's a struggle. Maybe it's self-defense. He lunges at you. You shoot him."

Still, Sandy held back.

For amusement. For the satisfaction of having cleverly pulled it off.

Suddenly, it occurred to Greg. Not a ploy, but the truth. An obvious truth.

"A woman killed the postmaster, Sandy. There wouldn't have been such a struggle if it had been a man the size of Ira. A big man like Ira would just have knocked Wilson out. Poor old disabled Wilson struggled with someone his own strength."

If only he'd thought of this months before.

"It's obvious, Sandy. A woman committed this murder. Everyone missed that, and you know why? Because they didn't want to think a woman could do this. They didn't want to think a woman can act like the big boys. They didn't want to think a woman can have it her way."

Sandy liked that. Her smile oozed mocking contempt. "Well, they were wrong, weren't they?" she gloated. "Because a woman did do it."

"Yes, Sandy?"

"I shot Wilson. I was there alone. I shot the postmaster."

Greg let her keep holding his hand. With his other, he reached into his shirt pocket, withdrew a small tape recorder, placed it on the table, punched a button.

"Tell me everything, Sandy," he said. "Tell me everything."

TWENTY-TWO

With Kim Rosen at his side, Greg awkwardly steered a borrowed dune buggy through the fog-enshrouded dunes. He couldn't get the hang of it, how to gun the whining machine up a steep slope, then hold it steady as it pitched down the far side. Nor could he see where he was going in the mist. It didn't make sense. Not only were they annihilating a pristine wilderness, they were also having a terrible time.

"Why would anyone want to do this for recreation?" Greg muttered.

Kim laughed as she blew the bangs off her forehead. "Such a moody man," she said. "Always ranting and grumbling at the elements."

"Why not?" he asked.

Kim nodded her approval. "Exactly so. Why not?"

They spent most evenings together now. Sometimes, when she was in the mood, Kim stayed over. In the mornings, she'd make a point of standing in the hallway talking on the phone to her office, dressed only in his unbuttoned shirt. Hand on hip, crisply delivering instructions to a paralegal, she'd pretend nonchalance as she watched him gape.

They were working now, though. June Blossom had disappeared. Nothing was missing, except for June. Two days ago, when he arrived at her cabin bearing an affidavit, Greg had found her animals wandering around, looking hungry and perplexed. He'd waited forty-eight hours before deciding she was gone.

It was Kim who suggested they spend this afternoon surveying the dunes. Maybe June didn't go far, she argued. Maybe June found another abandoned cabin. Maybe somebody has seen her crabbing in the surf. So they weaved now through willow and poplar and wax myrtle, past Venano Gordo Lake, across creeks, up and down the towering sand hills. In the damp haze, something with a motor seemed more suitable than hiking or horseback riding.

Time mattered. Ira, informed of Sandy's confession, had taken to showering Greg with ever more urgent proposals regarding both his case and his fellow inmates'. Illegal searches, confidentiality violations, common law privacy issues—Ira, camped out in the prison law library, delivered a brief on one topic or another almost daily. They looked coherent to Greg, but also tinged with a rising mania. Ira, he feared, was approaching a bursting point; Ira needed release.

So, for that matter, did Greg. The State Bar disciplinary panel was closing in. They'd finally filed a formal complaint in district court; a court date loomed in four weeks. He needed to prepare a defense, or else start thinking about handing over his license.

"What's the worst those State Bar cowboys could do?" Kim asked over the dune buggy's whine. "If you lose, you don't ever have to walk into a courtroom again. No briefs, no depositions, no Dennis Taylors. You should hope you lose."

She meant to make him laugh, but Greg scowled instead. There was a time he wouldn't have minded if she was serious. Now he did. To give up, to fold his hand, no longer even faintly beckoned.

They were almost where they wanted to be. Five days before, Greg had filed his motion for a new trial, based on Sandy Polson's confession. Within hours, Jimmy had started fanning the media flames. Within a day, the state press had descended on La Graciosa, big-city reporters and TV cameras and satellite trucks clogging the plaza around the *asistencia.* A witness's recantation was one thing, a familiar thing. But Sandy hadn't just recanted. She'd confessed. Holding back only the business about her drug dealings, Greg had attached a transcript of her taped statement to the motion he filed in county court.

The resulting thick black headlines proclaimed the news: WITNESS CONFESSES TO MURDER; NEW LEASE ON LIFE FOR SULLIVAN; JUDGE TO DECIDE SOON ON NEW SULLIVAN TRIAL; CONFESSION BRINGS MAN HOPE FOR DEATH ROW RELEASE. Knowing the media fires, once ignited, needed regular stoking, Jimmy had waited three days, then also leaked the June Blossom story to his colleagues. Even though they didn't have her affidavit, even though she'd gone missing on them. A phantom witness might not be good enough for the courtroom, Jimmy had explained to Greg, but the out-of-town reporters would devour it. Hell with bloody foreign conflicts over motherlands, or anguished national debates about health care. These fancy bigfoot correspondents realize what sells.

Inundated with media inquiries, Dennis Taylor at first held firm, insisting to all, "I would never have tried the case if I felt Ira Sullivan wasn't guilty." By the third day, though, a certain plaintive whine could be heard in his responses. "It wasn't my job to believe that Ira Sullivan committed this crime," he told one gaggle of reporters and TV cameras on the steps of the *asistencia.* "Based upon the evidence, it was always my understanding that he did it. But it was up to the jury to decide. It was the jury's job to believe or not believe he did it."

Publicly, Judge Hedgespeth maintained a solemn judicial silence. In his chambers, though, Greg and Jimmy heard that Hedgespeth was tearing up the furniture, ranting and fuming and pacing about. No one could get him to talk about the legal elements of Greg's motion for a new trial. For that matter, they couldn't get him to talk about anything on his docket. All he talked about was the news media. Who was there, what they were asking, what they were reporting. To one lawyer trying to discuss a scheduling matter, Hedgespeth pulled from his desk drawer a voter precinct list, showing how he'd carried every ward in the last election. "Every one," the judge informed his startled visitor. "That's what I did, carried every last one."

Through a discovery motion, after much delay, Greg had managed to get his hands on the Chumash County jailhouse logs for the weeks Ira, Sandy, and Paul sojourned together in the *asistencia*. The logs confirmed all that Sandy related. They moved Sandy and Paul to adjacent cells ten days after their arrests. Dennis Taylor visited Sandy and Paul frequently before Ira's trial, sometimes separately, a half dozen times together. Leafing through the logs, Greg whistled when he saw how Sheriff Wizen had managed to isolate Platt. "Paul Platt's relatives not allowed in facility for visitation," read one of his notes. "If Platt relatives appear, get in touch with the sheriff," read another.

Damning stuff, but by itself, not good enough. Peering into the mist, skidding and fishtailing, yanking his dune buggy to the left and right, Greg listened as Kim summarized her discouraging research.

"First of all," she advised, "don't count on being saved by the federal system."

McClesky v. Zant; Coleman v. Thompson; Barefoot v. Estelle. All were recent decisions sharply limiting efforts to get state murder cases reviewed by federal judges. The first effectively eliminated the filing of successive habeas corpus claims. The second closed the federal courthouse door even to some first-time habeas petitioners. The third, invoking "a presumption of finality," declared that "the role of federal habeas proceedings is secondary and limited . . . Federal courts are not forums in which to relitigate trials."

"*Herrera v. Collins* is the worst," Kim declared. "Basically it says it doesn't matter if your guy is innocent. Herrera turned up new evidence, but the justices weren't interested in even considering it."

Greg shook his head. "Read that one more closely, Kim. It's narrower than it sounds. Doesn't apply across the board."

Kim tapped her fingers on the dune buggy's front panel. "I don't know about that. Herrera had new evidence, but he didn't have an 'independent constitutional violation.' So the Court passed, and Texas executed him."

"What does it matter?" Greg asked. "We can win this in state court. We've got Sandy's confession."

"Maybe," Kim said. "But come on, Greg. You know judges hate recantations. Especially from convicts in prison. There's lots of case law saying recantations are to be viewed with 'suspicion and disfavor.' " She hesitated. "I have to admit, it's not hard to see why."

"Aha, Ms. Assistant U.S. Attorney. The prosecutor in you speaks." That came out a little more harshly than Greg had intended.

Kim glared. They were close enough now to fight. She relished a good fight.

"You don't have to be a prosecutor to understand, Greg. Even you can grasp it, I think. Convict recantations make it too easy to disrupt the system. You want to screw things, you just have to open your mouth. So little to lose, you're already sitting in prison. If judges jumped every time a convict recanted, prisons would have to be made with revolving doors."

Seeing Greg start to flush, Kim relented a little. "Look, okay, this is a tough issue. There does have to be some degree of finality, though, or else everything's pointless. If you play by the rules and the jury believes your witnesses, that's supposed to be the end of the story."

"Tell me about it."

Kim instantly understood. "Yes," she allowed. "Of course, you know."

"Once Frankie's testimony put Hilliard on Death Row," Greg said, "no one ever wanted to hear a different version from him."

A notion occurred to Kim. "Do you think you could go

through Hilliard's appeals process with me?" she asked. "Let's see if the version I heard in law school matches your version."

Greg stomped on the dune buggy's brake so sharply that Kim pitched toward the windshield. He grabbed for her, breaking her collision with his arm. "Version?" he sputtered. "Version?"

They were, without planning it, in an embrace, thrown together by the sudden stop. Greg felt her breath on his neck.

"Okay, wild man," she said. "Wrong word. Although I don't think it's grounds for crippling me. How about, 'Let's see if the version I learned matches the truth'? Will that do?"

They climbed out of the dune buggy and once again sat in the sand. This time it was Greg's turn to tell a story. He'd rehashed it countless times to himself and to attorneys in courtroom conversations, but never to a woman lawyer cuddled next to him in the Chumash Dunes.

Mr. Monarch, I assure you that I mean to finish this trial today. That's what the judge drawled when Greg pled for time to find the FBI expert. He meant it, too. After Detective Bobo hemmed and hawed, after the D.A. told the jurors, "A .38 killed the shopkeeper and here we have a .38," it was all over. Hilliard drew a conviction, his buddy Frankie, paper. Frankie didn't stay free for long, though. A month later, they picked him up in a bar carrying a gun. Probation revoked, he drew a twenty-year prison sentence. On his trips to see Joe at the state pen, Greg started visiting Frankie, too. Over and over, just as with Sandy.

"Frankie," he said at each visit, "Joe's sitting over there on Death Row." He could tell Frankie felt bad. So one day, Greg came in with a typed affidavit. Frankie had given false testimony, it read, in exchange for "favorable consideration." Frankie studied the piece of paper for a while. Then he signed it.

If only it had mattered. It hadn't, though. The judge

who'd presided at Hilliard's trial wasn't interested. The state supreme court made him hold a hearing anyway, but you couldn't say the Honorable Roland F. Wallace did so with much enthusiasm. In fact, he appointed a public defender to represent Frankie. Then he personally advised Frankie, from the bench, of his constitutional rights. The judge went on and on about the risk of being charged with perjury. At first, Frankie hung tough. Said he understood, didn't need to confer with his counsel. Identified the affidavit, admitted signing it, insisted its contents were true.

The judge again intervened. All these years later, Greg could still remember Wallace's words. *Let me again warn you, Mr. Frankie Frazier, you do not have to answer that question. You can claim your privilege under the Fifth Amendment if it tends to incriminate you, and it's obvious to the court that an answer to that question could incriminate you. I also warn you that any statement you make can be used in further prosecution for any charges. Most specifically, perjury charges . . .*

Still Frankie stuck to his story. Once more, the judge spoke, this time to Frankie's public defender. *Mr. Marshall, for the record, being the attorney for this witness: I am going to recess now and have you counsel with him. And I wish you would explain to him the consequences of perjury in a capital case. Perjury in a capital case carries a maximum penalty, I believe, under present Florida statutes, of life imprisonment . . .*

Judge Wallace had it flat-out wrong; the penalty for perjury in a capital case was thirty years, not life. Realizing as much a few minutes later, he reconvened the hearing, corrected himself, then sent Frankie back into recess to further reconsider. When they assembled for a third time in the courtroom, Frankie finally folded.

There'd been no deal, he testified, no nothing. His trial testimony was true. Hilliard killed the shopkeeper.

From his seat high on the bench, Judge Wallace smiled broadly. There'd be no perjury proceedings instituted against Frankie, he announced. There'd also be no new trial for Joe Hilliard.

Five years later, near Joe's execution date, Greg once more approached Frankie. Paroled, he was living up near Gainesville. Greg talked to his parole officer, who talked to Frankie, who said, yeah, he'd see Mr. Monarch again. "Whole thing still burns heavy in my mind," Frankie told Greg. "I have a conscience problem, a real weight problem."

This time, Greg videotaped the retraction. Then he filed a habeas petition in federal court and asked for a stay of execution. Again, it didn't matter. U.S. District Judge Thomas Horrell chose not even to hold an oral hearing. Nor did he choose to read or view Frankie's videotaped deposition. Horrell disdained recantations and habeas appeals. He read the court record and the lawyer's briefs, then issued his ruling: *I have concluded that none of the claims have merit and that the petition should be denied.*

Greg haunted the Eleventh Circuit after that, but could never provide them with the right procedural violation. The appellate judges just weren't interested in the missing FBI expert or the patently false murder weapon. That was a rookie defense lawyer's fumble, not a constitutional violation. That was how the adversary system worked.

"Joe wasn't scared until they came to measure him for his burial suit," Greg told Kim. "Then he was."

She tried to look into his eyes, but he kept them fixed on a pile of graying driftwood. "Greg, we can only try. As you saw in Florida, a trial judge is not likely to overturn his own proceeding. That we know. So we use the hearing to build a record for the appellate courts. What else can we do?"

Greg said nothing.

"You can't just shred the law," Kim insisted. "You can't just take the law in your own hands."

"Why can't you?"

Now Kim said nothing.

"If only June Blossom hadn't disappeared on us," Greg muttered. "She's not a recantation, she's new evidence. Hedgespeth would have to grant a new trial."

"Hedgespeth is the judge, Greg. As you've seen, judges don't have to do anything."

In the distance, Greg suddenly heard an all too familiar sound. He grabbed Kim's arm, softly covered her mouth. Together they listened. It was unmistakable: the whine of an approaching dune buggy. Yahoos out for a drunken spin? Tourists touring the dunes in the fog? Most likely so. But Greg didn't want to wait and see. Pulling Kim to her feet, he darted for their own vehicle. In an instant, they were rolling through the dunes.

"Aren't you being a little dramatic?" Kim asked.

"Probably, but I've had a dramatic experience out here."

Greg rolled down a hill, then turned sharply twice, tracing a zigzag line through the sand. He stopped to listen. The other dune buggy was still approaching, nearer now. Greg turned toward what he thought was the shore, aiming for flat, open sand where he could better maneuver. It took him a minute to notice he'd miscalculated and wasn't in fact heading toward the sea. A moment later, he realized he'd lost his bearings entirely in the fog and didn't know where he was. He could be going in circles; he could be heading directly toward what they were trying to avoid. The other vehicle's relentless whine sounded now as if it was just over the dune, and closing. In his rearview mirror, Greg noticed a wall of green foliage behind him to the right. Yanking his gearshift, twisting his wheel, punching his accelerator, he shot the dune buggy backward into a willow thicket. Then he jumped out, sprinted back into the dunes, turned and looked. The mist and the willows obscured the vehicle from view. Greg grabbed a loose piece of bark and dragged it lengthwise along the sand, wiping out their tracks as he retraced his steps.

Moments later, Kim and Greg watched in silence as a

stripped VW Bug rolled slowly by. Inside it, they could see two men's heads swiveling from side to side. For an instant, the vehicle passed through a clearing in the fog bank, exposing the heads to a clearer view. One was thin, with graying hair and a mustache. The other was round and bald, with a purple scar under his right ear. Kim gasped and clutched Greg's knee.

"I know him," she whispered.

"Which one?"

"The mustache."

"Who is he?"

By now the dune buggy had disappeared into the mist.

Kim shook her head. "I don't know his name. Don't even know who he is. But I think I know where I've seen him."

Greg waited. Kim sorted something out in her mind.

"The grand jury," she said finally. "During the Devil's Peak grand jury. He was there every day, out in the corridor."

"Who with, Kim? Who is he?"

Kim made sure to speak precisely. "I can't say. I only know who he stood next to in the corridor."

"Come on, Kim. Who?"

"Two guys from Rolfson Industries. Two guys in dark fancy suits."

An image from Ira's trial occurred to Greg. "Gray flannel suits?"

"Exactly. Gray flannel."

"What were they doing in your corridor?"

"It's a public building, I can't stop them. They showed up every day, a Rolfson lawyer and supervisor. I figure they were monitoring who we were calling to testify, because later I heard they'd visited with every Rolfson employee we brought in. Visited and debriefed them about what we asked."

"Mustache wasn't the lawyer or supervisor?"

"No, them I knew, they had business cards. Mustache

didn't have a business card. Mustache didn't have a name. Mustache didn't have an identity."

"Of course not," Greg said.

Faceless corporations had always been a favorite topic for him to rail about at JB's. Faceless corporations that conceal individual identities, individual responsibility. Poor Jimmy and Doc Lewis, they'd had to endure more than a few tirades. *If you plot in the barroom, it's a crime, but if you plot in a boardroom, it's not . . .* Now he had a faceless corporation actually stalking him in the dunes. A faceless corporation that Kim had found too powerful to bring down with all her majestic laws.

"You ever study how to prosecute a corporation's individuals?" Greg asked. "In that law school that taught you how not to practice like Greg Monarch?"

Kim ignored his tone. "We studied a federal case once. Trial judge wouldn't accept a settlement. One of the big pharmaceuticals meant to write a check, be done with it, no individuals charged. Except this judge said no, he wanted their top guys to take responsibility and repent right in his courtroom. 'Confession is good for the soul,' he told them. 'Face up to your misdeeds.' "

"What happened?" Greg asked.

"What do you think? Eighth Circuit reprimanded the judge under the Judicial Conduct Act. Reprimanded him and yanked him from the case."

"Should have guessed," Greg snapped.

Why was Jimmy so surprised that he didn't know the name Daniel P. Bellinger? Or that Bellinger was Rolfson's CEO? Rolfson put great effort into obscuring Bellinger's role, after all. Layers and layers of folks to insulate Bellinger and his colleagues from accountability. Layers and layers to insulate Rolfson from Ira Sullivan.

Greg twisted the dune buggy's ignition key, stomped on the accelerator pedal, punched out of the willow thicket. "Come on, faceless corporation," he shouted. "Show your face."

Up and down the sand hills he drove, sounding his horn,

gunning his engine, making their presence known to all inhabitants of the dunes. "Come on, damn you," he cried to the skies. "Show your face, show your face." He leaned on the horn, he banged the top of the buggy with a wrench, he howled his proposal. "Show your face, goddamn it, show your face."

Kim watched him with openmouthed wonder. She inched closer to him, put her hand on his leg.

"Real people have deliberately caused all this," Greg screamed. "Toxic contamination, missing plutonium, Ira on Death Row, Jenny Branson over a cliff. Individuals, making choices, taking actions. Not a process, not a system. Real people, who go home at night to their families. Real people, who hug their children. Real people, who kiss their mates—"

Honking and banging and steering, Greg eventually grew oblivious to his surroundings. So it was Kim who spotted the body first. She gasped, grabbed Greg's arm, pointed. There, against the rocks at the edge of the surf, it lay curled in the sand, one thin arm stretching stiffly toward the sea. Together Greg and Kim climbed from the dune buggy and approached. Well before Kim knelt and turned the battered, swollen woman faceup, Greg recognized the shawl and the long gray-black hair. He closed his eyes, drew a breath.

Was June Blossom's death punishment for letting her child perish? Or for wrapping her shawl around a weeping lost soul one foggy night? Or—Greg shuddered at the thought—for sharing her story on an afternoon with two strange men who appeared uninvited on her doorstep?

The dunes yielded no answer. The whine of the ATVs had disappeared. All was silence now, but for the roar of the surf and Kim Rosen sobbing at his side.

Maybe, Greg reasoned later that evening as he drove alone into La Graciosa, it hadn't even been a faceless corporation. Maybe what they'd seen had simply been a bald guy with a scar and a thin guy with a mustache, out for recreation on their day off. Maybe the surf had caught June Blossom unawares while crabbing, and dashed her against the rocks. Maybe Jenny Branson simply drank too much and braked too hard. Maybe he was inhaling too much of Jimmy's fevered exhaust.

It was well past dusk. Greg parked at the plaza and walked to the *asistencia*. Roger Kandle had the night shift tonight at the sheriff's office. Greg found him in the snack room, drinking vending machine coffee. Roger rose when Greg entered, almost spilling his steaming paper cup.

"Roger, this is important—"

Kandle cut him off with a hand on his chest. "No," he growled. "No. This thing has blown up now, TV cameras everywhere. Taylor is going nuts. No. Stay away. I'm not talking to you."

"A body was found in the surf this afternoon. A body of a witness who was with Ira at the time of the murder. June Blossom. Maybe you've heard the name."

Roger frowned. "Yes, forensics already checked in. Looks like an accident, they say. Battered on the rocks."

"Is that what they say?"

Roger backed away from Greg, moved toward the door, looked for escape. "I'm not talking to you anymore, Greg. I've never talked to you. Get out of here. Get away from me."

Greg started to argue, then stopped himself. He turned instead, and retraced his steps to the plaza. He'd spotted what he was after. A disturbed conscience, moral qualms, roiled nerves, call it what you will. Once he would have responded with empathy; now he saw it differently. Roger had shown him weakness.

Greg half skipped up the creek pathway, eager to meet his friends at JB's Red Rooster Tavern.

TWENTY-THREE

Greg flinched at the sight of the throng filling the steps of the *asistencia*. Reporters, camera crews, and curious spectators swarmed everywhere. Walking the creekside path from his cottage toward the plaza, Greg glimpsed them through the oaks before they saw him. Undetected, he scrambled up the grassy bank toward Carmel Street. It was early; he could retreat to a café, then later circle around to the sheriff's rear entrance. No one would spot him.

They'd gotten through the courthouse door: Judge Hedgespeth had grudgingly agreed to a hearing on their motion for a new trial. Even though Hedgespeth recoiled at the notion of altering a jury's decision, Sandy Polson's confession demanded at least some consideration. So the out-of-town journalists were in a frenzy. One witness confesses, another turns up dead—even a couple of correspondents from the august East Coast broadsheets had appeared in recent days to throw elbows with the raunchier tabloid hacks. Satellite TV vans had rolled as far as the state prisons, vainly seeking interviews with Ira and Sandy. Jimmy O'Brien was in his element—leading tours, dispensing tips, demonstrating the pleasures of JB's Red Rooster. Greg happily allowed him the spotlight.

The dubious worth of Sandy's confession appeared to have escaped almost everyone's attention. Sandy had now told three stories under oath. She'd certainly get hammered on the stand today. All the same, she was the only arrow in Greg's quiver.

He took a seat on the creekside patio of Stella's Café. He'd awakened at dawn to an uncommon morning sight—not fog, but dappled sunlight filtering through the oaks. On days like this one, he couldn't help but think of lazy summer afternoons past. He camping with his dad in the High Sierra, Ira fishing with Jeffrey at Los Osos Lake, everyone so unready for what was to come. Greg wished he could, just once more, talk to his father. Instead, he sipped coffee and watched the ducks fighting over the morning's crumbs.

At 8:30, he rose and crossed a small wooden bridge spanning the creek. On the other side, he turned up a path that circled to the rear of the *asistencia*, and the sheriff's private jailhouse entrance. Greg wanted to talk to Ira before the hearing. They'd brought him down from the state prison the evening before; he'd spent the night in the Chumash County Jail. Spent it there, but apparently had not slept. At least, that's how it appeared to Greg when a deputy led him to Ira's cell.

Ira sat on the edge of his cot, his bloodshot eyes restlessly scanning the room. They had him in his prison blues, the faded wrinkled uniform of Death Row. Despite his alabaster skin and gaunt profile, he looked afire.

"Ira," Greg said. "Dennis brought you down because of Devil's Peak. Because you took on Rolfson, because you fought for Jenny Branson."

They'd gone over some of this in recent days, but Ira was still laboring to grasp the shape of his ordeal. "Doesn't make sense no matter how long I think about it," he said. "Just hard to see."

"It's hard for anyone to see, Ira. That's the point. You goosed Rolfson, so Rolfson called Sacramento, and Sacramento called Dennis."

"Still hard to see."

"That's because there's more. There's Sandy. As powerful as everyone else was, they all needed Sandy to make this happen."

Ira pawed at his scalp. "Jesus, I can barely remember

that night at the Foghorn. I hardly know what I said to her. That woman is a lunatic."

"Well," Greg said. "It would be nice to think so."

Ira studied his ex-partner in silence. "However this works out," he said finally, "thanks."

Greg started to speak, but no words came.

"You fixed things," Ira said.

Greg tried to clear his throat. "Ira, we've a long way to go. Can't say we'll get there."

"At least we're trying."

"Yes, at least we're trying."

Ira exhaled and squeezed his eyes shut. Suddenly, he had no more strength left for bravado. "I'm scared, Greg. What if this hearing doesn't work?"

Greg searched for an adequate answer to the question that he'd been mulling all night long. It occurred to him finally that Sandy Polson must be just feet away, sitting in a nearby cell. They'd brought her down from the state prison the night before. Her proximity suggested the only response he could think of. He'd voiced it before, exuberantly; now he found himself forcing the words. "Nothing to worry about," Greg said. "We've got the perfect witness on our side."

Entering the courtroom through a side door, Greg flinched again at the throng before him. They'd packed bodies everywhere, the bailiffs bringing in extra chairs and roping off two rows for the press. Greg spotted Jimmy, who nodded and grinned and flashed a thumbs-up sign, not caring whether others thought him unprofessional. Looking about, Greg also saw Alison Davana, who for once didn't appear entirely bored and impatient, although she clearly was suffering from the courtroom's ban on smoking. Finally, scanning the spectators, Greg found Kim Rosen. You studied my last Death Row case, he'd told her. You might as well study this one. That's just what she appeared to be doing; she perched on the edge of her seat with a legal pad on her lap, a pen in her hand.

Across from Greg, at the single attorneys' table placed perpendicular to Judge Hedgespeth, sat not Dennis Taylor but Christopher Rawlins, an assistant attorney general from Sacramento. The state handled appellate motions in California; Rawlins was the A.G.'s chief death penalty specialist. Dennis Taylor instead would be a witness today, since one of the claims in Greg's motion involved prosecutorial misconduct. Specifically, the creation of perjurious testimony by Sandy and Paul.

For nights now, lying in bed, unable to sleep, Greg had imagined what it would be like to get Dennis Taylor on cross. Even if Judge Hedgespeth limited what he could cover, Greg relished the notion of grilling Taylor, of marching before him and compelling him to answer questions under oath. A tremor in Taylor's voice, or beads of perspiration on his forehead, would almost be reward enough.

The petitioner went first in a hearing like this. With Ira seated at his side, wrapped in manacles and leg irons, Greg rose to present his case.

Those among the spectators who'd watched Sandy Polson testify at Ira Sullivan's trial saw nothing different now. She walked down the aisle toward the witness stand much as she had so many months before. The cornflower-blue eyes, the tousled tawny hair, the easy, effortless manner. A simple blue dress this time, instead of white. She'd never looked calmer in her life.

On the bench, Judge Hedgespeth frowned as he watched her approach. At Sullivan's trial, it hadn't mattered if he thought Sandy dubious; it had been the jury's job to judge her. That notion remained for Hedgespeth a fixed article of faith. Yet today was undeniably different, for there was no jury in this courtroom. Today, he would decide; today, his opinion mattered.

What to think, though? If Hedgespeth didn't believe Sandy back then, how could he believe her now? Why believe what would be her third version of the postmaster-murder story? If he regarded her as fundamentally unreliable, why base anything on her testimony? Why not, in an objectively unknowable situation, cling to the system's one certain element—the jury's judgment?

Greg knew that such were Hedgespeth's inclinations. Yet the judge didn't strike him as being righteously inflexible; he just needed a compelling reason to step beyond the rules and procedures he genuinely revered. Nor did Greg think the judge corrupt. Half the state might be in Rolfson's pocket, but not Hedgespeth. The judge liked people too much to be their enemy. His flaws stemmed not from avarice or wild ambition or malevolence, but from the compromise required of anyone who'd devotedly toiled in the law for thirty years. Compromise that Hedgespeth now apparently wished to shed. He'd overruled both sides' preliminary motions, for they all were aimed in some fashion at limiting evidence. Maybe his impulse was partly self-serving, no doubt fueled by the media attention, but Hedgespeth plainly wanted to hear everything.

From the moment she began testifying, Sandy Polson appeared ready to oblige. As always, she spoke without hesitation or artifice. Except now, she told a wildly different story.

It was she who shot the postmaster, she declared, not Ira Sullivan. She alone. Mr. Sullivan wasn't there. She'd lied at Ira's trial because Dennis Taylor threatened her with the death penalty. She was a drug dealer, she needed money to cover what a supplier had fronted her. Scared and desperate, she thought of the Crocker postmaster; she'd heard that certain of his post office boxes held cash and drugs. She asked two men from the Foghorn to drive her up, meaning it to look like a night of barhopping. She left them at the Pozo Tavern, drove to the postmaster's home, talked her way in, tried to say she'd lost the key to a friend's box. He didn't go for it, he grew angry, he started pushing her. She pulled out a gun, ordered him to the post office. He lunged at her, they struggled, shots were fired.

She dropped the gun, they both went for it. She got to it first, pulling the trigger as she rose.

Sandy dabbed at her eyes with a handkerchief, swallowed, sighed. "I didn't mean to shoot him, but I did," she said finally. "There was no correcting that afterward, nothing I could do."

In the courtroom gallery, spectators began to stir. Some rubbed their jaws, some muttered to companions, some crossed and recrossed their legs. For so long, they'd thought they knew who killed the postmaster.

"What happened next?" Greg asked.

Carefully and precisely, Sandy explained. How she found the $33,000 hidden in the postmaster's fireplace. How she wrapped the cash in a dish towel, stuffed the towel and her gun into a paper sack. How Hutch and Linter drove her home. How she grabbed the sack from Hutch's car, walked inside, hid the gun, then left again in her own car. How on her way through Apple Canyon, on her way to pay off her debt, she drove off the road. How the deputies brought her to the sheriff's station.

"What did you do at the station?" Greg asked. This was so different, having Sandy as a witness for the defense.

"I made several statements," she said. "I told one lie after another. I told so many different stories, they got disgusted with me. Finally Dennis Taylor told me I better come up with somebody or it was all going to fall on me. So I came up with Ira Sullivan, Ira and Paul Platt. I thought that would save me, I thought I'd go free."

"Is that why you're testifying now, Ms. Polson? Is that why you've changed your story?" Greg knew the state would raise that argument, so figured he'd ask it himself.

"No, it isn't. The reason I've come forward is because I'm a recovering drug addict. Part of the therapeutic process is to face what you've done, to make amends to those you've harmed. I have harmed Ira Sullivan, I surely have. I cannot live with the fact that I helped put an innocent man on Death Row."

"You are telling the truth as you sit here today?" Greg asked.

"Yes I am," Sandy said.

"Thank you. I have no further questions."

From his seat in the press section, Jimmy caught Kim Rosen's eye. They'd never stopped circling each other from a careful distance, but they now understood they shared certain basic interests. Jimmy arched his eyebrows in inquiry. Kim shrugged. As soon as Chris Rawlins began his cross-examination of Sandy Polson, both had their answer. The rest of this proceeding was not going to go as favorably for Ira as had Greg's direct of Sandy.

Rawlins had a long face, a large nose, narrow eyes, and the phlegmatic manner of one supremely self-assured. He gunned straight for Sandy's history of multiple stories. He understood he did not need to prove her confession a lie; he needed simply to show her to be unreliable.

How many times have you testified about Postmaster Wilson's murder? How many times have you given statements? Each time you were under oath? Each time until now, you said Ira Sullivan was present? Each time until now, you said Paul Platt was present? Did you lie about how you got there? Did you lie about the route? Did you lie about the car? Did you lie about the gun? Did you lie about Mr. Sullivan grinning over Wilson?

Yes, Sandy answered, over and over. Yes, I did, yes I did.

"You were under oath each time you lied, were you not?"

"As far as I know."

"You held up your hand and swore to tell the truth?"

"Yes, sir, I did."

"Just as today you came up to the witness stand and raised your right hand and swore to tell the truth?"

"Yes, sir, just like today."

"But when you raised your right hand and swore to tell the truth at Mr. Sullivan's trial, then you were lying?"

"Yes."

"You were lying when you said Mr. Sullivan pointed a gun at the postmaster? You were lying when you said Mr. Sullivan pulled the trigger?"

"Yes."

"You lied to Sheriff Wizen? You lied to Detective Johnson? You lied to Detective Kandle?"

"Yes."

"You lied to Ira Sullivan's jury? You lied to Judge Hedgespeth?"

"Yes!" Sandy spat out the word this time, then looked surprised at what she'd done. Perhaps it was Greg's fault, for breaking her in their prison meetings; perhaps this interrogator reminded her of someone from the past; perhaps Sandy was playing one last game. Whatever the cause, she'd relinquished her constant composure. At the attorneys' table, Greg blanched and reached for Ira's arm. For so long he'd wanted Sandy ablaze; now he craved her cool, white ashes.

"Sir," Sandy told Rawlins, "I could probably save you and the court a lot of time here."

Hedgespeth glared down at her. He bit off his words: "I have a lot of time."

Sandy glared back, her composure now utterly abandoned. "It's just that I admit all this. Okay? I lied all the way through the interrogations and the trials."

Rawlins put his parched, gray face close to Sandy's. "Ma'am," he drawled, his narrow eyes expressionless, "you've got fifteen or so years to kill, so why the hurry? Just answer my questions."

From there, the situation deteriorated quickly. Rawlins fired question after question, barely letting Sandy answer. You're a drug dealer? You're a drug addict? You remained silent even though you knew that Ira Sullivan was facing the death penalty? You remained silent even as Judge Hedgespeth condemned him to die? You never told Judge Hedgespeth that you killed Bob Wilson? You let him make the hardest decision a judge can make? Isn't that right? Didn't you? Isn't that right?

Yes, yes, yes. Sandy was answering in a monotone now, barely hanging on. Greg slashed at a legal pad with a pencil. Jimmy and Kim stopped taking notes.

You're angry with Dennis Taylor because he wouldn't help you get off, aren't you? You're angry because you didn't get the leniency you expected? Your real motive is to get Dennis Taylor, isn't that right? You know you can't be retried and resentenced, don't you? You know the double jeopardy statute protects you? You know you can't get the death penalty? You know perjury would be the most you could face? Isn't that right, Ms. Polson, isn't that right?

At that last question, Sandy couldn't stop herself. "No, sir," she flaunted. "I can't even face perjury, as far as I know."

Greg slumped in his chair. *For amusement, for the satisfaction of having pulled it off.* Sandy, so proud of her achievements, so eager to display her legal knowledge.

"Because the statute of limitations has run?" Rawlins asked.

"That's right," Sandy said. "Because the statute of limitations has run."

"So you're free to get up here and say about anything you please, aren't you, ma'am?"

"No, sir, I'm not free—"

Rawlins wouldn't even let her finish. "There's nothing stopping you, isn't that so, Ms. Polson? Nothing to lose, nothing at all. You want to get Dennis Taylor and there's nothing stopping you? Isn't that so, Ms. Polson? Isn't that so?"

Two minutes before noon, Sandy's turn on the witness stand finally ended. Greg exhaled, squeezed Ira's shoulder, then rose slowly to approach the bench. Bide your time, he reminded himself. "Your Honor," he declared. "We may wish to recall Ms. Polson, and also call rebuttal witnesses, after we hear the state's case. With the understanding that we may do so, the petitioner rests."

Hedgespeth nodded his assent without looking up. "Ready with your first witness?" he asked Chris Rawlins.

On they came. The forensics technician, Matt Thomas. Sheriff Wizen. Buzz Johnson. Dennis Taylor. Each recalling the night of the murder and the following hours, each telling much the same story.

The forensics team and the sheriff's detectives didn't confer at the murder scene. None of them knew that first night how many shots had been fired. None of them knew about a missing bracelet. No one threatened Sandy Polson. No one coached Paul Platt.

When he was called, Buzz Johnson marched up the aisle to the witness stand looking even more menacing than usual. For an instant, he stood towering over Greg, his fists clenched. Then he sat down. Asked by Greg how he convinced Platt to talk, Buzz smirked.

"We just told him we knew he was there," the detective explained. "Once we told him that we knew how he came up there, he started talking and never stopped."

"He just started confessing after a few minutes? What do you attribute that to?"

Buzz's dull, round eyes glinted with amusement. "I have no idea," he said. "But it's not unusual. It's happened before in Chumash County."

Dennis Taylor looked at ease when he took the stand. He smiled, and exchanged familiar nods with Judge Hedgespeth. In the press section, Jimmy winced. He'd seen good-ol'-boy camaraderie like that often around courtrooms. How did Greg ever think he was going to bring down this D.A.?

Under Chris Rawlins's respectful guidance, Taylor carefully explained his prosecution of Ira. The key was Paul Platt's initial statement, he said. That eliminated Sandy as the killer. Yes, Sandy's story evolved over time, but that happens, that's not so unusual. Yes, he visited with Sandy and Paul at the jail, but that's not uncommon either. If you were a prosecutor you'd know—here Taylor pointedly looked at Greg—you'd know people sitting in jail, they want to talk. They send messages, we visit. We try to find out what's on their minds.

When it finally came time for his cross, Greg rose and walked slowly toward the witness stand. "Do you have any idea," he asked Taylor, "how or why Platt's and Polson's stories became more consistent?"

Taylor looked amused. "Maybe they were each deciding to tell the truth."

Greg kept his voice even. "And now Ms. Polson is telling lies, Mr. Taylor? Is that it? It was the truth then, now she's telling lies?"

Taylor glanced up at the judge. "I don't know whether she made them up or somebody else helped her make them up."

Greg now stood inches from Taylor. "Did you ever have occasion," he asked, "to meet with a woman named June Blossom?"

Taylor showed something, a hint of the tremor Greg longed to elicit. But only a hint. "No," he said, looking a little puzzled. "Can't say I've heard that name before."

Greg had nowhere to take this. He didn't even have Miss Elaine; he'd tried, but the motel manager had moved on long ago. He wanted Taylor at least to flinch, though. Flinch once before he let him go.

"Mr. Taylor, you never met June Blossom at the Day's Rest Motel at Clam Beach? You never want there to—"

"Objection," Rawlins interrupted. "No foundation, no relevancy, nothing. I have no idea where he's going with this, Your Honor."

"Sustained," the judge ruled.

After an hour, Greg gave up and sat down. Rawlins approached the bench, his usual drained expression colored now by a growing sense of satisfaction. "That is all for us, Your Honor. The state rests its case."

Judge Hedgespeth started to say something about closing arguments, but Greg interrupted. It was time now.

"Excuse me, Your Honor," he said. "The petitioner wishes to call a rebuttal witness."

Hedgespeth and Rawlins both gawked at Greg.

"You do?" the judge said.

"Yes, Your Honor."

"Is that person here?"

"Yes, Your Honor, I saw him in the corridor a moment ago."

"Who is it?"

"Detective Roger Kandle, Your Honor. The petitioner calls Detective Kandle as a hostile witness for the defense."

For years, whenever he relived his failings at Joe Hilliard's trial, Greg in his mind had always changed the ending. Late at night, lying in bed, he never trusted Bob Lasorda to call the FBI expert to the stand. He never assumed he'd get him on cross. He subpoenaed the expert himself, he called him as his own witness. In the dark, staring at the ceiling, Greg always made things right. He fixed the story.

Now, at last, it wasn't just happening in his mind.

Greg had served Kandle with a last-minute subpoena, and put him on his witness list. He hadn't counted on Rawlins calling Roger to the stand. If Greg could sense Kandle's weakness, after all, surely the other side could also.

He'd figured it right. Rawlins had steered clear of Kandle. It was left to Greg to invite Roger to the party.

Summoned from the corridor, Kandle frowned as he slowly approached the lawyers. He looked first at Rawlins, then the judge, finally at Greg. For an instant, Greg thought he was going to bolt. Then he sat down and gripped the sides of the witness stand.

Beginning his account, Roger appeared determined to tell the same story the others had. He didn't know the number of shots that first night, he didn't know about the missing bracelet, he never threatened Sandy, he never fed information to Paul. Kandle had done well enough at the trial, but he couldn't quite equal that performance now. He said the right words, but as time went on, he began to falter.

Poor Roger, Greg thought. Undone by his futile sense of right and wrong.

"Early that morning after the murder, Detective Kandle, you had an opportunity to pick up Paul Platt?"

"Yes."

"Initially, did Paul Platt deny any involvement?"

"Yes, he did."

"How did you get him to admit his involvement, Detective Kandle?"

Roger cleared his throat, reached for the glass of water at his side. "I wasn't interrogating Platt. Buzz Johnson had him."

Roger, oh Roger, Greg thought. Buzz taped his confession, but remember how it started? Paul Platt remembers. *Then they stopped threatening,* Paul had told Greg so many months ago in his jailhouse recantation. *Then they did more kind of trying to convince me. That Buzz Johnson left the room, another officer came, talked calm to me, asked me questions, nice and soft. Nice, strong, calm guy.* How long it had taken for Greg to figure it out.

"Isn't it true, Detective Kandle, that Buzz Johnson left the room for a while, and you took over the interrogation for a period of time?"

Kandle looked around for help, found none, reached again for the water glass. Roger could not lie, Greg was sure of that now. In a situation like this, he could not dissemble. No more than Greg could, once so long ago.

"Yes," Roger allowed, slowly feeling his way. "Yes . . . I spoke with Paul Platt for a few minutes."

"How did you get him to confess, Detective Kandle?"

Roger shifted, crossed his legs, tried to find a comfortable position in the witness chair.

"Detective Kandle, please answer the question."

"I told him I knew he was involved with Sandy Polson and Ira Sullivan in this murder."

An inch at a time, that's all Roger would move. But that's all we need, Greg thought. We need nothing big here. The legal system cared little about the monstrous acts of Rolfson Industries or Dennis Taylor. Nor did it much care about the cold, vacant machinations of Sandy Polson. What mattered to the system were procedural violations. So Greg would give them procedural violations.

"And what did he say?"

Roger pondered, chewed on the question. "He denied that, said no, he wasn't involved."

"After he denied that, what did you say?"

Roger seeped desperation now. He looked trapped, unable to breathe. Greg stared at him, trying to communicate silently. *Don't feel bad, Roger. When this is over, you'll be able to sit down with your three sweet daughters and look them in the eye. You'll be able to say something terrible happened involving your father, but it finally is over. Evil people do not win. Lies do not win. The truth wins.*

"I don't recall exactly," Roger finally answered.

"Detective Kandle, what did you tell him?"

"Nothing in particular."

"You are under oath, Detective Kandle."

Maybe Roger read Greg's unspoken message finally. Or maybe he just grew tired of trying to make his way in the world. Whatever the cause, Kandle began to signal his surrender.

He was looking straight ahead, into the middle distance, avoiding everyone's eyes. Then he was talking. "Well, I guess I told him something like 'Paul, Sandy says you came with her and Ira in a green Dodge van.' I . . . I, yes, that's what I told him."

Silence had fallen in the courtroom, punctuated only by an occasional cough and the faint sound of laughter from La Graciosa's plaza.

"So you told Paul Platt that you knew he went up to the

postmaster's house in a green Dodge van with Ira and Sandy?"

Roger hung his head, rubbed the back of his neck. "Yes, I did."

"You took that from Sandy's statement? Sandy gave you the green van, then when you talked to Paul, you gave that to him? You believed her, and gave that to him?"

"Yes, I did." A flat monotone now; something had unwound in Roger.

That the detectives were the link between Sandy's and Paul's initial statements had been Greg's theme, and a matter of common sense, from the start. Neither common sense nor a defense attorney's argument, though, had been able to transform the truth into a legal fact. Roger's testimony made provable what was once merely certain.

"Detective Kandle, when you learned Ms. Polson drove up to Crocker in a white Plymouth with two other men, once you took statements from Hutch and Linter, did you ever wonder whether you had the right story? Whether any of Sandy's account was true?"

Regret washed over Roger's face. "Well, yes, I wondered, but . . ."

It was the two-hour gap on the morning of the arrests that had finally opened Greg's eyes. From 4:00 to 6:00, a chunk of missing time after they'd brought Sandy and Paul to the station. A chunk of time before Platt started taping his confession. The police reports and jailhouse logs showed nothing for that two-hour period. But of course, they wouldn't have been inactive.

They would have visited the postmaster's family, the postmaster's two daughters. To tell them of the murder, and to debrief them. The jailhouse logs and police reports had Buzz doing this the next morning, after Sandy and Paul gave their statements. That didn't make sense, though; they wouldn't have waited so many hours to notify the next of kin. And they wouldn't have sent Buzz to visit them; they wouldn't have trusted Buzz to handle the bereaved relatives.

They would have sent Roger, calm, sensitive Roger. Who would have comforted the daughters in their grief. Comforted them, and ever so gently questioned them. About their father, about his friends, about what was missing from his house. Such as a cherished, valuable family heirloom; such as a scrolled diamond and emerald bracelet.

At Ira's trial, the daughters had avoided mentioning Kandle's predawn, unrecorded visit. Perhaps they'd forgotten, or perhaps Dennis Taylor had convinced them it would be best to remain silent on this matter. It would not have been hard to persuade them, Greg imagined. The grieving women understandably longed for the justice and resolution Taylor so earnestly promised.

"Detective Kandle, did you not, that morning of the arrests, meet the postmaster's daughters at their deceased father's house? To tell them the news and question them about his death?"

Roger flinched, even though by now he was prepared for the question. Greg was right; Roger could not dissemble. "Yes," he agreed, his voice just above a whisper. "Yes."

"Did the daughters mention in that interview what was missing from the house? Did the daughters mention a missing bracelet?"

"Not to my recollection. I can't recall." It was reflex, the standard response of the professional witness. Even now, despite everything, Roger clung to his training.

Roger, let's end this nightmare.

"Isn't it true, Detective, that the daughters told you a bracelet was missing, and you then told that to Paul Platt an hour later at the Chumash County Jail?"

Kandle surveyed the spectators with the look of a man who didn't understand how he'd come to be sitting in this room. "Yes," he said. "Yes, that's what happened."

Just how that bracelet disappeared, Greg wasn't sure. Sandy didn't take it, that much he knew, Sandy never realized it existed. Someone who came after Sandy. Someone who came to investigate the murder. Not Roger, surely not Roger. It had to be Buzz. Somewhere there amid the bullet holes and postmaster's blood, the big, thickset detective no doubt had found a bauble for his overflowing treasure chest.

All that remained was for Roger to dispatch the legal fiction about the bullet holes. The legal fiction that sheriff's investigators and a forensics technician would not talk the night of a murder, would not share preliminary impressions. June Blossom's death had reminded Greg precisely how absurd that notion was. Sitting in the sheriff's snack room just hours after they'd found June's body, Roger already had heard the forensics technician call it a probable accident. And yet, it had supposedly taken Matt Thomas almost thirty-six hours to discuss the postmaster's murder with the detectives.

"Detective Kandle," Greg asked. "When you finished visiting with the postmaster's daughters at the murder scene, isn't it true you then talked to your forensics technician, Matt Thomas? Isn't it true he was there at the house when you met with the daughters?"

Roger agreed to everything now. "Yes, yes he was."

"Surely you were curious about what he was finding inside? Surely you saw those bullet holes in the ceiling? Surely you wanted as much information as possible right away? Surely you asked him about the number of shots?"

Yes, Roger sighed. Yes. Yes. Yes.

"You then went back and provided Paul Platt with the information you'd just learned? You provided him with the details of his statement?"

Roger looked at peace; at last it was almost over.

"Yes, I did," he said. "Shortly after that, I left the room, and Buzz Johnson took over. Buzz taped the statement I gave to Paul."

"Why, Detective Kandle?" Greg asked. "Why?"

Roger surveyed the room, searching for an answer. "Because Dennis Taylor wanted it that way," he said finally. "Because Dennis Taylor wanted Ira Sullivan."

* * *

When Kandle stepped down from the witness stand, Greg approached the bench again. He thought he could see hesitation in Hedgespeth's expression, even resistance. Despite Roger's revelations, could it be that the judge was clinging still to a jury's verdict? If so, no matter. Greg was not through. Ira's freedom had long ago ceased being his only goal; he required also the district attorney's undoing.

"Your Honor," he said. "This morning, I reserved the right to recall Sandy Polson. With your permission, I'd like to do that now. But first, I ask leave to call one other witness, to lay foundation for the questions I plan to ask Ms. Polson."

Hedgespeth scowled. His gouty toe had started to throb. "Monarch, this better be good," he warned.

"Yes, sir, I know." With that, Greg turned from the judge. "Petitioner calls Alison Davana to the stand."

Greg's old girlfriend strolled down the aisle as spectators murmured, trying to determine this dark, lithesome woman's role in Ira's case. She wore a form-fitting black dress that startled against her olive skin. She slowly blinked her emerald-green eyes; she tossed her mane of jet-black hair; she watched people looking at her. Clearly, she was enjoying herself. Only Alison would feel no discomfort at revealing her vices, only Alison would enjoy shocking people. That's what Greg had counted on when he asked her last night to be a witness for the defense.

On the stand, she was shameless, intimate, and utterly precise. About her use of coke with Dennis Taylor, her purchase of coke from Dennis Taylor, her sexual relationship with Dennis Taylor. At each explicit description of lovemaking against office walls, of lovemaking while popping amyls, of lovemaking as payment for cocaine, Chris Rawlins barked out objections, but Hedgespeth kept waving him off. Perhaps the judge's prurient curiosity had kicked in, perhaps Greg's promises to "tie this all together" were prevailing, perhaps even the rule of law reigned. Alison had kept a diary, after all. Alison had dates, times, locations, amounts. *Foundation,* just as Greg had promised.

"Out toward Pirate's Beach," Alison said months ago, when Greg first asked where Taylor got his drugs. Greg had reminded her of that late last night. *I couldn't possibly tell you what to say tomorrow. But if you happened to recall more precisely? Something about Apple Canyon? Someone named Sandy?*

"Do you have more specific knowledge of where he went?" Greg now asked.

Alison nodded. "Somewhere in Apple Canyon. That's where he always said he was going. Someone named Sandy. Sandy in Apple Canyon."

With that foundation established, Greg recalled Sandy Polson to the stand. Sandy Polson, the district attorney's drug supplier. Sandy Polson, who, in place of the unprovable and invisible Rolfson Industries connection, could provide Dennis Taylor with a motive for what he'd done. For why he'd put not Sandy Polson but Ira Sullivan on Death Row.

Like Alison, Sandy favored precision and detail. How long her affair with Dennis lasted, where they did drugs, how much he bought. Snorting lines in restaurant bathrooms, snorting lines in cars roaring down state highways. Meeting suppliers, making buys. Dennis, her backer; Dennis financing her deals. With retaliation finally at hand, Sandy told it all with utter aplomb. Like a veteran actress, she'd regained her poise. Greg celebrated her lovely, empty soul.

"Ms. Polson," he asked, "when is the first time in your life that you ever met Dennis Taylor?"

"Ten years ago."

"Where was that?"

"At the Santa Theresa county fair."

"Have you had communication with Mr. Taylor from that point until you were arrested for the postmaster's murder?"

"Off and on, yes, sir."

"You knew Mr. Taylor when he first interrogated you about the postmaster's murder?"

"Yes, I knew him very well," Sandy said. "That's why Mr. Taylor wanted someone else to be the postmaster's killer. That's why he wanted Ira Sullivan instead of me. That's why I thought he'd let me walk free."

By now, the press section had emptied, the reporters scrambling to spread the word on phones and laptops. The murmur among spectators had risen to a loud hum. Up on the bench, Judge Hedgespeth banged his gavel wildly. It looked as if the custodian of the system finally had lost his faith.

"This hearing is recessed," Hedgespeth thundered, smacking his gavel one last time. "Counselors, in my chambers, immediately."

For days after that—in briefs, in the courtroom, in the judge's chambers—the lawyers wrangled and cursed and accused while Hedgespeth alternately calmed them and erupted himself. His outbursts mounted with the rising tide of scabrous media coverage. In the end, the judge was left sputtering at the shredded case before him. The shredded case, and his unfaithful, unchaste legal system.

He'd been naive about what was going on down there in the jail, Hedgespeth told the lawyers, mighty naive about that and other matters. The similarity of Paul's and Sandy's statements no longer looked like proof of Sullivan's guilt. Rather, the similarity looked like proof Platt had been coached and coerced. How could the investigators have ever believed Sandy Polson after her initial story proved false? Shocked, that's what he was, just shocked at the hearing's revelations.

Greg marveled at Hedgespeth's adroit transformation, but thought it wise to say nothing. Dennis Taylor, on the other hand, abandoned all pretense of lawyerly composure. He stomped about, he hurled threats and accusations, he quarreled and denied, he stammered and railed. In calmer moments, he leveled his cold, dead eyes at Greg and hoarsely whispered, *I know what you've done, Monarch, I know what you've done*.

It was no use, in the end. Paul Platt remained the crux of the case, just as everyone had always agreed. And Roger Kandle had effectively neutralized Platt's statement. Platt meant nothing now; Sandy had no corroboration.

Hedgespeth resisted the inevitable as long as he could. At first, only Sandy Polson drew his censure. She was a vicious, vindictive liar, that much he was willing to acknowledge. Here was a cautionary tale, indeed—a case study of what can happen when a witness expertly deceives, and is unfortunately believed by, well-meaning but imperfect investigators. Yet the legal system had worked as designed, the judge insisted. It wasn't Sandy Polson or Dennis Taylor who convicted Sullivan, Hedgespeth solemnly reminded the lawyers. It was a jury. We followed the system, we followed the process. Based on the evidence, the death penalty was warranted.

Greg understood Hedgespeth well enough now not to brood or protest over this prolonged discourse. The judge was simply reciting his psalms as he walked through a valley of legal ruin. The judge knew what had to be done. Without relinquishing his abiding faith, without recognizing his beloved system's failure, he would find a way to alter the law's natural course.

One early summer morning, Hedgespeth did just that. The judge's ruling sputtered out of Greg's aging, balky fax machine. Hedgespeth, Greg saw at a glance, had upheld all of his claims—perjurious testimony, new evidence, and prosecutorial misconduct. Dennis Taylor, Sheriff Wizen, Buzz, Roger—the judge had found them all accountable for creating witnesses' false statements.

"In reviewing the recantation testimony of Sandy Polson," Hedgespeth wrote, "the court is aware that such testimony is to be viewed with suspicion and that this testimony is not looked upon with favor. However, when viewed in light of all the evidence, this testimony should be presented to a jury. Therefore, it is the finding of the court that the petitioner, Ira Sullivan, be and is hereby granted a new trial."

It was a charade, of course, yet another legal fiction. How could there be another trial? The state's whole case had been Sandy and Paul. That case didn't exist anymore. They couldn't possibly retry him. And if they couldn't retry him, why string this out, why confine Ira any longer?

Yet trial judges never release those they've condemned to die. Trial judges leave that, if it's to happen at all, to appellate judges sitting hundreds or thousands of miles away. To judges looking at lifetime tenure and piles of papers, rather than at agitated communities and grieving families and upcoming reelection campaigns. Even appellate judges were loath to act in a situation like this one. Over the past quarter-century, California had never once freed a condemned convict because someone else recanted or confessed.

All the same, that was precisely what Greg asked of Judge Hedgespeth at Ira's bond hearing. Only a handful of spectators was sitting in the *asistencia* courtroom that early July morning, for few expected anything eventful from the proceeding. The state had sent only a young junior attorney to argue for Ira's continued custody. Greg didn't consider it likely he would prevail, but he also didn't consider his request quixotic. He'd provided Hedgespeth those compelling reasons he sensed the judge needed to abandon his faith. Whether to retry Ira would be the state's call, but Ira's present status remained in Hedgespeth's province.

"Without the testimony of its two eyewitnesses," Greg argued, "Ira Sullivan can't possibly be retried. So I ask for bail to be set for Mr. Sullivan. And because he is indigent, I ask that he be released on his own recognizance."

Standing beside his attorney in manacles and leg irons, Ira sighed audibly at this request. It sounded to Greg like a prayer.

Hedgespeth peered over his glasses at the two men

before him. He had presided over Ira Sullivan's trial; he had sentenced Ira to death. Now he was being asked to set Ira free.

"Like the Committee of Vigilance, Greg?" the judge asked. "To hell with the jury? Take the law into our own hands? Make sure truth and justice win? I decide who should hang, who shouldn't?"

He as well as anyone, Greg thought. An earnest family man who enjoys people, who understands the public arena.

"Something like that, Your Honor," Greg said gently. "We all love the good king."

Hedgespeth fidgeted with his gavel. "No apology is due from the sentencing judge," he declared sternly, his narrowed gaze swinging back and forth between Greg and Ira.

"No, Your Honor, of course not."

Hedgespeth nodded at the prison guard poised in the corner, then spoke his order: "Unshackle the prisoner."

The few spectators present murmured and shifted with wonder at the notion—from Death Row to freedom in a morning. The guard fumbled with his keys and the leg irons. Then the chains clanged to the floor. Ira studied them in disbelief. Greg embraced his client, kissed his cheek. "Come on, Ira," he said. "Let's go get a drink at JB's."

TWENTY-FOUR

On the night of Ira's release, for the first time in living memory, J.B. Baylor bought a round of drinks for every patron packing his Red Rooster Tavern. Then he bought another round. Then Greg bought one. Then, to the astonishment of all present, Jimmy O'Brien.

Half of La Graciosa appeared to be present. It was not that Ira had so many friends, or so many who'd always believed him innocent. In fact, Chumash County's favorable opinion of the death penalty, and fear of mounting crime rates, certainly endured. JB's boisterous crowd reflected more complicated impulses. It helped that authorities still had someone to condemn for the postmaster's murder; retribution remained at hand. Some at JB's had come to gawk, some to celebrate the undoing of institutional power, some to witness the resurrection of Greg Monarch. Dave at the piano and Shirley at the microphone serenaded them all. *Don't worry baby, it ain't nothin' new, that's just love sneakin' up on you . . .* For a time, Greg had Alison in one arm, Kim in the other, and old Doc Lewis roaring in his ear: *I told you so, I told you that Sandy Polson was one goddamn spectacular liar.* Finally Alison, with a fierce, saucy whisper—*You owe me*—drifted away to the potbellied stove where Ira sat, surrounded by well-wishers.

Ira brightened at her approach, which encouraged Alison to settle in the chair next to him. It was so like Alison, Greg thought. She knew everyone was watching her, many harboring lascivious thoughts. He'd already seen her dismiss a couple of liquor-sloppy cowhands with an "In your dreams." She cared about Ira, but soothing him publicly was also her way of taunting such guys. Greg had always marveled at Alison; he'd just never realized how useful he would find her one day. *Somewhere in Apple Canyon, someone named Sandy.* On the witness stand, she hadn't even blinked.

Bolstered by Alison's hand resting softly on his neck, Ira offered a lopsided grin. Although still unclear what to make of it, he understood he was free. He looked around and nodded at Greg with an expression only the two of them understood. Then he chuckled hoarsely as he spotted Jimmy, over by the piano, yet again spouting Yeats. *There is no witchcraft on the earth, or among the witches of the air, that these hands cannot break . . .*

Only Kim Rosen looked unamused. She finally pulled Greg to a table in the back, near the window giving onto the creek. "Very fine companion case for the law school textbooks, Counselor," she said. "We'll have to make sure my old professor includes this when they teach the Hilliard case." Greg noticed but ignored the edge in her voice, which, he knew, had been building ever since the hearing. He leaned over and pressed his lips behind her ear. She pushed his head away, managing at the same time to knock a half-full glass off the table.

"What do you think will happen to our unfortunate district attorney?" Greg asked.

Kim rubbed her palms along the whiskey-wet table, then raised a moist finger to Greg's lips. "Haven't you thought that out yet, Greg? You've figured everything else, after all. I'd say at the least, referral to the State Bar ethics committee, civil suit by Ira, kicked out of office. Maybe if you're lucky you'll get him disbarred."

"What can they do to Sandy?"

"Hard to call that one," Kim said. "As I'm sure you carefully explained to her."

"What about Roger Kandle?" Greg tried to sound casual. Word was, Roger planned to quit before being forced out. Also, unavoidably, before his pension kicked in. There was no chance he'd be able to find another job in law enforcement. A Realtor's FOR SALE sign now sat on his front lawn.

Kim peered at Greg, searching for something other than undiluted celebration. "I don't know," she said. "What does happen to Roger Kandle?"

Greg started to rise. Kim grabbed his arm, yanked him back to his chair. "I see now how I could have nailed Rolfson," she said. "Just point you at them. Let you prosecute them."

Greg searched the room for escape. "Roger will be okay. This is best for Roger."

Kim sighed. "Passion and honor, maybe they just don't mix."

Greg bolted from his chair this time, and headed to the bar. On the way, Doc Lewis stopped him to gloat again over Sandy Polson's exposure. Then Shirley wrapped herself around him, humming "I'm in the Mood for Love," lulling him into a slow dance. For a while, he relaxed into her arms, but soon grew restless. He pulled away and signaled J.B. for a drink. J.B. couldn't see or hear him over the crowd and its din. Greg suddenly felt an impulse to escape. He headed for the door. Kim cut him off.

"Where are you going?" she demanded. Greg heard the plea in her voice and felt her pressing urgently against him, but he pushed her away. He reached into his pocket, pulled out the keys to his cottage, handed them to her. "Go home, Kim. I'll be there soon." Then he turned and ducked out the door.

The fog hid La Graciosa in a thick gray camouflage. Greg picked his way carefully along the creek path to the *asistencia*. At the sheriff's entrance, he signed in, and for once met with no resistance. The deputy on duty, obliging his request, led him down the ancient hallway to Sandy Polson's cell. They'd be taking her back to state prison in the morning; this was her last night in La Graciosa.

It looked as if she'd been waiting for him. Wide awake, she sat on the edge of her bed, brushed and made-up, just as she was on the day he first visited her.

"No one noticed," Greg said.

Sandy made a stab at appearing puzzled. "Noticed what?"

"The county fair where you said you first met Taylor. The county fair at Santa Theresa. They didn't have fairs there ten years ago. Four years ago, that's when they started."

County fairs he knew about; his father used to take him every year.

Sandy shrugged. "So I made a mistake. So it was some other fair."

"Was it?"

"What do you mean, Mr. Monarch?"

"Your whole story about Dennis," he said. "The affair, drugs. Was any of it true? Did you even know Taylor before the postmaster's murder?"

Sandy's eyes widened with astonishment. "Of course, Mr. Monarch. That's what happened. Remember? We talked all about it."

Was Sandy even a drug addict? Her skin, her eyes, her hair—nothing reflected the ravages of coke or meth. Least of all, her nerves.

Had she really struggled with the postmaster? They'd seen not a mark on her that night.

"The postmaster's murder, Sandy. It happened just as you testified at the hearing?"

She reached out, put her hand on his. Her eyes softened in a way he defied anyone to call false. "How do you want me to answer these questions, Greg? You tell me how I should answer them."

"Tell the truth."

She laughed gently, tilting her head in that way of hers, cementing their complicity with a stark, intimate gaze. "You've won, I've won," she murmured. "That's the truth."

Greg started to respond, then stopped. Some things were beyond understanding, it occurred to him. Some things, some people. He was trying to make sense of what he couldn't. *An attorney shouldn't hear what he didn't need to know.* A basic lesson of Professor Hammilberg's. Greg was forgetting his teachings.

Greg rose, recoiling from their bond but unable to deny it. "Good-bye, Sandy," he said, backing out of her cell. "Good luck to you."

From the *asistencia* Greg drove northwest through the pass toward Pirate's Beach, then turned south at the coast, winding his way slowly in the thick fog along the steep cliffs overlooking Clam Beach. So easy to spin out of control here; so easy to share Jenny Branson's fate. Greg held the steering wheel with two hands. Soon the cliffs descended and the beach widened into the start of the Chumash Dunes. Greg continued south, following a bumpy dirt road through cabbage fields. At its end, he parked and entered the dunes near Venano Gordo Lake, just as Ira had done so long ago with Planet and Moose. He hiked until he found the great golden hill full of towering coreopsis. He climbed halfway up, then sat down amid the plants to listen to the dunes at night. To listen, and imagine the utopia that had once flourished here, ever so briefly. The long-vanished utopia, the utopia that in truth never existed.

"I thought this is where I'd find you." Jimmy O'Brien's booming voice startled Greg so badly, he jumped up, then tripped in his haste and started rolling down the hill.

"Goddamn it, Jimmy, can you never let me sit in peace," he gasped, lying on his stomach in the sand.

Once again, Jimmy had a bottle of Black Bush in his hand. "My hill as much as yours," he grunted. "Saved your ass not far from here, didn't I?"

They sat together in the fog, sipping from Jimmy's bottle, listening to the distant roar of the surf. The wind had picked up, driving a sudden chill into the summer night.

"We did it, Greg," Jimmy said. "Had to be done, just like the Committee of Vigilance. For the good of Chumash County. 'So the citizens of Chumash County could walk about unarmed, transact their business, and feel at ease. So Chumash County could become a fit place to raise an American family.' "

Greg took a pull on the bottle. In his mind rose images of June Blossom's swollen, curled body, of thermal white streams crawling from Devil's Peak, of venal hands clutching missing plutonium containers. "Is that so, Jimmy?" he asked.

Yes, it was so; Jimmy was certain of that. Surely Greg wouldn't regret this; surely he had helped Greg.

"Come on," Jimmy urged. "Detesting the jerks isn't enough."

Greg said nothing. He stared into the fog, looking vainly for sight of a star. A gull calling somewhere drew his attention. Perhaps it sensed peril, perhaps it sensed a peregrine cruising cannily above him. What to feel, awe over the falcon, or pity for the gull? A foolish question, of course. They were both just facts of nature to observe and understand. Hunter and prey; the stronger, the weaker.

Although rejoicing in Ira's salvation, the rot of his opponents' corruption weighed on Greg. He had toppled his adversaries with their own tools, making their weapons his. For that, he'd been showered in recent days with accolades, none more glowing than those from his professional colleagues. With Ira free, the State Bar had dropped its formal complaint.

"Greg, come on, now, you won," Jimmy begged. "Let's keep this going, let's go get Rolfson. You and me and Kim. We can bring those guys down."

Maybe they could, and maybe they would, Greg thought. Just now, though, a modern-day Committee of Vigilance appealed not at all to him. Neither, for that matter, did clinging to this golden hill in the dunes. What truly beckoned was his cottage on a creek, and the urgent, cross woman awaiting him there. He understood the edge in Kim's voice tonight at JB's. She was far too sharp a lawyer not to grasp what had happened in Judge Hedgespeth's courtroom.

They would examine that matter, surely they would. There would be plenty of time to analyze and speculate and debate. There might even be time to reach an answer.

Greg reached for his friend's arm. "It's okay, Jimmy," he said. "It's all right."

Special advance preview from
Barry Siegel's new novel

ACTUAL INNOCENCE

Available in November 1999 from Ballantine Books.

"Okay now, Sheriff, let's go back to the evening of the murder."

"Yes, sir."

For a moment, Greg Monarch let Roy Rimmer ponder those critical hours on his own. He turned slowly, walked to the lawyers' table, picked up a file, flipped through pages. The sheriff's studied deference was getting on his nerves.

"Now then," Greg continued. "At Sarah Trant's trial you testified that when you went down to the river that night, went to search the river—"

"Yes, sir . . ."

". . . That you were specifically looking for footprints. Isn't that right?"

"Yes, sir."

"Good . . . Glad we agree on that much."

In truth, Greg wasn't glad about anything. He chafed at the need to be in this courtroom. With the fire thoroughly contained, Judge Solman had resumed the habeas hearing long before he could finish pursuing all that still intrigued him in El Nido. Clearly, Brewster Tomaz's murder and Sarah Trant's prosecution were mere props in some larger contest that stretched well beyond the Camp Mahrah conflict. To save Sarah, Greg needed to uncover everything that remained hidden to him in El Nido. Yet there was little chance to do so within the confines of this habeas hearing. He planned to feel his way, kick up some dust, keep his eyes open—and hope Judge Solman didn't hold too tight a rein.

"Now then," Greg continued. "Sheriff Rimmer, isn't it true that at Sarah's trial you testified that you found only her footprints and Tomaz's at the river?"

"Yes, sir."

"And that was a flat-out lie, wasn't it, Sheriff Rimmer?"

Rimmer started to show some flash, then regained control of himself. He reached for a glass of water. "Not at the time, sir. When I testified at the trial, I totally forgot about the other set of boot prints we'd found."

"I see," Greg said. "So, you went to the river that evening looking for footprints. You already answered yes to that. Do you want to change that answer?"

"No." Rimmer stared at Greg. "I went there looking for footprints."

"Okay. Besides the footprints of Sarah Tant and Brewster Tomaz, you found a third set, did you not? Boot prints?"

"Not the ones I was looking for. Those were old ones—"

"Hold on," Greg interrupted. "Please just answer my questions. That last required only a yes or no. Now. You saw a set of boot prints and you thought, Well, those aren't the ones I'm looking for. Is that your testimony?"

Rimmer went back to sipping his water. "Yes, it is."

"Tell me, Sheriff. Did you misunderstand the defense attorney's question at Sarah's murder trial? Is that your testimony?"

"No, I understood the question. I just had totally forgotten about the boot prints. If I'd remembered, I would have answered differently."

Greg frowned and paced. As he passed the lawyers' table, Sarah caught his eye. In her expression he saw growing hope. He touched her shoulder, then wheeled toward the witness stand. "Okay, I see. Okay. So you forgot about the prints. Let's just accept what you're saying; let's assume that it's true. But you surely would have put it in a report right then, right after you first saw the boot prints. Wouldn't you?"

Rimmer turned to James Mashburn with a silent command in his eyes. Greg stepped between them. Next Rimmer glanced up at the judge. Solman's hand rested on his gavel.

"Wouldn't you, Sheriff?" Greg demanded. "Wouldn't you put it in a report?"

"I supervise, Mr. Monarch. I wasn't the one actually on the line down there in charge of the operation. I wasn't the one writing the reports."

"So you didn't do a report on what you found at the river?"

"No."

"Did you take notes?"

"Yes . . ."

Before Greg could frame his next question, Judge Solman intervened. "Excuse me, counselor, may I contribute here?"

In a habeas proceeding, federal judges were allowed and often did interrogate witnesses directly. Solman had made little use of this power so far. Now, apparently, he meant to. Greg fumed. He'd been on a roll. Apparently, too much of one.

"Of course, Your Honor," he said.

Solman leaned forward, nodded at Rimmer. "Sheriff, didn't someone write up a report about these boot prints?"

Rimmer nodded vigorously. "Yes, Your Honor, the

forensic technician did it. There was a forensic write-up on those prints."

"And was there a reason why you didn't consider that forensic write-up to be of any importance?"

"Yes, sir. The forensic team told us those prints were three days old. They could tell because there'd been a freeze earlier in the week. The prints were set in icy mud. I'm not sure of all the technical details, but it's in the report, which you have among our submissions. Bottom line is, we knew they weren't from the murder night."

"And did you make this report available to Ms. Trant's defense attorney?"

Rimmer appeared shocked at the question. "Of course, Your Honor . . . I handed it to Reggie Dodge myself."

"Did Mr. Dodge ever bring it up again?"

"No, sir. He seemed to agree the boot prints weren't relevant. He said something like, Well this isn't anything. Never heard any more from him about it."

Judge Solman removed his reading glasses, wiped them, put them back on, and turned to Greg. "Counselor, you may continue. But I wouldn't use up much more time on this matter if I were you."

Greg stared at Solman. The judge looked away and began scribbling on a pad. Greg turned next to James Mashburn. The district attorney was busily leafing through a sheaf of documents.

"Okay then," Greg said slowly. "I'm finished with this witness."

BARRY SIEGEL is the author of two previous books: *Shades of Gray: Ordinary People in Extraordinary Circumstances* and *A Death in White Bear Lake*, which was nominated for an Edgar Award in the Best Fact Crime category. He is an award-winning reporter for the *Los Angeles Times.*

Printed in the United States
by Baker & Taylor Publisher Services